Walking Together

Translated by **Laya Zryl**

JERUSALEM
PUBLICATIONS

Walking Together

A novel by
Yehudit Schreiber

First published 2001
ISBN 0-9707572-2-0

Copyright © 2001 by JERUSALEM PUBLICATIONS

All rights reserved.

No part of this publication may be
translated, reproduced, stored in a retrieval
system, adapted or transmitted in any form or by any
means, electronic, mechanical, photocopying,
recording, or otherwise, without permission
in writing from the copyright holder.

JERUSALEM PUBLICATIONS
Jerusalem, Israel

Distributed by Feldheim Publishers
202 Airport Executive Park, Nanuet, NY 10954
www.feldheim.com

10 9 8 7 6 5 4 3 2 1

Printed in Israel

𝒯o my wonderful grandparents

Mr. and Mrs. Rechnitzer

who always show
so much love and affection

May they be blessed with
long life, good health and
much *nachas*.

Contents

1	Face-to-Face	11
2	Just Plain Shuki	17
3	Tzachi	23
4	Only in Arazim	31
5	Where Is Yossi?	37
6	One Hour of Searching	43
7	Bitter Disappointment	50
8	The Heart of the Tragedy	57
9	The Locked Door	64
10	A Need to Cry	72
11	Spoken from the Heart	80
12	No Reason to Feel Bad	86
13	When Are We Going to Talk?	92
14	Mixed Emotions	98
15	A Moment of Togetherness	105
16	More Than Enough	112
17	Back to the Past	120
18	In Moments of Danger	128
19	Forgotten Letters	133
20	"I Went owt — Don't Worri"	141
21	It's Got Nothing to Do with Him	146
22	When Father Knows Best	152
23	After All That Hard Work	160
24	Just Like Manny	168

25	Change	. . . .	176
26	A Strong Backbone	. . . .	183
27	Never Give Up	. . . .	190
28	A Lemon-Flavored Candy	. . . .	197
29	A Discerning Eye	. . . .	204
30	Unbelievable!	. . . .	212
31	Not My Type	. . . .	219
32	True Stories	. . . .	226
33	The Price	. . . .	233
34	Life's Purpose	. . . .	240
35	A Big Mistake	. . . .	247
36	A Heavy Responsibility	. . . .	254
37	Zigzag	. . . .	260
38	A Tangle of Lies	. . . .	267
39	Chalk on the Blackboard	. . . .	274
40	All in One Night	. . . .	281
41	Operation Tears	. . . .	288
42	Bitter Smile	. . . .	295
43	Blue-Brown	. . . .	302
44	Words That Hurt, Words That Heal	. . .	308
45	Solution in Sight	. . . .	317
46	First Steps	. . . .	323
47	A Lot to Talk About	. . . .	329
48	Changes	. . . .	336
49	Newfound Pride	. . . .	344
50	In Pursuit	. . . .	349
51	Irrefutable Evidence	. . . .	355
52	Footsteps in the Sand	. . . .	361

My gratitude to the daily newspaper *Hamodia*, in whose Hebrew edition this story first appeared, and to its international edition for providing a distinguished platform for the English version. May both continue to be blessed with success.

1

Face-to-Face

The vigorous tugs at his sweater sleeve persisted. "Well, Shuki, are you coming with me?" Shuki Katz cast a worried glance at the gray clouds slowly rolling toward the classroom window. They seemed threatening, as if they were about to fill the entire window with their sad grayness. His eyes darted to the hands of the wall clock, which showed that recess was almost over. "I...I don't...," he stammered, "I don't really...I..."

Shuki continued looking feverishly for his coat among the other twelve. He searched for the right words to tell Meir that he wasn't exactly interested. Yet despite his reluctance, even Shuki knew what Meir knew — that he, Shuki, would do what he was asked. After all, that's why Meir had addressed his request specifically to Shuki and not to any of the other boys.

"Well?" Meir opened the the door. "Are we gonna run?"

Shuki slipped on his purple jacket. They would run.

The peaceful morning's silence enveloping the small settlement was broken by the rhythmic crunch of their shoes on the gravel path. Moving at a gentle clip, they crossed the open square at the village's center, squeezed through a hole in the fence and found themselves on Arazim's main street.

"It's a good thing the Gemara lesson comes after this break." Meir was panting heavily. "Can you imagine Rabbi Gold's reaction if it had been during the last period? He'd come into class, see Aryeh's and Dovi's Gemaras covered like they should be. He'd look at the second row and see Tzviki's and Chaim's, also covered. Then he'd stop short at the third desk, ours."

Meir laughed lightly in relief. "Boy, would I have been in trouble — especially after he warned us three times that we were starting *Hameniach* today and everyone had to bring the right Gemara."

Shuki laughed too, but his laugh was strained. Meir's description had made him nervous. He could already envision a new scene: Rabbi Gold walking into class and finding two empty seats, his and Meir's.

Unlike his other classmates, Shuki never ran home during breaks. Sure, the school's big gate was always open, but he had nothing to look for at home during school hours. In school, all he wanted was to see a smooth blackboard and the colorfully decorated walls. As for whatever he saw at home, he had more than enough of it when he was there.

Now, though, he had run through the cheder's gates. Not for himself, for Meir. Actually, he would have done the same for almost anyone else — but not for the reason everyone thought. While the whole world might praise him for his good nature, in his heart of hearts, he knew the truth. Such behavior didn't come from the better part of him. Not at all.

He half-listened to Meir's cheerful chatter and hoped he wasn't mistakenly sighing at the end of a joke. All he wanted was to make it back to class in time. Rabbi Gold was a stickler for punctuality and rules.

They were almost there. A little farther and they'd be in the newer section of Arazim, slightly distant from the main cluster of houses — as distant as possible in a settlement of only seventy families. There, right at the beginning, was his house. Meir lived on the street after that.

The gray clouds grew heavier, sinking down until they seemed to be resting on the red tiled roofs that ran along the length of the street. The wind whistled closer, shrieking in their ears. Shuki shivered.

"Winter's suddenly come back." Meir rubbed his hands to warm them.

"We'd better hurry," was Shuki's answer, even though it had nothing to do with what Meir said. He glanced nervously at the long row of houses looking like sparkling white blocks trimmed in green. "The bell's going to ring soon."

Meir rolled his coat sleeve back slightly to reveal a black wristwatch equipped with an impressive assortment of buttons. Somewhat importantly, he informed Shuki that his watch showed another six minutes until the end of the break.

"We'll make a quick run to the end of the street," Meir decided. "After that, we'll cross the park, pass another three houses and we'll be there."

The two ran as fast as they could. Another eight houses — Shuki counted the white blocks rushing toward him — another seven, six. There was his house, similar to all the other houses but so different. It stuck out a mile away. It didn't have a simple wooden fence or a creaking, rusty iron gate. No, his house was surrounded by a perfectly pruned hedge, behind which lay a beautiful garden and the best-kept lawn in Arazim.

Without stopping, Shuki mentally waved hello to the house and to whoever was inside, and ran on.

Strange, but he felt no pride in the garden, in the flower beds bursting with color, or in the garden everyone admired. He would have gladly traded it all — from the marigolds to the bougainvillea — for the sand and junk of Meir's or Tzviki's yard.

Face-to-Face ♦ 13

It wasn't that he didn't love the garden and everything growing there. Not at all. Every new leaf unfurling toward the sun opened something in his soul too and warmed his heart. Way before he noticed an open shoelace or a stain on his shirt, he'd see the blue cornflowers that had sprouted only a day earlier, seemingly waving to him in greeting.

He guessed it was because of Abba that the garden was precious to him. Still, there were other, more important things. Recently, Shuki had been feeling that it was between the walls of the classroom that he could find one of those things that was especially meaningful to him.

Another four houses, another three — Shuki stopped short. His right foot hurt. Something was bothering him. He leaned over his brown shoe, streaked with mud stains from the garden, and crouched to open the knots in the laces. A small pebble had probably gotten inside.

Meir kept on running. "Hey!" he called to Shuki as he sped down the street, a step or two away from the corner. "What happened? Did you fall?"

Shuki stood up immediately and continued to run with difficulty. It wasn't worth drawing Meir's attention to his shoes. True, now Meir was friendly, chatting and joking, but you could never know what tomorrow or the day after or next week would bring. Then, when a few boys were sitting on the school steps or walking home together, Meir could suddenly act differently. He could laugh or make some comment poking fun at Shuki.

Facing the park, they hurriedly crossed the street. The low hill, covered by carpets of damp, slightly yellowed grass, beckoned to them. Shuki noticed that some of the blades of grass had turned green again. Winter was coming to an end. A warm ray of sunlight lit up his heart at the thought.

Then he spotted the playground. It looked a little strange on this wintry morning, as if some mysterious hand had painted its usually colorful swings and slides gray. Suddenly, the playground looked to Shuki abandoned, orphaned, desolate. Right then, Shuki realized something else. His heart was also gray, shadowed by heavy gray clouds. "Uh, I'm going to wait here for you. I...I'll start going around," he said to Meir. "You go on ahead and get your Gemara."

Meir stared at him, uncomprehending. "But it's getting late," he urged.

"You keep going," Shuki answered, his eyes scanning the hill restlessly. "I'll meet you on the path that circles the park. Besides, what difference does it make? Do you need someone to escort you right up to your desk?"

"I don't need anybody to escort me at all," Meir laughed and tugged at Shuki's purple coat sleeve in a friendly gesture. "I know the way myself, *baruch Hashem*. I just thought it would be more fun to walk together. I didn't know it was such a problem for you to go out for a run on a morning like this."

Shuki was silent. With faltering steps, he dragged himself after Meir on the familiar, beloved path leading up to the hill. Now he didn't love it at all. The hill seemed like a threatening mountain. Wide-eyed, he stared at the big tractor mower standing there peacefully on the hilltop.

Yesterday, Abba had talked about the approaching spring. Today, he had probably gone out to greet it. Why did Shuki have to leave the cheder during the hours that Abba worked — and especially with Meir?

Shuki smiled bitterly. Especially with Meir? Because of Meir.

Shuki could just imagine Abba's surprise, his eyes twinkling with happiness when he saw him. He could almost feel Abba's hands hasten to hug him warmly, while his own body tensed. Oh, how he loved Abba's hugs. But the thought of the same warm hug that gave him such a good feeling in their small, cozy kitchen every lunchtime, now caused a cold shiver to run down his spine.

He would race down the hill at lightning speed, without looking to the side or in any other direction. He didn't want to meet Abba when Meir — or any other friend — was with him.

True, there were no secrets in Arazim, and everyone knew

his father since even before Shuki was born. But that didn't mean he wanted to suffer the stares of pity sent his way, even if they were behind his back.

Yes, Shuki was all too well aware of the painful truth: people might see his father hundreds of times, but they would still prefer to focus on the pavement rather than look directly at his face.

2
Just Plain Shuki

Shoelaces open only when you're in a hurry, Shuki concluded, *just like briefcases that refused to close or zippers that got stuck at a minute to eight.* Why couldn't they be more considerate? In the afternoon, he'd have lots of time for them, plenty of time to tie and untie and then retie again.

In honor of Rosh Chodesh, cheder let out early that day. Shuki still didn't know how he was going to fill the hours that stretched ahead of him, long and empty.

He walked faster and caught up with his friends. Everyone was feeling great. What could be better than a few hours of vacation? They decided to get together after lunch and ride their bikes around Arazim. Spring was in the air. It was the perfect time to drag their bikes out of storage, pump air in the tires that had gone flat during the winter and put them to good use.

Shuki was happy. *Good thing they decided on bikes,* he thought with satisfaction. After all, they could have just as easily decided on a ball game or hike. Now, without asking his opinion and without him having to say what he felt, they had done just what he wanted.

Shuki pictured his new, shiny BMX racing bike. Abba had bought it at the end of the summer, right when the other kids had gotten bored of riding their bikes, and ball games had taken over every spare minute. Well, happily for him, they had remembered the bikes. Shuki liked to ride. He also knew how to ride well.

Once, he had asked himself what came first. Did he like to ride his bike because he was good at it, or was he good at it because he liked it?

He still didn't have an answer to the question. He wondered the same thing about playing ball. Did he hate it because the ball tended to bounce out of his hand instead of staying put, or did the ball refuse to cooperate because he was so tense?

He decided it didn't matter. Why tax his brain with questions that were too hard. (Maybe they were hard because he didn't like them?) The main thing was that today it was bikes and not ball, and he looked forward to having fun that afternoon.

At noon, sleepy Arazim bustled with activity. Apple-cheeked preschoolers walked home in groups of twos and threes along with flocks of schoolgirls in their blue uniforms chattering away. The boys rushed out of cheder and took over Arazim's pathways as if they owned the place in contrast to the pairs and trios of serious *kollel* members who walked home for their short lunch break with quick, yet measured, steps.

Shuki and his friends reached the center of the settlement, the place where what Shuki had once dubbed "family reunions" took place daily.

"There's my dad!" Tzviki cried out. "I think that's yours, Aryeh, walking next to him. I recognize him by the glasses."

Shuki looked at the group of men. He thought he saw Dovi's father, maybe Chaim's too. He didn't say anything. He knew his father wasn't one of the group — not today, not yesterday and not tomorrow, either. Nope, he wouldn't be walking home with Abba.

Plenty of times, Moishe's father, who was the third grade teacher in the cheder, waited for Moishe near the entrance to walk home with him. Bentzi's father, who worked in the cheder's office, often made a surprise visit to his son. He'd knock on the classroom door right after the bell rang, and, with a wink at Rabbi Gold and the other boys, say, "What, you're still learning in here?" Then he'd pretend to be looking for someone. "I need one boy in particular," he'd say as he gazed around the room. "I'm looking for—" he'd make a dramatic pause — "for Bentzi Guttman."

With all eyes on him, Bentzi would stand up happily and run over to his father.

Shuki wasn't jealous. Why should he be jealous? His father would have been more than willing to come get him every day. His father could have easily brought him in the morning and walked him home at lunchtime and when the day ended. Once — and suddenly Shuki felt it was ages ago — once it really had been like that.

Shuki remembered how in kindergarten, he'd eagerly run to his father's open arms. Proudly, he would open his book bag and take out the day's arts-and-crafts project for display to his admiring father. Then he would be lifted up in strong arms, sure that there was no happier boy than he in the whole world.

Back then, he didn't notice Abba's scarred, scarey face. It was as if it didn't exist for him. He saw only the laughing eyes filled with love and felt only the warmth and concern. He saw Abba and nothing more.

But all that had been a long time ago. Suddenly — and he couldn't pinpoint the exact day — suddenly he began rushing to pack up his things ten minutes before dismissal. He'd hurriedly get up from his chair the minute the bell rang, and dash outside as if he were escaping from a fire. Gasping and panting, he would run toward Abba, trying to walk quickly, wanting to see himself at home already, far away from his friends and everyone else.

Just Plain Shuki ♦ 19

Then, he had also begun to leave earlier in the mornings. First five minutes earlier and then another five and another five. When the street was quiet and still, and only the chirping birds observed them from above, it didn't bother him to walk with Abba. Birds don't flinch at the sight of scars; they don't look with pity at regular faces. He wasn't embarrassed in front of the birds, nor was he afraid of them. He'd walk with his backpack on his shoulder alongside Abba holding his tefillin bag under his arm, and together they would begin a new day.

But even this belonged to the past. After that, he started walking alone to an empty classroom. All the pretexts and excuses about learning and reviewing and other urgent tasks fell away in the face of his growing tiredness. His classmates would arrive to find him dozing on his desk. There were jokes and quips about the boy who didn't have a bed — until one wintry morning, cold and teary, Shuki knew there would have to be an end to it.

Even now, his sensitive soul twisted inside him as he remembered those moments, as he weighed his father's impending pain against his own. When Shuki finished speaking, Abba understood what he had said. He son was a big boy already. Big boys don't need their fathers to walk them to cheder and back. Big boys' fathers wait for them at home. That's how it went. To this very day, Shuki didn't know if Abba had realized then what was behind it all. In any case, that night, Shuki's pillow was wet with tears, and he was afraid his father's pillow hadn't remained dry either.

But after that night, the tears during the day had lessened. Mainly, they were tears that stayed inside his heart, because Shuki had never been one to cry much. From then on, he didn't have to make up excuses, go to cheder early or rush. He wasn't forced to deal with the stares that he hated so much, those in which he found countless unspoken messages, none of which enhanced his peace of mind — from then on, until today.

Suddenly, he noticed that he had already turned into the long street and was very close to home. None of his friends were with him. Various appetizing aromas tickled his nostrils. Shuki found himself busy thinking about them. *Onion soup*, he decided resolutely. *Onion soup and grilled hamburgers.*

All the houses on the street resembled each other, as alike as Siamese twins. All had the same small kitchen with a big window facing the street. All the stoves were in the same place: under the window, where the smells of cooking wafted out to passersby. And in all of the kitchens, people were now eating lunch.

Had he wanted to, Shuki could have easily watched the Weiss family contentedly eating the onion soup he smelled. But he didn't. His imagination drew the picture for him, down to the youngest child whose soup dripped from his spoon without his realizing it. The scene amused him.

Later, Abba would tell him that it didn't matter what "everyone" did. But it did matter. In Arazim, everyone did the same things. Everyone was now sitting in a small kitchen near the window and eating, everyone had covered the window with small-mesh screen, a tried-and-true solution against the insects that filled all the settlements in the Galilee. The few that had not yet done so would pay for their neglect that summer or the next. Everyone had ordered the screens from Levi the handyman in the nearby town because everyone said that he was the cheapest and most reliable. Besides, he did good work.

Sometimes, Shuki felt like he was part of one big happy family. That feeling was actually pleasant, because he had never had a big family. Then he immediately remembered that it wasn't exactly like that. In Arazim, he was part of the family, but different, sort of on the sidelines. His father wasn't like all the other fathers in Arazim, that was for sure. That meant that he, as his father's son, couldn't be like all the other boys in the settlement. Maybe he was the stepson in the Arazim family.

"Good afternoon, Shuki," his mother greeted him from behind the steaming pot.

"A good Rosh Chodesh, Yehoshua," his father said, glancing up from the newspaper.

Shuki sat down near the table, trying to guess what kinds of food were producing the aromas in his own house. He didn't have to guess too hard. Still sizzling chicken cutlets, fluffy white rice and cooked vegetables smiled up at him from his plate.

"Enjoy, Shuki," his mother said. "Would you like something to drink first?"

"It's a Rosh Chodesh meal. It's worth washing your hands, Yehoshua." That was his father speaking.

Yehoshua. As much as Shuki loved the name "Shuki," that was as far as he felt from "Yehoshua." *When I grow up, I'll be Yehoshua*, he had often thought. "Mr. Yehoshua Katz" wasn't a bad combination. But now it was much more comfortable and right to be just plain Shuki.

He remembered Tzviki's visit a few years ago. They had been playing on the red rug in his bedroom when Abba had called him from the garden.

"Yehoshua!"

"Your father is probably angry at you," Tzvika had said then knowingly. "When my mother tells my father that I played ball in the living room again or that I fought with my brother, he calls me Tzvi in the same serious voice."

But Abba hadn't been angry at all. His father almost didn't know how to get angry. Abba had only wanted to tell him to pour a cold drink for his friend and to take some cookies too, so that the two of them could enjoy themselves.

Abba always called him Yehoshua. To everyone else, he was always Shuki, but to his father he was still Yehoshua. He had gotten used to it. In the end, you get used to everything. But that didn't mean he wouldn't be happier if even once Abba would call him just plain Shuki.

3

Tzachi

The blue compact car pulled to a stop, finding a place alongside similar late-model cars in the Raanana parking lot. The door slammed shut with a bang that shook the quiet street, accustomed as it was to its prolonged afternoon siesta.

Brosh jabbed a finger at the round elevator button of the three-story apartment house. What was taking it so long? He heard the elevator door open on one of the upper floors. How long did it take the thing to get to the ground floor? He pressed down hard on the button and kept his finger there.

It's faster to take the stairs, he decided, heading for the stairwell.

"Elevators are for lazy people," Tzachi had always said. "I'd rather take the stairs. It gives me the feeling that I'm doing something productive, climbing instead of waiting."

Yup, that was Tzachi, all right. Brosh couldn't help but smile. *You always were a hopeless philosopher, Tzachi, so dreamy and unrealistic. And look what happened. In the end, where did your desire to climb get you? You're still standing in the same place.*

"Hello!" He flung the door open without knocking.

"Brosh?" His father rose from the easy chair to greet him, a wide smile spreading across his tired face at the sight of his son. It was a smile reserved for sons who lived far away and seldom visited.

"Is that Brosh?" his mother called as she hurried out to greet the tall guest in the doorway. "How was the trip here? How are you?"

Brosh shrugged. "Okay," was all he said, but privately, the fuss his mother still made about the drive from Tel Aviv to Raanana amused him. She forgot that he hadn't gotten his driver's license yesterday. She also forgot the kind of job he had. Why, he flew from one capital to the next as often as she went to the supermarket.

Yes, that was his mother. She treated her grown sons as if they were still small boys in her care, anxious for her motherly love and concern. To her, the Brosh of today, a senior diplomat at the Israeli Embassy in Germany, was still the toddler who had to be spoon-fed to put some weight on him.

Brosh strode into the spacious living room, his head almost scraping the ceiling. "Truth is, I'm in a big rush today. But don't worry," he added at the sight of his mother's disappointed look, "I'm planning a real visit at the end of the week. I just stopped by for about fifteen minutes or so.

"Ima," he said, getting straight to the point of his unexpected visit, "maybe you remember where I put my notes from the last semester in college? They were in three big binders, two green ones and a yellow one."

His father sunk back down in the easy chair. Finding things in the big house had never been his department. It was enough that he knew where his glasses were.

Brosh's mother quickly brought the small step stool. "It's all here," she reassured him. "You know me, I never throw anything away. I have all your notebooks, all the papers and reports. I used to have Tzachi's books and notebooks, too, all packed and organized, but he came and threw them all away. He told me he didn't need them anymore, and then he burned them in the backyard. 'I don't need them, and I don't want to need them ever again' is what he said." His mother sighed and motioned Brosh to climb up and look for the notebooks himself.

Brosh moved the step stool out of the way. He didn't need it.

"Still growing, Brosh?" his father teased. From where he sat in the armchair, Brosh loomed even larger.

Brosh chuckled amiably. "That's already become a regular question in the embassy in Bonn," he said, his head deep inside the small storage space at the top of the hall closet. "Everyone wants to know how I got my name and if the cradle was already too small for me when I was born."

His parents nostalgically recalled the distant memories. "Tzachi was four years old then. We asked him what he wanted to call his new brother," his father said, repeating the familiar tale. "We were sure he would suggest a fairly common name, like the ones his friends had. But Tzachi looked out the window and said decisively, 'Brosh.'"

"You were actually quite a small baby then, only six pounds eight ounces." His mother smiled. "No one would have guessed that you would grow as tall as your namesake, the cypress tree."

Brosh's father was still thinking about his other son, Tzachi. "No one would have guessed where Tzachi's originality and independence would lead him either. I figured it began and ended with picking the name "Brosh." Little did I know that was only the beginning."

Esther frowned. She didn't like that he saw Tzachi as some kind of tragedy. True, at first she had been angry when Tzachi had come home with his strange ideas. Insulted was more like it. What was so terrible about the lifestyle she and Binyamin had given their children? In time, though, she had made peace with it.

Today she had a smart grandson who sometimes came to visit. There were clever remarks to laugh over, someone to give presents to, someone upon whom to shower love, and that's what counted. Even Tzachi's side curls and the *kippa* didn't bother her the same way they once had. Besides, not much remained of Tzachi's looks anyway, including what had been his face. She had always said there was something special about his face — and now that something special was even more exceptional than it had been, even nobler if possible.

As Brosh pulled himself out of the closet, two arms laden with books and notebooks came into view. Several slipped and landed on the marble floor with a bang, raising clouds of dust. His parents rushed to help.

"What exactly are you looking for?" his father asked, smoothing a book cover that had almost been severed from its binding.

Brosh bent over the heap. "I'm only missing one course and one project to get my doctorate in oriental studies. During the three months I'll be here, I'd like to finish and finally get my Ph.D."

His father looked up from the pile from which he was busy retrieving more books. "But didn't you decide two years ago that you wanted to devote more time to economics and languages?"

"Yes," Brosh shot back, "but recently I decided to find out what's happening in the area of oriental studies as well. I didn't sign a lifetime contract with the embassy in Bonn." He winked meaningfully. "So it's best to be prepared for all eventualities."

His parents nodded their heads. Yes, that was the motto they lived by, and that's what had bothered them about Tzachi. Why did he have to burn all his bridges? Why couldn't he keep on living as he had and also keep mitzvos? Why suddenly start everything anew? Why did he have to be so extreme?

Now his mother thought that maybe Tzachi had been right about something. When she had visited his house on one of those rare visits, she sensed something different going on there. The air seemed somehow purer. To achieve this, a person probably had to live a life without compromises. He probably had to make a fresh start, exactly as her Tzachi had done.

"Two green binders and one yellow, you said? Maybe it's this green one?" Binyamin handed Brosh a thick loose-leaf notebook.

Brosh flipped through the pages. "What's this? It's not my handwriting. I think this must have been Tzachi's."

His mother grabbed the notebook out of his hands. "Tzachi's?" She thought Tzachi had finished with his studies, his books and notebooks, his old world. Yes, it was Tzachi's, a botany notebook from twelfth grade.

"This too," said Binyamin. "Look, there's a few of them." He leafed through the binders slowly. "Look how organized these are," he showed his wife proudly. "Look at the flawless penmanship."

"So he didn't burn these," Esther murmured. "In spite of everything, it was still hard for him to part with botany and agriculture."

"But he left them here," her husband said, an angry bitterness in his voice. "Why did he have to quit? He could have excelled in his studies!" Both their sons were gifted and talented, but Tzachi had always been the more diligent and ambitious of the two. "He could have gone far."

"You're mistaken, Binyamin," his wife said softly. "He wouldn't have succeeded even if he had continued. He couldn't bring home such notebooks today or achieve the grades he once did — and it's not because he changed his lifestyle. They're two unrelated events that took place at the same time, that's all."

Brosh searched feverishly for the binders. He wasn't sure

they were there. Maybe he had lent them to a fellow student when he thought he wouldn't need them anymore. What would he do if they weren't there? Where would he start looking? He had so little time to familiarize himself with the material again, to begin planning the project and immerse himself deeply in the subject.

Ah, there they were, two blue loose-leaf binders and an orange one. He had been mistaken about the colors, that's all. Pleased at finding them, he threw the binders into a bag he had brought along and waved goodbye to his parents as he made for the door. "See you." He turned around and gave one last smile before closing the door.

Esther tackled the pile of notebooks. Those belonging to Tzachi she put, with a measure of reverence, into a separate bag. "How about visiting Tzachi tomorrow?" she suggested to her husband. "We haven't been there in a long time. We could bring him these notebooks. Maybe he can use them. We'll buy the boy something too. Why not? Do you have anything better to do?"

Her husband shrugged his shoulders. *Visit Tzachi, just like that, at a moment's notice?* He didn't think so.

"I need two weeks' advance notice before I visit Tzachi. After all, you don't want our visit to annoy him, do you?"

His wife shook her head.

"Well, then, that's the way it is. I have to remember that at his place, you wash your hands and recite blessings before eating, and I have to find the small white yarmulke, which I have no idea where it is. I also have to remember that Tzachi is called Yitzchak. I have a lot to remember."

Esther sighed. Why did her husband love to make such a big deal out of every little thing? He had no problem remembering about washing his hands and saying the proper blessings, and Tzachi always received them with a smile. Every time they visited, he tried to give them the feeling that they were welcome guests. So why was Binyamin so reluctant to go?

As for calling Tzachi Yitzchak, what was so hard about that? Who, if not Binyamin, had given him the name Yitzchak at the bris? What was wrong with him using it?

She understood Tzachi. He wanted his son to see him as he was now, without a complicated past. So why not respect his wishes?

"Well, Binyamin?" she persisted.

Her husband scratched his forehead. "We'll see. Maybe in another six or eight weeks I'll take a day off and we'll go. Remember to buy a nice present for our grandson."

Esther sighed. She would remember. She didn't have that many other things to remember anyway.

In the small house in Arazim, Shuki sat near the window waiting for his friends to come by on their bikes. He thought he saw Meir's striped shirt in the distance, so he stood up, ready to take out his bike too. The phone's ring stopped him. He picked it up. "Hello."

"Hello." There was an urgency to the voice on the other end of the line. "Is Tzachi there?"

"Who?" Shuki was sure he hadn't heard right.

"Tzachi. Is Tzachi there?" This time the tension and impatience were unmistakable.

"Sorry, wrong number," Shuki said confidently and hung up. He had known right away that it was a mistake. The breathlessness, the sharp tone — what would anyone who talked like that have to do with his father?

He was almost out the door when the phone rang again.

"Hello, can I please speak with Tzachi?"

"You have the wrong number," Shuki repeated.

"Is this the Katz family?" the voice asked, slightly less confident.

Shuki nodded slowly, forgetting the caller couldn't see him.

Tzachi ♦ 29

"Is this 987–7435?"

"Yes it is."

"Then it's the right number. Who are you? His son?"

Before Shuki could answer, he sensed his father behind him. He covered the receiver with his hand and whispered, "He called twice already. He doesn't believe me that it's a mistake. He keeps on asking for someone named Tzachi."

"Tzachi?" His father's voice boomed, and Shuki flinched. "He asked for Tzachi? Why didn't you call me right away?"

4

Only in Arazim

Some people don't like the darkness of evening, when a chill wind rustles through the trees, and the solitary street lamps light up one after the other. They find the time when sidewalks empty, doors are locked and the world waves farewell to another day depressing.

Right then, Yitzchak Katz was one of them. He sat on the white plastic chair in the garden, the comfortable chair with its added cushions, sunk in gloom. As his gaze lingered on the last rays of the sun that had vanished somewhere on the horizon, he thought about other disappearances. Another day was gone.

"Shalom, Reb Yitzchak!" A familiar pair of laughing eyes smiled at him from between the fresh green leaves of the well-kept hedge. "Shalom," the friendly greeting was repeated. "What's new? Resting a bit? Gathering your strength?"

Yitzchak twisted his mouth into a half smile. What was he supposed to answer? That he hadn't known the taste of true rest for the past fifteen years? Yes, he was gathering his strength —

or trying to. If things worked out as planned — and the hope given him yesterday on the phone did not end up another shattered dream — he would need much of his strength in the coming days and weeks.

With three strides, Reb Yankel Miller was standing at the entrance to the garden, looking as if he owned it. "You weren't at the *shiur* yesterday," he suddenly recalled. "Is everything okay?"

Yitzchak nodded. He understood Reb Yankel's surprise. He was surprised himself. He could count on the fingers of one hand the number of times he had missed a *shiur* over the years. He was as inseparable a part of the scene as the lecturer who took his place faithfully every evening, as the tables, benches and slightly peeling white walls.

The second image was much more on target than the first, he thought bitterly. He was more like the walls and benches than the man who gave the lecture. The thought tore at his heart — not because of the insult to his self-image but because of the reality it reflected.

// // //

While his father was sitting in the garden, Shuki was in the house, busy straightening up his room. Moishe Levin had said he would come at 6:15, but it was already 6:20 and he still wasn't anywhere in sight. Where was he?

Actually, Shuki hadn't been that anxious to have him come. He didn't like having friends over. He was more than happy to study with them, play or just talk, but he'd rather do it at the friend's house or somewhere outside.

But Moishe had insisted on coming to Shuki's house, and Shuki hadn't been able to put him off any longer. Shuki wanted to be friends with Moishe. Moishe Levin was one of the best, most popular boys in class, and it was a big honor to be his friend. That's why Shuki had given in this time. Soon, all too soon, Moishe Levin would knock at his door.

Shuki stood in a corner of his room trying to look at it as if he were seeing it for the first time. It looked nice to him. The closet, desk and bed were all made from matching pinewood, accented with a deep green trim. There was a small plant in one corner and window boxes of flowers on the windows.

He went over to his desk. On the first shelf, standing like soldiers, were his *sefarim* and notebooks. On the second shelf were the books he loved to read, the ones he knew almost by heart. And on the third shelf, well, the third shelf was buckling under the load of games. He had tons of games.

Shuki wondered what Moishe would say about it. He probably didn't have nearly that many games. Shuki doubted there was a single boy with as many games as he had. Even Fun City, the toy store in the regional shopping center, didn't have as big a selection. Once he had gone there with Abba and hadn't found even one that he didn't own. In fact, he even had some the store didn't have. Maybe only the really big stores, the huge department stores where his grandmother did her shopping, had a bigger selection.

Shuki took a look at the games. Each one brought back memories, because every time his grandparents visited, they brought a present, and every time, the present was a rectangular-shaped box, wrapped in colorful wrapping paper and ribbon. Even before he opened it, Shuki always knew the present would be a game.

He knew his grandmother loved him very much. She would have liked to bring him mouth-watering treats or buy him new clothes or books, but she was afraid. "All the kosher symbols are so similar," he had once heard her say to his father. "If you would tell me that everything that says kosher is good, I could manage, but this way…" her voice had trailed off in helplessness.

But Abba didn't make do with just kosher, thought Shuki with pride. Abba was strict about having only the best *hechsherim*, and he carefully inspected every food that entered the house. So, despite all her good wishes, his grandmother couldn't buy candy or other treats.

She couldn't buy clothes either. Once she had brought a

warm blue sweater with four big gold buttons. The sweater was so pretty, and Shuki had looked forward to wearing it for the first time on Shabbos. Then he had suddenly discovered a big smiling Mickey Mouse on the back, so that was that. The sweater wasn't suitable for Shabbos or for during the week, either. His grandmother couldn't understand why she never saw Shuki wearing the sweater and how such a big sweater had become too small for him so fast.

Since then, she had brought him games. Every box reminded Shuki of a different visit. The game of checkers was from Chanuka two years ago, the Monopoly from when they had visited during summer vacation four years ago, the Rummy was for his ninth birthday and the Game Boy was given on an ordinary visit. Battleship, Trouble, Risk — the list was long. There hadn't even been so many visits, but even the few that had taken place had added up to a shelf full of games.

Just then, there was a knock on the door.

Shuki invited Moishe in. "Wow! So many games!" Moishe stood in the doorway with a look of pleasure on his face. "You've got more games than all the boys in the class," he said to Shuki, his eyes sparkling. "Why don't we ever come to you to play? Tomorrow, I'll tell everyone how many games you have," he said, suddenly excited. "Wait till you see what a line there'll be outside your house!" Moishe laughed, oblivious to Shuki's silence.

Shuki felt like someone who had just smelled a sweet rose in full bloom only to feel a thorn dig deep inside his flesh. He enjoyed the pleasant thought about the lines of friends leading up to his door, but he would have preferred to keep them that way — outside. It was fine to imagine them knocking on the door, but the last thing he wanted was for them all to walk into his house where they'd see his father.

Moishe and Shuki bent over the desk, reviewing the material as they had learned it in class, delving into the Gemara. "I didn't understand this point completely," Moishe said. "When Rabbi Gold explained it in class, I thought it was a cinch, but when I got home, I couldn't figure it out."

Shuki focused on the small letters, and the explanation flowed easily from him.

Moishe stared at him, stunned. He was learning a lot during this visit. He never knew Shuki could understand a *sugya* like that, thinking so deeply, grasping the idea and drawing connections. Why, Shuki hardly ever raised his hand during class. Moishe wondered why.

They continued to learn, not realizing how fast the time was passing. Finally, Moishe yawned and stretched. "How about going out to your garden for a short break?"

Shuki shook his head resolutely. "Let's finish first."

Moishe gave in. He turned his eyes away from the scene beckoning through the window and tried to involve himself once more in the topic under discussion.

A few minutes passed. "Let's take a break now." Moishe stood up resolutely. "Now we can go out to your garden. Whenever I pass by, I can see some kind of red and purple flowers behind the hedge. Now I want to see the garden from the inside."

"Okay," Shuki said. "We'll go out in a minute. You're sure you don't want to play one of the games you were so excited about before?" Shuki was already standing on a chair, pulling down a pile of games that he deposited on the floor with a flourish. Moishe sat down nearby, examining the profusion of boxes with eager eyes.

"I'd like to stay and play all of them," he said longingly, "but it's too late. I've got to get home. I'll come another day, just to play. Maybe tomorrow. Let's go — you can walk me through the garden."

Shuki hesitated. This was exactly why he didn't like to invite friends home. If only he could have kept Moishe in his room until a quarter to eight. That's when Abba went to shul for Maariv and his *shiur*, staying there until late at night. Then he could take Moishe around the garden and proudly show him

Only in Arazim ◆ 35

the beautiful gladiola. Just that day he had noticed how tall they had grown and how their red and orange flowers had started to open. He would stroll with Moishe alongside the pink and yellow rosebushes until they got to the gate that was covered by purple bougainvillea. How nice it would be to walk with his guest on the stone path that wended its way through the lush green grass, so neatly trimmed. They would breathe in the fragrant aroma of honeysuckle, his favorite flower, as he identified each flower by name for Moishe and expertly answered his questions.

But it was only seven-thirty now. Abba was still in the garden.

"Okay, I'll walk you. But we might as well go in another ten minutes. That way, we can daven Maariv with the minyan at a quarter to eight."

Oh no! What did I say? Shuki bit his tongue, but he couldn't take the words back.

"Great," Moishe exclaimed. "We'll go out now and that way we'll get to Maariv just in time. Didn't you once say that you could spend hours in your garden?"

"Uh, sure. I'm just...I'm just putting on my shoes."

"Okay," said Moishe, already at the door. "I'll wait for you outside." Before Shuki could say a word, Moishe was on his way to the garden — to Abba, who was sitting there as he always did at this hour.

Shuki remained frozen in place. *It could only happen in Arazim,* he thought to himself gloomily. Only in the tiny village of Arazim, where everyone was like one big family, could an otherwise polite kid behave as if his friend's house were his own.

He went after Moishe, slamming the door to his room behind him. Maybe he could still head him off.

At the entrance to the garden, he stopped. Moishe had been too fast for him. He was already standing there, near the plastic lawn chair, talking to Abba.

5

Where Is Yossi?

Nissim mopped the beads of sweat trickling down his forehead and sighed. The whole country was just one big traffic jam. Even this usually quiet road leading up to Arazim was suddenly congested.

He stuck his head out the window and pulled it back in quickly. It looked hopeless. The long line of cars stretching all the way to the intersection showed no sign of going anywhere within the next few minutes. Nissim leaned his weary head against the steering wheel and closed his eyes. If not for the traffic, he could have been outside Arazim's supermarket by now, unloading the goods and getting ready to continue on his way.

Some new driver who had just gotten his license had probably crashed into a pole, or maybe some blabbermouth who couldn't part with his cellular phone had rammed into the car in front of him. Nissim sighed deeply. If only everyone would drive as cautiously as he did, there'd be a lot less accidents and traffic jams.

The car crawled along with the rest of the long line at a snail's pace. Nissim felt a grudging gratitude for the lack of patrol cars or ambulances. "It's probably a broken headlight or dented fender," he grumbled sagely. "Maybe some teenager who just got his license scratched his fancy new car. Oh, well, what can you do?" he announced to the empty truck cabin, as if it wasn't the tenth time he was saying it.

"What can you do?" he repeated and answered himself, "Learn a lesson for the next time and free up the highway already. Why does the whole country have to suffer because of a few reckless hotheads?"

The driver of the gray Volvo behind him got out and walked toward the intersection. Deciding anything was better than sitting in the overheated metal contraption any longer, Nissim climbed down, slamming the door behind him. Besides, he had to find that driver who was the cause of this mess. He had a few choice words to say to him.

Fists tightly clenched, Nissim set off to give the guy a piece of his mind when he was suddenly struck by the strange silence. As he got closer to the intersection, he came upon a crowd — other drivers who, like he, had abandoned their cars to see what was going on. All were listening intently. Surprisingly, there were no flare-ups, raised voices, accusations or name-calling — only looks of empathy and commiseration directed toward the man addressing them.

Without his realizing it, Nissim unclenched his fist and let it hang limply at his side. This time, he was wrong. It hadn't been just another thoughtless driver blocking the road.

He pushed his way to the improvised platform set up between a small kiosk and a hitchhikers' stand. "Yosef is still alive!" a banner proclaimed.

A man with a terribly scarred face was handing out pamphlets to passersby. Nissim took one.

"Where is Yossi?" screamed the cover. Staring Nissim in the face was a young man looking as if he didn't have a care in the world. Yossi Nir. You hardly heard his name mentioned any more. Nissim had almost forgotten who he was altogether. How many years had passed since then?

He was spared any strenuous calculations by the man on the platform. In a voice poignantly full of hope, he told the crowd, "The Peace for Galilee War ended fifteen years ago, but the battle for Yossi Nir is still going on.

"Fifteen years have passed since his disappearance, and we still haven't heard from him. Is he dead or alive? We don't know." The speaker paused. "The United States is now interested in achieving an understanding between Israel and Syria. We say there will be no agreement before Syria gives over the information we know it has about Yossi Nir." Here his voice grew louder. "The government must make this its top priority. It was this country that sent him out to battle, and it is this country's responsibility to bring him back!"

The speaker paused and reached for a paper cup filled with bottled spring water. Someone began to clap but stopped. Something in the atmosphere made applause seem an unsuitable gesture. Instead, he took out his checkbook and wrote out a check. The big box emblazoned with the words "The Association on Behalf of Yossi Nir" was filling up fast.

As a petition passed from hand to hand, a growing sense of unity swept the crowd. Who could return to his car, step on the gas and drive off with equanimity after hearing about one of their own whose fate was still unknown?

More and more people resolutely signed their names on the paper. By doing so, they were declaring themselves part of the groundswell of public opinion that insisted on government action — now, before the present opportunity, like so many previous ones, slipped through its fingers. The man in the street wanted freeing Yossi Nir made a top priority, with all other items on the agenda put on hold until progress was achieved on this sensitive issue.

Angry honking from somewhere down the road forced people back to their cars. One after another, the vehicles started moving, some to climb up the road that led to Arazim.

Yitzchak Katz sat down on the folding chair he had brought with him, opened his small *Tehillim* and began to recite with deep concentration. In a little while, when the congestion cleared up a bit, he would once again take his place at the intersection and wave the placards.

He was aware of the powerful impact he was making. He could see the understanding and empathy in people's eyes, their flickering anger when he spoke about the government's lack of action, and their desire to help in some way. That's exactly why he was there.

Even now, he still wasn't sure why he, out of all of Yossi's friends, was the one who remained an inseparable part of the family, the battle, the hopes and the disappointments. Maybe it was because he was one of Yossi's closest friends. Maybe it was because the friendship between them had affected them both deeply, touching an innermost layer of their souls — the part that would relentlessly search for the good and the right thing to do, with no compromises.

Maybe it was also because he had come to the Nir family after everyone else, after six months that were one long question mark tearing at people's hearts, six months that were long enough for some people to begin to forget. By the time he showed up, there were no longer any Knesset members or government ministers sitting in the living room, no reporters or photographers. Even the friends and acquaintances had long since gone home. All that remained in that room echoing with emptiness were parents who didn't know whether they still had a son.

Yitzchak's words had fallen on anxious ears. He had become close to them then, a true partner in their struggle. His sincere willingness to do whatever it took had gained their trust.

Many years had passed since that first visit. Only a few weeks ago, Daniel Nir, Yossi's father, had called him after a long period during which they hadn't spoken. There had been a faint undercurrent of hope in his voice. "One of the various officials we have connections with is about to pass us some information," he said, "information that will give us a new chance of discovering Yossi's whereabouts."

The information had been handed over. That very same day, Daniel had reported the details to the army's human task force, a special government-appointed committee to handle all matters related to soldiers missing in action. He was convinced of the reliability of the testimony, which stated that Yossi had been seen in Hizbullah captivity two years after the war. He was also convinced that the disclosure would send all those officials running to deal with the matter immediately.

But that's not what happened. The document was photocopied and the copies transferred to some of those same officials. The original copy was dutifully placed in the neglected file — that of the missing Yossi Nir. This brief flurry of activity was followed by several vague promises but nothing more.

The Nir family decided not to remain silent. Yitzchak was brought into the picture to help launch a massive nationwide campaign. Volunteers took to the highways with placards and petitions, and the public responded. Although it had been fifteen years since Yossi was taken captive, an impressive number of people signed and contributed. The poster of a smiling, perpetually youthful Yossi engraved its heart-rending message on the consciousness of an entire nation.

The Nir family planned a huge rally in a month's time, scheduling it on the anniversary of the war from which Yossi had never returned. The entire nation would unite for Yossi's sake and for the sake of his unknown fate. Tens of thousands, if not hundreds of thousands of people bearing placards demanding that the battle for Yossi be renewed could not easily be dismissed. Media coverage was assured, not only in Israel but around the world. Public pressure on the government would have to bring results.

Yitzchak painfully smoothed the creased pages of his small *Tehillim*. No, he wouldn't argue with the Nirs over the effectiveness of a demonstration. But he knew that his suggestion could have accomplished a lot more. The power generated by a nationwide day of prayer would have done wonders.

Too bad. Daniel Nir had rejected the idea outright. "I'm looking for a popular activity, something that will appeal to everyone," he had told Yitzchak. Yet, what could be more suitable for such a situation than a few heartfelt chapters of *Tehillim* or earnest words of prayer?

For his part, Yitzchak had kept quiet. Some things couldn't be forced, nor did it make sense to try. The soul itself had to yearn for the balm that had no equal when it came to healing a wounded heart.

Yitzchak sighed. He pitied those who thought they were punishing G-d and didn't realize they were punishing themselves. Even if the whole world went out to protest, it would never have the same power as prayer.

Hot tears dripped down onto the page. Had he also once looked at it this way, through Daniel Nir's blurred vision? Had he thought the same years ago? No, he knew he hadn't. His sensitive soul had always carried him along spiritual paths. There hadn't been specific words or defined prayers, but a genuine plea that spiraled upward from a soul slowly feeling its way through the world.

It was prayer that had opened the first door and led him step by step to his new life.

Yitzchak returned to his *Tehillim* with renewed vigor. A general day of prayer had not been called for, but that didn't mean he couldn't make one of his own — a private day of prayer, a day of beseeching, of offering up prayers that a lost son be returned home, with a silent entreaty that all lost sons return home. If not that, let them at least find comfort in the ancient words that were their inheritance.

6
One Hour of Searching

"You're sure you didn't see it, Ima?" Shuki looked forlornly at his mother, who was standing near the *fleishig* counter. "You're sure you didn't see the small green note anywhere?"

His mother didn't answer. If the situation hadn't been so annoying, she would have laughed. On the other hand, if it hadn't been so funny, she probably would have let her irritation show through. Now she only gave Shuki a long look and said nothing.

Shuki wasn't waiting for an answer. If his mother had something to say, she would have gladly told him earlier. She wouldn't have waited for him to repeat his question another half dozen times.

"So you didn't see any green paper?" Shuki sighed heavily and stared at the floor, as if trying to decide whether the ground had swallowed it. "No green paper with names and prices?"

He dragged himself out of the kitchen, mumbling unintelligibly. "I've gotta find it — and now. If I don't bring it to school this afternoon..." With a look of determination that barely hid his growing despair, he set off on another round of searches.

Yesterday, during recess, Chaim Neuman had asked him to do something he loved. Before Pesach, the Neumans had gotten rid of the junk piled in a corner of their yard, and now Chaim and his brothers wanted to plant a small garden there. Chaim had talked a lot about his plans for the garden to anyone willing to listen, but when it came to practical advice, it was Shuki he turned to.

Shuki was flattered. He had promised Chaim that he'd ask his father about what to plant and where to get it when he went home for lunch.

"You won't forget, will you?" Chaim had asked as they left school.

Shuki had laughed. Forget? Chaim sure didn't know him. How could he possibly forget something like this? As soon as he said walked in the door to his house and said hello, he'd start getting the information Chaim needed right away.

But it hadn't worked out that way. His ringing "hello" had hung in the air unanswered, like the steam rising from the soup on the table that was slowly getting cold and the oppressive silence that filled the room until he felt like he was choking.

What happened? Shuki had wanted to ask, but the question remained unspoken. Somehow, Shuki had felt that it was the wrong time for questions. Abba was sitting at the table, ignoring the bowl of soup in front of him, his face buried in a newspaper. Shuki sensed his father's thoughts were a million miles away.

Ima was sitting at the table, too, stirring her soup back and forth. Shuki knew she had no intention of eating. She was tense — and all because of Abba.

Shuki ate his soup quickly and quietly, glancing at his father surreptitiously every so often.

"How are you, son?" his father addressed him suddenly, folding the paper.

Shuki's eyes lit up for a moment. Surely now his father would turn back into the Abba he knew. But one look at his father's face showed him he was mistaken. Abba still looked distracted and nervous, totally preoccupied, as he had been for the past several days.

In the afternoon, an embarrassed Shuki was forced to tell Chaim he didn't have an answer.

"What happened? You forgot?" Chaim asked. "That's okay. Don't worry about it. You can ask tonight. Do you want me to come with you and ask your father myself?"

No way! That was the last thing Shuki had expected. "It'll be okay." His voice sounded shrill to his ears. "It'll really be okay. I didn't forget. It's just that my father was busy, and it didn't work out."

Shuki knew he had no reason to feel uncomfortable. After all, Chaim had only asked him that day, and the day wasn't even over yet. But he couldn't think logically when he felt that sinking sensation in the pit of his stomach. It was a vague uneasiness, as if he had somehow lost out. Shuki was a boy who tried hard to please. He made supreme efforts to be liked, wanted and accepted by his friends — and he had just ruined a perfectly good opportunity sent his way.

"I ruined everything," Shuki muttered to himself, almost in tears, still running from room to room in a frenzy. "Where is that note Abba wrote for me?"

He flung open closet doors one after another only to angrily slam them shut a second later. He emptied his drawers and shook out each notebook, hoping against hope that the note had slipped inside one of them. But it was all in vain. The paper was nowhere to be found.

He moved the beds and checked behind them. He found a copy of a children's magazine he had read two days ago and searched for since but no trace of a green piece of paper.

One Hour of Searching ✦ 45

Shuki dragged the gray stepstool through the house. He looked on top of the refrigerator, on top of the dining room breakfront and on the game shelves, but except for some dust, he found nothing. Where was the note?

Last night he had asked Abba to write down his suggestions for the garden on a piece of paper. Abba had been anxious and distracted then too, but he had promised to do it. This morning, when Shuki was still in bed, Abba had come into the room holding a small piece of green paper from the stack they kept near the phone to jot down messages.

"I wrote down some ideas for your friend," Abba had told Shuki, who was still rubbing traces of sleep from his eyes. "I'm putting the note here."

But where exactly had he put it? Shuki was sure he had heard his father tell him. It had been such a logical place that he hadn't made any effort to remember it. After all, would anyone think of remembering to put the bread in the bread box or the milk in the refrigerator? Did it take effort to recall that glasses belong on your nose and a scarf goes around your neck?

He was positive Abba hadn't gone far. He had stood in the entrance to the room, moved slightly and put the note somewhere. But where?

Shuki sat down and tried to think clearly, but the chair felt like a patch of thorns. He couldn't sit; he couldn't concentrate. He had to find that note fast. The night before, Chaim had called, and that very morning he had come over to him before class to ask about it.

"Too bad you don't have it," Chaim had said. "My father said he had time today to take me to buy what we need."

What would Shuki tell him now? He just had to find the note before he went back to school.

Various possibilities flashed through his mind. Time after time, he jumped up only to sink back down onto the edge of the chair like a worried old man.

Was it near the telephone? No. On the magnet attached to the refrigerator door? Nope. On the kitchen table near the door? No again. One by one, Shuki's bursts of inspiration met with defeat.

Enough! He decided not to think about it anymore.

"When is Abba coming home today?" Shuki called in the direction of the kitchen. "Are you sure he won't be here by the afternoon?"

Ima dried her hands on a towel. "I don't know what's gotten into you today, Shuki," she said. "You know Abba is in Yerushalayim now at the demonstration outside the Knesset for Yossi Nir. He'll probably be home late, and he'll be tired. I think you should get ready to go back to cheder now. Tell your friend what happened and bring him an answer tomorrow. What's the big deal?"

Shuki sighed. It wasn't really a big deal, but then again, it was. Too bad that today of all days Abba wasn't home. Abba could have written him another note in no time and solved all his problems. "Too bad Abba doesn't have a cellular phone," he said suddenly. "Too bad they had to pick today for the demonstration, too bad —"

Suddenly he thought of the small drawer near the telephone crammed with all sorts of notes and invitations. It seemed most logical that his important note would be there too.

He threw open the drawer and pulled out papers one after the other. There was the water bill and the telephone bill, an assortment of receipts, an invitation to the Weiss's bar mitzva and — a small envelope caught his attention. He opened it and found a stiff white card, embossed with a somber black border. On it was written:

In June 1982, your loved one went out to war in Lebanon. A month later, he had already returned home. He came back to you and has been with you until today.

Our beloved Yossi also left in June 1982 to fight in Lebanon. He hasn't returned since. We have been standing by the door and waiting for fifteen years, but our Yossi hasn't come home yet.

One Hour of Searching ❖ 47

Please stretch out your hands to Yossi, who wants to come home.

On Wednesday, June 5, 1997, a large demonstration will be held outside the Knesset for Yossi. Be with us at this difficult hour. Remember Yossi who left together with you and still hasn't come back.

In gratitude and hope,
Daniel and Efrat Nir

Yossi crumpled the card in his fist. A burst of emotion suddenly flooded his young heart. "Your loved one went out to war…" Had Abba been in the army together with Yossi Nir? Had he fought alongside him? Talked to him?

Shuki tried to envision his father walking at Yossi Nir's side. He had no problem imagining Yossi. The publicity photos during the last few weeks had caught his attention too. It was easy to picture the tall, handsome soldier, a broad grin on his face and a gun slung over his shoulder. Imagining his father as a soldier was much harder. His father a soldier? Not as far as he knew.

Abba didn't like to talk about the past. For the longest time he had even managed to hide the fact that things had once been different. But why?

"What difference does it make?" he always said, cupping Shuki's chin and smiling warmly into his eyes.

Shuki would give in immediately. "It really doesn't matter," he would tell Abba, returning the smile. "I was just curious."

Okay, so his father had probably been a soldier once. He had fought in difficult battles. His friend, a friend who had been in combat with him, had been taken prisoner, and Abba had come home.

Shuki shivered. Where was he now, this Yossi Nir? What was he doing? What was he thinking about? Was he still alive somewhere? How had the family found the determination not to give up after fifteen years of searching?

Oh! Searching! What about his own search?

Shuki opened the drawer again to look for the green note. It wasn't there. Slowly, he closed the drawer. Suddenly he didn't care so much about what Chaim would say. The note assumed its real proportions. It was only a small square piece of paper anyway.

If one hour of searching had made him frantic, what could be said about fifteen years of searching for a lost son?

7
Bitter Disappointment

The evening air was warm and humid. Even the open shutters brought no cool breeze to the large room, only flies and other buzzing insects.

Yitzchak Katz straightened his black yarmulke, glanced again at the letter in front of him and wondered what had brought him to the Nir residence that evening. Had the morning sun whispered in his ear that somewhere in the north of Israel there was a dark, gloomy house that saw no sunshine? Maybe it was because of his son Yehoshua who found the daily newspaper excellent for drying windows and ideal for protecting the table during arts-and-crafts projects.

That morning, Yehoshua had stood by the kitchen table trying to deal efficiently with two crackers generously spread with cheese. He had smoothed the unruly *peyos* that refused to stay in place and stared at the newspaper open in front of him.

"They don't say a thing about it," he had said angrily, flinging the paper aside. "What's going to happen now that the big demonstration is over?" he had demanded. "What did all those important Knesset members decide? That's what I'd like to know."

Yitzchak had stared out the window, a bitter smile twisting his face. *My Yehoshua is still so innocent,* he remembered thinking as he lovingly stroked his son's velvet yarmulke. *With his child's eyes, he sees a world that's only good.*

Back then, Yitzchak hadn't thought of himself as naive. Looking back, he realized that he and Yossi had been too innocent. They had put too much faith in the lengthy army training, the rigorous preparations for the war, the camaraderie in arms.

Daniel Nir got up stiffly from his chair and went over to the walnut buffet. Almost automatically, he opened it and took out two crystal glasses.

Yitzchak moistened his lips. He hadn't realized how dry they were. The dreadful dryness in his heart as he read the letter had made him forget everything.

The letter lay, cold and official, on the table.

June 12, 1986
Dear Mr. and Mrs. Nir,

The government of Israel, the Israel Defense Forces and the soldiers and citizens of the country share your pain for your son Yosef, missing in action since the Peace for Galilee military campaign in 1982.

The Israel Defense Forces will continue to do everything possible to locate the missing soldiers.

The demonstration in front of the Knesset building on June 8, 1996, was an expression of deep, searing pain, yet it is not within our power to do more than what has already been done.

There is no doubt that if and when new avenues of approach open up they will be pursued by all parties concerned to bring about a positive turn for the best.

With words of encouragement, we remain,

Sincerely yours,
The Government of Israel

Yitzchak turned his eyes from the black letters to the crystal glass. He clutched the delicate glass so tightly between his fingers that his thumbs turned red. What a beautiful glass, he tried telling himself. But it sounded hollow even to him. When your hopes and dreams shatter before your eyes, can a crystal glass stand peacefully in front of you?

With great effort, he focused on a small green leaf on the embroidered tablecloth. It was only a leaf, a green leaf that drifts on the wind to some unknown destination in an unknown land. Yes, once there had been a fresh green leaf, but it fell off a tree, turning yellow before its time....

Enough!

He set the glass down hard on the table. Yes, it was enough. His thoughts were again leading him to a dead end, before which lay only a gaping abyss. Better for him to stop and think of other things.

The truth was, he couldn't think of anything else — but at the very least, he could think about it differently, maybe try to find a new angle.

Trust in Hashem. The magic words echoed in his mind, bringing a semblance of peace and tranquility. His tension eased, as if a heavy burden of responsibility was lifted from his shoulders.

Have pure, unquestioning faith in Hashem. He found solace in those words and the gift of meaning behind them. He would never forget the moment when he had first understood them. Then, he had been the unhappiest person in the world. He saw his future being destroyed before his eyes. More than once the thought had crossed his mind that he would be better off if his mind were duller, if only that would allow him to escape to a world of blessed delusion, a place where he wouldn't feel the searing pain.

But it was not to be. He didn't lose consciousness, not for a minute. Even when his face went up in flames, his mind remained clear. His eyes were open every waking moment to the sudden new reality thrust upon him.

He had nowhere to escape the first time they placed the small round mirror in front of his eyes. His mother sat by his side, sobbing uncontrollably. His father had bitten his lips and left the room shouting, "Why did you bring him this? Take that mirror away immediately!"

They tried to fool him. They brought him a tiny mirror that was half covered with cheerful-looking clowns painted on it.

It didn't help. The little he saw reflected in the mirror was more than enough. He was too smart to be fooled. As for what he didn't actually see, his imagination easily filled the gap.

What did they think? That he didn't notice the frightened expressions on their faces when they entered his hospital room after the bandages were removed? Did they think he was blind? How could he not see their eyes dart from place to place trying to avoid eye contact, turning to the white walls, the metal bed, the sheet with the hospital logo — anything but the blotched, peeling, horrible face distorted beyond recognition?

Coming as it did while he was in a state of severe depression, the second piece of bad news — that his memory was gone — was the last straw. If at first he had occasional moments of optimism when he imagined himself sitting in a library immersed in thick tomes, doing the research and experiments he had always dreamed about, the bitter truth blasted his hopes, turning them to whispering embers.

He sat for long stretches of time, his head cradled in his hands, crying and silently screaming. *There's nothing left of you,* he muttered over and over again. *Neither on the outside nor within. On the outside, you have turned into scorched red dough, and inside there are only burnt cinders. Nothing is left of who you were, absolutely nothing.*

He was filled with questions in those difficult days, filled with "whys" and "how comes," "ifs" and "buts." People tried to help him, to offer comfort, encouragement and support, but nothing helped him as much as those three little words: "Trust in Hashem."

He had discovered Hashem even before what happened, but now he wanted to know Him even more. He now saw Him for the first time as a merciful Father Who lovingly watched over him from on High. He no longer felt disappointed, cheated by life and full of complaints. No, he felt more like a small, dependent child burying his scarred face in the loving embrace of his Father, no questions asked. Trust in Hashem. Whatever happened was His Will. Even if you can't understand, you must believe that whatever happens is what is best for you.

Yitzchak knew that words mean different things to different people. For him, these were the words his wounded soul blindly followed. There was no reason to question, no need for defiance. Instead, all he had to do was bow his head and accept it all with humility and faith.

As time passed and such faith became his way of life, these words remained his guiding light. They guided him to Arazim, an out-of-the-way settlement, and to his garden and his quiet, peaceful life, as calm today as yesterday and as tranquil yesterday as last week.

Those who hadn't known Tzachi would never have believed that the Yitzchak they knew had once been ambitious. They would never have dreamed that the quiet, gentle person they knew had once craved, even thrived, on challenge, and was aggressive in the pursuit of knowledge to the point of arrogance. Now he was content to remain out of the limelight and had no interest in what others said or didn't say about him, what they talked about and didn't talk about. All that mattered to him was to follow Hashem as a son follows his father.

Yitzchak lifted his head. The sudden movement jostled the pitcher of orange juice in Daniel's hand. The small round ice cubes sparkled through the glass.

Taking the glass from his friend's hand, Daniel filled it. "To your health," he said with forced cheer, willing Yitzchak to smile.

Yitzchak took the glass, conscious his hand was trembling.

"Thanks, Daniel." He set the glass down on the table.

"Drink," his host urged him gently. "Yosefa is bringing cake too."

"Uh, everything's okay. There's no need for it." Yitzchak wanted to say that he wasn't hungry, but that wasn't true. He actually could do with something to eat. "Do you have some cold water?" was what he finally said.

A shadow crossed Daniel's face. No longer the friendly host, he assumed his official persona as the nondescript clerk sitting behind the desk at the local bank branch. A reserved coolness crept into his voice as he asked, "Is it the *hechsher*?"

His voice contained no trace of derision, only hurt, surprise and distance.

Yitzchak wondered how he could ease the tension. He tapped his fingertips on the side of the glass, searching for the right words. It wasn't the time for lengthy explanations or long speeches. Something else was needed — but what?

Yosefa came into the room carrying a plate laden with delicious-looking cakes and pastries. Her golden curls bounced as she put the plate on the coffee table.

"Should I bring more juice?" she asked, noticing their guest's still-full glass of juice. "You didn't drink anything. I know why," she smiled mischievously. "You don't like this kind of juice. I don't either. Abba always says I don't have good taste. But Abba, look, our guest doesn't have good taste either. Or maybe he really does know what tastes good."

She quickly ran back to the kitchen without waiting for an answer. "I'll bring you a glass of cold water." Her voice rang through the house. In a flash, she was back in the living room holding a paper cup.

"I hope this is good enough." With her large green eyes, she looked directly at her father. "You know Ima doesn't let me touch the crystal glasses. That's why I brought a paper cup. Is that all right?"

"It's perfect," Yitzchak wanted to say, but for some reason

the words stuck in his throat. The parched feeling in his throat was paralyzing his vocal chords. Instead, he slowly enunciated a blessing and sipped the cool, refreshing water.

Yosefa was no longer in the room, but the light of her golden curls lingered in the air.

A faint smile flickered on Daniel's lips. "If I don't have Yossi," he said, "at least I have Yosefa. She looks just like him. She keeps alive the dream even in the most difficult moments.

"I'll tell you quite frankly," he continued, "there've been plenty of difficult moments in the past fifteen years. There were times when the pain and worry tore at my heart. Then, too, there was the anger and a sense of numbness.

"But I'll tell you something, Yitzchak, if ever there was a difficult day, a day of gut-wrenching disappointment, this is one of them."

8
The Heart of the Tragedy

"Will you make the light?" Yitzchak asked as he fixed his gaze at the blinking yellow traffic light. "I sure hope so," he continued the small talk, taking advantage of every possible moment to defuse the heavy silence. "You know this congested intersection as well as I."

Daniel turned his head from the road momentarily to face his passenger. Yitzchak was frightened by the empty look he saw in Daniel's eyes.

"I don't hope for anything," Daniel said flatly, staring once again at the heavy traffic in front of him. "It's foolish to build your life on hopes. It may give you momentary pleasure, but it ruins your life. Hopes tend to explode in your face."

Yitzchak swallowed hard. He hadn't thought the last disappointment was such a blow. The light turned red, giving Daniel time to cast a tortured glance at Yitzchak's scarred features.

"Seven years went by, just like that," Daniel painfully reminisced. "For the first seven years we lived our private pain, waiting from letter to letter to hear even a shred of news from the Ministry of Defense. We would sit in the living room for hours on end, although we knew it was unrealistic, even childish, imagining the moment when Yossi would fling open the door and appear. In our mind's eye we saw him just as he was on the day he left — standing in his pressed army uniform, with a wide, confident smile on his face. Oh, the illusions of aging parents." His voice trailed off.

"We were never the kind of people who knew how to get things moving in the establishment. Sure, we had our criticisms and complaints, but that was as far as we went with it. Mentally, I wrote letters to bank presidents, the labor union, city hall, the school principal, the bus companies. All the letters had the same opening sentence and the same closing one — I knew them by heart — but not one of them ever got written down on paper, let alone sent."

Yitzchak nodded, identifying with every word. He once read a saying on a wall calendar: "The only thing tension does is stretch the shoulders." How many pages had been torn off calendars and thrown away since Daniel's shoulders were taut with tension? Fifteen years of pain and longing had the power to totally change much more than a person's shoulders. The Daniel Nir of today was not the Daniel Nir that once was.

Yitzchak couldn't help but reflect that, no matter what happened, Daniel would never be that person again. The years that passed were gone, but the wrinkles they had added to Daniel's forehead would remain etched there forever.

"We wasted seven crucial years," Daniel said. "We were convinced the government was doing its utmost. Other than writing letters to the various prime ministers and attending one useless meeting after another, we didn't do a thing."

Yitzchak sighed. From the corner of his eye, he suddenly saw Daniel as fragile, as a person who had been tossed into stormy waters and told to sink or swim.

Daniel had jumped into the water with Yitzchak at his side. They had done everything humanly possible, but all their efforts ended the same way — in one big zero.

The red light had long since turned green, and the compact car surged forward. *You move ahead,* thought Yitzchak glumly, *yet the monotonous black asphalt road with its metal guardrails gives you the feeling you're getting nowhere.*

Yitzchak thought of all the many meetings with international VIPs, key figures with extensive connections in the Arab word. He saw in his mind's eye the heavy file of letters in Daniel's desk drawer. Where was Yossi in this seemingly unending mass?

The sharp odor of gasoline hit his nostrils.

"The tank is almost empty," Daniel informed him as he pulled into the gas station. "It'll be just a few minutes, okay?"

Yitzchak took advantage of the stop to get out of the car and stretch his legs. He straightened his aching back, a pleasure he wouldn't allow himself when Daniel was by his side. How could he stand tall when only inches away there was a pair of shoulders weighed down with sorrow?

He tried to organize his thoughts. *Daniel is hurt and troubled. He's been slapped in the face today by another wave, and he's struggling to keep his head above water with the bitter taste of salt in his mouth. I'm right here, standing by his side. I can't let Daniel give up.*

These past months, Daniel had put all his energy into the publicity campaign. He had pinned all his hopes on its success. But the campaign was a disappointment. There was the mass rally, but it didn't have the effect he was hoping for — to move the government to do something. It was no more than another letter to add to the overflowing file. *Well,* Yitzchak thought to himself, *it's never good to put all your eggs in one basket. You have to leave room for other options, for another way out. You've got to reach for the last life preserver.*

His mind raced. Again he felt that nagging ache that engulfed

The Heart of the Tragedy ♦ 59

him whenever he pushed himself to analyze a situation. He reentered the car and sat down. He would ask Daniel for a complete up-to-date list of all his previous efforts. They'd go over it together, check it out and send more letters. They'd set up more meetings.

He pressed his forehead against the car window, trying to cool off the thoughts burning in his brain. *No, he chided himself. That's not enough. You have to look for a new angle. You've got to come up with a brilliant idea that's never been tried. What you need is a breakthrough.*

Nervously, he gnawed on a fingernail. When something is beyond reach, what's there to lose by dreaming even the wildest dreams?

If I were today as I once was, if I had the head today that I had years ago, he thought, his eyes growing misty, *everything would be different. Maybe then I'd be able to come up with an ingenious plan. Back then, I would have been able to find the right person in the right place to put in a good word. I'd have found the right approach to get him involved and to get the information needed to locate Yossi. Is he dead or alive? More important — where is he and who is holding him captive?*

Yitzchak rolled down the window. No, there was no chance he could mobilize Tzachi's brilliant mind to search for Yossi Nir. That mind belonged to the past. Once it had been his mind, a bright mind with extraordinary powers of concentration. Today his face was covered with scars, a memorial to the brilliant mind that once was and is no more.

But what he could give Daniel he gave — his outstretched hand, another shoulder for support, his two feet that were willing to run anywhere and, most of all, his heart.

Looking out the car window, he saw Daniel pay the gas station attendant, take the change and pocket it.

You fool, Yitzchak chided himself, a bitter smile on his lips. *You connect everything — the damage to your brain and Yossi's last appearance — to that ill-fated battle. If you're cry-*

ing over your injury because it's preventing you from helping Yossi, shouldn't you cry over Yossi himself? Even better, maybe you should look to the Hand that took Yossi to some unknown place and decreed that your mind should suffer. Pray for a kind, loving caress, a bandage, a soothing salve for your wounds, and daven to bring Yossi back from the distant unknown to all those waiting for him.

Yitzchak lifted his eyes toward heaven with renewed trust and faith.

Daniel returned to the car and hurriedly put the keys in the ignition. "Sorry for the delay," he said. Despite the apology, his voice held a note of satisfaction. "Someone recognized me from my picture in that newspaper interview and wanted to know what's happening."

Yitzchak heard in his friend's voice the new lease on life the attendant in the oil-stained overalls had managed to impart as he filled up the tank. As Daniel pulled onto the main highway, Yitzchak could almost feel the wheels effortlessly flying over the road, so unlike the heavy drag of only a few minutes earlier.

"Let's start from scratch," he said aloud, trying to inject optimism in his voice.

Daniel nodded in agreement. "Here's where we turn right, isn't it?"

"Yes."

Daniel relished these moments behind the wheel. He always said that driving gave him a sense of moving forward. Yitzchak never took his car to Daniel's. He'd rather let Daniel drive him home.

A red light stopped the car at the junction leading to Arazim. The intersection was busy as usual, and Daniel, no longer disinterested in his surroundings, scanned the countryside with interest. At the sight of a large billboard to his right, he did a double take.

His face white, he pulled over to the side of the road and

opened the car door.

"Do you see this, Yitzchak?" he cried.

Yitzchak remained silent. The sign was enormous. Yitzchak himself was the one who had gone to Media Ads and paid for the billboard. It was one of many in the country, all situated at major intersections as part of the publicity campaign to arouse public awareness of Yossi's plight.

"Is Yosef still alive?" the bold black letters screamed. At the bottom, against the yellow background, was a picture of Yossi Nir in his army uniform smiling his sweet smile. "Yossi wants to come home. Help him!" read the plea in smaller letters.

Daniel was overcome with emotion as he stood looking at Yossi's smiling face. Tall ladders leaned against the billboard as four workers pasted new sheets of a fresh ad. Two colorful rectangles were already hanging on the left showing a bottle of cola resting in someone's palm. An ad comes and an ad goes, but the billboard goes on forever.

Daniel tried to ignore the new sign. He stood close to his Yossi battling for his life beneath the wide brushes that plastered the surface with a thick coat of paste. The missing words of his plea were hidden by a carefree hand waving the bottle of cola.

"Is Yosef still" was all Daniel saw. "Is Yosef still alive?" Daniel wanted to shout. Why are you blotting out the word "alive"? My Yossi is alive! Let him stay here on the sign alive and smiling! Why are you burying him beneath the silly slogan about the taste of life from this or that drink?

"I, too, once liked days bubbling with activity," Daniel gave voice to his feeling. Yossi too loved life, his heart cried. But our taste of life was different from theirs.

"What do they know?" Daniel suddenly screamed in a voice full of pain. "What do they know about the taste of life? Yossi," Daniel's voice turned soft and pleading, "give me one last smile before they erase you from here too."

Yossi smiled. It was a half smile. He looked at his father with one eye and seemed to take his leave peacefully, a second before the carefree youth with the cola took his place in the public eye.

Daniel stood as if rooted to the spot. Hypnotized, he stared at the workers silently pasting away. They pasted the last two sections on the billboard. Now the words "Yossi wants" disappeared. So did the word "still."

"Yossi no longer wants anything," Daniel whispered as he slowly walked to the parked car.

Yitzchak walked beside him in silence. Daniel cast one last glance at the sign before he turned the key in the ignition. He saw the young boy joyfully drinking his bubbling cola.

"All the cars behind us," Yitzchak said, "will see this boy and the bottle of soda in his hands. They won't even know that a few seconds before another young boy was here — Yossi Nir, a boy pleading for his life."

The car surged forward. "It's like a story," Daniel continued the thought. "Once upon a time there was a boy. The boy's name was Yossi Nir. He walked through the streets happy and smiling, dreaming of the future, wanting to live life to its fullest. Then one day the boy disappeared. They searched for him one day, a second day, perhaps even a year or two. Then they stopped searching. In the street where he walked, the cars continued to travel, their horns blaring. On the sidewalks where he had once walked, people continued to walk and laugh and enjoy life. They all forgot that there was once a Yossi Nir."

Daniel wiped away a tear.

"Perhaps that's how all those whose loved ones are no longer with them think," he said suddenly. "But they at least can visit their final resting place. They have a place where they can go talk to them, a place where they can mourn.

"My Yossi is alive, and if not – we don't know about it. And this," he concluded, "is the heart of the tragedy."

9

The Locked Door

The soft pile of the carpet absorbed the nervous tapping of Yitzchak's shoes. None of the clients in the small waiting room could detect the tension in his moves. Each was filled with hope, expectation and a strong will to leave the place a calmer, more relaxed and happier person.

Yitzchak took a seat. In a woven straw basket on the floor lay various medical journals. He absentmindedly reached for one of them. The thin paper was just the thing to relieve his fingers' restlessness. What was written on the pages didn't matter. He leafed through them, thinking about Dr. Malin and why he was there in his office.

On the wall was a blowup identical to the smaller version in his pocket explaining the new treatment. "Dr. Malin," it said, "heals with the positive energy flowing from his hands. He administers a series of ten treatments tailor-made for each patient based on the ailment. In many cases, Dr. Malin's treatment works wonders where conventional medicine has failed."

In smaller letters was an extensive list of problems that Dr. Malin promised to alleviate in his Tel Aviv clinic. The list was long: migraine headaches, backaches, hearing loss, ulcers, high blood pressure, stress and memory disorders. The words that had caught Yitzchak's attention were "lack of concentration."

It hadn't taken him long to remember how hard he had tried over the years to regain his powers of concentration. He had jotted down the name and address and called for an appointment. Now, there he was. He had momentarily set aside all his plans regarding his best friend, Yossi Nir, whom he thought of day and night, and had gone to the doctor's office in Tel Aviv. Everything else could wait but not this.

What would happen, Yitzchak savored the possibility, *if Dr. Malin is really Hashem's messenger to cure me? What would it be like if I left this office today or tomorrow or next week with my mind functioning as it once did?*

He tried to imagine the scene. He would come home and go straight over to the large bookcase in the living room. Crammed with books, it was his pride and joy. Those sacred volumes added sanctity to the room, the house and his soul, he was wont to say. He remembered the day he had unloaded a large set of Shas, the most recent deluxe edition, from his car. Shuki had been standing in the doorway, watching. He was about four years old at the time, maybe five.

"Abba, why do you need so many books?" he had asked. "You'll never read them all."

He knew the boy hadn't meant to embarrass him. Every child, at one stage or another in his life, looks at the bookcase in his home lined with wall-to-wall books and finds it overwhelming. Nevertheless, for Yitzchak the words had a deeper, more painful meaning.

If Dr. Malin succeeded where others had failed, Yitzchak's first steps would be toward that bookcase. And if it were up to him, he would stay there, with Hashem's help, for a long, long time. Even now, he spent hours with his *sefarim.* He breathed their holiness, lovingly caressed the binding and the embossed letters on the covers.

Opening one, he would mobilize all his powers of concentration, however minimal, to understand the depth of the words written. Five, ten minutes would pass until, his eyes burning red and his head pounding like a sledgehammer, an inner voice would mock, "You thought you had the same mind you once did, but times have changed."

Yitzchak suddenly realized that the man next to him was talking. "You're here because of a hearing problem, aren't you?" he bantered. "This is the fifth time I've tried talking to you."

Yitzchak blushed.

"Is this your first visit?" asked the friendly stranger.

Yitzchak's nod disappointed him.

"Too bad," he continued. "I was hoping to hear what someone who was already treated by Dr. Malin had to say. Everyone sitting in this room, including you and me, is here for the first time."

The young man sitting opposite, who looked to be about twenty, joined the conversation. "I think," he said in a stage whisper, an ironic smile on his lips, "that everyone comes here only for a first time."

The two of them laughed, others in the waiting room smiled, but not Yitzchak. He wasn't about to let his hopes be dashed by cynics. He was determined to find the right treatment for his problem right there in that office. He had lived through enough disappointments.

"What do you say to all these letters of thanks?" Yitzchak asked, trying to convince not only them but himself as well. He glanced at the various diplomas on the wall, all of them bearing impressive seals and signatures. Proudly displayed next to them were thank-you letters from grateful patients.

"It's not that hard for someone to write effusive letters of gratitude and sign them with whatever name he chooses," said the skeptic.

Yitzchak made no reply. He wondered what had brought the man to the clinic. Perhaps he was one of those who had just about given up all hope and wanted to give it one last chance.

He stood up to inspect the framed documents on the wall. He wasn't willing to give them that much credence, either. Yet, still, maybe one of them would mention regaining lost powers of concentration.

He read each and every letter. Two were from patients who had a weight loss of forty-five and sixty-five pounds respectively and couldn't say enough in praise of the doctor. Another was from someone who had been cured of an ulcer, and one was a grateful letter from the mother of a child who had stopped stuttering. There was not a word about concentration.

Too bad, Yitzchak thought as he went back to his chair. Well, if things turned out well, he would be the one to write the next letter — in large, gold-embossed letters on a silver background. He'd willingly pay anything to the person who could restore his ability to immerse himself in the depths of Torah study.

His thoughts went back to the days before it all happened. Then he had been able to sit for eight hours a day in front of an open Gemara, concentrating on the tiny print, understanding all the difficult concepts. Nothing could distract him.

Oh, how his heart cried. He no longer basked in the sweetness of Torah. In those early years, his mind had been open, but his heart had been closed to Hashem's ways. Then, when his heart was open and ready, his mind was no longer capable.

He remembered as if it were yesterday those first Gemara lessons. The difficulties seemed insurmountable, but he didn't despair. He attributed it to the new style to which he was unaccustomed. But when it lingered on and on, Yitzchak understood that it wasn't the new style that was the source of the problem.

He had then turned to one of his books from "back then," one of the books he had promised himself he would never touch again. He opened the book to the fourth chapter and tried to study as if preparing for a difficult test. The memory of what had happened then made him shudder even now. The bald truth had stared him in the face, leaving him nowhere to escape.

He tried to evade its message by rationalizing that he was tired, hungry and tense. He opened the book the next day and the day after that — but truth was stronger than he. Yitzchak knew, without a doubt, that his powers of concentration were severely damaged. He could no longer concentrate on the printed letters for more than a few minutes at a time.

Frantic, he ran from doctor to doctor. All he got from the medical experts was cool detachment.

"The war, no doubt, caused this condition," said one.

"It's only natural. It will improve with time," said another.

"It's not something we can quantify," said yet another. "Try to get more rest."

Frustrated, all Yitzchak could do was leave, slamming the door behind him. *Why do they refuse to understand?* he cried bitterly. The door to a wonderful world was finally open before him, a world full of light, and suddenly the door was slammed shut in his face, locking him out. Why wasn't anyone trying to help him break down the barrier so he could move forward?

Yitzchak was stubborn. He went from neurosurgeon to neurosurgeon. At first, the routine testing didn't show a thing, but after a series of complex scans, the cause was detected. The doctors noticed that a small blood vessel had burst, leading to pressure buildup on the brain cells in the area where the powers of concentration are located. There was nothing to do. All that could be offered him was medication to thin the blood so there would be no more damage. That was it.

"Do you mean to say there's no cure?" Yitzchak practically shouted at the neurosurgeon.

"I didn't say that," came the answer. "The annals of medicine tell of cases where the blood was reabsorbed by the brain tissues, and the stricken section returned to normal. But this has to happen naturally, without medical intervention."

Yitzchak had just sat there, overwhelmed.

"Be happy that nothing worse happened," the doctor added, trying to soften the blow. "Sometimes stuttering or even loss of speech can occur. At other times, partial or complete paralysis or even complete loss of memory can result. Be thankful the pressure is localized and affects only your ability to concentrate."

Only, Yitzchak thought bitterly. Later he found out that this was the standard approach. Live with it, the doctors said.

At the sight of an elderly gentleman leaning on a cane walking out of the doctor's office, Yitzchak returned to the present, to Dr. Malin's waiting room. Yitzchak studied the old man carefully. He thought he detected a measure of satisfaction on his face.

Dr. Malin is a G-d-fearing Jew, the thought popped into his head. Maybe he will understand the impact this disability has on my life. Maybe because he's religious, he'll make an extra effort to restore to me some of the ability I once had. They say he tries to improve the quality of life for his patients, even for those whose life expectancy may be short, so they can enjoy their remaining days as much as possible. Well, is there anything that would improve my quality of life more than this? What can give my life more meaning and quality than long hours of sitting over a Gemara?

He suddenly thought of his son. Shuki had so many questions. There was so much he wanted to know. Wasn't he entitled to a father like all other boys had?

Shuki could sit and learn with his father, but for his father to be able to teach him and explain the hard points, that was a different story. He had spoken to the Rav, who agreed to help Shuki. The Rav said he was willing to sit with the boy from time to time and explain the difficult passages. But his Shuki was so shy. He would rather leave homework unanswered than ask the Rav — or anyone else — for help.

Yitzchak felt a sudden surge of pity. A father is supposed to teach his child Torah, he thought sadly. How he davened to Hashem, hoping that he would at least be able to pass on to Shuki the feelings that were inside – his love for every letter of the Torah, his yearning, the burning desire in his soul that gave him no rest. If only he could pass this on to his son, Shuki would see that the desire to learn melts all barriers of embarrassment.

His turn came to go into the doctor's office. Slowly, he crossed the floor and opened the door to the inner office, his pounding heart sounding loud to him.

He sat down in the chair in front of Dr. Malin's desk, waiting.

The doctor looked him straight in the eye, slowly taking him in. "What's the background?" he asked, without preliminaries.

"Wounded in action," Yitzchak replied quietly.

Dr. Malin continued to study him wordlessly as he glanced at the medical reports on his desk. He opened and closed a file, adjusted his metal-frame glasses and cleared his throat.

"In all fairness," he said, looking anywhere but directly at Yitzchak, "I must be perfectly honest with you. I have no way to treat your condition."

Yitzchak turned white. He was about to get up when he realized that he hadn't told the doctor anything about his problem.

"Scars are a problem for conventional medicine," Dr. Malin said.

"That's not why I came to you," Yitzchak said, cutting the doctor short as he painfully touched his scarred face. "I have a different problem, one that's even more painful."

A heavy silence hung in the room. Yitzchak knew it was his turn to speak, but he felt drained. Human beings see only the outside, but *Hakadosh Baruch Hu* sees beyond, deep into the brain, deep within the heart. He knows that the facial scars go much deeper, and that they will never totally heal. They will always remain fresh, mourning the loss.

Would he find a cure here in this room? Would the locked door finally open, letting in a world full of light?

10
A Need to Cry

Shuki looked at his watch. In exactly another seven minutes, the bell would ring and science class would finally begin. For the past six days, he had been waiting impatiently for his favorite class. He glanced at the small open Gemara on his desk and tried hard to concentrate. Paying attention was usually no problem for Shuki, who understood everything taught. He really enjoyed learning, *baruch Hashem*, and usually asked his rebbe good questions. But right now, he just couldn't concentrate.

Meir read off his homework answers. Shuki noticed how Rabbi Gold's eyes lit up as he slowly nodded his head in rhythm to Meir's words. *Meir gave a great answer*, Shuki thought, aware he was jealous. Meir wasn't as smart as he was and paid a lot less attention in class. Meir could go bike riding before finishing his homework or even before reviewing the material. But now it would be Meir who would get a good mark in the rebbe's notebook, and he would be the one showered with praise in front of the whole class, not Shuki.

So what's the big deal? thought Shuki. Meir himself admitted that his father helped him with the homework. So what was it worth? He, Shuki, prepared the answers all by himself. His feelings of envy were bitter.

Without realizing what he was doing, Shuki felt under his seat for his brown leather briefcase. His fingers sought the metal buckle, and before he knew it, he was holding the meticulously covered notebook in his hands. The large round sticker on the cover of his precious science notebook was staring at him.

Shuki felt compelled to hold his science notebook in his hands. Meir's voice droned on as he continued to recite the answers. *Actually,* Shuki thought, *there's nothing wrong with his father helping him, is there?* Wouldn't he, Shuki, run to his father every night, Gemara or *Chumash* in hand, if only his father could help him? Why, that's exactly what he had done last Wednesday with his science project.

Shuki looked at his watch again. Only another five and a half minutes were left. *If only the science teacher picks me to read the second answer out loud,* he hoped. He had spent a lot of time preparing it with his father. The assignment was to identify leaves and bring a labeled sample of each variety. But Shuki had done more than that, much more.

He couldn't help but peek. Two full pages of dried leaves in a multitude of shapes and sizes appeared before him. Under every leaf, in clear, precise lettering, Shuki had written the plant name and identifying characteristics. If only the teacher would call on him to read this answer, Shuki hopefully thought, he'd raise his hand high, as high as he could. If only...

Shuki closed his eyes. He envisioned the teacher taking the notebook from his hand and showing it to the class as he walked down the rows, stopping at every boy. He could already hear his classmates' oohs and ahs. Imagine — Shuki Katz! He relished the compliments the teacher would shower on him. He could almost hear him say, "Excellent, Shuki. Very nice."

"Very nice, Shuki," an angry voice thundered at his side.

Shuki opened his eyes, trying to get his bearings. Rabbi Gold was standing right near him, grasping Shuki's science notebook tightly in his hands.

"Very nice, Shuki," he repeated, his tone rising a notch or two. "A science notebook during the Gemara lesson?"

'It's not...," Shuki stammered.

"What's not?" Rabbi Gold asked, as Shuki's shrinking heart skipped a beat. "It's not a science notebook, or it's not a Gemara lesson?"

Shuki held back the words as well as the tears that were ready to burst forth. *It's not what the rebbe thinks.*

There are things that can't be explained, certainly not by a boy burning with shame as the whole class stares at him.

Rabbi Gold held the notebook for another endless minute, as if wondering what to do next. After looking into Shuki's eyes and noticing his trembling hands, the rebbe put the notebook down on the edge of the desk. "What a pity," he said, walking back to his desk at the front of the classroom. "I am very disappointed in you, Yehoshua Katz. A science notebook during the Gemara lesson?"

Shuki sat huddled at the edge of his chair, curling up like a wounded puppy, vulnerable and utterly embarrassed. *I am very disappointed in you, Yehoshua Katz.* The words echoed in his mind over and over. Disappointed...disappointed... In the background, as if to complete the scenario, he heard his classmates whispering, "Imagine...Shuki Katz."

He needed a tissue to wipe away the tears but was afraid to bend down to his briefcase, so he sat up straight and remained silent.

Rabbi Gold continued talking, and one could detect the excitement in his voice. All the boys sat up in their seats, highly interested in what was being said. Shuki wanted to elbow Bentzi to find out what was going on, but he didn't. Instead, he perked up his ears trying to catch what the rebbe was saying.

"...in another three weeks," Shuki heard the tail end of the sentence. Every one started clapping. "In the cheder's auditorium," the rebbe continued, surprising the students with every word, "the principal will address the student body, and a special guest speaker, a very important Rav, will give a lecture. Valuable prizes will be awarded...."

Shuki desperately tried to piece together all the stray bits of information. He had only missed a sentence or two, so why couldn't he figure out what the rebbe was talking about? What had Rabbi Gold just announced? Was there going to be an assembly or a *siyum*? Was it going to be just for his class or for the whole cheder?

"As far as the class speech is concerned," the rebbe said, talking quickly since it was almost time for the bell to ring, "think about it tonight. Tomorrow I want to make the final choice as to which two boys will represent the class. Saying a *dvar Torah* of this kind is not something that can be prepared in one day."

The boys all nodded their heads in agreement. Shuki noticed his classmates exchanging glances. Meir was interested, that was for sure, and so were Bentzi and Chaim. Avreimi probably wanted to be picked and Nati, too.

Wait a minute — what about me?

Shuki really wanted to be chosen. Rabbi Gold said it wasn't the kind of thing you could prepare in one day, and Shuki sure knew how to work hard. He was ready to sit day and night to prepare something special. Was there a chance of his being picked?

By the time Rabbi Gold left the classroom, eight minutes of the science class were gone.

"Who needs it?" complained Bentzi. "What do we need science for anyway? What do we have to learn about some pointy old leaves for anyway?"

"Especially now," Chaim continued, "right when we're in the middle of something interesting. Who cares about Mr. Weiman's boring leaves?"

Shuki didn't say anything. What could he say? That the leaves interested him now and had always interested him? That for a whole week, ever since the last science class, he had been looking forward to this science class?

No, he couldn't say anything. If he did, he'd only make a fool of himself in front of the others. The safest thing was to be quiet.

Mr. Weiman, the science teacher, rushed into the classroom. "Take out your homework," he said without any preliminaries, probably unwilling to waste any more time than the eight minutes he'd already lost.

"The first question," he said, scanning the room. "Avreimi, please."

When Shuki heard the teacher say, "The second question," he felt himself tense. He raised his hand, waving it frantically in front of the teacher's eyes.

"You don't have to wave so hard," Shuki heard a voice behind him whisper. "No one but you is even interested in reading the answer."

Shuki lowered his hand.

"Have you changed your mind?" the teacher asked him.

'Uh...no," Shuki stammered, "not at all. Of course not."

Shuki stood up, nervous yet anxious to give the answer. He read aloud his comprehensive explanation, not skipping a single detail of any leaf. Shuki's eyes were glued to his notebook. He was concentrating so hard on the leaves pasted on the page that he missed seeing his teacher's face glowing with satisfaction.

But it was a good thing Shuki was oblivious to what was going on in class. That way he didn't notice his classmates' bored expressions.

"That was an excellent answer," the teacher exclaimed as he took the notebook. "I see Shuki has even gathered the different leaves, dried them and pasted each leaf near its description. If we had time," he said turning to Shuki, "I would show your wonderful work to the class. But since we're running late, I suggest, class, that you all go over to Shuki's desk to see for yourselves the wonderful job he did."

Shuki modestly lowered his head, thrilled at the honor bestowed on him. He put his notebook aside, carefully closing it so that the pages didn't crease. *I'd better be careful with the leaves, he thought. When all the boys crowd around to look, the pages might get crushed and stained or even torn.* He'd have to guard it carefully. Too much work and effort had gone into that assignment.

In the end, Shuki didn't have to guard the notebook. The second the bell rang, all the boys took their schoolbags and ran out of the room, busy talking about the topic that had been cut short when science class began.

"I wonder who the rebbe will pick," Bentzi said, his eyes sparkling.

"I wonder which Rav will be the guest speaker," Meir said. "If he didn't tell us a name, it means he probably doesn't know yet."

Shuki slowly put his rejected science notebook back into his briefcase. He closed the big metal clasp with an angry snap and dragged himself out of the room after the rest of the boys.

"What interests me the most," Avreimi was saying, "is what the *siyum* will be like. How will we sit? Will it be rows of kids and then rows of fathers, or will each of us sit near his father?"

"I guess," suggested Shmuli, "we'll sit in separate rows."

"Who says?" Bentzi retorted. "It's much nicer sitting together. If my father comes to the *siyum*, why shouldn't he sit with me?"

Shuki stuck close to Meir and Bentzi. He thought he had understood everything, but now something didn't seem right. What were they talking about?

"Are fathers coming to the *siyum*?" Shuki asked incredulously, his usually quiet voice now loud.

"Of course," they answered, looking at him suspiciously. "That's the whole idea. How can we have a *siyum* by ourselves? Besides, what's the big deal?"

Shuki was glad he was almost home. At least he wouldn't have to keep on listening to their happy chatter anymore. He needed to be by himself to think about what he had just heard. He was no longer sure he wanted to be the one to say the *dvar Torah*. He was no longer sure he even wanted to have this *siyum*.

He went into the house. His father was standing next to the door, hanging his hat on the rack. Shuki compared his father's tall stance to his own at that moment. Here he was, hunched over and eyes downcast, when probably all the other kids had burst through their front doors loudly announcing the *siyum*. He too wanted to tell his father about it, but the words stuck in his throat. Instead, he mumbled a greeting and headed for his room.

It didn't take Yitzchak Katz much longer than it had Shuki to sum up his son's gloomy mood. He forced himself to smile and tried to forget his disappointing visit to Dr. Malin's office in Ramat Gan.

"How was your day, Yehoshua'le?" he asked warmly, turning to his son.

"*Baruch Hashem*," Shuki answered, his voice barely audible.

Yitzchak wanted to ask him what they had learned that day in Gemara, what *perek* they were up to in Mishna, what interested them most in Rashi. But he didn't ask any of these questions. He wasn't about to ask a question when he knew he wouldn't be able to understand the answer.

That morning he had been full of hope that he would one day be able to study Torah in depth, but Dr. Malin hadn't given him much of a chance. "After ten treatments you may notice some minor improvement," was all he would say. "When the powers of concentration are impaired due to pressure from blood buildup on the brain, there is not much that can be done."

Shuki took his briefcase and headed for his room. Yitzchak wanted Shuki to remain at his side for one more minute. He wanted to get close to him, to be with him. All of a sudden, he remembered. Today was Wednesday, the day of the science lesson.

"Yehoshua," he asked, this time with a genuine smile on his face, "what did the teacher say? How was the science lesson?"

"Great," was all Shuki would say. His voice broke, and all he could do was rush to his room. The lesson really had been great, but for some strange reason, he felt a strong urge to cry.

11
Spoken from the Heart

Yosefa Nir sat on the top bunk, wide awake, and looked around the spacious room when she was supposed to be sleeping. He mother had told her repeatedly that it was important for her to rest before the long trip they would soon be taking. They were going to meet some very important people, and Yosefa would have to talk to them.

She really didn't want to upset Ima or make her angry, but she just couldn't fall asleep. As if Abba and Ima were resting! She had seen for herself how Ima sat in the living room nervously biting her nails. Sleep, at least in her family, didn't come on demand.

Yosefa's bed creaked as she turned over. *That's the story of my life,* she mourned. *Not only is the closet ancient, the chest of drawers practically falling apart and the paint peeling off the desk, but the bed is just a tired old creaky thing.*

No one else in the class has a bedroom like this, she thought with a rush of self-pity. Last week, when Orna and Shira had come to visit, she had taken them to her room, the room that once belonged to Yossi. They didn't sit down.

"Is this your room?" Shira had asked incredulously. "It sure doesn't look like a girl's room."

She was right. Yosefa didn't think it looked like a girl's room or even a kid's room. All her friends had bright, colorful rooms decorated in pink, orange or yellow. But in her room, everything was brown, old-fashioned and sad. Her mother refused to change a thing. She wouldn't even buy a new chest of drawers, even though the old one was falling apart.

Once a carpenter called in to fix a broken drawer had laughed at it. "Lady," he had said, "are you sure you want to fix this piece of junk? How long do you think it will last? It's seen better days," he said with a chuckle.

Ima hadn't found it funny at all. She had opened the top drawer, still untouched since Yossi had last used it. Looking at Yossi's clothes, organized in neat piles, she had begun to cry. "I'll never get rid of it," she had said, tears streaming down her face.

Yosefa sometimes wished she had a new room with a new desk and chest of drawers. She wanted shiny new Formica in the bright, happy colors she loved. Still, the old one reminded her of the big brother she had never known. The marks that couldn't be cleaned off were places where Yossi had pasted on stickers, her mother told her.

Yosefa loved to think about Yossi, and looking around the room helped her. Everything was waiting for the day he would return. She tried to imagine his laughing face, the one she knew only from photographs. A strange thought suddenly occurred to her. *These clothes may not even fit him. How old is Yossi right now?*

Yosefa jumped off the bed excitedly and ran into the kitchen.

"Ima, hold old is Yossi now? He stays the same age in the pictures, but how old is he really?"

Spoken from the Heart ◆ 81

"He's thirty-four, Yosefa'le," her mother answered, her eyes suddenly moist.

"Thirty-four?" That sounded very old. "Ima, I don't think the clothes in the closet will fit him, and if we're going today to that man who will help bring Yossi home, maybe we should buy him some new clothes."

Her mother didn't answer. Yosefa saw her wipe away a tear.

Everything makes Ima cry, thought Yosefa. *Everything reminds her of Yossi. Every word makes her miss him more.*

"Yosefa," her father called, "come here for a minute. I want you to listen carefully to what I'm going to tell you now."

Yosefa turned to see her father sitting at the kitchen table.

"We will soon be on our way to a very important meeting with the American secretary of state. We worked hard to arrange this meeting, and we want to take full advantage of the opportunity we've been given."

Yosefa listened carefully. She understood more from her father's tone than his actual words the great hopes pinned on the meeting.

"You'll hold this red rose in your right hand," he continued. "Then, take two steps toward the man and speak to him in your beautiful English. Start out by saying, 'Welcome,' and then say this."

Her father handed her a small piece of paper on which the following words were written: "My name is Yosefa Nir. I'm called Yosefa so that I will always remember my big brother, Yosef, whom I have never met. Yossi is somewhere far away, and he wants to come home. I know that you can bring Yossi back to us. I so much want to see him. Please help us as much as you can."

"Now," her father told her, "stand by the kitchen door, hold the flower and let's pretend that I'm the American secretary of state."

Yosefa took the rose and held it carefully. She took two steps forward and began the speech with a very polite "Welcome."

Looking older than she really was, she finished the short speech.

"Excellent!" her father exclaimed.

"That was very good," her mother said, giving her a hug. With a caress that bespoke a mother's love for her daughter and a longing for her missing son, she stroked the little girl's golden curls.

"I'm not sure I'll be able to say it like that when I'm there," Yosefa said, digging her hands deep into her pockets. "Now, I'm talking to you, here at home. But there I'll be talking to a stranger who maybe isn't even interested in Yossi."

Her father nervously drummed his fingers on the tabletop. "Let's hope it will go over well," he said. "Yosefa," he cleared his throat several times, but the words still wouldn't come. How had Yitzchak Katz put it? We'll pray to Hashem, and He will help.

The words remained unsaid as he and his wife and daughter got into the small car and drove onto the winding road leading to Jerusalem. A heavy silence, a silence that not one of them was interested in breaking, settled in the car. Great hopes are often best expressed in silence. Prayer stays in the heart during such private moments.

Yosefa broke the silence by practicing her speech. Before the end-of-the-year performance of the school play, she had also practiced her part. Then it had been only a minor role. The teacher had warned the girls that whoever didn't know her lines and made mistakes would ruin the play.

Sitting in the car, Yosefa felt shaky. She didn't want to forget her lines and get mixed up. She couldn't make mistakes and ruin everything. This time it was for real.

Abba and Ima were also practicing their roles. They weren't rehearsing like she was, but they were planning every move. Just before they left the house, her father had taken out his thick folder with all kinds of documents and letters in it about Yossi. Over the years, he had carefully

Spoken from the Heart ◆ 83

amassed testimony from Yossi's fellow squadron members, reports by experts and scraps of information.

The Nirs knew exactly what they wanted from the American secretary of state who was in Israel as part of his Mideast shuttle. His next stop was Syria, where he would be meeting with Assad and other top Arab officials. The Nirs had one request, a request they had placed before the Israeli government and shouted out at massive rallies. Now they were going to tell the American official that they were certain Syria had up-to-date information on Yossi's whereabouts. All paths led to Syria, a country with great power over Arab terrorist organizations. Syria held the answers to what had happened to Yossi, where he was or if, G-d forbid, he was no longer alive.

Before every peace negotiation with Syria, Mr. and Mrs. Nir planned to say, human decency required, at the very minimum, that the case of the missing Jewish soldier be brought up.

"We've asked this so many times." Yosefa's mother broke the silence in the car. Her husband's only answer was to step on the gas. He too saw in his mind's eye all the images that never left them, day or night. To whom hadn't they talked? They'd talked to cold, disinterested European diplomats, to ambassadors and heads of state — to anyone who had any measure of influence on Syria and the Arab terrorist organizations.

Now they were on their way to tell yet another diplomat. It took all their inner strength to convince themselves that this time it would be different. It was a good thing Yitzchak Katz stood with them. His firm faith allowed them a window of hope for a brighter future.

Yosefa's father parked his car outside the luxury hotel, and the three of them entered the lobby, where they were directed to a suite reserved for visiting dignitaries. After a seemingly endless wait, they were ushered inside to meet one of America's most influential officials. The meeting they had worked so hard to set up was about to begin.

Yosefa held the red rose tightly in her right hand and took

two steps forward. "Welcome," she said in her sweet child's voice, just as she had practiced. She paused, ready to continue according to plan, when the secretary of state stood up and walked over to her.

"You're the little Nir girl, aren't you?" he asked.

"Yes, I'm Yosefa," she replied, nodding her head.

"Yosefa — that's nice. Yosefa," he said, "what can I do for you? What is the thing you want most in all the world?"

Yosefa wanted to continue with her prepared speech about Yossi, but suddenly she saw her father bent over, heavy with the burden of sadness and her mother's eyes always wet with tears, and the words escaped her lips of their own accord. "I don't want my father and mother to be sad anymore," she said. "I don't want Ima to cry anymore because of Yossi. I want us to be a regular, happy family like all families in the world. Just like yours, Mr. Secretary of State."

Yosefa felt weak. She sat down and burst out crying, not knowing if she should have said what she did. Actually, she didn't feel she had anything to do with what she had just said. Her heart had spoken, not her.

And that's how the meeting began.

12
No Reason to Feel Bad

Shuki took his time walking along the familiar path that led from his house to Arazim's cheder. It was the same path he took every day, and every day he was amazed at how one path could be filled with so many different plants and rocks.

He walked slowly, breathing in the cool, fresh morning air that carried the fragrance of wildflowers — all the familiar scents of Arazim proclaiming a bright new day full of promise.

Oh, how Shuki hoped the new day would be full of promise. Yesterday Rabbi Gold had spoken to the class about the *siyum* and the *hadran*. Today, he would not only talk about the *hadran* but would actually choose two boys to say the *dvar Torah*. Shuki knew that lots of boys in the class wanted to be picked, but that didn't stop him from having high hopes.

Yesterday he had spent hours pouring over his Gemara looking up the different *mefarshim*, figuring out the meaning all by himself. His father had passed by several times, even stopping to see what he was doing.

"More science homework?" he had asked. The sparkle in his father's eyes hadn't escaped Shuki. Shuki hadn't wanted that sparkle to disappear, but the truth was he wasn't doing science homework.

"Uh, I'm just going over something," Shuki had said, pushing away the Gemara. "It's nothing important. I'm just...uh...thinking."

"What are you thinking about, son?" his father had asked as he sat down on the bed across from where Shuki sat at his desk. Even though he wasn't right next to him, Shuki felt that his father was very much there for him.

Shuki had wanted to answer, he really had, but instead, all he could do was bite his bottom lip. He knew that if he told Abba what he was really thinking, the words would come rushing out, unchecked, followed by a flood of tears. It wasn't his tears that concerned him, though, as much as it was their effect on his father.

After a few minutes of sitting in silence, his father had gotten up and left the room, leaving Shuki feeling more frustrated than ever. *He loves me so much,* Shuki had thought then, angry with himself, *and I love him so much, too. Why didn't I say anything to him about the siyum and the hadran?*

Now, as Shuki walked the path to cheder, he tried to forget the events of yesterday. Today he would wave his hand with all his might, hoping Rabbi Gold would pick him. But then what would he do? Would he really be able to do it if he was chosen?

He'd worry about that when the time came. The main thing was to be chosen.

"Hi, Shuki." It was Chaim and Bentzi.

"Good morning," Meir and Tzviki chimed in.

"Hi," said Shuki as he joined the group walking to cheder.

"Yesterday," said Meir, "my father spent the whole afternoon going over the Gemara with me, and we found a great *vort*."

"Hey," Tzviki sounded slightly irritated, "who says the rebbe will pick you?"

"He's not saying the rebbe will pick him, but he can plan ahead just in case, can't he?" It was Bentzi. "My father and I also thought of an idea yesterday. My father even said that when he sees Rabbi Gold in the office, he'll ask him what he thinks of the idea."

Shuki walked alongside the group in silence. Actually, he also had an idea of what to say for the *hadran*. He had fallen asleep trying to think of a topic, and in the middle of the night, he had suddenly woken up with an idea. Why not find a connection between the last words in the final *perek* and the first words in the new one that they were going to learn?

He had gotten out of bed, turned on the night-light next to his bed, and tiptoed into the living room. He didn't turn on any lights there because he was afraid it would wake up his parents. They'd for sure get a shock seeing him roaming around the room at two in the morning looking for a Gemara.

Even in the dark, he found what he was looking for. He was so excited he couldn't fall asleep. One thought followed another until he hit on the connection that tied it all together. But he had no one to talk it over with. Who knew if his idea was a good one? Who knew if he was making the right connection? Maybe he didn't understand a point.

Sure, Meir and Bentzi could sound confident – they had their fathers behind them. What did he have? Only some half-baked idea.

Shuki tuned back in to the conversation.

"I wonder when Rabbi Gold will do the picking," said Aryeh as they reached the school yard.

"Yeah, it'll be interesting to see who he picks," Shuki said.

"What's so interesting about it to you?" Meir gave Shuki a look.

"What do you mean?" Shuki looked at him incredulously. "The same way Aryeh's interested, I'm interested."

Meir snickered, and Shuki heard some of the other boys trying to stifle giggles.

"How can you compare yourself to him?" Meir said. "Aryeh has every chance in the world of being chosen. Rabbi Gold is going to want the *hadran* to be on a high level of learning. You know as well as I do that Aryeh's father is a Rav and can help him prepare a *hadran* that'll be as good as anything you could hear in the best yeshiva. How can you even consider yourself in the running?"

The blood drained from Shuki's face. He really couldn't compare himself to them. He knew, just as Meir knew, that Aryeh's father was a big *talmid chacham*. But so what? Two boys were going to be chosen, and besides, the rebbe had specifically said he was choosing boys not fathers.

Shuki slunk into the classroom, practically unnoticed. He quietly took out his siddur and began to daven. He remained silent even when Rabbi Gold sat down at his desk and in a voice bursting with enthusiasm said to the class, "Boys, what have you thought about at home? Who wants to prepare the *hadran* for the *siyum*?"

Hands shot up. There were confident hands, demanding hands and one hand hesitatingly raised somewhere over on the far side of the classroom — the hand belonging to Shuki Katz. He raised it and then lowered it, raised it again and then lowered it again. He looked furtively around the room to see if any of his classmates saw his raised hand and, if they did, how they reacted.

Rabbi Gold continued talking, emphasizing again what a responsible role it was and reminding the boys that he allowed and even wanted fathers to help. He looked again at the hands still up. Second thoughts had lowered some hands. The remaining ones belonged to Meir, Aryeh, Bentzi, Dovi and Shuki.

No Reason to Feel Bad ♦ 89

"Let's let Aryeh do it," someone called out. "He's the best one."

A chorus of voices agreed and the rebbe nodded. Aryeh, not at all surprised, accepted.

"Who else?" asked the rebbe slowly. Shuki sensed that the teacher was looking at him, and he felt embarrassed.

Maybe I'll really be picked, he thought, as his emotions once again got the better of him. Then he suddenly remembered Meir's pointed look and his cutting remark. He was right. How could he compare himself to the others? What could he, eleven-year-old Shuki, do in comparison to others who had fathers who were *talmidei chachamim*? There was no comparison.

His hand dropped.

Shuki imagined he saw a look of relief in the rebbe's eyes, but then the rebbe said, "Shuki is an excellent student. It would be fitting for him to prepare a *hadran* for us."

Before Shuki could change his mind, the rebbe continued. "However, since Shuki does not want to, we'll choose Dovi instead. He got over 90 on all the Gemara tests this year, and you all know how much effort he puts into learning. It is only fitting that he should be the one to say the *hadran* now that we finished the *perek* in *Mishnayos*."

The clapping of hands echoed in the small classroom. Shuki felt his thundering heartbeat blending in, like the ticking of the clock announcing that they had passed the moment, like the sound of receding footsteps. He had missed his golden opportunity. Shuki knew that he had only himself to blame, but that didn't change anything.

He put his head down on the desk, thinking of the original idea he had worked on last night, remembering the night-light that burned through the dark night, a silent partner in his search and discovery.

"It's a good thing Shuki wasn't picked," he heard a whisper behind his back. Shuki waited for the voice to continue. "What could he prepare, anyway? My father learns in the *kollel* with Dovi's father, and he always says it's amazing how much Dovi's father knows. It sure is lucky Shuki changed his mind at the last minute."

"You don't think the rebbe really would have picked him?" asked a voice Shuki recognized. "Don't make me laugh. It's a good thing he put his hand down. That way he's got no reason to feel bad."

The last sentence rang in Shuki's ears for hours afterward. How ironic. Right. He had no reason to feel bad. Sure.

13
When Are We Going to Talk?

Shuki's mother entered his room holding his six-month-old brother, David, in her arms. "What are you doing now, Shuki'le?" she asked.

"Nothing special," answered Shuki, standing by the window, bored. "Just looking out at the street."

"Wonderful," continued his mother, obviously delighted. "How about taking an even closer look at what's going on outside? I want to straighten up the house, and David needs some fresh air. The weather's nice out, Shuki. The stroller is in the shed outside, remember?"

Shuki didn't answer. He continued to press his nose against the window, wondering what to say. "I can play with David here in my room, Ima," he suggested. "Right, Duvi?"

"It's stifling hot in here at this time of day." Shuki's mother opened the windows wide. "Outside there's a nice breeze.

Duvi will enjoy watching children playing and seeing people. It'll do you both good to go out for a while."

Shuki reluctantly took his baby brother in his arms. Duvi was the cutest baby in the world, and Shuki could spend hours watching him in his crib, but to take him out, well, that was a different story. What was he anyway, a sissy? Only girls went out wheeling strollers, not boys. Okay, so there were no girls in the family, only two boys and one of them was a baby. But did that mean he had to act like a girl?

Ima didn't understand it at all. Shuki was more than willing to help by washing the windows or peeling vegetables, even if in most families the girls did such jobs. That was okay because inside the house, where no one saw, he didn't care. He enjoyed helping. He liked standing next to a mountain of potatoes, for instance, and watching the pile get smaller and smaller until it practically disappeared while on the other side of the counter the smooth, pared potatoes formed a new mountain. That was fine.

But to go for a walk outside with Duvi?

Five minutes later, Shuki was holding Duvi in one hand and maneuvering the stroller out of the shed with the other. He adjusted the backrest and gently put the baby in. Through the bushes surrounding the garden, Shuki could see his friends riding their bikes. Just what he needed! How embarrassing it would be to have them see him wheeling his baby brother in the stroller. In his mind's eye, Shuki saw them whizzing down the hill, ringing their bicycle bells while he trailed after them pushing the stroller like a girl.

"What's new, Ma?" they would probably taunt him as they passed by.

They might as well send him to Arazim's central square, he thought. At that time of day in the summer, toward sunset, it was filled with carriages and strollers. All the babies sat and watched their sisters jump rope. Every once in a while, a baby would cry and one of the girls, his sister, would go to give him a drink or something to eat. After a few minutes, she could return to play.

Yes, Shuki knew the scene by heart. He and the other boys often rode their bikes around the square. Lots of people used to pass by there on their way to the supermarket, him included. The other boys in his class probably never thought about what went on there, but Shuki was one to notice.

He had always loved babies, the kind that smile right back at you from their carriage. He had liked them even before Duvi was born. Yup, he knew exactly how things went in Arazim when it came to taking babies for an outing. Well, as long as he wasn't a girl and his friends didn't play jump rope but rode bikes instead, he sure didn't feel like taking Duvi outside where he could be seen.

Shuki walked slowly down the gravel path that led to the street. He stopped just before the gate and leaned against the low stone wall, absentmindedly crushing some dry leaves with his fingers. To Shuki's delight, Duvi gurgled happily in the stroller.

This is a great spot, thought Shuki. Duvi had plenty of fresh air and could "see the world," as Ima put it, while he could breathe some fresh air too, in peace and quiet, without pressure and without having to hide. The only problem was that it was pretty boring standing there in the same spot. How long was it going to take to clean the house? When would he be able to go back in?

Ah, there's Abba! Shuki was happy, just as he always was when his father came home at night. But this time, his joy was compounded by knowing that he would finally have someone to talk to after spending so much time sunk in boredom.

"Hi, Abba," came Shuki's friendly cry as he ran to greet his father.

"Hello, Yehoshua," his father replied.

Shuki was taken aback. Something in his father's tone of voice didn't sound right. His hello hadn't been the usual warm, loving hello of always. There was something else in his voice.

Shuki's father didn't even stop when he reached Shuki, but

continued walking toward the house with slow, heavy steps.

"What's wrong?" Shuki blurted out. "Did something happen? Was there another disappointment with the Nirs' son?"

"No," his father said, pointing an accusing finger at Shuki. "Something about my son disappointed me."

Shuki paled.

His father stepped close to him. "You're having a *siyum*, aren't you?" he asked, placing his hand on Shuki's shoulder. "Why do I have to hear about it in shul?"

"Uh...I...uh...I wanted to tell you about it," Shuki stammered. "It's just that..." His voiced trailed off.

"It's just that what? You see me in the morning, you see me in the afternoon, and you see me at supper time and at night. So what was the problem?"

"I...uh...I for—" Shuki had started to say that he forgot but stopped himself. That would be an out-and-out lie. He hadn't forgotten the *siyum* for even one second, not the *siyum* nor the fact that fathers were invited.

Yitzchak Katz sighed. He hadn't meant to sigh loudly enough for his son to hear, but he did. The sound cut through Shuki like a knife.

"I don't understand." The pain in his father's voice now overpowered any lingering anger. "Why are you so withdrawn lately? Why don't you come and tell me about your day? Is something bothering you, Yehoshua'le?"

Shuki looked down at the pebbles that formed the path he was standing on. Like some problems, they were small, but that didn't change what they were. Just as a stone is a stone, a problem is a problem.

His father gave up on getting an answer. He went over to the blue stroller and gave Duvi a hug. As the baby smiled up at him, his own face softened. *Yes*, he said to himself with another sigh, *that's how it is. With these small angels, everything is so much simpler. Yehoshua was also once a happy child. And*

Duvi will also one day be Shuki's age. That's how it is.

With a third sigh, this one heavier than the others, Shuki's father opened the creaky wooden gate.

Shuki stood glued to the spot, tightly gripping the stroller's handle, not taking his eyes off his father.

"Abba," he called out, wanting to say something but not knowing what.

"Yes?" His father turned around.

"You're going into the house, aren't you?" Shuki continued. "Can you please ask Ima if she's finished cleaning?" After he said it, he realized it wasn't the right thing to say just then. "Uh, never mind. It doesn't matter."

"What's doesn't matter?" his father asked, not quite understanding what Shuki wanted.

"Nothing matters. Don't ask Ima if she finished cleaning. She'll call me herself, I guess." With that, Shuki turned the stroller around and pushed it toward the lawn.

It was getting dark. The deep colors of sunset cast gray shadows over the garden. Shuki took the faded pink blanket he sometimes used for playing outdoor games and spread it out on the grass.

"Come on, Duvi," he said to the baby as he undid the safety strap. Duvi babbled and the joy endeared him to Shuki, who squeezed him in wordless thanks.

Putting the baby down on the blanket, Shuki sat next to him cross-legged. Duvi tried to get up on all fours and crawl over to his big brother, but each time he tried, he fell back down on his stomach laughing.

"You sure are a happy kid," Shuki said aloud. "I cry whenever I don't succeed, but look at you. Abba really loves you a lot, do you know that? I think he once loved me like that too. Maybe he still does, but today he's disappointed in me. I don't think disappointment leaves much room for love.

"You won't disappoint, Abba, will you? I'm the only one

who's like that. What can I do? I love Abba a lot. I don't even mind that he looks so scary with all those scars on his face. People who don't know him sometimes cross over to the other side of the street. They probably think he's dangerous or something. But you and I, Duvi, know the opposite is true. Abba's the best father in the world, but... What can I say, Duvi, I'm ashamed of him in front of my friends. And I sure can't tell him, can I?

"You won't be like me, will you, Duvi. You'll go everyplace with Abba, and you won't care what people think or say. You won't be a scaredy-cat like me, will you?"

Duvi gave a long gurgle in reply.

"There are a lot of things you have to know in this world, Duvi." Shuki intently shredded a blade of grass. "First of all, you have to know that our father won't be able to help you with your *Chumash*, Mishna or Gemara — but he'll be really happy when you learn and succeed.

"I don't know how it is with other fathers. Maybe every father loves his son this much." Shuki spread his arms wide to show just how much. "But I know that our father loves us a lot. If you have more brains than I do, you'll be able to feel very proud of him."

Duvi gave another of his wide, toothless grins, as if dismissing his big brother's all-too-serious philosophizing about life and its problems.

"You...you," chuckled Shuki, unable to keep a straight face as he lifted his little brother. "To you, everything is one big joke. All I want is a brother I can talk to and discuss things with, the kind of things you can't talk to your friends about, the stuff you can't ask your father or mother.

"There's all kinds of things only brothers can talk about. So when will you grow up? When will we be able to sit down together and have a serious man-to-man talk?"

14
Mixed Emotions

Daniel clutched the steering wheel tightly in an effort to drive slowly and carefully. He glanced to his right, expecting to see Yitzchak sitting there and instead saw a car window half covered with a heavy curtain.

"I got confused again," he smiled ruefully. "Everything here is so different."

Yitzchak agreed with him. He had wanted to take a taxi, but Daniel hadn't agreed. As soon as they arrived at the Park Lane Hotel, Daniel had contacted the car rental agency and rented a new compact car.

"I've been to London before," he continued, "but I guess I'm so used to driving on Israeli roads that I forget that in England the steering wheel is on the right, and you drive on the left side of the road."

Daniel glanced at the map that served as his guide. On both sides of the road tall white buildings sprouted up around them, each one identical to its neighbor.

Yitzchak surveyed the area with interest. The houses seemed old-fashioned, with a certain impressive dignity. He could readily envision the majestic white houses as ancient castles and wondered who inhabited them.

"Mussa Salim probably lives in one of these houses," Daniel said as if reading Yitzchak's mind. "And he's not the only one. Plenty of rich Arab sheiks have recently bought up houses here."

"A home like that must cost plenty."

"You're not kidding," Daniel agreed, his mood more cheerful than usual. "That's why Mussa Salim agreed to meet us. He hopes we'll finance his house and much more."

Yitzchak made no comment. He pulled aside the curtain that covered the car window and looked out at the spacious lawns. The deep green grounds ringed by shrubbery seemed bursting with life and promise of renewal. Salim's motivations were of no importance; what mattered were results.

"This is Regency Park," Daniel noted. "Mussa is waiting nearby. There should be a small café in the vicinity and a yellow sign with red lettering."

Yitzchak spotted the place and told Daniel to park.

When they entered the café, they found Mussa waiting there for them. His fingers cupped a tall, thick glass. He smiled nervously.

Daniel and Yitzchak sat down quickly and waited for Mussa to speak.

They had come to the meeting to listen. Mussa had told them he had information for them. He didn't want to send it to them in writing, and he refused to disclose his knowledge over the phone. Face to face was the only way, he insisted. Daniel well understood his real reason. This way Mussa was sure the money would make its way directly to his hands.

Mussa spoke in a whisper. "Proof?" his voice was hoarse and emotional. "You want proof that the boy is alive?"

Daniel opened his mouth to answer but not a sound emerged. Did he want proof? How inadequate the word sounded! Was there anything in the world they wanted more?

Yitzchak hesitated before turning to Mussa.

This wasn't the first time Daniel had met with Mussa. Several months after the first encounter, which had taken place several years earlier, Mussa had sent him the first message and arranged a meeting. In those days, Mussa was still the owner of a luxurious villa in Beirut. Still, the scheduled meeting had taken place in London.

Mussa had babbled on and on in long-winded speeches — but he had given real information. True, it hadn't been much, but when all you have is a jumble of confusion, any shred of information is invaluable.

Mussa had promised Daniel that his son was alive, held captive by Palestinian terrorists operating in Lebanon. A wad of dollar bills had loosened his tongue enough to disclose the source of his information.

"The caretaker of my villa," Mussa had explained, "is a Muslim from one of the local villages. I don't remember exactly how it all started. We were always having arguments, but this one turned more serious. In the midst of the screaming and shouting, the scoundrel threw his wages down on the table and started to storm out of the house.

"'You...you...,' he began to curse, 'you good-for-nothings! We Muslims know what war is and the meaning of victory. My oldest brother, for example, is holding an Israeli soldier captive. As for you and your kind, except for knowing how to furnish a villa, you don't know anything!'

"I wanted to grab the rascal by the collar," Mussa had told Daniel at that meeting, "give him a few good shakes and throw him down the thirty-six steps of my villa. But then I thought of the poor Israeli soldier and decided that if what he was saying was true, I shouldn't let him get away that fast.

"So that's the story," Mussa had told Daniel then. "I

checked out a couple more details he told me, and I'm convinced that the soldier he was talking about is the one you look for. To me it doesn't matter – Israeli or Christian, they're all human beings who deserve to live."

Years had elapsed since that meeting. Daniel Nir passed on the name Salim gave him but nothing much had come of it. It contradicted army intelligence information and so, except for adding a line to the report in the file, nothing happened.

Now Daniel again found himself sitting across from Salim who, judging by the look on his face, possessed secret information. This time Daniel decided to take along with him not an important government official or politician but Yitzchak Katz, whose slight figure conveyed great strength and commanded respect. Yes, his son's friend had true strength and courage, just the qualities he so sorely needed at this trying time. Daniel couldn't deny that he, tall, broad-shouldered pillar of strength that he was, relied totally on the quiet person now sitting beside him in a London café.

"All along you demanded proof," Mussa said, turning to Daniel. "Well, I have it. To be precise, I almost have it. I know how to get hold of it, but it will take some — how shall we say? — some greasing of palms. Not everyone is dedicated to the cause, as you well know. Some people are only interested in money."

Daniel and Yitzchak nodded. Yes, there certainly were people who were interested only in money. And one of them was sitting across the table from them at that very moment. Despite all the noble-sounding words, his eyes gave him away.

"I have kept up my contact with Farouk Abu Mazruk," Mussa said. "He's Yassar Abu Mazruk's brother, the one who was holding the soldier captive."

"Was?" Daniel paled.

"Correct." Mussa shrugged. "Farouk told me that not long ago the captive Israeli soldier was handed over to someone else, but the documents were left with his brother."

"Documents?" Daniel asked.

"Yes." Mussa explained, "These documents are worth their weight in gold. They are army documents and government certificates."

Daniel and Yitzchak exchanged glances. "That's exactly what we've wanted all along," Daniel said hoarsely to Yitzchak. "Documents will give us written proof that there is a substantial reason to pursue this new angle." Turning to Mussa, he asked, "How much do you want?"

Mussa didn't miss a beat. He wrinkled his brow and scribbled something on a scrap of paper. He pushed it across the table to Daniel. "We meet here tomorrow, same time, same place. Make sure you bring the money."

"You'll get half tomorrow, and the rest when the documents are in my hands. Agreed?"

Mussa took Daniel's hand in his right hand and Yitzchak's hand in his left. Rubbing them against each other, he said with obvious pleasure, "Agreed."

※ ※ ※

Shuki paced back and forth in the kitchen. "When is Abba coming back from London?" he finally asked.

"I still don't know," his mother answered from her spot at the sink washing the supper dishes. "You know as well as I do, Shuki, that when Abba travels abroad he has no idea how long he'll be away."

Shuki nervously bit a fingernail. The *siyum* was next week. All the fathers were coming. Would Abba make it in time?

"Too bad he doesn't know when he's coming home," Shuki muttered to himself. "If only I had some idea. Is he coming back this week, next week or next month? This way, it's all so complicated."

His mother dried her wet hands on the blue-checked terrycloth apron tied around her waist. "It's hard for you, isn't it?" she asked softly. "You miss him, don't you?"

Shuki nodded. It was the truth. It was very hard without Abba. He missed him a lot. True, he had left only two days earlier, but Shuki already longed to hear his father's warm good morning and hear him ask how Shuki's day had gone when he came home.

Today and even the day before, Shuki had opened his eyes and wondered what was missing. He was so used to waking up to his father's footsteps, meeting his encouraging look and starting the long school day with his father's warm wishes.

Abba would stand by the door as he left for cheder, reminding him to learn well, wishing him good luck on his tests and saying that he hoped Shuki would know everything and have time to write everything down. Abba always reminded him not to be embarrassed to raise his hand if he knew the answer or if he had a question. With Abba around, Shuki found it easier to part from the warm comfort of his bed and set off for cheder enthusiastically.

Take today, for example. Without his father passing by his room and poking his head in the doorway, Shuki had found it hard to wake up. He had tossed and turned until finally, much too late at a quarter to eight, he had dragged himself out of bed.

"I'm sure Abba misses you a lot, too," his mother continued. "He asked about you over the phone yesterday and sends you his warmest regards. But you know as well as I do," here she lowered her voice as if afraid someone would hear, "that he didn't go to London for a vacation, don't you?"

"Sure," Shuki hastened to answer. He hadn't expected any explanation. He was no baby. He knew why his father went. Besides, his mother didn't know why he was asking. She thought his only problem was that he missed Abba.

Actually, an idea had occurred to Shuki moments before, when he was sitting in his room thinking about when his father would come home. *If Abba stays away in London for another week and a half,* he had thought, *the whole problem will be solved. I'll go to the siyum alone and tell everyone that my father is traveling abroad. Maybe I'll sit next to Nachum; his father probably won't come.*

The idea began to sound plausible. It was then that he went to his mother and asked his question. Naturally, he didn't tell her why he was asking when his father was planning to come home. Let her think it was because he missed him. It was true. But even more true was that he was willing to wait a little longer and miss him another week and a half.

The telephone's ring broke the silence. Ima's hands were full of soap so Shuki answered.

"Hi, Abba!" Shuki's voice was bursting with excitement. "How are you? When are you coming home?"

"I have a surprise for you, Yehoshua," his father replied. Shuki could hear the joy in his voice. "Tomorrow night we'll be boarding the plane for home. Where's Ima?"

Without saying another word, Shuki handed the phone to his mother, who was already by his side. His father would probably interpret Shuki's giving over the phone so quickly in a positive light, as not wanting to run up a big phone bill.

"Wonderful," Shuki heard his mother say. "Everything here is fine, but best of all, it's wonderful that you're coming home so soon. I'll tell Shuki," she continued. "He'll be delighted. Oh, you already told him?" Shuki's mother asked in surprise, glancing at Shuki's worried look. "You told him you're coming home soon?" she repeated.

Shuki turned away and, seeking escape, quickly ran out of the kitchen.

15
A Moment of Togetherness

The sound of his home fax beeping startled Daniel. He rushed over to the machine, tense. The paper slowly rolled off the fax, and the words began to appear. Daniel gripped the page as it came out, as if afraid it would slip out of his hands.

He had anxiously awaited this fax. From the moment he and Yitzchak had returned from London he had done nothing but wait for this message.

He had known it would take a few days before the fax arrived, but for a person in his state even two days was a lifetime. He had spent much of the time sitting in his black leather recliner deep in thought, impatiently awaiting the fax with good news from Mussa Salim in England.

Daniel held the thin paper and gave full rein to his imagination one last time.

By nature, Daniel wasn't a socializer. When he came home from a long, nerve-racking day at the bank, he didn't want to be disturbed by annoying phone calls or ringing doorbells. Every so often he would actually disconnect the phone. "A little peace and quiet never hurt anybody," he would say to his wife, Efrat. Then he would sit back in his favorite recliner, slowly sip a steaming cup of coffee accompanied by two squares of the finest Swiss chocolate and relax. Sometimes close friends would visit, but more often it was just the three of them – he and Efrat and their Yossi, the most wonderful boy in the world.

But when Yossi disappeared, all that changed. The first fax machine in the neighborhood was theirs. Unfortunately, it hardly ever ran out of paper. Of the messages that did arrive, only a few made their way to the precious file. Most were thrown directly into the wastepaper basket. The Nirs often wondered how people had the nerve to waste their time and that of others when they had nothing to say.

Still, Daniel agreed that it was all worth it for the one page that might mean something to them. All the fax machines in the world, all the international phone calls and plane flights were worth it for Yossi.

More than once Mussa Salim had told them that he was afraid to talk over the phone. It was safer, he said, to send confidential information by fax. He had promised Daniel that the minute he had his hands on the documents, he'd let him know.

"He kept his promise to get hold of the documents as soon as possible," Daniel murmured to himself, remembering the cloudy skies of London earlier that week. "Actually, why shouldn't he?" Daniel smiled bitterly. "Half the money is already in his pocket."

I wonder if he already has the documents or whether he'll only have them in a couple of days? Daniel mused. If he already had them, then the first flight out of Israel to Heathrow wasn't fast enough.

Daniel put on his reading glasses and read the fax. When he got to the end, he reread it, refusing to believe his eyes.

What has he written here? Daniel looked for a date but there was none.

There was nothing about a meeting written there. Mussa was no longer interested in them. "They're on my trail, and my life is precious to me. Sorry," was all that was written in the fax.

Daniel angrily crumpled the paper into a ball and threw it into the wastepaper basket in the corner. The basket was empty. Jennie, their devoted cleaning lady, had been there that morning. The crushed ball of paper landed at the bottom of the basket with a rustle, echoing the sense of empty disappointment and frustration Daniel felt.

He reached for the phone and quickly dialed the familiar number. It seemed like the wait for someone to pick up was endless.

// // //

At that very moment, in a small house in Arazim, Shuki sat with his father basking in a rare moment of togetherness.

Not that it was unusual to see the two of them sitting side by side. After all, Yitzchak Katz made it a point never to miss family meals. He always came into Shuki's room in the morning before his son left for cheder, and he regularly spoke to Shuki in the evening. Nevertheless, this was a special moment of togetherness.

Today something suddenly opened up. Shuki wasn't sure how it came about, but he was elated that it finally happened. His father had come into the room, just as he did on other evenings, and sat down on one of the desk chairs next to Shuki.

"How's everything, Yehoshua?" he had asked, a routine question.

"*Baruch Hashem,*" Shuki had replied.

"So when is the class *siyum*?" his father asked. "Have they given out invitations yet?"

Shuki squirmed. He had hoped his father had forgiven him for not telling him about the *siyum*. He had hoped he had forgotten about it. Why was his father bringing it up, anyway?

Yitzchak noticed the gloomy look in his son's eyes and put his arm around Shuki's shoulder. "I'm not trying to cross-examine you, Yehoshua'le. I just want to tell you that if you have something to say I'm here to listen. Okay?"

Shuki smiled. What Abba said made him feel good. "You mean our class *siyum*?" Shuki asked. "It will be, *be'ezras Hashem*, next week, sometime in the beginning of the week. I'm not sure if it's Monday or Tuesday. If it's really important for you to know, Abba, I'll check in my school diary," Shuki offered, making a move to get up.

"To you it doesn't matter?" his father asked.

Shuki didn't answer. He looked down at the floor. "Not really," he said, the words barely audible.

Yitzchak Katz felt that here was an opportunity. "Why, Yehoshua'le?" He leaned forward expectantly. "You don't feel like being part of this class celebration, do you?"

Shuki felt a dam burst open. The words began to flow one after another. He was surprised at the relief he suddenly felt. Yes, he would share his thoughts with Abba; he would tell him about it. He would get it off his chest once and for all.

"Why aren't you interested in the *siyum*?" his father prodded.

Just then, the telephone rang. It was a startling shrill ring that cut through and destroyed the beautiful, rare moment of understanding.

Should I pick it up? Shuki's eyes asked wordlessly.

Pick it up, his father wordlessly signaled.

"You know what?" his father suddenly called after him. "Tell them I'm busy and can't come to the phone. Take a message, okay?"

One hundred percent okay, Shuki agreed, angry at the phone for taking his father away from him when he needed him most.

※ ※ ※

Daniel Nir didn't mean to sound so aggressive, but that's how it came out.

"Is your father home?" his voice boomed over the receiver.

"Abba is busy now," Shuki said. "Who's calling?"

"Daniel Nir," the voice sounded irritated. "Tell him it's urgent."

Shuki handed the phone to his father and watched as the softness in his father's face totally disappeared. The scars turned redder each passing minute until they were a deep purple. *That's how he looks when he gets excited*, Shuki remembered.

He waited for his father to hang up but instead saw him pull over a chair, sit down heavily and begin a lengthy conversation. Shuki went to his room and locked the door. *Even if Abba finished talking right this minute*, Shuki undeniably knew, *we won't be able to continue where we left off*. Not every moment is meant for openness, not every minute is right for the outpouring of a closed heart. The rare moment had passed, gone forever.

"What will happen now?" Daniel shouted into the phone, his voice cracking in anguish. "What now?"

Yitzchak thought for a moment. He, too, understood deep down in his heart what Daniel knew. All the efforts had a dual purpose. Not only were they efforts on Yossi's behalf, they were for his father as well. Yitzchak knew that Daniel was no longer able to sit idly by. The never-ending attempts – in spite of all the bitter disappointments – were what kept Daniel going.

Both of them had had hopes that this fax from London would be an omen, the optimistic beginning of the end to a long, drawn-out process. They had planned a second trip to England and counted on coming back with documents they could show to expert graphologists for analysis. These experts would draw their conclusions, and the Nirs would take it from there. They would turn again to government officials and ask them to reopen the investigation.

"So what do we do now?" asked Daniel, not willing to give up.

"Now?" Yitzchak slowly repeated. "What do we do now? The first thing you do now," he went on, the decisiveness returning to his voice, "is get some rest. When the brain is exhausted, it can't function properly. Unplug the phone, turn off the lights and lie down for an hour to get some sleep. In the meantime, I'll try to think of new ways to handle this."

Daniel resisted the idea of resting, but Yitzchak was adamant. "Call me in two hours," he said, "not a minute before."

Yitzchak clicked off the phone. Yes, Daniel would probably try to rest, but the chances of his succeeding were slim. Yitzchak wouldn't be able to rest now either. He had to think of a new angle to replace the aborted plan. But what?

The two hours passed for Yitzchak all too quickly. All sorts of thoughts crossed his mind, but there was not one reasonable idea among them. Despair was beginning to set in. *Maybe our whole approach has to change,* he suddenly thought. *After fifteen years of disappointment, perhaps we should abandon the hope of ever seeing Yossi again? Perhaps it's time to help Daniel come to terms with reality and try to teach him how to live with his terrible loss?*

Or could it be, Yitzchak asked himself, *that Heaven is waiting for one more attempt, one final step that will fill the cupful of tears to the brim with all our efforts?*

This was a hard question for Yitzchak to answer. Those bigger and greater than he would have to decide.

A quick glance at the wall clock showed that the two hours had passed and the phone would ring any minute. *What will I say to him?* Yitzchak was nervous. What indeed would he say when he was again asked the painful question, what now?

Daniel rubbed his eyes. The rest had done him good. He had fallen into a deep sleep the likes of which he rarely experienced these days. But what would happen at night?

I'll call Yitzchak now and hear what he has to say, he thought as he reached over to plug in the phone. *He always knows what to say. Maybe he'll give me something to think about in the long night ahead, a new idea that needs mulling over, a plan that needs to be developed.*

Just as he was about to dial, the phone rang. He picked up the receiver and heard a voice ask, "Is this Daniel Nir?" The tone was official yet at the same time softened by the words that followed. "We've been trying to reach you for the past two hours," the unknown voice continued. "I'm speaking from the army personnel office in Jerusalem. I have the representative of the U.S. secretary of state here with me. We have news for you. How soon can you get here?"

"Is it good news?" Daniel practically shouted.

"Right now, we don't know if it's good or bad. We do not have the information in our hands yet. But," the voice continued, "the mere fact that there is new information is in itself good news, don't you agree?"

"What's it all about?" Daniel could hardly contain his impatience.

"All I can tell you right now," the voice answered, "is that it concerns documents in Syrian hands. The pressure exerted by the U.S. State Department bore fruit, and the Syrians will be handing the papers over to the secretary of state. More than that we can't tell you over the phone. You will hear the rest when you get here."

So that's it. Daniel hung up without saying another word. In a few minutes, after he calmed down, he'd call Yitzchak — not to hear what his friend had to say but to share the good news. His heart was filled with gratitude. It's Yitzchak's G-d Who didn't forsake us.

It's my G-d too, he whispered to himself.

16

More Than Enough

The festive atmosphere in the cheder's auditorium was almost tangible. One could sense a smile in the air as the boys ran around setting up the refreshments, their joy and excitement reflecting an aura of brightness that covered the scratched wooden tables in pure snow-white tablecloths.

"The soda should be kept cold," Meir suggested. "Is there enough room in the kitchen refrigerator, Rabbi Gold, or should I run home?"

"Should we cut the cakes now?" asked Bentzi, looking hungrily at the chocolate cakes tantalizingly within his reach.

"Who had the nerve to bring popcorn?" someone complained. "It's not fancy enough for this occasion."

Rabbi Gold wandered among the boys, no less excited than

they and perhaps more so. He hadn't planned on such a formal affair, but the youngsters set the tone. Their anticipation of the event, the discussions and the preparations had turned a small simple *siyum* into an attraction that involved all the families in Arazim.

"Do you have a piece of paper?" asked Tzvi, walking over to Aryeh.

"I think so," Aryeh answered, going through his pockets. "What do you need it for?"

"I want to reserve three seats," Tzvi answered. "One for my father, one for me and one for my big brother, Moishe."

"What a great idea," Aryeh said, handing Tzvi a crumpled piece of paper, but not before tearing it in half. "When you're finished writing, give me the pencil for a second. I need more than three places. My two grandfathers are coming, and then there's my three brothers besides me and my father, of course."

"Of course." Tzvi smiled magnanimously. "You're giving the speech, so they have a real good reason to attend. They're coming to *shep nachas*, and why not?"

Shuki stood at the side, listening to their conversation. The festivities that were part and parcel of the room, the excitement that permeated the atmosphere, all eluded him.

"Do you want a piece of paper too?" Aryeh generously offered Shuki.

He just shrugged his shoulder without answering.

"Come on," Tzvika prodded, "reserve a few places. Look, everyone is using my idea. In a few minutes, all the best front-row seats will be taken."

Shuki shrugged again but on second thought took the paper he was offered and mumbled his thanks. *Which places should I reserve?* he wondered. *I guess a seat on the outer aisle. That way my father and I can enter the auditorium and go directly to the seats without anyone seeing us.*

Shuki mechanically taped the slip of paper to one of the

chairs. He was totally unenthusiastic about the event. Too bad he hadn't gotten a chance to explain his feelings to Abba that evening when they were talking together and were interrupted by the phone call from Daniel Nir. At least then his father might have understood him and maybe, just maybe, might have helped him change his perspective.

"You know what, guys?" Chaim proudly announced. "We're in today's newspaper. There's a small ad on the last page saying all of Arazim sends us best wishes."

The boys were suitably impressed. Getting in the newspaper was pretty good.

"I have the paper right here," Chaim continued. "I thought it might be a good idea to cut out the ad, blow it up and hang it somewhere on the wall for everyone to see."

The newspaper was spread out on the table, and all the boys crowded around. Some had already seen the paper that morning but were still excited to read it again. The others weren't willing to be left out, Shuki among them. He didn't utter a word but just looked at the paper. Even when Chaim read the headlines out loud, Shuki kept silent.

"The weatherman says that today will be 'unseasonably hot,'" Chaim quoted. "Father and son injured in a car accident."

"Look what it says here," he said as he continued to read the smaller headlines, oblivious to the hum of activity in the room. "It says that today the documents and diaries of Yossi Nir will be handed over to Israel. Do you all know who that is?" Chaim asked, pushing up his sliding eyeglasses. "He's a missing soldier."

Shuki perked up. Unlike Chaim, he wasn't interested in the daily news, but Yossi Nir – that was a different story.

What's that Chaim said? What will be handed over today? All of a sudden, Shuki began to connect the recent telephone calls to his house, the longer-than-usual conversations and his father's expressions of faith in Hashem brimming with hope and fervent prayer. So that's what it was all about!

In a flash, Shuki realized that the news Chaim had just read would affect him. Where would Abba be in four-and-a-half hours? Would he be at his side as they walked together into the auditorium, or would he be on his way with Yossi's father, Daniel Nir, to Jerusalem? During the past months, all he had heard at home was Daniel this and Daniel that.

Shuki started to put all his thoughts in order. Abba would go to Jerusalem and leave him to attend the *siyum* alone, exactly as he had wished when Abba was in London a week and a half ago. No one would look at his father, and he wouldn't have to maneuver inconspicuously to get a side seat. To any questions he would simply explain that his father couldn't come, and that would be that. Even Nachum told the class that his father might not make it. He was a *maggid shiur* in one of the nearby settlements and made it a point never to miss giving his lesson.

Well, my father may not be a maggid shiur, Shuki rationalized, *but he is also entitled to be absent, isn't he?*

"Okay, boys," Shuki heard Rabbi Gold say as he was still caught up in his thoughts, "we'll be seeing each other in exactly another four and a half hours."

The boys dispersed, going home for a short afternoon rest.

Shuki did likewise, anxious to know if his father had left for Jerusalem or was waiting for him at home. He had to know for sure – would his father be going to the *siyum* with him or not?

With each step he took toward the house, the fateful question beckoned. What was in store for him? Would his father give up being at the *siyum*, the celebration all of Arazim had been talking about?

Shuki couldn't make up his mind whether he wanted to go to the *siyum* alone, without having to contend with the stares, or if he wanted to be reassured that his *siyum* was the most important thing in his father's eyes? The decision wasn't his, yet the burden of it weighed heavily on his shoulders.

Shuki dragged his feet along the long path, crossed over to his garden and opened the door, putting off the final answer, whatever it would be.

Shuki found his father sitting in the kitchen, smiling. At that moment, Shuki's heart filled with love, and he knew what he preferred. In spite of everything, he wanted to go together with Abba.

/// /// ///

Yosefa tiptoed into the spacious dining room. She stood there gazing at her mother, a faraway look in her eyes, and stared at her father nervously drumming his fingers on the table. She waited to be noticed, but neither parent paid her any attention.

"I'm thirsty," she said half aloud, walking over to her parents.

There was no response.

"I'm thirsty," Yosefa repeated, this time in a loud voice.

Daniel got up and walked over to the kitchen counter. He took the bottle of raspberry syrup out of the refrigerator and opened a cabinet to take out a glass. When Yossi was her age, there had been none of this syrup in the house. His wife, Efrat, would squeeze fresh lemons for lemonade and make homemade apple juice too. "We aren't going to feed our children this synthetic poison," she would declare. "In our house, it's a matter of principle."

Daniel poured some raspberry syrup into the glass. As the years passed, the principle flew out the window. Efrat no longer squeezed fresh lemons. With time, the house filled up with more than enough sour lemons, squeezed to the hilt. They could no longer be choosy. Every ounce of sweetness was a blessing, be it natural or synthetic, as long as it sweetened the palate and the heart.

Daniel filled the glass with water and handed it to Yosefa, all without saying a word. *Yossi grew up in the same house with the same parents*, he thought as he patted his daughter's curls, *but his childhood was different – happier and sweeter, even without the sugary syrup.*

Daniel suddenly felt a strong urge to make this charming, innocent daughter of his happy.

"Does it taste good?" he asked tenderly.

"Yes," Yosefa said. "I know how to pour it myself but," she handed her father the glass, "thanks. I'm finished."

Absentmindedly, Daniel took the fragile glass. "Do you think...?" he said, turning to his wife, Efrat.

Shattered glass broke into his sentence.

There were times when broken glass brought a smile to his lips, times when Efrat, sweeping up the slivers, would say, "My mother always said that broken glass is a sign of good news in the offing."

Daniel would good-naturedly dismiss her comment with a wave of his hand and say, "Silly superstitions. But if you believe in it, what does it matter? Who's against receiving good news?"

Now, as Daniel swept up the glass, the memories returned. Lots of glasses had crashed to the floor of their house in recent years. It's understandable that in times fraught with tension one's grasp is relaxed and the mind wanders. Many glasses were broken and Grandmother's saying, may she rest in peace, was forgotten. The good news they so hoped for was long in coming.

"This time, Efrat, it may be symbolic," Daniel said as he picked up the slivers. "Broken glass, two hours before the appointed time, will surely bring good news in its wake."

"I hope so," Efrat sighed. "Which reminds me, it's time for us to get going. Yosefa'le, you're going to your friend's house, aren't you?"

"I'm tired of sleeping over at other people's houses," the girl said with a shrug of her shoulders. "I want to sleep in my own room, in my own bed."

"If that's the case," her father suggested, "why not invite a friend over? Or do you want a babysitter?"

Yosefa made a face. She never did like babysitters. But to invite a friend over? That was a different story. She'd ask her mother to call up Orna's house or maybe Shira's. She'd see who wanted to come.

Yosefa quickly opened her briefcase and took out the typed page the teacher had distributed — a list of addresses and phone numbers of all the children in the class — for just such occasions.

"What will happen," Yosefa suddenly remembered, running to her parents with outstretched arms, "if Yossi comes home with you tonight?"

"Yossi won't be coming home so fast," her father answered gently.

Yosefa wanted to ask how fast is fast. Were all the years of her life and the years before she was born — was that called fast? But she didn't say anything. Her father and mother were sad enough. She certainly didn't want to be the one to cause them more sorrow. She wouldn't ask any more sad questions about sad subjects.

But she had to ask one more question. "Why are you going to Jerusalem now? Why are you so nervous?"

Daniel sat down on the sofa and motioned for Yosefa to sit next to him. Too often he paid scant attention to this little girl of his who was growing up practically alone. Good-hearted and understanding as she was, mature beyond her years, she always tried her best not to be a bother.

"This is the first time in all the years of Yossi's absence," her father explained, his voice cracking, "that we are about to get some real information about him. Do you remember our meeting with the American secretary of state?"

Yosefa nodded vigorously. How could she forget? Did her father mean to say that it was all connected with that meeting? *Maybe, maybe,* she allowed herself to think, *it is all because of what I did? Maybe what I said then wasn't as bad as I thought?*

"Yossi's story touched the heart of the American secretary of state, and he put heavy pressure on Syria," Daniel continued, as if lecturing to a classroom of students.

Yosefa didn't quite understand how one person could put pressure on a whole country, or how this pressure was related to her brother, but she continued to listen with interest to the next part of what her father was saying.

"After much negotiation," Daniel went on, "and after Israel gave in on several points, Syria promised to hand over information and documents related to our Yossi. There is his personal diary from the time he was in captivity and many more papers. Do you understand what this means?"

He stood up. "We will be able to unearth a lot of information about Yossi — who held him captive and for how long, where he was taken and more. Until now, all we had were bits and pieces of information riddled with contradictions."

"Do you think Yossi writes how he was treated?" Yosefa asked, beginning to get caught in by her father's excitement. "Do you think it says what kind of food they gave him? When I lie in bed at night, I think about him and wonder what he is eating and if he has enough food. Do you think he's hungry?"

"It's possible," her father answered, his voice subdued.

"No, it can't be," Yosefa said, tears rolling down her cheeks. "A person can be hungry for a day or even for a week, but how can you be hungry for years? Just imagine what it would be like for me if all my life I wouldn't get enough food, and I would be hungry all the time. Just imagine."

"I can imagine," Daniel said his voice barely audible. "I think about it a lot. Too much."

17
Back to the Past

Shuki's mother stood by the kitchen door *shepping nachas* as she shared her son's excitement. "Tuck in your shirt, Shuki," she said, unable to refrain from typical motherly comments. "And your collar needs straightening. Good luck and enjoy the evening, Shuki."

Shuki nodded and straightened his clothes. But what did she mean by "good luck"? What did he need that for? If he had been chosen to say the *hadran*, then he would have needed her good wishes. But now? Why does a boy who sits in the audience need good luck? As for enjoying the evening, well, he for one had no such expectations. He could hardly wait for the evening to be over. He wasn't going to this *siyum* to enjoy it.

Where was Abba? he wondered. Too bad. He had wanted to leave at exactly seven o'clock. That way they wouldn't be too early and at the same time they wouldn't meet all of Arazim on their way to the cheder. Shuki's plan was to arrive at the last minute, quickly walk into the hall and, without making a commotion, find their seats. What was taking Abba so long?

Oh, there he was.

"Did you reach him?" Shuki heard his mother ask anxiously.

"No." Shuki could see his father was upset. "His cell phone is off. It's a shame because I wanted to give Daniel a few last-minute words of encouragement. It's bad enough that I'm not there to give him moral support."

He noticed Shuki staring at him, listening to every word. "That's how it is," he said, talking now to both his wife and his son. "Tonight I'm all yours, Yehoshua'le." Taking Shuki's small cool hand in his big warm palm, he added with a broad fatherly smile, "It's getting late, isn't it?"

They walked to the front door. Shuki reached out to the doorknob, turned it, opened the front door wide — and stopped in his tracks. His father took a step forward and then he too stopped as if struck by a bolt of lightning.

"Oh! Dad, Mom," Shuki's father exclaimed. Flustered and confused, the words finally came out. "How nice to see you. What a surprise!"

Standing there were Shuki's grandparents, Binyamin and Esther Katz. Shuki leaned against the doorjamb, trying to calm down. His mind was racing. Who told them about the *siyum*? Had his father invited them as a surprise? His hands hung limply at his side. *What's going to happen now? Will Savta stay home with Ima and Saba want to come and join us at the siyum?* A lump lodged itself in Shuki's throat. He couldn't take it. It was too much for him.

He could just see what would happen. He'd walk in the crowded auditorium with Abba on one side and his grandfather, a small white *kippa* pinned to his thin gray hairs, on the other. Everyone would see that the *kippa* looked out of place perched on his almost-bald head, and they would realize that Shuki's grandfather was likewise out of place at a *siyum*.

No, it wasn't only because his grandfather wasn't religious. If it would be his grandmother joining them, that would be different. Sure, he loved his grandfather when he

Back to the Past ❖ 121

was on the living-room couch or sitting on the lawn, working at the computer or playing games.

But there, in the cheder, Shuki knew his grandfather would turn into a different person, someone bitter and angry. He would complain that it was hot, and he would make comments about how uncultured it was the way they packed so many people into such a small auditorium. He'd be bored by the long speeches and dismiss the *siyum* and what it signified with a wave of his hand. At the end of the evening, his grandfather was liable to walk over to Rabbi Gold, politely shake his hand and tell him exactly what he thought of the whole evening, including a full dose of critical comments and complaints.

No, Shuki wouldn't be able to stand it.

He wouldn't be able to sit next to his grandfather knowing that all his friends and their fathers were following their every move. His grandmother, at least, was the gracious type, smiling all the time, nodding her head and warmly thanking everyone. But grandmothers, as everyone knows, aren't invited to *siyum* celebrations in the cheder.

Shuki, standing in the doorway, lifted his gaze to look at his grandparents standing there with their gray carryall bag.

"Binyamin," his grandmother said, as though she was in seventh heaven, "do you see how surprised the boy is? I told you it would be a delightful surprise for them all. Wasn't I right?"

Shuki's grandfather murmured something and turned to enter the house.

"It's really a wonderful surprise," Shuki's father said, recovering from the shock as he ushered them into the house. "We...ummm...we didn't expect you."

"I said to your grandfather," Shuki's grandmother told him proudly, "that grandparents don't always have to call first before they come to visit. I know that you, Tza— uh, Yitzchak, I know you are usually home with Bruria and the children. I even remembered that Shuki finishes school late in the afternoon, so we came just now. I see I was right. Shuki is already home."

"How about going out to the garden?" Shuki's father suggested. He had quickly brought a pitcher of juice from the refrigerator. "The weather is quite pleasant at this time of day."

Shuki blinked. "Wouldn't it be better to sit in the living room, Abba?" he asked. "There are so many people outside now. We won't have any privacy. There's plenty of time to go out later on."

His father heard the pleading note in Shuki's voice and paused. His parents' unexpected visit so shook him that he couldn't think of a way out of the predicament. Since when did his parents just drop by? The answer was never. His parents visited very infrequently, and when they did, it was always preplanned for definite times — Chanuka, Sukkos and Shuki's birthday.

"I've been wanting to pay you a visit for the past two months," Shuki's grandmother said, making herself comfortable on the couch. "It's not easy to convince your grandfather to come." She smiled at Shuki, who stood in the corner like a statue carved out of stone.

"I'm still not convinced that this visit today was a good idea." These were the first words Shuki's grandfather had uttered since their arrival. "Why are you dressed up, Shuki?" he asked. "We'll soon hear that today is some holiday that we don't know about or that Yitzchak and Shuki are on their way to perform some mitzva and we are disturbing them."

Shuki's already white face paled several degrees more. His father's eyes avoided his. Shuki could see he was wondering what to say at this awkward moment.

"There's a small get-together tonight here in the moshav," Shuki said, trying to sound casual. "Abba and I thought of going, so we didn't make any plans for this evening. Now we can spend the free time together. How did you know when to come, Savta?"

Shuki sounded convincing, not because he was a good actor — acting was never one of his strong points — but because it was the truth.

Back to the Past ♦ 123

His grandfather accepted the explanation and allowed himself to relax, sinking into the easy chair. "Where is the present we brought for Shuki?" he asked his wife.

Shuki's grandmother stood up dramatically, as if waiting for the cue, and opened the zipper of the gray carryall bag. She took out a large rectangular box – what else would it be? — gaily gift wrapped.

"Where is Duvi?" she asked, suddenly remembering the baby. "We brought him something too." She took out a colorful rattle and shook it.

Shuki politely thanked his grandparents for the present and opened the package, wondering if there were any games still left in the store that he didn't already own. He sat down to read the instructions, thus allowing the adults to talk undisturbed. His present, a new version of the classic Monopoly, looked exciting.

Who will play it with me? Shuki thought. Too bad Duvi is still too young and all that interests him are rattles and bells. Here he finally had a brother, and he couldn't even play anything with him. Shuki started calculating. When Duvi would be old enough to play Monopoly, Shuki would be far, far away in yeshiva bent over a *shtender*. No chance of them playing then.

Shuki thought of his friends. Take Moishe, for example. He had been so excited when he saw Shuki's collection of board games that time he visited. Maybe Shuki should invite him to come to his house again instead of always going over to his friends.

It took him a split second to remember that last visit and how Moishe had insisted on going out to the garden. Just remembering how embarrassed he was when Moishe set eyes on his father was enough to make Shuki abandon the idea. This new game, like all the rest, would lay on the shelf unused. His grandmother had no way of knowing that Shuki didn't like inviting friends over.

My friends, Shuki thought. What were they doing now? They were probably in the middle of the *siyum*. Maybe the Rav of Arazim was speaking. Maybe Rabbi Gold was making a short speech. Was Aryeh or Dovi saying a *hadran* that very minute?

Oh, how Shuki wished he could sprout wings and fly to the auditorium to be together with his friends — with Abba or without, with his grandfather or without him, it didn't matter. Why was he sitting at home when his class was having its big moment, his big moment?

He put the game down on the couch and went over to the table. What would he say to his friends tomorrow? What would he tell Rabbi Gold?

He'd say that his grandparents paid a surprise visit, which was the truth. But when Rabbi Gold asked, "So why didn't you bring your grandfather to the *siyum* like some of the other boys did?" what would Shuki answer then? He certainly wasn't going to tell the whole class that his grandfather was different. Would he say that a *siyum* on *Mishnayos* was not exactly his grandfather's cup of tea? Could he admit that his grandfather didn't even wear a yarmulke all the time and only carried a tiny white one in his pocket for his occasional visits, so as not to offend Shuki's father?

No, he wouldn't say a word. Rabbi Gold would probably shrug his shoulders, Meir would whisper something in Moishe's ear, Aryeh and Nachum would exchange glances and someone was bound to say that Shuki had always been strange, somewhat odd and unpredictable.

No one could understand him. Kids who fit the norm can't understand kids who are different, nor can they empathize with a kid whose father is different...and whose grandfather is different too.

At a quarter to nine, Shuki's grandfather yawned. "It's getting late, isn't it?" he said to his wife, who was still sitting on the couch. She got up reluctantly.

Tzachi's living room is different from mine, she thought. *Tzachi himself is different, and so are his children, but I love them just the same and I love being here with them. You can feel the warmth and serenity within these walls. There's simplicity*

Back to the Past

and contentment without pretentiousness. Oh, how the time flies here, and how it creeps at a snail's pace at home in Raanana.

Shuki's grandparents got ready to leave, bidding everyone goodbye.

"It was wonderful having you, Dad," Shuki's father said. "You'll visit again soon, won't you?"

"Come again," chimed in Shuki, knowing it was the right thing to say. "It doesn't matter if you tell us ahead of time or come as a surprise, the main thing is for you to come."

His grandmother smiled a broad smile full of *nachas* and started to walk down the path. Shuki and his father accompanied them, with Shuki's mother following, pushing the baby in the stroller. They watched as the car door closed, the motor revved up and the car drove off in the distance.

"You did a good job, son." Shuki's father gave him a pat on the shoulder and then, after taking a deep breath, he asked Shuki in a barely audible voice, "Do you want to go now?"

Shuki stood frozen in his place, unable to speak. "Now?" he asked incredulously.

Pausing for a second, Yitzchak realized there was no point in pressing the issue.

"I think your impeccable behavior had a big effect on your grandfather," his father said with uncharacteristic candor. "Just think for a minute how he would have felt if you had wanted to go to the *siyum*. He would have taken a few steps backward in his *Yiddishkeit*."

Shuki accepted the compliment in silence. Didn't Abba see that there was nothing meritorious in how he had behaved? A mouse running for cover doesn't deserve a medal for outstanding behavior — not by a long shot.

They were about to enter the house when Shuki's father stopped.

"I'm going to Daniel's," he said impulsively. "I want to be there to greet him when he gets home from Jerusalem. I want to be there to share the latest news, good or bad." He kissed the mezuza and turned to leave.

Traffic was sparse, and Yitzchak increased his speed. During the past few hours he had put the latest developments regarding Yossi out of his mind to concentrate fully on his parents' visit. Now, as soon as he was free, his tension was palpable.

Authentic documents. Yossi's personal diary.

He saw the handwriting in his mind's eye. The letters would be small, straight and perfectly formed. They would reach high as if to go beyond the present, uncompromising as they reached below the line. Yitzchak longed to see those letters, to once again hold a page written by his friend and see his handwriting. Would the letters look the same, or had years of suffering eroded Yossi's determination? Would the high aspirations still be there, or had the agony of torture taken its toll?

Suddenly the road ahead fogged, and Yitzchak couldn't see out the window. The pane was no longer clear but cluttered with black specks fluttering in every direction. He pulled over to the side of the road, well knowing that he couldn't continue to drive in that state. The air was suddenly full of small, densely printed letters, lines and lines of them with hundreds of letters going around and around in jumbled confusion.

There was a time when he and Yossi sent each other long letters discussing penetrating questions, with answers even more profound. There was a time when they talked deep into the night on the sands of the army camp. Their discussions carried onto the written page an ocean of words, words that set a fire burning in their hearts.

Yitzchak wiped his brow and massaged his forehead, but the memories were stronger than he was. He slumped in his seat, knowing he couldn't drive in that condition. Navigating the sharp curves of the northern highway is tricky even when you're fully alert; it's impossible when your mind is in a different place. Yitzchak's mind was now far, far away, back in those distant times, reliving the experiences all over again.

18
In Moments of Danger

Yitzchak pulled hard on the hand brake and turned off the motor. He lay his head down on the wheel and shut his eyes. He felt himself shaking as he relived the Peace for Galilee War.

※ ※ ※

On that Sunday, the second day of the war, the sky above was clear blue. On the horizon one could see beautiful mountains dotted with white houses that looked like toy building blocks peacefully laid out on the steep slopes.

"You'd never know there's a war going on," Yaakov, the tank commander, remarked as he looked out of the tank's turret.

"As if there's no war," Yossi Nir whispered to Tzachi, gripping his buddy's arm.

Yossi Nir looked straight ahead. His eyes were full of prayer and hope, but his hands shook uncontrollably. They were nineteen. Sitting inside the armored steel tank, the atmosphere unbearably close from lack of air, they were on their way to their first battle. It would turn out to be their last.

The long line of armored vehicles moved forward along the main road in Lebanon between Tzur and Sidon. The mission: to penetrate the route from the west. They were four soldiers in the tank, each one at his position, tense and alert.

"Now is the time to daven," Tzachi said to Yossi. "Let's pray that we return home safely. We'll ask Hashem to be with us at our side."

Yossi turned for a split second toward Tzachi, a worried look in his eyes.

"You still don't know the proper way to pray? Well, neither do I," Tzachi said reassuringly. "The one thing I managed to learn during the past weeks were the two blessings before eating bread, but they don't seem appropriate for these circumstances. My small *Tehillim* is right here in my breast pocket," he added, "close to my heart. As for me — I'm praying in my own words."

"Too bad the war didn't wait a few more days," Yossi said with regret. "Then I could have put on tefillin a few more times and made more progress along this path I've recently discovered. Do you think Hashem will already consider me a son," Yossi asked, "even though I haven't yet had a chance to look upon Him as a Father?"

Tzachi somehow managed an answer, sorry that their Rav was not with them now in the tank moving toward the battlefront. What a Rav! His soft, penetrating answers satisfied the soul thirsting for Torah.

His phone number is probably somewhere in one of my pockets, Tzachi suddenly remembered. They had parted, promising to stay in touch.

"The first Shabbat I get leave, I'll come to you," Tzachi had promised the Rav, making what was really more of a promise to himself. Danny, the medic, and Yossi were standing there.

"Maybe I'll join you," Danny said.

"Maybe I will too," Yossi added somewhat hesitantly.

Tzachi didn't pin much hope on Danny. Danny took an active part in their late-night discussions, but when morning came, at the first cynical comment of one of the fellows, he would do an about-face. "It's nothing," he would say with an elegant wave of the hand.

All he wants is to be one of the boys, Tzachi thought. *Danny has no backbone.*

But Yossi was different, serious and unwilling to compromise. "I have to be 100 percent sure of myself before taking such a step," he explained afterward. "I feel there's a part of me that's not ready yet. But I do have a strong feeling," he reassured Tzachi, "that it won't be long in coming."

"Will you be coming for Shabbat?" Tzachi asked.

"It's only Sunday," Yossi replied. "A lot can happen by the end of the week. Who knows what we'll be like after a week under fire?"

"Zebra, this is Concord," a voice came over the transmitter. "Zebra, do you hear me?"

"Concord, this is Zebra. Go ahead. Over." Tzvi's voice was coming through loud and clear.

"Zebra, this is Concord. The tank battalion is proceeding. There are Arab civilian villages on both sides of the road. Don't open fire. Over."

"Concord, this is Zebra. Message received. End."

The pale faces of the soldiers turned even paler. The road narrowed, and the massive tanks that until now had sped along started to wobble from side to side in the winding turns. The serene countryside suddenly changed, replaced by small, crowded stone houses with a string of dirty courtyards that turned the area into one stretch of ugliness.

Barefoot Lebanese children stood by the roadside staring at

the tanks that passed their homes. They reached out to touch the sides of the tanks as they went by.

"This village is crawling with terrorists," Yaakov, the tank commander, told his men. "The PLO established a base of operations here long ago. I myself participated in actions against it. But just look at all these civilians coming out of their houses now with friendly waves."

Yitzchak lifted his head from the steering wheel and sighed audibly.

The serenity didn't last long. There were friendly waves and broad smiles — but that was at the beginning. When the first tank reached the center of the village, armed men in civilian clothing jumped out from behind a building. The commander of the lead tank was the first casualty. He was standing on the platform, looking out of the turret and waving back to the welcoming civilians — and that's how the whizzing bullets found him.

Another RPG rocket hit the tank fourth in line. It burst into flames, sending billows of thick black smoke rising from within. The third tank had no means of escape.

They were difficult minutes. The confusion was terrible. The children ran wild when the first shots were heard. Suddenly, bursts of gunfire from behind the houses raked them. They had no choice but to return fire without stopping to think where the next round of shots would come from.

The order came. "Zebra, this is Concord. Return fire."

"Tira, this is Concord. Return fire."

"Shamir, this is Concord. Return fi—"

The sound of shooting was louder than the commander's instructions. Yossi, the tank's ammunition officer, loaded the gunner. Tzachi kept on driving as fast as the tank in front of him would allow. The last tanks were supposed to clean up the area,

In Moments of Danger ❖ 131

according to the standard army training manual.

Suddenly the sound of an explosion raked the air.

"It's a bomb." Yossi froze.

"No," said Yaakov, the tank commander, "it's one of their antimissiles for knocking out tanks."

The crew sent out heavy fire, but it was too late to prevent what had happened. The second tank was also hit. Yaakov helplessly saw his crew jump out of the tank, one soldier after another, trying to escape the flying bullets, seeking refuge in the vehicle at the head of the line.

"Drive fast," he commanded the tank's driver. "Move. Drive around the burning tank ahead of us and keep going. If we don't make it," he warned, "we'll find ourselves trapped under fire."

The tank charged ahead. But it headed straight into a trap — into the heart of the fire.

What does man know of success? What does he know of the trap waiting to ensnare him?

It is the Hand from Above that is holding onto the tank, and blessed is he who merits to realize that, in time of danger, it is the Hand of Hashem navigating it all.

Yitzchak knew. And so did Yossi.

19

Forgotten Letters

A blue compact car pulled over to the shoulder of the road and stopped next to Yitzchak's car. "Need any help?" the friendly driver asked after he rolled down the window. Yitzchak practically jumped out and in so doing, banged his head. He stared blankly at the fellow who had appeared out of nowhere. What was he doing there?

The owner of the blue car opened his door and got out. He was determined not to be like the tens and hundreds of drivers who passed by a lone parked car without giving it a second thought.

"Mister, do you need any help?" he asked kindly.

This time the look in Yitzchak's eyes was clear and sober. "I need help," he said. "I need a lot of help. But you can't give it to me."

The man shrugged, got back into his car and slammed the door shut. *Maybe all the other drivers who whizzed by ignoring that guy were smarter than me,* he thought as he cast a final glance at the strange man parked along the highway.

Yes, he needed a lot of help.

※ ※ ※

The tank rolled forward. Yaakov, the commanding officer, spurred Tzachi to drive as fast as he could. It wasn't only the commander's words but his urgent tone that bespoke fear. Yossi cracked his knuckles nervously. His face was as white as chalk and his lips trembled.

Gabi didn't say a word. Ever since the first bombshell had exploded he hadn't uttered a sound. The spark in his eyes died, leaving a blank look.

"It's shell shock," Yossi whispered to Tzachi.

This was their first encounter with live fire, the cruel shooting that knew no mercy, that didn't discriminate between tank and tank, soldier and soldier.

"This shooting is bound to have an effect on a person's heart," Yossi said. "Only if a person has a heart, of course."

Tzachi's mind couldn't function. It was a race for survival as he pressed his foot down on the gas pedal, expending all his effort in getting the steel tank to take them far from death. He didn't have time to think, but one sensation enveloped him – the strong feeling that Hashem was watching over him from above. He felt Hashem was with him.

"We made it!" Yaakov let out a sigh of relief. "Now we have to catch up to the rest of the battalion." With a smile on his tense face he added, "I was afraid I wouldn't get out of here alive."

At that very moment a thunderous boom interrupted the lull in the battle. The third tank, the tank that held Yaakov, Gabi, Yossi and Tzachi had suffered a direct hit by an RPG rocket.

"Command headquarters!" Yossi called over the radio transmission. "Respond!" But there was no answer.

"We have to jump out and find cover," Tzachi yelled as he grabbed Yossi's arm. "The tank is going to explode any minute."

He pushed Gabi, who stood frozen, stiff as a statue, out to the open field and, climbing out, called to Yossi, "Get going!"

In recalling the events of that day, Yitzchak thought, reliving those moments of fear took longer than the actual incident. In reality, it took a fraction of a second from the moment the tank suffered a direct hit till it moved forward out of control.

Gabi was on the outside with a chance of staying alive. For Yaakov, trapped in the turret, it was too late. Two soldiers were left in the tank, fighting for their lives, two men whose hearts beat as loudly as the ear-splitting gunfire that surrounded them, two young men in a runaway burning tank on a wild ride between life and death.

"This must be how people feel before they die," Yossi said, his lips trembling with fear.

This is probably how my grandfather felt in the gas chamber in Auschwitz, Tzachi thought. But at least my grandfather knew what to think, what to say, what to expect. As for me, who am I? I'm heading toward death without knowing a thing. Why did I live and why am I dying? Who and what am I?

The flames rose higher, effortlessly enveloping the armored tank, trapping Tzachi and Yossi inside. Thick, heavy smoke filled the burning vehicle, but it's impossible to jump off a swiftly moving tank. Totally engulfed in flames, the tank rolled down the hill and smashed into a small stone house, battering one of its walls, before coming to a halt.

Tzachi fell back, his head badly injured. For a minute he lost consciousness and saw himself in another world, a better, more pleasant one. But the next moment, after regaining consciousness, he found himself facing the cruelly bitter reality.

"Get out fast," Yossi shouted. He pulled Tzachi toward him.

He didn't know where he was, but he knew he had to escape the blaze that was quickly consuming the steel tank. Yossi jumped out, running away from the fiery flames.

"Tzachi!" he screamed. "Tzachi, get out!"

"I can't," Tzachi replied, his voice barely audible amid the thick smoke. "Tell my parents..."

Yossi dashed back into the blazing inferno. "I won't tell your parents anything," he said, grabbing a hold of Tzachi with all his might. "You can tell your parents and my parents anything you want."

The flames were roaring on all sides, but Yossi was oblivious to them. The heavy smoke blinded him as he grabbed hold of Tzachi and dragged him out of the tank.

A second later, the armored vehicle turned into a flaming torch.

Yossi looked at his friend, whose clothes were aflame, and knew that every second was crucial.

"Lie down on the ground!" Yossi screamed, rolling Tzachi on the sandy surface. He acted without missing a beat, amazed at his own presence of mind and the cool he never realized he possessed.

The flames died down. Yossi was now able to take a look at himself. His shirtsleeve was torn, but aside from a few minor burns, he wasn't hurt. Not so Tzachi. For Tzachi, it was a different story.

"Are you okay?" Yossi asked his friend, turning his head aside so as not to see him.

So as not to see, he told himself as he wiped away his tears with his tattered shirtsleeve. *Tzachi will need a strong will to remain alive. If I'm not careful, I may add to his despair.*

"Are you all right?" Yossi asked again. Not being a doctor, he couldn't diagnose the degree of the burns, but even to him it was obvious how severe they were.

"Are you okay? Do you hear me?" Yossi asked. "Are you with me?"

Something flickered in the red, swollen face. "Okay?" Tzachi whispered. "I wish I didn't know how I felt. I'm burning! I can't take the pain! Make it stop!"

Yossi crouched down, helpless to assuage his friend's agony.

"You know something," Tzachi whispered, partly to himself, partly to his friend and partly to Hashem, "if I get out of here alive, my life will be different. It will be a life that will teach me how to live and how to die, a life with meaning, not just a life in passing."

In those moments of pain and anguish, the words barely made an impact. It was only later, weeks, months and years later, that he found meaning in them.

"How long will we be able to hide here?" Yossi wondered aloud as he surveyed the destroyed, abandoned house. "How will we be able to hook up to the battalion?"

He looked at his wounded friend and knew that finding the rest of the troop was just one problem. Tzachi needed medical help urgently. If not, he would die. What should he do?

From afar, Yossi heard the sound of gunfire. He wasn't about to stay put in this hut and have the enemy soldiers find him, their rifles drawn to shoot. He lifted Tzachi and half-dragged him to the doorway.

Tzachi would never forget that moment. His feet were on the hard ground while one hand of Yossi's supported his head and the second was raised in surrender.

The enemy soldiers lay down their weapons when they saw the two Jewish soldiers, one wounded and a second surrendering.

Tzachi, looking from the side, saw things differently. He saw a hand raised toward Heaven in prayer and pleading, a silent prayer, a cry to Hashem, the Omnipotent, Who can do everything.

Later, Tzachi was taken to the Palestinian's medical tent, and Yossi was taken elsewhere, to some unknown destination. He was never seen again.

The vision of Yossi that stayed with Tzachi was the last one he remembered: right hand lifted toward the heavens in fervent prayer, left hand tenderly supporting his friend's scorched face.

※ ※ ※

Yitzchak blinked a few times, trying to see if the lights of vehicles passing in the darkness weren't hiding armed Palestinians or burning tanks. He remained another minute staring into space and then returned to the present, to the ongoing traffic speeding along the black asphalt.

What information had Syria passed on to the Israeli government? he wanted to know. What details were disclosed? What documents were handed over? Most of all, of what value would they be during the coming days in the renewed efforts to locate Yossi?

The last stretch of the journey passed quickly. It was nearly midnight when Yitzchak found himself near the cold, forlorn stone home of Daniel Nir. He knocked on the door impatiently. The sound of slippers slowly shuffling could be heard.

"So?" Yitzchak said as soon as the door opened, skipping formalities. After all, midnight visits aren't included in the book of etiquette.

Daniel took a batch of papers out of his robe pocket.

Yitzchak's hands trembled. He fingered the pages, wondering how he would be able to read over all of them right then without missing a single word. But the task proved easier than he had anticipated.

There was a small diary, the blue binding torn and its pages yellowed and creased. One glance was enough for Yitzchak to know what it was. His heart beat fast, and his fingers moved uncontrollably. Yossi's smiling eyes were reflected between the lines, those bright eyes, questioning, seeking answers to the ways of the world.

Yossi had started keeping the diary a few months before the war broke out. There were pages that he addressed to himself, and there were pages addressed to Yitzchak, his best friend, to whom he could pour out his heart and with whom he could share his innermost thoughts. Yitzchak quickly flipped through the pages, his heart racing.

But there was nothing. Daniel's blank expression told Yitzchak he wouldn't find what he was looking for.

"Sunday, June 7, 1982. Today is the day I'll be going to fight the first battle in my life. I pray to G-d that He help me. When I come back from the war, dear diary, I'll no doubt have lots of stories to tell you."

These were the last words in the diary. Not a word about the blank darkness in his life. Not one speck of information on the unknown that followed. Yitzchak put down the diary on the coffee table.

"When you come back, Yossi," he said, his voice cracking, "you'll have lots of stories to tell. But what do you have to tell now, this very minute? What can you tell us so that we will know how to reach you and how to bring you back to us?"

The question remained hanging in the air, unanswered. Yitzchak looked at the last pages. There was the printed prayer that the army rabbinate distributed to all the soldiers before going to battle and a request form for equipment that Yossi had started to fill out. That was all.

"That's it?" Yitzchak asked in disbelief.

"That's all," Daniel answered.

"This is what Mussa offered us in exchange for that astronomical sum of money?" Yitzchak asked, dumbfounded. "This is what the whole country was in an uproar about yesterday?"

They had anticipated more recent documents, excerpts from a diary written by Yossi in captivity or documents with information. The yellowed pages in their hand would wring the hearts of all who read them, but how would it help them find Yossi?

The one who held these old documents no longer held Yossi. The faded pages must have passed through many hands before reaching theirs. How would they be able to point an accusing finger at the guilty party? How would they be able to identify the hand grasping poor Yossi by the neck and holding him prisoner? It was impossible.

"This is what Salim offered us." Daniel spoke brusquely but his fingertips caressed the wrinkled pages.

"What did the American secretary of state have to say?" Yitzchak demanded. "What did he say when he saw these earth-shattering papers?"

"The American secretary of state doesn't read Hebrew," Daniel answered in the same tone. "He strutted around the hall like the groom at a wedding and left others to inspect the documents after he left."

A heavy silence reigned in the room. Then, suddenly, Daniel broke down and cried. The long-lost handwritten pages carried him to his beloved son, who for fifteen years had shown him no sign of life.

20
"I Went Owt — Don't Worri"

Ripples in the blue drapes gave the illusion of a refreshing breeze outside. But the wind was still. The heavy heat of a *sharav* filled the air, carrying with it fine yellowish sand that filtered through the open windows. Rabbi Gold stood up to close the window, but the oppressive heat had already permeated the room.

The sixth-grade cheder rebbe looked again at the principal, who was sitting at his desk talking on the phone, deeply absorbed in yet another conversation. Rabbi Gold had been sitting there for over half an hour. Save for a nod acknowledging his presence when he entered the room, no communication had taken place between them. The calls came one after the other.

Rabbi Gold began to wonder if it was worth the wait. He could see lines of fatigue forming around the principal's eyes reflecting the tiredness felt after a long, tedious day.

Rabbi Gold admired the man sitting behind the desk. He knew how many problems made their way across this desk every day and how many calls from people in distress reached that phone and found their way straight to a listening ear and an understanding heart.

Beads of sweat formed on the principal's forehead. *It's high time an air conditioner was installed in this room*, Rabbi Gold thought, not for the first time. No matter how hot it was outside, it was always hotter inside the principal's room.

But Rabbi Gold knew the man he admired so much would never agree. When was it that the teachers had taken the matter into their own hands and collected money to buy the principal an air conditioner? Why, they had even called in a technician to check out the room. When was it? Yes, two and a half years ago, that was it. The whole staff had chipped in. It was going to be a Purim surprise, but somehow, the secret had gotten out, and the principal put a stop to the project.

"As long as there is no air conditioning in all the classrooms for the children and their rebbes," he had said adamantly, "I won't have it in mine. If they have to learn in the heat of summer and the cold of winter, I won't be any different. I will continue to do my job, with Hashem's help, just as faithfully without an air conditioner."

Three boys ran past the window. Rabbi Gold's glance met Nachum's as he scampered by. *My students*, he thought with pride.

"Rabbi Gold is in the principal's office." The whisper was loud enough for him to hear.

It was only natural for his students to be curious. They must wonder why he was in the office. He heard the trace of fear in their voice and knew why. The heavy blue curtains hid the room from passersby. Every boy knew where the principal's office was located, but none of them wanted to see it from up close.

They don't really know the principal, Rabbi Gold thought sadly. *They think I'm here to discuss some unruly pupil, a boy who disturbs the class with his rowdy behavior. How wrong they are. They have no idea that the real reason I'm here is to discuss one of the quietest, most well-behaved boys in the whole school, a boy who is a teacher's dream.*

Nevertheless, there he was. Shuki Katz never caused a disturbance in class, but Rabbi Gold wanted to talk to the principal about him and hear his experienced opinion. The boy definitely had a problem.

The principal clicked off the phone and put it down. "What can I do for you?" His smile was the smile of a person with all the time in the world.

As Rabbi Gold began to explain the situation, he found himself at a loss for words. What could he say about Shuki? What was the underlying problem that seemed to be bothering the boy? So what if he hadn't come to the *siyum*? And what of it that he had been very quiet during the weeks of preparation preceding the *siyum*? The boy had never been one of the class leaders. What else? Oh, yes. Shuki lacked self-confidence. His eyes always darted around the room before he raised his hand to answer a question. That was no real proof of anything, but, nevertheless, Rabbi Gold had an intuition, a strong gut feeling that something was bothering the boy.

"I sense that the boy is suffering," he said finally. "Peer approval determines his every move. What his friends think and say is at the focal point of his life, even though he himself is on the periphery socially. I have the feeling that the boy wants to talk much more than he does, but he's so afraid of what his friends will think and say that he holds himself back. He's so unsure of himself."

Rabbi Gold paused. "It's strange," he began slowly. "Shuki never mentions his father, neither in class nor outside the classroom. Maybe he is afraid that his friends won't accept his father's looks, which are unusual. The boy may come up with all sorts of excuses, but I am convinced that that is why he didn't participate in the *siyum* yesterday. It could be," he concluded, "that he didn't even tell his father about it."

Rabbi Gold sat back, waiting for the principal to give him direction. Would he call Shuki into his office for a talk? Would he tell him to talk to the class and at the same time work to build Shuki's self-confidence? Or maybe he would advise him to let the situation ride, hoping that with time it would straighten out by itself?

The principal furrowed his brow. What he said next surprised Rabbi Gold. "I think you should have a serious talk with Shuki's father."

// // //

When it came to serious talks, Yitzchak Katz had had his fill. He was all too used to weighty conversations — but on a totally different subject. In fact, at that very moment he was in the midst of one such extremely serious conversation.

Daniel clutched the worn diary, the one with the torn blue cover, close to his chest. Yitzchak sat next to him, saying nothing. After fifteen years of silence and a total blackout on any information about Yossi, Daniel was overcome with longing as he held these first tangible regards from his son.

"It was you who wrote these words, my precious Yossi." Daniel's tears fell on the letters, smudging them. "These pages I'm holding are pages you held, Yossi. Oh, Yossi! What did you think about as you wrote these lines? What are you thinking about now?" His voice cracked; he couldn't go on.

He stood up suddenly and strode into Yossi's room. At the flick of the light switch, Yosefa opened her eyes, startled.

She sat bolt upright in the bed. "Did Yossi come home?"

Her father didn't answer. He walked over to the old wooden chest of drawers and opened the bottom drawer. It stuck, but he persisted. Tonight he was opening shut doors, entering rooms that had been closed for years under lock and key. As for opening old wounds, never mind. He was one big open wound anyway.

His hand had no trouble finding the brown briefcase. Just

touching it sent an electric shock through him. He shut the light and returned to Yitzchak in the living room.

"Do you see this?" Daniel asked without waiting for an answer. "These are Yossi's old notebooks. It's the same handwriting, maybe more childish, but his. Here's his second-grade notebook, full of 'Excellent, Yossi,' and 'Keep up the good work.' Here's his third-grade notebook, and his history notebook from the sixth grade."

Daniel stopped, reluctant to further intrude on this private domain.

"Here." His voice grew quiet as he reached into the inner pocket. "Here is where Efrat saved the little notes Yossi used to write us. Efrat's a great saver of mementos. She photographed, videoed and taped everything. There wasn't a moment in his life that she didn't capture for posterity. The shelf in Yossi's room has a whole row of albums — and that's in addition to all the photos you see around the house. Yosefa, on the other hand, has only one album, and it's not even full."

Daniel's voice cracked. "I want Yosef here live, not as a picture or a memento."

Yitzchak lowered his eyes and read the small notes Daniel silently passed to him. Birthday greetings, "sorry" notes — all cute and candid. There was one last note, a scribbled page full of a child's spelling mistakes. The handwriting was precise, the formed letters unmistakably Yossi's.

"Deer Abba and Ima," it said. "I went owt. Don't worri. I'll be bak soon. Yossi."

Daniel buried his face in the pages of the diary and cried uncontrollably.

We know you went out, Yossi. We know and we're worried. Many years have passed and we're still worried. Will you ever come back? Ever?

21

It's Got Nothing to Do with Him

Daniel's heartrending sobs shook the quiet house. Efrat's silent weeping in the living room added to the gloom. Nor did the blessed silence of night spread its wings over the children's room. The bed creaked. Yosefa lay there, eyes wide open, listening to her parents and knowing it meant that once again all their hopes were shattered. Yossi's empty bed still awaited him and would probably stay that way for some time to come. Otherwise, Yosefa realized, her father wouldn't be so sad.

The room was dark. Yosefa pulled aside the curtain and looked out at the smiling moon. In school that day her language teacher, Kochava, had told the class a story. Shira and Orna loved it, but she thought it was a little silly and childish. Besides, she didn't like make-believe stories. Why do all the good things happen in stories and not in real life?

The tale was about a poor boy who had no house or family,

neither a bed to sleep in nor friends to play with. The small boy slept in the street with only the sky above him for shelter. The only friends he had were the moon and the stars.

One night, when it was very dark and cold, the boy, shivering and alone, turned to the moon and poured out his heart, saying how hard his life was, how lonely and sad. The moon felt sorry for the young lad and shed tears of sadness. Lo and behold, the tears touched the small boy and turned into candies. The boy ate the sweet candies and felt better. The sweet taste in his mouth even made him smile, and he was no longer so unhappy. He knew that he had a friend above who took care of him and wouldn't ever leave him.

The next night, the moon called to some of his friends among the stars and they went over to the small boy. They covered him so he wouldn't be cold and shed their light so it wouldn't be dark.

At the end of the tale, the boy became the happiest child of all. He had a small house made out of stars that shone like diamonds. Everyone looked at the bright, shining house and wanted to be friends with the happy boy who lived inside. The boy was no longer lonely, no longer cold at night, no longer hungry and unfortunate. And so, the boy lived happily ever after.

Yosefa yawned. Kochava sure knew how to tell a story dramatically. Whenever she told a story, all the girls sat mesmerized, drinking in every word. But when the story was over, and the teacher began asking questions in her regular teacher voice, Yosefa felt that the magic was gone, and she decided she didn't like the story at all.

She now thought of the small boy. She loved him and pitied him. The small boy could sometimes be Yossi, even though Yossi was big, and could sometimes be her, Yosefa, even though she was a girl and had a house to live in. She thought about the small boy and felt exactly like he did, wishing she had someone to talk to.

She couldn't talk to Abba or Ima. They themselves were looking for someone on whose broad shoulders they could cry.

It's Got Nothing to Do with Him ◆ 147

They too wanted to unburden their innermost feelings to someone who would understand. She couldn't talk to Shira or Orna or any of her other classmates, and she couldn't tell Yossi how she felt. Even her teacher Sigalit, the one she loved so much, had patted her curls and said, "You're a real heroine, Yosefa, and your parents are heroes too. Everyone is trying to do whatever they can to bring your Yossi home. You know that, don't you?"

Just hearing those words had calmed her down, even though she didn't agree that she was a heroine. *Heroes are strong, brave men aren't they?* she thought. *Abba is so helpless and broken. Right now he's even crying out loud. If only my teacher Sigalit were here now, maybe she would come over to me again and say something encouraging. That would be better than nothing.*

But now, it was the middle of the night, and Yosefa was alone in her dark room. Until morning came, when it would be time to see Sigalit, many hours would have to pass, and every hour has seemingly endless minutes. Who could she talk to now?

Yosefa opened the window and again looked out at the moon. She stared and stared but found no inclination to talk to it at all. The moon can't talk and it can't throw down candies. The moon can't build a house of stars and can't watch over Yossi. It's all just a fairy tale.

Yosefa knew Who she wanted to talk to, but she didn't know how. This friend of her father's, the one in the black suit, always talked about G-d. "Pray to Him," he would say to Abba when he was sad. "Pray," he would tell Abba when he was worried. "Hashem hears you. He's waiting for you."

Too bad Morah Kochava doesn't teach us how to pray to G-d, Yosefa thought sadly. But she wouldn't give up. She would pray to Him in her own words and tell Him exactly how she felt.

Standing there by the open window and looking up at the indifferent moon, Yosefa thought about the One Who is higher than the moon, much much higher. She would talk to Him.

"Hashem," she began, her voice trembling. "Hashem, do You hear me? Do You hear a little girl with tears in her eyes talking to You? Please, Hashem, You see Yossi. You know where he is. Please watch over him and bring him back to us soon."

Yosefa crept back into bed and snuggled under the quilt. She felt much calmer than before. Now she would probably be able to fall asleep.

Poor Morah Kochava, Yosefa had time to think before closing her eyes. *When she is sad, who does she talk to? To the moon, like in the fairy tales? Too bad her father doesn't have a friend like my father does — a friend who will teach her how to talk to Hashem.*

Yosefa closed her eyes. The smile on her face bespoke peace, faith and security all wrapped up into one.

※ ※ ※

It was the usual end of a very ordinary lesson. The weather was hot and dry outside, and the students in the classroom had other things on their minds besides the different kinds of triangles their teacher was discussing in math class. The water fountain at the end of the hall beckoned to the children's dry throats. Recess, with its snacks, playground and bright blue sky, was much more inviting than the lesson.

The math teacher was too tired to fight them. He stood at the blackboard lecturing on geometry, knowing well how difficult it was to teach not only at the end of the day but at the end of the year.

"Do you have a red Magic Marker?" Nachum asked Dovi, poking him to get his attention.

The teacher shot the two of them a look. "I just want you to know, boys," he said, raising his voice, "that the material we are now learning is the basis for the geometry you will be learning next year. So don't come to the teacher next year and say—"

"Next year we won't be learning here," a voice piped up from Bentzi's direction somewhere in the last row.

"What do you mean?"

"It's true," Bentzi went on. "Efraim Ganz, Nachum, Chaim and I are leaving the cheder."

It was if a bomb had been dropped. The thirst, fatigue and exhaustion caused by the heat dissipated in a split second, and a tumult erupted in full force.

"What's he talking about?" Chaim wanted to know. "Who are you to decide that I'm leaving the cheder? To which cheder will I be going, in your humble opinion?"

"Just wait till you get home." Bentzi was grinning from ear to ear. "You'll see. Your father'll tell you all about it. All week long our fathers have been talking about it. They talked to the principal to ask his advice. My father works in the office, so he was really involved. Our fathers decided that it would be a waste of time for the four of us to continue here in seventh grade, since really, according to our age, we should be in eighth grade. They had a hard time deciding, but in the end they came to the conclusion that next year the four of us should learn together in the eighth grade somewhere outside Arazim. That way when we go to *yeshiva ketana* we won't have missed anything important and we'll be ready."

The class exploded. No one was more surprised than the three other boys.

Sure, they were all used to Bentzi being the cheder's unofficial spokesman. He tried to overhear every phone conversation his father got at home and managed to piece together the fragments, along with the help of his father's facial expressions, into news he could tell his friends.

Bentzi would be the first to know about a forthcoming class trip, when it would be and where they would be going. Bentzi would know if a teacher was going to be absent, who the substitute would be, if the Mishna test would be two full pages or only one and a half pages long and if it would be given during the first period or the last one before going home.

What they couldn't believe was that Bentzi knew something that involved them that they themselves didn't even know about.

"Actually," Chaim suddenly remembered, "my father did hint at something. He asked me how it is learning in the same class with boys almost two years younger than I am. He even said he wanted me to be in a class with boys my own age. But, he didn't go into details, and I didn't ask any questions."

"It's all because Arazim is such a small place." Nachum explained knowledgeably. "There were only four boys who belonged in seventh grade, and you can't open a class just for four. That's why we're learning with all of you now in the sixth grade."

"I've known about it for a week already," Bentzi boasted. "You can't keep secrets in my house 'cause it's too small. Boy, was it hard not to say anything. This morning, my father told me the decision is final and that the news would soon be out. So that's it. I couldn't hold it in any longer."

The bell rang, but none of them heard it. They didn't even notice that the teacher was gone. All they could think about was next year and the minivan that would be taking the four boys — Bentzi and Chaim, Nachum and Efraim — to their new cheder. These boys, who were such good friends of theirs, who had been together with them from the beginning, would now be the friends of other boys in another class in a new cheder far away.

Shuki listened to all this from the sidelines. He stayed out of the conversation. It was interesting news, but it had nothing to do with him.

He didn't know yet that his father had spoken to Rabbi Gold. And he had no idea what an effect this latest piece of news would have on him personally.

When Father Knows Best

Shuki's father sat on a low folding lawn chair in his garden. His fingers absentmindedly reached out for a lump of dirt and crumbled it. It was hot outside at that time of day, and the evening breeze didn't promise any coolness. He looked at the yellowing leaves. They turned their faces to the ground as if ashamed of being caught off guard in their difficult hour.

It wasn't his favorite time of year for being in the garden. The sun beat down mercilessly on the foliage and the parched earth, drying the fertile soil. Yitzchak, his soul bound to all things green and alive, felt their distress keenly.

Although he knew summer would eventually end and the plants would once more turn green with the winter rains, he preferred to sit inside his cool home rather than see the suffering of the parched vegetation. Now, though, he chose to sit outside in the garden. He looked down the path impatiently, wondering when he would see the familiar figure with a brown briefcase on his back.

He was tense, tense because of what he wanted to say to his son and even more nervous because of what his son might have to say to him. How would Yehoshua react? Would he like the idea, or would he totally reject it?

He found himself sweating at the thought of his son biting his lips and holding back tears of shame. Who knew? Maybe he would be insulted and take it as a sign that something was wrong with him, that he was different, not like everyone else, a problem case.

Just then Shuki came down the road. Strolling along the road, he hummed a pleasant tune to himself. How great it was to come home after a satisfying day at school!

Shuki tried to pinpoint what exactly was so wonderfully different this day from the previous day and the day before that. What had happened to make his briefcase feel light on his shoulders and his heart burst with joy? Was it the fact that he knew the answer to a question in the oral quiz ahead of Aryeh and Dovi, Meir and Moishe, in fact ahead of everyone? Can knowing the right answer to just one question, can a warm smile from the rebbe and rare looks of approval from friends put a person in such a good mood?

Shuki turned the bend. Soon he would reach the familiar path that led to his house. Would his father notice the sparkle in his eyes? Would he tell Abba why he was so ecstatic?

Maybe he would. After all, his father would no doubt be happy to hear what had happened in class. How was it that he was the only boy to know the answer to the rebbe's question? Thinking about it now, Shuki realized he had found the answer the night he had looked up a *vort* to say at the *siyum* just in case he was chosen to say the *hadran*. The rebbe's question turned out to be on that very passage, and he remembered it practically word for word.

There's Abba. Shuki's bouncy steps lightened tenfold as he spread out both arms to greet his father. When things went well and his friends smiled at him approvingly, Shuki felt that the whole world was on his side. Then life became wonderful, and everything seemed as bright and shiny as a brand new penny.

His father returned his hug but Shuki sensed a certain tension.

"What's new, Yehoshua'le?" his father asked as he placed a loving arm round Shuki's shoulder. "Come sit here next to me and tell me how your day went."

Shuki sat down on the edge of the chair and looked around his beloved garden. *Should I tell Abba what happened?* He sensed his father had something on his mind and wasn't listening to him at all. Maybe this time Abba wants to tell me something. Maybe he has something to say about Yossi Nir.

"You tell me something, Abba," Shuki said, settling comfortably in the chair. "Tell me something about the son of that man you went to. What's happening? Is there anything new?"

His father didn't reply. Forcing a smile, he turned slowly toward his son. "We'll talk about him some other time, Yehoshua," he said. "Now I want to talk about someone else."

"Who?" Shuki was really curious.

"About my son." He smiled "What do you have to say, Yehoshua? What's new in the sixth grade? Soon you'll be in seventh grade, won't you?"

"Uh, yeah," Shuki answered, not quite knowing what to make of the conversation. "Tzviki is already marking off the days on the class calendar." Shuki figured he might as well say something. "I never count the days. What for? It just makes time pass more slowly."

"Do you want the time to pass quickly?" his father asked.

"Not always," Shuki answered. "For sure not always. And besides," he brushed off some dried grass from his pants, "all the days go by whether you want them to or not, so why think about it?"

"Some of the boys in the class are going to be learning in Haifa next year," his father abruptly changed the subject. "Do you know who?"

"There are four," Shuki said authoritatively. "Bentzi, Efraim, Nachum and Chaim. They don't really belong in our class because they're a year ahead. They're really going into eighth grade. Just think, Abba," Shuki said, "this year they're running around, playing with us in the sixth grade and next year they'll be sitting in eighth grade practically like *yeshiva bachurim*. What do you say to that?"

The last words flew by Yitzchak unnoticed. "Without those four, your class will be tiny. A class with only eight boys can be pretty boring at times, can't it?"

Shuki didn't answer. He hadn't thought about that part of it before. The class hadn't stopped talking about the four boys who would be leaving to learn in the big city. They hadn't really discussed the boys who would be remaining in Arazim and the effect it would have on them.

Come to think of it, he wondered, *what's it going to be like? Will we sit in only two rows? Will the one sitting on the second bench be in the last row?* He found the thought amusing.

"They'll be commuting every morning," his father said, breaking the silence. "There's room in the van for you." He looked straight into his son's eyes, which were now wide open in surprise. "How would you like to join them?"

"What?" Shuki asked, incredulous. It wasn't an exclamation of surprise but one of total lack of comprehension.

"You heard me," his father replied. "Actually, why not? You'll be able to learn in seventh grade with new friends in a big class that's more challenging. You won't be tied down to seven boys who have known you since you were born. How does that sound, Yehoshua'le?"

Shuki's jaw had dropped in astonishment. "Me?" he finally managed to croak. "Learn in Haifa? Leave my class? Leave all the boys and the cheder in Arazim? Why?"

The why came out sharp and harsh sounding, filled with bitterness and pain. It was a why that demanded an explanation.

His father lovingly patted Shuki's head, hoping the strong emotion in his heart would somehow filter through. *Let Yehoshua feel it,* he thought to himself. *Let him feel some of the love I have for him. Let him understand the anxiety and concern.*

But Shuki's father knew that it would take many years before his son would be able to understand the depth of his feelings. When the time came and his Yehoshua held his own son in his arms, then and only then would he understand. That's how it is.

"But why," Shuki asked again. "Why?"

"Why?" his father echoed, wondering how best to handle it. "Actually, why not? Isn't it better to be in a big class, with lots of different types of boys? Eventually you'll have to leave the sheltered environment of Arazim, so why not now? Look, Bentzi, Efraim, Nachum and – "

"But they're in a different grade," Shuki broke in. "What about Tzviki and Meir and Moishe and Dovi and Aryeh and the others? How come a small class is okay for them?"

"Maybe for them it is okay," his father answered. "Listen, Shuki, we thought about this a lot. Naturally, we won't force anything on you. We, that is, Rabbi Gold and I, think that it may be very good for you to leave Arazim, to get out in the world and learn in a big city. Haven't you complained plenty of times about how the moshav is so confining and limited?"

"Maybe." Shuki felt as if the world was closing in on him. How could Rabbi Gold and his father do this to him? How could they have kept him in the dark about the plans? His father sounded so reasonable, with his soft, mellow voice, as if Shuki's leaving his class in Arazim was nothing major but just an everyday occurrence.

What would all the other boys say? What would he tell them — that his father decided to have him switch schools just like that, for no good reason? That the class had suddenly become too small? They would all burst out laughing. He could just imagine the scene: on the way home after school, as soon as he turned off the road to walk down his path, all the boys would start talking about him and his father.

No! Under no circumstances would he agree to it. It was bad enough to be born different. Why make things worse?

His father's voice continued, trying to convince him of the advantages of a large class, new friends, new surroundings.

"I'm not going."

Yitzchak wasn't surprised by his son's reaction and didn't press the issue. He stood up, taking Shuki's hand in his. "Let's go into the house. We'll talk about it some other time."

For the rest of the day, they talked about other things. No one mentioned the earth-shattering conversation.

But Shuki couldn't get it out of his mind. Underneath his fear, he found the idea exciting. At the same time, it was as if a huge boulder stood between him and the cheder in the big city.

Shuki knew what the kids in his class would say. They'd say his father wanted him to switch schools because his father had never studied in a cheder. They'd say that maybe in a school where history and math were important, a big class might have its advantages, but in a cheder, where Torah and Gemara are the most important subjects, what difference does it make if the class is small? The main thing is wanting to learn and understand!

The boys for sure would say it's because his father wasn't completely accepted in Arazim, that he's different, only a simple gardener who attends *shiurim* at night. That's why he doesn't feel any attachment to the moshav or a sense of responsibility for the community's development. It wouldn't be a big deal for him to take his son out a year ahead of time because, after all, what does he care if the class is even smaller?

The boys would say... The thoughts wouldn't leave him alone. He knew he wouldn't be able to stand up to the social pressure. He would tell his father that he didn't want to leave. He just couldn't. Didn't his father say that no one was going to force him?

The next morning, Shuki went to cheder just like he did every day. His pace was more snail-like than ever, and he walked as if in a dream. One by one, the other boys arrived — Meir and Dovi, Chaim and Aryeh.

"What's new, Chaim?" Dovi asked. "Getting ready?"

"Of course," Chaim sounded excited. "Tomorrow I'll be going to Haifa with my father for an interview with the principal. They don't automatically accept every boy, you know. Each boy has to come with a parent to be tested. They have to see what your level of learning is. They want to know what kind of boy you are and if you come from a good home.

"The cheder in Haifa is outstanding," Chaim said with not a little pride, "and it's very choosy about who it accepts. It's only here in Arazim that every boy in the moshav gets in."

Dovi and Meir looked at Chaim in admiration. They could just picture Chaim standing before the stern principal being asked question after question.

What if he doesn't measure up to the standards? Shuki worried. *Will he have to return to Arazim in humiliation?*

"Are you excited?" Dovi asked. "Are you scared?"

Shuki figured that they, too, were thinking the same thoughts he was. How lucky it was that the cheder in Arazim didn't have any entrance exams.

Chaim barely got a chance to answer their questions when Aryeh, who until then had stood quietly by the side, took over. "It's exciting, but scary too," he said. "It's not only the interview. It's that it's such a big change in our lives. I know exactly how you feel, Chaim."

There was a moment of silence. The boys looked at each other, both wondering what Aryeh was hinting.

"Yes, my father decided that the class is too small for me,"

Aryeh said. "He says it's better for me to be in a bigger class. He has other reasons, too. He registered me in seventh grade in a cheder in Yerushalayim. I'll be staying with my grandfather and learning there."

This piece of news created an uproar. Aryeh? Was he also leaving?

Shuki started to say something. He wanted to tell the boys that he too was leaving, that his father was thinking along those same lines. How logical everything sounded when it came from Aryeh quoting his father. Aryeh's father didn't have a different background; his father was part of the community. Besides, he was a *talmid chacham* and knew all about *chinuch*.

At that moment, Shuki knew he would leave. He had been tempted to make the decision himself the night before. It was just that there had been a barrier, a boulder in the road between him and the new cheder. Now, with this one sentence from Aryeh, the barrier was removed.

All at once, Shuki felt relieved. Everything was now clear and simple.

But a minute later, when he reconstructed the events of the previous twenty-four hours, he felt a weight settle heavily on his small heart.

Why? he tormented himself bitterly. *Why couldn't I hear it when Abba said it? After all, I know he has my best interests at heart. Why did I value the idea only when it came from Aryeh's father?*

23
After All That Hard Work

Shuki's mother energetically kneaded the ball of dough. Shuki stood by her side, following with great interest every move of his mother's expert fingers. He watched as she carefully poured the oil drop by drop onto the thin layer of dough. The cocoa-sugar mixture sprinkled on the lightly oiled pastry turned it a beautiful light brown. His mother rolled it all up and put it into the oven. Shuki's favorite cake would soon be ready.

"Interesting, isn't it?" his mother said.

Shuki replied with a smile. This yeast dough was part and parcel of Thursday night preparations for Shabbos, inseparable from the small homey kitchen. The Katz family wasn't one for culinary experimentation. If a recipe came out tasty, it became a perennial favorite, and if a recipe failed once, it was bound to fail again. Why make changes when you have something tried-and-true?

His mother took an egg out of the refrigerator and cracked it open into a glass to check it for blood spots.

"Do you remember, Ima," Shuki asked out of the blue, "what we discussed about my teeth?

"Your teeth?" his mother asked incredulously, glancing at her son's pearly white teeth. *Of course!* she suddenly remembered. The side molars were coming in crooked. Now was a good time to go to the orthodontist for a professional opinion. Eleven is considered the ideal age to start with braces, she had explained to Shuki.

"We really do have to find a dentist," she sighed. "We have to find the time to take care of it. Here at the small clinic in Arazim there are no orthodontists yet."

"I asked around and found the name of a dentist," Shuki said. "I even found out when it's a good time to make an appointment."

"You did?" Bruria exclaimed, putting down the sugar that was in her hands and looking directly at Shuki. No, he wasn't joking. His face was serious as always. When had her little boy become so mature and independent? She wasn't sure if she was pleased with the change or not. And what made him all of a sudden so interested in his slightly crooked teeth?

Her husband had told her about his talk with Rabbi Gold. Maybe that had something to do with Shuki's concern. Could it be that the boys made fun of his looks?

Ridiculous. Bruria was sure there was no basis for such a thought. Would anybody, other than a caring mother like her, notice that the inner molars were growing in a bit crooked? Why, compared to the buck teeth of some of the other boys, Shuki's teeth were positively straight as a ruler.

Shuki took advantage of the moment of silence to continue. "In two weeks I can have an appointment on Tuesday or Thursday. Can you come with me to Haifa? There's a dentist there who's highly recommended — Dr. Yarkon. Tzviki told me that all his brothers and sisters had crooked teeth and they're very satisfied with his treatment. Next week, he's going there and in another month he'll be wearing braces. He has the phone number and address. Do you want to call and make an appointment for two weeks from now?

"The timing is just right, Ima," Shuki rushed on, "because the new cheder in Haifa told Abba that the entrance exams are during the last week of school. This way you'll be able to come with me to the interview too."

Shuki finished his long speech and looked tensely at his mother.

Something is not quite right here, she thought, *but I can't quite put my finger on it*. Shuki's flow of words and his super self-confidence, so untypical of him, suddenly confused her.

"Is it okay, Ima?" Shuki pleaded.

"Okay? Well, we'll see. Maybe," was all his mother said.

"So it's all right?" Shuki wasn't about to give up easily. "You'll call the dentist's office and make an appointment for Tuesday or Thursday in two weeks, won't you?"

"Probably."

"Why aren't you saying you will, Ima?" Shuki practically whined. "I want to know now. I need to know that you're going to make the appointment and come with me to the orthodontist and that as long as you're in Haifa, you'll come with me to the interview. I have to know now," Shuki's tone rose to a demand. "I have to have an answer!"

"Why is it so important for you to know right this minute. We're talking about two weeks from now, aren't we?"

"Yes," Shuki replied, nervously pacing the kitchen floor. "But...but I have to know now. I..." Why did he have to have an answer right now?

He couldn't tell his mother the real reason. How could he say he wanted to be sure she would come and not his father, that he was ashamed to go with him?

// // //

"How did the interview go yesterday?" Bentzi asked Chaim and Nachum, curious as to how things went.

"*Baruch Hashem*," Chaim replied. "Everything went okay. You have nothing to worry about, Bentzi."

"I'm not worried," Bentzi laughed, "My father will take care of everything for me. Were you tested?"

"Barely," Nachum replied. "It was nothing serious. They asked me what *mesechta* we're learning now and what topic we studied last. It was as simple as pie."

Shuki took in every word. He would be going on Thursday. His mother had made an appointment with Dr. Yarkon for ten o'clock, and afterward they would be going to the cheder. It's a good thing Nachum and Chaim said that the interview wasn't as bad as people thought. Shuki hoped and prayed that all would go without a hitch, and that he wouldn't make a fool of himself in the new surroundings.

"Who went with you?" Shuki said quietly.

"What do you mean?" Bentzi started to answer. "Obviously—"

A piercing look from Nachum stopped him short. Shuki blushed in embarrassment. He really hadn't meant to interrupt their conversation. Even in class, during the most boring lessons, he tried to pay attention and be careful never to disturb. Now they weren't even in class. They were getting ready for a very interesting program being put on for the fifth and sixth grades. Shuki had merely wanted to ask a very important question. Too bad the conversation was cut short and he didn't get his answer.

The summer vacation for the cheder in Arazim was very short. There wasn't a real day camp program but instead there were three weeks of light learning interspersed with recreational activities. At the moment, the boys were sitting in the large fifth-grade classroom getting ready for an interesting program. At the front of the room, a guest lecturer was explaining how one can learn a person's character traits from his handwriting. The lecturer's voice was monotonous, and some of the boys were getting restless.

"This is pretty boring," Bentzi whispered as he turned around in his seat. "This is for girls! How can you call this an interesting camp activity?"

"You're right," Chaim agreed as he stifled a yawn. "Who's interested in my handwriting anyhow? What difference does it make if my letters are big or small, slanting to the left or to the right, extending above the line or below? I wish he would finish already."

Shuki, on the other hand, was enthralled. Was it really possible that the lecturer was right? Can you really tell from densely written letters, from the pressure and the size of the script whether a person was honest or a liar, consistent or always changing his mind? How come he had never heard of such a thing before?

"I see that you don't believe me, boys," the graphologist said, "but I have proof."

The bored boys came to life.

"I need five volunteers who will each give me a notebook. It doesn't matter which one. I'll look at the notebook and analyze the person's character based on his handwriting."

You could feel the suspense in the air. Now it wasn't just meaningless theory — now the graphologist was talking about their notebooks, their handwriting, their very own character traits, and that was bound to be very, very interesting.

"Who's ready to volunteer?" the lecturer asked his by now enthusiastic audience. Shuki bit his fingernails nervously. Oh, how he wished the graphologist would analyze his handwriting. How he wanted to know if what the expert said was true. Could this man know who he really was, what his real character traits were?

He glanced around the room. Was anyone volunteering? If others raised their hands, he would volunteer too, but he wasn't about to be the first one. No, not him.

"I'm willing to give my notebook, " Meir said, opening his briefcase, "but what is this graph-graphologist going to say? All I need is that he should tell everyone that I get mad fast or forget to do my homework. I'll be embarrassed in front of the rebbes, and besides, I wouldn't want all the kids in both classes to hear."

Meir has no problem talking about all this, Shuki thought with envy amid the burst of laughter that followed Meir's remarks. He would never be able to be so candid. But Meir was right. Even if the entire class volunteered, he wouldn't want the graphologist to broadcast all his faults in front of the entire class.

Rabbi Gold saw all the children hesitate, reluctant to volunteer. He whispered something in the graphologist's ear. "Of course, by all means," the expert said. "Boys, I want you to know that I will only mention the positive points I see."

Shuki was aching to raise his hand, but he forced it to stay down. It was only after Chaim and Nachum raised their hands followed by Bentzi, Aryeh, Yehuda and Dovi that Shuki finally got up his courage. But by that time it was too late. The graphologist had quickly picked five boys and that was that.

All the boys leaned forward to get a good look. You could have sliced the silence with a knife. The lecturer took one of the fifth-grade notebooks, opened it at random and placed it on the projector. The page appeared large on the screen making every row of Yehuda's rounded handwriting clear for all to see.

It didn't take more than two seconds for the graphologist to begin. "Yehuda is a well-behaved boy. He likes to smile and laugh. He enjoys a good joke and has a great sense of humor." The room rocked with laughter. Was he ever right! How had this stranger known that Yehuda was the class clown?

Rabbi Landesman, the fifth-grade rebbe, quieted down the class so the graphologist could continue.

"Yehuda is easygoing and doesn't tolerate unfairness, be it to himself or to others. He's always ready to help those in need of assistance." Cries of admiration and surprise rippled through the room. Yehuda turned red as a beet, and his shoulders practically sagged from all the pats on the back he received from his friends.

"Let's go on to the next one," Rabbi Gold announced as he brought Dovi's *dinim* notebook.

"Dovi is a serious boy," the graphologist said, "well balanced and a deep thinker. He's also mature for his age. Dovi is diligent, persistent and ambitious." The sixth-grade boys could barely control themselves and a round of applause echoed in the room. Dovi modestly lowered his eyes, somewhat embarrassed by the outburst.

Time flew as the boys' enthusiasm grew with each passing minute. The analysis was accurate down to the last detail.

"We want a turn too," shouted Meir and Nachum

"Me too," chimed in Shuki, his voice barely audible.

The two rebbes exchanged looks.

"Okay," Rabbi Gold acquiesced. Turning to the three boys he said, "The graphologist will write an analysis of your handwriting, too. Hurry — where are your notebooks?"

Scrutinizing Meir's notebook, the expert began to quickly write a few brief lines. "Should I write everything?" he mischievously asked.

"Everything!" answered Meir.

Shuki stood restlessly nearby. All he wanted was for the handwriting expert to hurry up and go on to the next boy so he could see what he'd say about him.

Finally Shuki's notebook was returned. He quickly closed it and hid it deep inside his briefcase. He wasn't going to read it right then and there with everyone shouting.

The boys left the building one by one talking about what they had just experienced.

"I can't wait to tell my father about this," Bentzi said excitedly. "I hope he's home."

At Bentzi's mention of his father, Shuki remembered that he hadn't gotten an answer to the question he asked.

"Who," he said, turning to Nachum, who was standing next to him, "went with you to the interview in Haifa?"

"What do you mean, who went with him?" Chaim asked, butting into the conversation. "His father, of course. No one goes to an interview alone."

"What about going with, uh, your mother, for example?" Shuki cautiously asked, choosing his words carefully.

"With your mother? Are you kidding?" Nachum burst out laughing. "Why would someone go with his mother to an interview at the cheder? Especially a boy going into seventh grade. It's absolutely ridiculous."

Shuki flushed. *Let him stop talking already. All I need is that all the other boys should hear my question and start laughing too. I'd better get home fast.*

Shuki wasn't rushing because he wanted to show his parents what the graphologist wrote in his notebook. No, he had something much more urgent to attend to. After all the trouble he had gone through, after all the energy he had put into arranging for his mother to go with him to Haifa, now he had to cancel the whole plan and go with his father.

How was he supposed to go about making a last-minute change like that?

24
Just Like Manny

Shuki sat in the living room easy chair, looking at the cleared dining room table. *Wednesday is the only day you can see the tabletop*, he thought to himself, looking at the worn wooden walnut table. Until Wednesday the table was always covered with an off-white embroidered tablecloth, and on Thursday morning, the first thing his mother did was spread out the snowy white lace Shabbos tablecloth. Shuki had expected to hear the washing machine thumping away, but instead he heard his father turn to him with a question.

Yes, it was Wednesday, seven o'clock in the evening. Tomorrow his mother would fold up the freshly laundered weekday tablecloth and put it in the closet. Tomorrow was the day Shuki had to show up for the interview at the new cheder in Haifa. Now his father was asking all sorts of questions. Didn't he understand what Shuki wanted deep down? Or was he just pretending not to know?

"What's going to be with the orthodontist, Shuki?" his father asked, tapping his pen on the table. "You know that's your mother's department. I don't even see what you need to go to him for. As far as I can tell, your teeth are perfect. Why do you need braces?"

Shuki was getting ready to answer when he noticed his father's smile.

"You're right, Abba," he said as the idea hit him. "Let's cancel the appointment. It's not worth missing school, is it? How about putting off the appointment until summer vacation?"

"What about the cheder interview?" Shuki's father asked, stroking his beard.

"That's exactly the point," Shuki said excitedly. "You can call the principal and ask if we can come in the evening when classes are over. Maybe we could even go to his house."

"Why would you want to do that?"

"Uh," Shuki squirmed, "because of what I just said. It's a shame to miss classes — and all the other activities. I heard there's a great program planned for tomorrow.

"I'll be leaving all my friends," he continued with great pathos, playing his last card. "I'll be leaving my friends, leaving the cheder — leaving them all forever. The least I can do is spend what little time is left with all my friends."

His father played along. "Here's the phone." He handed Shuki the receiver and took a small crumpled piece of paper from his pocket. "And this is the number."

"What?" Shuki asked, taken aback.

"It's very simple." He father stood up as if to leave the room. "Dial and talk."

Shuki looked at the small note and then at his father standing in the doorway. Tears welled up in his eyes.

"But, Abba," he pleaded, "you know I don't know how to talk to principals. How will I know what to say? I don't know how to begin."

Just Like Manny ◆ 169

"You managed to explain yourself just now," his father said tersely. "A young boy who finds every minute of learning so precious can make a wonderful impression."

He took the phone back from Shuki's hand and dialed. Shuki shrank back in his chair, wishing the earth would open up and swallow him right then and there. He had never been one to use deceit to get his way, but what was he supposed to do? He was willing to bear the embarrassment of going with his father to meet the principal, but not the shame of hundreds of strange boys staring at the scars on his father's face.

"So it's set then?" The sound of his father's voice woke Shuki from his reverie. "Tomorrow at eight P.M. in your office. Thank you!"

Shuki gave his father a look of gratitude. *It's better for him this way too*, he rationalized. After all, how would he feel having a troop of boys staring at him? Some would probably point at him, some would stop and stare, and for sure there'd be those who'd whisper loud enough to hear, "Do you think he was born that way or was it an accident?" Others would turn away. Then there were always those whose expression would turn to one of pity and they would sigh, "What a shame. Just see how he looks."

Shuki's imagination worked overtime, and he soon felt quite noble. He, Shuki, was an exemplary son, full of care and concern for his father. Why, he was preventing his father from suffering mental anguish and sparing him heartache and pain. The past few minutes that had at first felt so unpleasant now took on a different, rosier hue. What wouldn't he do for his father?

Shuki got up and went over to his briefcase. Now he could finally take out his nature study notebook and see what the graphologist had written in it. He had purposely given him this particular notebook because it was the neatest. The lines were the straightest, the handwriting precise and even.

He sure hadn't wanted the graphologist to see his other

notebooks, the ones he took notes in during class, for example. There he had to write very fast as he tried to keep up with Rabbi Gold, and lots of times he didn't even have a chance to sharpen his pencil, so the letters came out thick and ugly looking. Besides, they were full of black blotches from the eraser marks. If he had given them to the graphologist, he might have said that Shuki was disorganized and a boy without any sense of esthetics.

He pulled his nature notebook out of his briefcase. It was so clean and organized, no graphologist in his right mind would say it wasn't neat. What could the handwriting expert say about him? But despite his burning curiosity, he clenched the notebook in his hand tightly and didn't open it.

What comments could the expert have written? Shuki tried to guess. *He must have seen my yearning to succeed in learning and do well on tests,* he mused. *And he surely noted my fear of failure and getting low grades. Maybe he wrote that I dream of being more a part of the gang, and maybe, just maybe, he saw in my handwriting that the relationship between me and my father is so...so complicated. I love him a lot, but... And that's a big but!*

Then, as if making a weighty decision, Shuki opened the notebook and flipped it quickly to the last page. There, in small, precise letters (what does that say about the graphologist himself?) were five short lines. Shuki scanned them, trying to absorb it all in one glance — everything, the compliments and the criticisms.

He took a deep breath. At first glance he saw nothing terrible. There was nothing about him being bad or wicked, boastful or jealous. He took the notebook and sank down onto the living-room couch. His breathing was as shallow as if he had just finished climbing five flights of stairs.

"A pleasant type, somewhat easygoing," the graphologist's comment began. "Lacks independent thinking, pays extreme attention to what others think. His friends have a great influence over what he does, how he acts, his opinions and his outlook on life."

What? Shuki was suddenly uncomfortable. He shifted positions and reread the words out loud. "A pleasant type, somewhat easygoing." That's right, he smiled. "Lacks independent thinking." What does that mean? "Pays extreme attention to what others think. His friends have a great influence –"

"Are you studying?" his father asked as he entered the room.

Shuki sat there frozen in his place.

"Uh, it's just...," Shuki stammered, closing the notebook, his face turning beet red, "uh, it's just a notebook. It doesn't even have any homework inside."

"What's so interesting about just a notebook?" his father asked, taking it from Shuki's hands and slowly opening it.

Shuki's beet red cheeks turned an even deeper red. "Oh no, Abba. It's just...it's not important...there's nothing interesting."

"Who says?" his father asked as his eyes scanned the pages. "Whatever pertains to my son and is of interest to him is important and of interest to me."

Shuki kept silent and still. Only his eyes darted to and fro like two scared rabbits looking for a place to hide. His father stopped turning pages. "Shall we look at it another time?" he asked. Then, without waiting for an answer, he gave Shuki a warm smile, put the open notebook on the table and left the room.

It was only later that night, when Shuki was sound asleep, that Yitzchak went over to his son's briefcase. He knew that if something silly had been written in the margins of the nature study notebook, they would by now no longer be there. There had been ample time for Shuki to erase anything embarrassing, time he had given him. He had no wish to catch his son unaware.

He quietly tiptoed over to the desk and riffled through the contents. Hadn't he said he would look at it some other time? Well, now was another time, and here was the opportunity.

The nature notebook was in his hands. He looked at Shuki peacefully sleeping in his bed, and something tugged at his heartstrings. He covered his son with the thin blanket and hurriedly left the room.

He sat down in the living room. It didn't take long for him to find the right page. The words were waiting. He stared at the lines for a long time.

"So that's how it is," Yitzchak murmured, his eyes scanning the lines.

Just as his son, Shuki, had reread the words out loud so that his mind and heart would absorb them, so did Yitzchak. A dormant memory struggled to rise to the surface of his consciousness. The words, the context, the sharp uncompromising analysis — all were familiar.

He closed his eyes to let the memories return. "Lacks independent thinking, pays extreme attention to what others think. His friends have a great influence over what he does, how he acts, his opinions and his outlook on life." Back then, these were the same words, the same sharp analysis.

He remembered how Manny had become confused. With a wide grin, he had opened the page and begun to read out loud, sharing the words with all his friends around him.

Manny was very protective of his image as one of the boys. He was always smiling, backslapping and joking with his friends. When he discovered what the graphologist had written, it was too late to take back the words. His friends heard every word.

Yitzchak recalled the smiles he later exchanged with Yossi. "I never did believe in graphologists," he had said. "I thought they were quacks. But Manny just made me less suspicious of them," he concluded, with Yossi nodding his head in agreement.

He suddenly saw Manny in his mind's eye. The three of them, Yossi, Manny and he had much in common. The same questions, the same doubts disturbed their peace of mind. The

Just Like Manny ❖ 173

three of them were aware of the void in their lives and tried to fill it with meaning.

Nevertheless, their differences overshadowed what they shared in common. They were like tall mountains — all seemingly the same but each unique. One was carved out of stone, while another was made up of grains of sand, prey to the blowing wind.

Although Manny was older in years, it was obvious to Yitzchak and Yossi that time alone doesn't account for accomplishments. If your inner self is weak and shaky, achievements will be a long way off.

Where is Manny today? Yitzchak suddenly wondered. *He had been a medic in the army reserves. He was the first to bend down and see my burnt face,* Yitzchak remembered. *Although he was used to seeing wounded soldiers, there was fear and aversion in his blue eyes when he first saw me.* The scene was still vivid and Yitzchak shuddered.

He had been in enemy hands for thirty-six hours. Manny was the first to come over to him when he was released and returned to the Israelis. Until that moment, he had felt the heat of his burned skin. But when he saw the shocked look in his buddy's eyes, something wounded his sensitive heart.

They never met again. Like all his army buddies, their ways parted.

Yitzchak again looked at the open notebook. He suddenly understood the shadow that passed over Shuki whenever they spoke. Why hadn't he realized it before? His Yehoshua, his beloved son, reminded him so much of Manny, his army buddy. Who said children resembled their parents? Yehoshua was so different from him. Manny's insecurity, so unlike his own self-confident nature, was deeply implanted in his son.

Manny had proved to him for the first time that graphologists know what they're talking about. Now, Yitzchak sadly thought, he had more proof. But this time the pain was greater. Manny was a friend. But Yehoshua? Yehoshua was the essence of his hopes and dreams.

It is impossible — and this Yitzchak knew without a shadow of a doubt — it is impossible to realize dreams and expectations, to soar and reach lofty heights, when the soul is dispirited.

25

Change

"What a great program!" Meir gestured enthusiastically. "I can't wait to tell everybody at home about it."

"Yeah, it was really something," agreed Chaim.

"Now we can understand what we learned in the parasha better," Dovi added. "We saw pictures of the *Mishkan* when we learned *parashas Tetzaveh*, but there's no comparison. The explanations the lecturer gave, how he knew every detail. I feel like I saw the real *keilim*, the *shulchan*, the menora right in front of me."

The boys all nodded vigorously in agreement. Shuki, his mind elsewhere, nodded too. He knew that the class had seen colored slides. The screen was on the wall right in front of his eyes, so he couldn't help but see the pictures being shown one after another. He knew that they were of the *keilim* of the *Mishkan*, and he was aware of the accompanying explanation along with the background music. But his mind was elsewhere. He was sitting is some strange principal's office somewhere in Haifa, answering questions being shot at him from all sides.

What time is it? Shuki wondered. *It's been a long time since I looked at a watch*, he thought as he glanced at his digital wristwatch, realizing that time was very relative. Only five minutes had passed. Another two and a quarter hours to go. He felt the butterflies in his stomach fluttering away.

It had started that morning. The minute he had opened his eyes, he felt something deep inside. "Today is the day," he whispered over and over to himself. He got dressed, drank a glass of hot chocolate, went off to cheder like every ordinary day, davened and attended classes. But he wasn't himself. Shuki Katz wasn't in the cheder in Arazim — he was on his way to start a new chapter in his life, off to the unknown.

The interview totally occupied his mind. He would enter the principal's office with his father. What would the room look like? Would it be friendly, warmly welcoming every boy, even one as nervous as he, a boy who just might stammer from bashfulness? Would there be a square black desk piled high with papers and files behind which sat a busy principal, studying some forms as his glasses slid down his nose?

What about the windows, what would they look like? Were they large ones facing a bustling play yard or main road? Or maybe they were small and unobtrusive, covered with curtains waving in the breeze as if protecting those within from curious eyes outside?

Shuki glanced at his watch again. Another three minutes had passed. Actually, the type of room wasn't important. He must focus on the interview itself, think about the questions that would be asked and start preparing some answers. He'd be starting in a new school, and first impressions are crucial. It was important to start off on the right foot.

"What sort of questions were you asked at the interview?" Shuki asked Bentzi and Chaim who were walking home with him.

"At the interview?" Chaim repeated. "Oh, yeah, the interview," he reminded himself with a smile. "What made you think about that all of a sudden?"

"I think about it all the time," Shuki answered, blushing slightly. "Soon" — he looked yet again at his wristwatch — "in another two hours and seven minutes to be precise, I'll be there."

Chaim and Bentzi chuckled. "Once you get there, you'll have to wait at least another half hour, so it doesn't pay for you to count the minutes. As to what questions the principal asked, well, they were nothing special. He's more interested in talking to you, so there's no point in preparing ahead of time."

Shuki pursed his lips in silence. No, he wasn't that type. He preferred to prepare all the answers to every possible question ahead of time. He went over the last *daf* of Gemara three times. He once heard that it was customary to be tested on the material you were currently learning. If the principal asked him a question on that *daf*, he'd be prepared. He would have no problem repeating word for word the question Tosafos asks and the answer, or presenting the conflict and the differing opinions on it.

"Tell me anyway," Shuki begged them. "What questions do you remember? At least I'll know what to think about." His voice pleaded for an answer, and his face reflected the great tension he was under at that moment.

"I'm really scared," he said with a candor unusual for him. Perhaps the tension over what the future held provoked the last remark. "I'm afraid that because I'm so nervous I won't be able to answer any of the questions," he confided.

Shuki remembered the dream he had had the previous night. In his dream he sat on a small stool in front of the big tall principal, his whole body trembling.

"What is your teacher's name, Yehoshua?" the principal had asked.

Shuki opened his mouth to answer but the words wouldn't come. His mind was a total blank. His eyes darted around the room looking at the blank white walls, the gray tiled floor and the high ceiling, but for the life of him he couldn't remember his rebbe's name. He pinched himself, desperately tapped his feet, but nothing helped. This simple, basic fact eluded him.

The frustrating situation came to an end with the buzz of the alarm clock. But what would happen with the real principal in exactly another two hours and one minute? There wouldn't be any alarm clocks ringing to turn reality into a dream.

"What do you say?" Shuki again prodded Bentzi and Chaim. "What did the principal ask?"

Bentzi couldn't be bothered to answer. Chaim scratched his head trying to remember the exact wording, when behind them the grumbling of complaining voices were heard.

"Shuki, do you really think that's all we have to talk about?" Meir attacked him. "How many times can we talk about the same subject? You'd think that the only thing in the world was some cheder in Haifa and a miserable interview."

Shuki bit his lower lip hard.

"Yeah, enough is enough," chimed in Dovi. "We finally have an interesting topic to talk about, the fantastic slide presentation, and you bring up your new cheder again."

"Go there already." That was Meir trying to be funny.

Shuki turned white. Without thinking, he looked at his watch again. In another two hours minus four minutes — that made it one hour and fifty-six minutes. *It's a good thing I'm going for this interview*, he thought. *It's a good thing that's what Abba decided for me.*

He'd leave Meir and all the others behind and start from scratch. Of course, in Haifa there would probably be boys more or less like Meir. After all, the boys in his class in Arazim were no worse than the boys in a big city.

Still, the long years of being together established certain norms that Shuki had neither the courage nor the power to change. It was okay for Meir to throw out nasty remarks but he wasn't allowed to answer back. Dovi could say what he wanted, but Shuki wouldn't react. In Haifa, in a new cheder with new friends, maybe things would be different.

The group around him continued to talk about the slide presentation and about the summer activities in general. They continued their conversation as they came to his corner and didn't notice when he mumbled a quiet goodbye.

Once he was home, the minutes crawled. Shuki looked from his watch to the round clock on the wall. He practically counted the seconds as he paced the floor, wandering from one room to another, opening and closing doors without knowing why. The minutes dragged by until his father appeared as if from nowhere.

"Are you ready, son?" His smile was a broad one. "Come on. Let's go."

Finally, after a drive that went by all too fast and a short wait in the office behind closed doors, the moment arrived. Shuki wondered how people managed to contain themselves in dramatic moments such as this. How could a person suddenly feel hopeful and fearful at the same time — and all in the split second it took to open the door to the principal's office?

The principal wasn't at all as he had imagined. He was short and round with a warm smile on a face that exuded friendliness.

"Hello," he said cheerfully, pointing to the two chairs in front of his desk. "You must be Yehoshua Katz."

Shuki nodded his head, trying to remain calm.

"Fine," the principal said. "In what cheder have you been learning, Yehoshua? What grade are you in? What are you learning? Where are you holding?"

As the questions were asked, Shuki began to forget that he was at an interview. The conversation was so pleasant that he felt as if it was an ordinary amiable conversation between friends. His answers flowed, and there was no need for his eyes to dart nervously about.

The time passed quickly. After sitting in the office for ten minutes, the principal took out the registration forms from the drawer and began filling them in. His name, address, telephone number, age... For the first time, his father joined the conversation. Until then, he had sat with folded arms, a slight smile on his face.

The long page gradually filled up with the pertinent information, and the principal then gave Shuki the school's code of rules.

The principal talked a bit with his father as Shuki glanced over the paper. Shuki's eyes reached the third line: "It is forbidden for any student to leave the cheder premises without permission. Every absence must be reported to the administration..." Reading the code, Shuki didn't pay any attention to the conversation between his father and the principal until he suddenly perked up. What was the principal asking? Suddenly he was all ears.

"I am a gardener," he heard his father calmly respond.

Shuki looked at the principal, trying to decipher his reaction, as he nervously clenched his fists.

"A gardener. That's interesting." The principal tapped his pen on the light oak desktop. "What would you say," he continued "if I asked you to do some work for us? The past few weeks I've been looking for someone to take care of the grounds, someone reliable and dedicated but most of all someone who likes children and whom children will like in return. We have quite a bit of property around the building, but it's been neglected for the last couple of years, and that's a pity.

"What do you say, Mr. Katz? You could have a free hand to plant greenery and flowers, nothing too expensive of course, and once you establish a garden you would continue with the maintenance. Having foliage would add a lot to the atmosphere."

Shuki's father looked out the window at the gray drab building with its stone entrance and enclosing wall. He agreed with the principal that greenery was missing and that flowers would definitely enhance the building. Green creepers for the wall, perhaps, with small orange and pink buds, purple flowers in the far corner and a splash of orange along the walkway would bring life to the drab building.

Shuki sat very still, following every word. *What?* his thoughts started to run wild. *Abba will be the gardener at my cheder? Abba will be in the yard together with me where hundreds of boys can see him? We'll both arrive together every morning and walk together through the big gate? We'll be together every recess, he'll talk to me between class breaks?*

Oh, no! Anything but that, Shuki wanted to scream. *Don't do this to me! I'll go back to the cheder in Arazim. I'll go to Yerushalayim and live with Aryeh at his grandfather's. Anything but this!*

Yitzchak didn't hear Shuki's silent plea, he didn't notice his son's eyes turning into balls of fire, nor did he see the clenched fists and the increasing frustration. Nevertheless, he shook his head.

"No, not right now," he answered the principal. "Not in the near future."

"Whew!" The sigh of relief came unbidden. His father and the principal looked at him.

For a split second, Shuki's father was taken aback. *It's a good thing I declined the offer,* he said to himself, *but it's even better that I agreed to send him here to Haifa. I wasn't sure at first, but now I don't have a shadow of a doubt. Hopefully, changing schools will bring about other changes too. Because Yehoshua needs these changes — more than he can ever know.*

26
A Strong Backbone

Yitzchak sat down on one of the hard wooden benches along the long corridor. He kept his eyes moving, taking in the closed white doors with their small metal plaques that identified the room's occupant and studiously avoiding eye contact with anyone else. In such a place, it was best not to look at other people. Otherwise, you might be confronted by tears or a look of deep worry. Sometimes you might rudely trespass on a moment of personal sadness or see that which a person wanted to hide — deep red scars, for example.

Yitzchak was no stranger to the plastic surgery department of the Rambam Hospital in Haifa. After receiving emergency first aid from Manny, the army medic, he was brought there by helicopter. He spent weeks and months inside that very building, weeks of hellish pain and stress so severe he knew he would never be the same again.

He remembered the day he was released for the final time. He went out into the street and looked up at the sky. It was still blue, filled with puffy white clouds, soft and dreamy as they had been since time immemorial. He took in the ground at his feet, the asphalt roads, the cement sidewalks, the sand along the roadside. He knew he should feel happy and grateful that he could see it all, that he could again feel the warmth of the blazing sun and hear the beeping of car horns interspersed with the twittering of the birds.

Yaakov, my army commander, would give everything in the world to be standing in my place, just to be here, to be able to hear and see all this even if they couldn't do anything else, Yitzchak thought morosely. *And so would Yossi.*

But even though he realized all this, his heart at that very moment lacked any shred of happiness. He may have successfully overpowered the fire that engulfed him there on the battlefield, but the fire had won certain victories over him too, turning a part of him into whispering embers.

From the hospital he went home to the house that awaited his return, unchanged save for one small difference. At first, he couldn't quite put his finger on it. It was only when he went to brush his teeth that he noticed something was missing.

His father and mother had meant well when they removed all the mirrors from the house. They wanted to make things easier for him. All at once he realized what was missing in the entry hall, between the wicker basket and the philodendron plant, and why the wall above the living room couch suddenly seemed so empty.

The wave of love and appreciation that gripped him at that moment was swiftly overcome by one of bitterness. *I'm not a child!* he thought angrily.

"Where's the oval mirror?" he demanded loudly. "Where is it? Where's the big mirror with the gold frame and the long one that used to be in the entrance hall? Where are they all? I want to see how frightening I look! I want to see myself with all my scars."

His mother pretended not to hear, and his father buried his face deeper into the newspaper. But Yitzchak would not be put off. The strength of his emotions proved stronger.

"When I went to the clinic today, I was the only one on the sidewalk," he said, practically in tears. "Do you hear me? Alone on the sidewalk. Across the street, the sidewalk was full of people. But on my side, I was alone. So where is the mirror? Do you really think that if I don't look at my reflection I will be a happier person? Never! Not as long as others look at me and stare."

His mother closed the kitchen door, fighting back her tears.

Let them cry, Yitzchak thought heartlessly. *Let them all cry. Let them mourn the war that took their healthy son, whole in mind and spirit, and gave them back a broken vessel, crushed and bitter, consumed with frustration.*

※ ※ ※

Yitzchak stood up in the hospital corridor, a smile on his face.

In spite of everything, the gloomy predictions hadn't come true. True, there had been no miracles. His face was still scarred, and people still stared. But after a brief period of withdrawal from the world, he stopped shutting himself away in his room. He went on with his life — the real life, the life he had so longed for even before the war. The life he had wanted to experience from up close waited for him. He savored it and wanted to taste more; he studied, and his knowledge knew no bounds.

He would walk the streets and not even notice the people around him. It made no difference whether they were staring at him or pointing a finger, whether they were taking a step back or crossing the street to the other side. He was too preoccupied with his own thoughts, too busy occupied with building his new world. His eyes were focused on High, toward the blue sky and what was beyond.

Why care what people in the street did? Let them fill their empty lives to their hearts' content, and if his looks aroused their curiosity, that was their business. He certainly wasn't willing to waste even a second of his time thinking about it. No, he didn't want to waste even a fraction of a second of the wonderful gift G-d gave to man — life.

From then on, Yitzchak visited the plastic surgery department several times. His parents pushed him, went with him, made the appointments. He was too busy with other, more important things.

He underwent several plastic surgery operations that improved his appearance only slightly. His father and mother were very frustrated in those days. The last crisis coming on top of the previous ones was too much for them and made their life unbearably dark and gloomy.

While his parents were frustrated and dispirited, he was strong and sure — and happy. It was the happiness one finds in those who are convinced of the righteousness of their ways. Occasionally he would visit the hospital ward to give moral support to those who had suffered severe burns. Only someone who had been through the same trauma could understand their suffering, sometimes even more then they could themselves while they were going through it. Every visit filled him with a warm feeling of gratitude toward Heaven for sending him a life preserver of faith when the stormy waves threatened.

He was drawn back to the present when the door he faced opened. A young boy went in and quickly closed the door behind him.

Yitzchak tried to think. More than once his mind betrayed him by making it hard to follow a thought through. He would reflect on one thing, trying to delve into it deeply, but his thoughts would flee as if they were feathers shaken out of a pillow. He furrowed his brow, trying to concentrate.

What indeed had given him the strength to leave his cozy warm life where he was loved and secure to set off on a new way of life that was so different? What was it that enabled him to stand up against those who mocked him to cling to his faith?

If he hadn't recently thought about this character trait of his, he probably wouldn't have thought about it now. But this trait, which had come in handy in recent weeks, stubbornly came to the forefront.

"You have a boy here with a strong backbone," the surgeon once said to his mother when she came into the postoperative waiting room. As if in a deep dream, he heard the words and was glad. Yes, this was also a gift he received from Hashem, and perhaps he should be grateful for it more than everything else.

He sighed as he slowly walked down the hall. He was here again after so many years of absence. He had come to terms with his appearance years ago. Seeing his scarred face in the mirror no longer bothered him.

But Yehoshua, his sensitive son, was a softie, a boy pushed this way and that with every turn of the wind. It was because of him that Yitzchak was there. The field of plastic surgery had developed over the years. Maybe the doctors would have something new to suggest, a treatment that wasn't available years ago, an operation that would somewhat improve the existing condition.

He wasn't affected one way or another. He didn't care what people thought. But what wouldn't he do for his suffering son!

At the end of the corridor, near the long windows, stood an automatic drink machine. He was looking for a brand with a good *hechsher* when his eyes caught sight of the newspapers and magazines strewn over a table in the corner. They used to be on the other side, he remembered.

Yes, he would know. How many hours had he spent sitting and waiting for appointments? He walked over to the table. Did they still have copies of *The World of Nature*?

He wasn't disappointed. On the table lay the latest edition of what used to be his favorite magazine. He opened it and flipped through the pages. He had first discovered the magazine there in the hospital. Reading it helped make the long hours of waiting pass more quickly. He enjoyed the articles on topics so dear to his heart, and he especially took pleasure in enriching his knowledge by reading about the latest experiments and discoveries in the field.

Years ago, he had turned to the first page and jotted down the address, surprised that such a fascinating publication wouldn't advertise itself. Subsequently, he had subscribed to the magazine for several years, saving every edition. He had all his copies of *The World of Nature* neatly stacked, hidden away on the top shelf of a bookcase at home.

Thoroughly familiar with the publication, he knew that even someone as careful as he was about what he read could read it. He picked up the latest edition and sat down to read. *I wonder what they have in this issue about plants and agriculture?*

He spotted a caption. "American experts arriving for a tour of the Negev. Israel continues to be among the most advanced countries in the world in developing agriculture under desert conditions. The visit is under the auspices of the Ministry of Agriculture."

He continued reading. "Last year, American experts helped set up magnificent gardens in Saudi Arabia. They ran into great difficulties due to the desert climate. This is the first time the Saudi princes are being assisted by Israeli know-how, albeit in a roundabout way."

Yitzchak stopped in his tracks. Something lit up in his brain, a flash of intuition telling him the article shouldn't just be put back on the table. There was an idea here. Maybe, with a lot of *siyatta diShamaya*, he could do something with it.

In a mad rush, Yitzchak ran down the stairs, magazine in hand. On the first floor, he'd ask at the information desk where there was a Xerox machine he could use. He must have a copy of the article to read later, when he'd be able to concentrate on it better. He'd need the name of the author, too, to contact him for more details.

With a copy of the write-up in hand, Yitzchak returned to the fourth floor and put the magazine back in its place. By now impatient, he went over to the nurses' desk to find out if the long line was moving. He suddenly had no patience to wait. Something new was burning inside, demanding his attention. If he hadn't spent two and a half hours waiting and six weeks in anticipation of this appointment, he would have gotten up and gone home. But since he had invested so much time and effort, he made peace with the situation and sat down on a bench with his *Tehillim*.

He davened for himself, he davened for Yehoshua and he davened for Yossi, his best friend who was always in his thoughts.

27

Never Give Up

Dafna sat hunched over the keyboard staring at the screen trying to decide which picture to choose for the cover. She opened photo after photo, waiting until each was displayed entirely. There was a magnificent picture that Dvir had attached to his article on waterfalls. It was a photo taken by the famous outdoor photographer, Dan Ariel. Like all his work, this one was so lifelike you could practically touch the water cascading down the mountain cliffs. The magazine's logo, *The World of Nature*, in bold blue, would blend in perfectly with the photograph.

There was also a close-up by Y. Ra'anan of a lone deer with the caption "Let me also live on the land!" Dafna was charmed by the soft dewy look in the deer's eyes — even though she knew it wasn't only wildlife that was threatened, according to Ra'anan's critical article on ecological dangers.

Dafna couldn't decide which photo was more suitable. The one of the cascading waterfalls begging to be touched would be a real eye-catcher on the cover. On the other hand, the deer was related to the actual article. Ra'anan's stories always drew attention, capturing a prominent place in the magazine. Perhaps the deer should be chosen.

Dafna looked around the office to see whom she could consult, but the room was empty. *How can I work this way?* she grumbled. *If Tammy or Galit were here, I could ask them. How can I work alone?*

But Galit and Tammy weren't there. At exactly five o'clock, after a long tiring day in the office, they closed their computers and went home. Only she remained, even though her job didn't require her to do so. True, today was Tuesday and tomorrow night was the deadline before they went to press. But she didn't have to take more responsibility than anyone else. Not at her present salary, in any case.

Dafna sighed. What could she do? The boss had asked her to tie up all the loose ends. What could she say to him? That she wanted to be there for her son Shai when he came home from the day care center? Excuses of that sort were not acceptable to Eliyahu Zamir, editor-in-chief of *The World of Nature*. The bimonthly publication was his whole life.

She turned away from the computer to reach for the phone. She quickly dialed home, knowing Betty, her cleaning lady, would pick up the phone.

"Is he home yet?" she asked without any preliminaries. "What? He's not home yet?"

Dafna was worried. "What are you doing in the house? Go downstairs again and wait for the minibus. I'll call you again in five minutes."

Dafna clicked the phone off, her heart skipping a beat. It was already four-thirty. Shai was usually dropped off by four-twenty. Maybe Betty wasn't there when the bus came? Maybe the bus passed by without her noticing? Where could he be? Was he wondering why his mother wasn't downstairs waiting for him?

The waterfall and the deer no longer held her attention. To get it over with, she picked the waterfall, adding the magazine logo without any further consideration. With several clicks of the mouse, she colored the text deep blue, added more space between the letters and saved the file. Any other day, she would have given more time and attention to setting up the cover page. She would have enjoyed playing with colors and positioning the artwork to bring the cover into sharp focus. But not this time.

Suddenly the phone rang, startling her. *Shai must be home. It's Betty calling to let me know.*

"Hello?" Dafna answered, expecting her housekeeper to be on the line.

"Hello, have I reached the editorial department of *The World of Nature*?" a hesitant voice asked, surprised by the tone of her hello.

Dafna bit her lip in disappointment. "Yes," she answered as briefly as possible without being rude.

"Good. I read Mr. Ra'anan's article in a recent edition of your magazine on "Experts Touring the Negev" and I am very interested in the topic. May I please have his phone number? I'd like to contact him for some additional details."

"No, I'm sorry." Dafna was not interested in being helpful right then. "We don't give out the phone numbers of our writers. Goodbye." She looked at her watch again. It was already four-forty. *I'll just finish up the border graphics for page five and then give Betty another call.*

She picked a simple border, one that she had already used on page twenty and copy-pasted it to page five. She changed the color, saved the file and picked up the phone.

She clicked it on, but before she could dial, she heard a voice say, "Hello, have I reached the editorial department of *The World of Nature*?"

Dafna swallowed her anger. The voice, if she wasn't mistaken, was familiar.

"Yes." *Just let him be quick about it!*

"I spoke to you just two minutes ago, but you hung up before I finished. I wanted to ask — "

"I already told you," Dafna cut him short. "It is against our policy to give out the phone numbers of our journalists. You can write a letter or fax your request. Goodbye."

"Just a minute." It was more a plea than a demand. "Could I ask a special favor? I must have — "

"I'm very sorry," Dafna interrupted again, but this time in a softer tone, "but the office is actually closed now. You can phone in the morning and speak to the secretary. She may be able to help you. Thank you for calling."

She hung up without waiting for a response. What was happening with Shai?

Once more the phone rang. She suspected it was that nudnik again and was tempted to hit the "do not disturb" button. How did her boss expect her to get any work done? Since when does a graphic artist have to do the work of two secretaries?

Despite her indignation at the injustice of it all, she dutifully picked up the phone. Maybe it was Betty or the editor-in-chief himself wanting to hear how things were going. If she didn't pick up, he might suspect her of having left before four forty-five.

Dafna picked up the phone, tension and impatience evident in her every movement.

"Hello. You have reached the editorial office of *The World of Nature*," she said automatically.

"Hello," the calm even-toned voice answered. "I spoke to you a minute ago about Mr. Ra'anan's article in your recent edition. I want to briefly explain to you the importance of the matter. Do you know what I am referring to?"

Dafna tried to remember which article he was talking about. She remembered Ra'anan's article on the danger of extinction facing some of the wildlife in northern Israel. That was the article she had just seen, the one with the accompanying photo of a sad-eyed deer. But what had Ra'anan written about last month?

Never Give Up ✦ 193

She tried hard to think, but none of the familiar photographs that she had scanned and processed crossed her mind. Wait a minute! She finally remembered. The last issue had included his article on the ecological problem of garbage dumps. But she didn't remember that the accompanying pictures were particularly colorful.

"I think you are mistaken, sir," she said to the anonymous caller. "The last issue carried an article on the ecological hazards of garbage dumps. You must be referring to an old issue."

Dafna heard the rustling of pages. "In the recent issue that came out eleven days ago, issue number 387," the voice answered, "there appears an article, 'Experts Tour the Negev.' I have the magazine right here in my hands."

Oh! To me, the last issue is the one I'm working on, which goes to print tomorrow morning or at best the one that went to print two weeks ago. Who can remember a magazine from so long ago?

"Even if you don't remember exactly which article, it doesn't matter," the voice went on. "You can help me anyway. I understand that it is against your publication's policy to give me Mr. Ra'anan's phone number, but you can do me a favor. You can contact him and impress upon him the urgency of the matter. I am sure that if he hears that, he will contact me himself and be happy to provide me with the information."

Dafna was not taken in by his enthusiasm. She was still cool and distant. Yigal Ra'anan occasionally stopped by the office. He was tall and formidable looking. She wasn't quite sure he would be thrilled to go out of his way to help some unknown caller.

"Ra'anan wrote in the article," the caller began to explain, "that in a few days American experts will be arriving in Israel to tour the Negev. I am very interested in meeting with these experts or with the representative of the American Department of Agriculture who will accompany them. These experts will be wanting to get a firsthand look at how Israel overcomes the great lack of water in the arid south.

"I think I have information that will interest them, and I don't want to lose time. They may be ending their visit and about to go home in a day or two. Have I made myself clear? They are planning to provide expertise to Saudi Arabia in setting up gardens, and this is an unusual situation where an Arab country is being helped by Israel. I want to take advantage of this opportunity in order to — "

What? Dafna definitely thought that she missed something in the enthusiastic speech she just heard. Something seemed out of context. *What does this left-winger want? Is he asking me to help him assist the Arabs? What's it my business? Why am I wasting my precious time listening to this gobbledygook?*

"I am very sorry." Her voice sounded harsh. "I cannot help you at this time. Try again tomorrow morning. You can send a letter or fax. Goodbye."

The telephone continued to ring but Dafna ignored it. She became totally absorbed in getting her work done. She went through the magazine on screen page by page, making the necessary graphic changes.

At five-fifteen she closed the computer and stood up to leave the office. Now she would hail a taxi and head for home. She hoped that her son, Shai, was home by now, and if not, that Betty would have had the presence of mind to handle the matter. Oh, how she hoped she wouldn't arrive to an empty house with Shai waiting at the day care center crying. She had no more patience for tension and worries. The last hour had sapped all her strength.

She got into the taxi thinking about the caller. What could be so important about experts touring the Negev? People think they can call the office at all hours and expect you to be at their service. They forget that you're finished with your work for the day and have turned into a concerned mother, worrying about your son who is late in coming home from day care.

Dafna didn't know that it was as a concerned parent that she would have been most helpful to the unknown caller. Yitzchak Katz had hoped that the story of Yossi Nir would touch her, whoever she was, and that she would want to help. After all, who wouldn't be touched by the story of the missing Yossi, whose mother longed for him day and night.

But the phone at *The World of Nature* had been picked up by Dafna the professional, whose workday was over.

// // //

Yitzchak clicked off the phone, disappointed. No one was answering. Too bad they had already gone home. His dejection lasted no more than half a minute.

Pulling himself together, he opened the bottom desk drawer, took out pen, paper and two thick phone books. He would write a letter and fax it to the magazine. Maybe Ra'anan would walk into the office that very night. Maybe. Yitzchak didn't get his hopes up; he knew he had only a small chance of success.

He could always give up later if the plan didn't work out. He could have given up before he even started back there in Rambam Hospital when he first saw the magazine. He could have given up fifteen years ago, as had so many others.

But that wasn't his style. He didn't want to give up. Being full of hope and faith, he wanted to keep on trying. And he would.

28
A Lemon-Flavored Candy

Shuki couldn't sleep. His bed creaked pitifully again and again, collapsing under the heavy strain of the heart that slept on it. When the early morning rays of the sun crept into the room, the youth bed, along with Shuki in it, breathed a sigh of relief.

How do people begin a new chapter in life? Shuki wondered as he washed *negel vasser*. Was he the only one in the world made out of putty, soft as butter, burning with excitement and tense with worry?

He had gotten up early that morning, very early. At half past six he had already kissed his siddur and put it back in its place in the front compartment of his brown briefcase. On the first day of school, classes began at nine-thirty. The silver gray minivan that would be picking him up every day from here on in, taking him from tiny Arazim to big, unfamiliar Haifa, was due to arrive at eight-thirty.

Shuki opened his bedroom door and went out into the hall. He heard the electric kettle boiling in the kitchen. Either Abba or Ima was already up. Shuki took comfort in the thought. Another person was awake in the house, someone who could share his trepidations.

"Good morning, Shuki'le." His mother stood in the kitchen pouring herself a cup of coffee. "Already up and dressed?"

"I davened, too."

"It's a shame Abba didn't know you were up. He didn't want to leave without first saying goodbye and wishing you well on your first day. He was about to open your bedroom door when I stopped him. I heard you tossing and turning all night, so since you were finally in a deep sleep, I thought it best to let you get your rest."

Too bad, Shuki thought. What he really needed was some warm words of encouragement from his father.

"Want a hot glass of cocoa, Shuki?" his mother offered. "Before a long trip, it's important to eat and drink. Will you wash for bread?"

Shuki shrugged. Just thinking of bread made him queasy. How could anyone think of eating now?

"How about some cookies or crackers?" his mother asked. "Here, sit down and have something."

Shuki couldn't help but smile. Ima was excited too. She was fussing over him as if he were a little kid.

"What kind of sandwich should I prepare for you to take along to cheder?" she asked.

Shuki shrugged again without answering. He thought about the cheder every waking minute, but not about the kind of sandwich he would take there. Anyway, he was sure he wouldn't have an appetite to eat anything.

"That's it, Shuki." She wrapped the peanut-butter-and-jelly sandwich. "From tomorrow on there will no longer be breakfast in this kitchen, nor lunch prepared by your mother. You'll be leaving very early in the morning and returning late at night, almost like a *yeshiva bachur*."

Shuki imagined he heard a crack in her voice. Was the change having an effect on Ima too? He had assumed that only he was finding it so hard. A surreptitious glance at his mother showed her eyes glistening with tears. Shuki felt a stab in his heart. His parents were so caring and devoted to him while all he thought about was himself.

Wanting to please his mother, he took a bite of the cookie, hoping it wouldn't get stuck in his throat. He had felt as if a lump was stuck there ever since he woke up. Maybe after he met his new friends and exchanged a few words with them things would be different. Maybe after he sat at his new desk and introduced himself to the rest of the boys in the class and explained why he had transferred to the new cheder, maybe then the lump would disappear and he'd be able to munch on Ima's delicious cookies.

He barely swallowed the third cookie, feeling fuller than he ever had in his life. He took two sips of the cocoa and stood up to leave.

"I know I still have time," he replied to his mother's unspoken question, "but I can't stay in the house. It's cooler outside. It's better to wait outdoors." Taking his brown briefcase, he said goodbye to his mother and kissed the mezuza.

"Start out on the right foot," his mother said fondly, giving him one last smile.

Shuki looked at his watch. It was already seven-thirty. There was another hour left. He decided to walk around the moshav and wait for the van at the first stop, near Nachum's house. That way the time would pass more quickly.

His brown leather briefcase swinging from his shoulders, Shuki trekked along the paths of Arazim. *The village is still sleeping*, Shuki thought as he looked at the small houses, most of them with their shutters still closed.

Summer vacation was almost over. His classmates – his

former classmates, that is — would begin learning in another two days. They had two more days to sleep an extra half hour and to leisurely ride their bikes.

But not he. No, he wouldn't be able to sleep peacefully or indulge in carefree play — not now, with this new beginning looming over him like a frightening shadow.

Shuki walked straight ahead, not taking the shortcut but continuing on the long path that passed by the last row of houses. The sun began to rise high in the sky, its rays announcing that autumn had not yet arrived. The prolonged coolness of the morning put off, for a few hours, the summer heat wave.

The swaying branches of the trees seemed to be smiling at him. Shuki glanced at his watch. There was still plenty of time. He would do something he hadn't done in a long time. He would walk to Nachum's house by way of the grove.

The tall trees cast deep shadows. A song burst forth from Shuki's lips, and he allowed himself to sing louder than usual. A small bird flew from branch to branch listening to the melody. Shuki smiled at the bird. Do winged creatures understand the thoughts of human beings?

Let's say that I'm in class right now, Shuki suddenly thought. *Let's pretend all the trees are the new students. They're standing together, tall and important looking, knowing each other, recognizing and being recognized. As for me, I'm standing by the side, shy and new. What will I say?*

He clutched his familiar brown briefcase tightly, took a few steps forward, plastered a smile on his face and said in a loud voice, "Hello. My name is Shuki Katz and I live in Arazim."

He took a deep breath. Too bad trees can't talk. If they did, they would have been able to tell him if his opening introduction was impressive enough or if he had to polish it up a bit. Don't be silly! He smiled. If these trees could speak or hear or feel he would never have practiced on them in the first place.

He walked the rest of the way in silence. He suddenly felt self-conscious in front of the green-leafed trees and the brown earth below his feet. Deep inside he felt the turbulence of a stormy sea.

I hope I have lots of friends, he silently addressed a nearby tree that looked as if it could be trusted. *I hope they will know me as I want to be and not —*

He didn't finish the sentence or even the thought. He just looked at the tall tree whose loosely hanging branches belied understanding.

He kicked two fallen leaves with his toe. "Let me have more courage," he announced, "courage to say out loud what I always keep to myself."

His voice seemed to echo in the void and he stopped talking, looking around to see if anybody was a partner to his monologue. *The courage I am wishing for is yet to come,* he sadly thought, hoping that the new situation would bring about miraculous changes.

At eight-thirty the gray minivan stopped by Nachum's house. Shuki got on and sat down in the empty vehicle as the driver started to move.

"Hey," Shuki yelled. "Wait a minute!"

"They told me one boy would be getting on at this stop," the driver explained.

It didn't take more than a few seconds for Nachum to appear red-faced, running toward the van.

"Whew!" He plopped down on a seat. "I always have a hard time adjusting to a new schedule at the beginning of the school year. It takes ages until I get up on time and get organized.

"This morning," he continued, "I couldn't find my briefcase and suddenly I remembered that my lunch bag was torn. Today we had to daven at home, and then Abba reminded me about the list of things we have to bring for the first day!" Nachum tucked in his shirttails and took a bite out of the apple his mother had given him at the last minute.

A Lemon-Flavored Candy ♦ 201

How different can one boy be from another! Shuki thought in amazement.

※ ※ ※

In the big school yard of the Haifa cheder, groups of boys stood around in animated conversation. No one paid any attention to the small gray minivan that had just pulled up with its five nervous passengers who eyed the crowd with trepidation.

Four of the boys walked together toward the building, as if they were a troop, to see what their eighth-grade classroom was like. One boy stayed outside, his eyes taking in the boisterous activities in the yard. Would he ever be part of the crowd?

At the sound of the bell, the groups of boys formed one long line and filed inside. Shuki maneuvered himself between two boys and, together with them all, entered the building. Once indoors, the boys went down the hallway to their classrooms and Shuki found himself alone in the empty corridor with the principal by his side.

"Good morning, Yehoshua," the principal smiled as if talking to a old friend. "Come, let's go to your seventh-grade class.

"This is your new classmate," the principal said to a group of tall boys who were standing by the door deep in animated conversation. "Introduce yourselves until Reb Moishe arrives." He hid a smile under his beard and quickly returned to his office.

Shuki cleared his throat, organizing the words he had practiced saying, but the last four words that the principal had dropped like a bombshell were so dramatic that the boys forgot the introduction.

"Reb Moishe!" The boys clapped their hands in enthusiasm.

"Reb Moishe! Why did everyone say that this year we would be getting Reb Tuvia?"

"Reb Moishe explains the Gemara so well that there is no one who doesn't understand," a red-headed boy called out, his voice echoing from one end of the hall to another.

"There's no one like Reb Moishe when it comes to class trips!" another said, positively jumping for joy.

"What a great way to start the new year," a few boys said practically in unison.

Shuki felt invisible. Why was he being totally ignored? Next to the legendary Reb Moishe, do new, bewildered, bashful boys vanish into thin air?

He found himself looking forward to having this Reb Moishe arrive to save him from the awkward situation. Maybe he would take care of the introductions.

Shuki stuck both hands in his pockets, a sure sign of embarrassment. He felt something hard and round rustling inside.

He pulled out a folded piece of paper and opened it. Inside was his favorite kind of hard candy, a sweet-and-sour lemon drop. On the paper was a message from his father: "Shuki'le, I'm with you all the way. Abba."

Was his father trying to tell him that all beginnings were sweet and sour? Clenching both the candy and the note, Shuki suddenly felt a surge of newly found strength flowing from his palm straight to his heart.

29
A Discerning Eye

Shuki stood alone at the side, looking on. What a big group of boys, full of real camaraderie like one big happy family. Yet Shuki felt no affinity with them. What's more, he had no desire to be part of the group.

A few boys did attract his interest — the tall one, for instance. His eyes sparkled and his long black curly *peyos* bounced every which way when he spoke.

He looks as if he comes from a fine home, Shuki thought. *He's so self-confident and sure of himself.*

A chubby redhead also caught his attention. His cheeks were so full of freckles it looked like an artist had sprinkled paint across them. He looked kind and happy, the kind of boy who takes things as they come and doesn't get upset easily.

Shuki found he was enjoying his new hobby. It was fun studying his new classmates' faces and trying to figure out what their personalities were like. *Do I have a sharp, discerning eye?* he wondered. Time would tell.

One of the boys left the crowd and walked over to Shuki. The spectacled boy was so quiet and serious looking that Shuki almost didn't notice him until the last minute.

"You must be the new boy," he said with a shy smile. "We heard that someone like you was arriving."

Really? Shuki was all ears. He had barely arrived and already they were talking about him. What could they have heard?

"Yes, that's me." Shuki smiled without realizing that his smile looked as forced as that of the boy facing him. "My name is Shuki Katz. Or do you already know that, too?"

The boy's smile became even more strained. "No, of course not. Someone said that a few boys would be coming here from Arazim to learn in the eighth grade and that one boy is in the seventh. We figured out that the boy — you — would be in our class, because the parallel class has thirty-eight boys and ours has only thirty-five."

"Thirty-five?" Shuki was stunned. "Thirty-five boys in one class? How will I remember everyone's name?"

The boy with the glasses burst out laughing. "Start out with an easy name. How about Shloime Levy?"

"Shloime Levy," Shuki mumbled, "and I'm Shuki Katz. Remember?"

The ice was broken. Shuki made a mental note that getting to know new boys could be a pleasant experience, one full of surprises.

A tall, impressive person entered the noisy classroom. His steps were slow and deliberate, conveying to the thirty-six students that it was time to quietly take their places.

That must be Reb Moishe, Shuki noted, and there in the fourth row in the second seat is Shloime Levy. The happy-go-lucky redhead sat in the first row, and directly in front of Shuki sat the boy with the bouncing peyos. *I'll probably soon discover that he's the principal's son or that his father is the Rav of the community. He looks the type, like Bentzi, Meir and Aryeh all wrapped up in one.*

A Discerning Eye ✦ 205

Shuki glanced at the seat to his right. A dark-skinned boy with a shy smile sat next to him. *Why doesn't he ask me anything?* Shuki wondered. *Why doesn't he say even one word, anything to break the tension? Maybe I should go first? Is it proper etiquette for a new student to start conversations?*

The decision would have to wait. The boy to his right, like all the other boys in the class, sat up straight, his eyes glued to Reb Moishe. Shuki made a supreme effort to gather his wandering thoughts and shove them to the back of his mind. Enough. He had already spent too much time and energy on analyzing his new classmates.

Today was the beginning of a new school year, time for a new start, a new *mesechta* in the Gemara and a new *perek* in Mishna. Shuki desperately wanted to learn properly, to get ahead and succeed, to merit tasting the sweet taste of Torah, to go in the right path. He hoped to present his father with good marks, marks that would light up his father's dark, shadowed eyes.

Friends aren't everything, no, not at all. But he knew now, just as he had known in the past, that when friends are at your side you have the strength and energy to pursue your goals, and if not — it's a short distance to failure and defeat.

Reb Moishe's words were clear and to the point, making it easy for Shuki to concentrate and keep all other thoughts at bay. He sat mesmerized for over an hour, his only movement an occasional enthusiastic nod of the head. When Reb Moishe stood up and opened the teacher's attendance book, it was a signal that the marvelous talk was over and he would now take care of some necessary technical details.

Shuki was already impressed. *The boys sure hadn't exaggerated,* he agreed, stretching as if waking up from a magical dream. *If all his lessons are like this, there's what to feel happy about.*

Reb Moishe went straight to roll call. He called out the names of the boys one by one, looking directly at each student. Following him was another pair of eyes, those of a curious

Shuki. He wondered what the name of that tall boy was, the one with the dark black *peyos*, and that of the friendly smiling redhead. Maybe he would recognize the names of some of the boys in this big strange class. Maybe there'd be cousins of former classmates or former classmates of cousins.

Pinchas Aharoni, Moshe Binder, Yonasan Ben Shlomo, Eliyahu Davidowitz, Reuven Horowitz, Gedalia Dalinsky – the chubby redhead raised his hand and Shuki wondered if there wasn't some mistake. He never expected this jolly looking freckled-faced fellow to have such an important sounding name as Gedalia Dalinsky. No, never in a million years.

Reb Moishe managed to read off a few more names while Shuki was still occupied with being surprised at Gedalia's name. He came out of his reverie to try to catch the many new names that were being called. The boys would be impressed if he knew their names the very first time he talked to them.

Tzvi Isaacs, Binyamin Jacobson — Shuki was ready. His name was about to be called. Just a second. Not yet. Yerachmiel Kahn (the boy sitting at his right answered), then Avraham Shimon Kahn and finally Yehoshua Katz. Shuki raised his hand, hoping he wasn't shaking. Was anyone wondering what he was like, or was it only he, Shuki, whose mind was occupied with all these myriad thoughts?

He didn't have the courage to look around and see anyone's reaction. He stared at his desk in typical bashfulness.

Shlomo Levy, Shmuel Naor, Yona Prager... It was getting to be confusing. Every minute another hand was raised. The names were beginning to sound alike — and there were so many of them. What was with the tall boy sitting in front of him? Shuki wanted to know. *I'll try to remember just his name. Maybe it'll be an easy one to remember.*

This assumption proved to be the only one that Shuki correctly guessed. "Avner Shaked," Reb Moishe called out and paused momentarily before continuing with the rest of the names.

Avner Shaked — the name rang in Shuki's ears. It was a bit different and didn't quite fit the tall boy who had stood before him with his long bouncing *peyos.*

Avner Shaked sat down in his seat. *I guess I'll probably remember this name,* Shuki thought as he continued to stare at him.

Avner, sitting in the front row, probably felt the stares. He waited for Reb Moishe to leave the classroom, took his sandwich out of his schoolbag and turned around.

"Hi," he said with a smile. "We didn't get a chance to introduce ourselves. How do you like our class? What do you think of the boys?"

"It's a bit confusing. I was used to a class a third the size."

Shuki had an urge to answer Avner's last question with a question of his own. It might be fun to make conversation by nonchalantly asking, "What do you think of the new boy?" But Shuki wouldn't do anything of the sort, of course. You don't ask a question like that.

A few more boys gathered around his desk.

"You'll get used to things pretty fast," the redhead said with a wink.

"You'll adjust to a class like ours, one, two, three," one of the other boys — which? — said.

"Did you move here?" Avraham Shimon Kahn, the boy they called Shimi, asked.

"No," Shuki explained, blinking nervously. "We still live in Arazim. Four of the boys in my class came here to learn in the eighth grade. My father, and one of the other fathers, decided that the class would now be too small, so..."

He stopped to catch his breath and took advantage of the momentary break to utter a silent prayer. He himself had no problem with the reason for his transfer or with the result. He had mulled over the reason dozens of times in his mind. To him, the honest truth was reasonable. But would his new classmates also accept the reason?

"Let's go wash," one of the boys said (was it Yona Prager?). "When a guest comes to town you offer him food and drink. Come on, everybody, to the sink."

Shuki stood up. Yes, this Prager was a nice kid. *I guess my father was right in sending me to this cheder. In all of Arazim, as nice as the boys are, there wasn't a single one who would have said something like that. It's good to get to know a lot of different types of people.*

The boys washed their hands, dried them on the large checked towel and went back to the classroom to eat their sandwiches. Shuki was the last one to wash, with only Avner standing near him at the faucet.

Avner took a step toward him and in a low whisper asked, "When exactly did it happen?"

"When did what happen?" Shuki asked, not having the faintest idea what Avner was getting at.

"You know," Avner winked. "I already heard everything. I'm curious. How did your family take it?"

"Take what?" Shuki practically shouted.

"Shh, lower your voice," Avner hushed him. "How old were you when your parents became *ba'alei teshuva?*"

Shuki looked down wishing the ground would open and swallow him. He was in a state of shock. How could this be happening to him?

"What makes you think we're *ba'alei teshuva?*" Shuki asked, holding back his tears. "Why are you making up stories that aren't true?"

"I didn't mean to insult you or anything," Avner apologized, leaning closer. "If I would think that I was saying something insulting, I would never have asked you in a million years. You can ask all the boys, they all know how proud I am of —"

"I'm not interested in asking any of the boys anything," Shuki broke in. "Do you mean to tell me that the class already talked about this even before I got here?"

"No, of course not. Someone from the eighth grade came over to me and told me what he had heard. It was only because of —"

Shuki didn't want to hear another word. "I don't get it. Is this how you greet a new student?" Looking Avner straight in the eye he added, "Just don't talk about this to anyone, okay?"

Without waiting for a reply, Shuki stomped off toward the classroom without washing. He had lost his appetite.

// // //

It was still afternoon when Shuki arrived home after the first day of school.

"How was it?" his mother asked as she greeted him, anxious for a full report.

"*Baruch Hashem*," Shuki said out loud while thinking, *It depends what.* Reb Moishe's lesson had been super, and getting to meet Shloime Levy and Yerachmiel Kahn was also nice. Talking with the boys was fun, and it was interesting to meet lots of different types of boys, like Gedalia Dalinsky and Yona Prager.

But those moments at the sink with Avner Shaked had been horrible. He hadn't been able to look Avner in the eye for the rest of the day. Every time Avner turned around to look at him, Shuki had purposely rummaged around in his briefcase or pretended to be busy with his notebook.

Wait, what about the note from his father with the sweet-and-sour lemon drop – that certainly was a good part of the day.

"Where's Abba?" Shuki asked.

"Abba went out," his mother replied. "There's been a new development with Yossi. Abba has high hopes. He'll be busy for the next few days. He'll probably come home late tonight."

Shuki suddenly had a brainstorm. He took out of his pocket the small scrap of paper that had been wrapped around the sweet-and-sour lemon drop, with its message from his father: "Shuki'le, I'm with you all the way. Abba." He turned it over and wrote, "Thanks, Abba. I'm with you all the way too. Shuki."

Then he put the note on his father's pillow.

30
Unbelievable!

The seventh grade class in the Haifa cheder was quietly humming with activity. *Sefarim* were open and worksheets rustled as the boys poured over their assignment. Reb Moishe sat at his desk in front of the class, his hands folded as he studied the faces of his students, trying to discern what was going on in their minds.

"Yes, Shaked?" he asked as a hand was raised. The student looked puzzled.

Shuki held back a smile. He still wasn't used to being called Katz in place of the familiar Shuki. Even his father's Yehoshua sounded better than this new strange way — Katz.

"Yes, Shaked, how can I help you?" Reb Moishe repeated.

"Some pages are torn out of my *sefer*," Avner explained. "Can I go to the other classroom for a *Kitzur*?"

"It's a shame to waste the time," the rebbe said, glancing at his watch. "Cohen and Katz can look on together. Katz, please give Shaked your *Kitzur*."

Shuki took the open *sefer* and handed it over. "Take it," he muttered, without looking at Avner.

The brief break was enough of an excuse for the rest of the class to momentarily stop what they were doing. Heads turned as the boys took the opportunity to follow the short conversation. Many eyes were witness to this short interlude. Taking it all in, the boys noticed how the *sefer* had been passed and wondered what it all meant.

"Did they have an argument?" Gedalia Dalinsky asked, poking Yonasan Ben Shlomo with his elbow, surprised that something could have happened that he wasn't aware of.

"They didn't fight." Pinchas Aharoni turned around. "But something did happen."

"What?" Gedalia demanded. He didn't have to add another word. More than he wanted to know, Pinchas wanted to tell.

"Katz insulted Shaked," Pinchas said. "I heard him shouting. They were standing there next to the sink, and his fist was clenched. I couldn't hear everything," he went on, "but I definitely heard him saying something about *ba'alei teshuva*. I guess Katz was insulted by something Shaked said and got back at him by referring to his being a *ba'al teshuva*."

"That's ridiculous," Yonasan interrupted. "It's not like Shaked to make a big deal about something like that. He's pretty open about everything."

"It all depends," Gedalia answered. "It depends on what's being said and how. Katz looked real aggressive when he entered the classroom, not the way he looks now. And besides," he continued, "maybe Katz finds it hard to look Shaked in the eye after he talked to him that way. Don't you think so?"

Yonasan Ben Shlomo and Pinchas Aharoni were about to express their opinion of Gedalia's supposition when they noticed Reb Moishe giving them a look telling them to get back to work.

But Yonasan couldn't concentrate. At recess, he went over to

Unbelievable! ♦ 213

Avner. "What happened with Katz? Did you fight?" He had to know.

"Oh, it was nothing." Avner dismissed the question with a wave of his hand. "He's a sensitive kid. I think he sort of blows things out of proportion."

"What was it about?" Yonasan wasn't about to let the subject drop.

"It doesn't matter." Avner wanted to evade the issue.

"It was about you-know-what, wasn't it?" Yonasan whispered with a knowing look. "Someone heard him mention the words *ba'alei teshuva*, right?"

Avner didn't deny it.

"Don't take it to heart," Yonasan said sympathetically as he placed his arm around Avner's shoulder. "Whoever says anything is really being childish, like a baby who doesn't know how to look at life. We all know who and what you really are."

Avner smiled. The backing Yonasan gave him, even if he wasn't quite sure of the reason behind it, was in place. It took the edge off the hurt he felt following Shuki's disparaging look.

"How could I have known he would react that way?" Avner shared his frustration with Yonasan. "I thought that a seventh grader, a boy that makes an impression of being serious, would have a more mature attitude, like me."

Shuki sat at his desk eating his sandwich. His eyes wandered over toward Avner's direction, just as they had done many times during the past few days. Sometimes he felt like transferring to the parallel class, or alternately, having Avner transferred there. His first meeting with this boy didn't follow the planned scenario. Too bad you couldn't erase things and start over from scratch.

But Shuki just couldn't bring himself to talk to Avner, and it seemed that for Avner, too, a conversation at this stage was out of the question — all this complicating the matter even further.

Avner spoke freely with all the boys. He was always at the center of every discussion — and Shuki felt threatened. Any shred of self-confidence he might have had was slowly eroding. He was worried Avner would go back on his word and talk, letting out the secret. He felt as if Avner held the key to his future in the class and was holding him captive. Everything was in Avner's hands.

What's this? Shuki felt a bitter taste in his mouth and spit out the bite of sandwich. But it wasn't the mayonnaise or the sliced tomato that his mother had devotedly cut that morning that was to blame. It was the conversation taking place between Avner and Yonasan.

※ ※ ※

Once again Shuki came home to find the living-room door closed. Ever since he started the new cheder he hadn't had a chance to have a decent conversation with his father. He still hadn't told him about his friends, about Avner or about all his new hopes and his inability to turn them to reality.

True, his father had spoken to him twice. On Shabbos they sat together, just the two of them, his father wanting to hear how things were going. On Tuesday night, Abba was home, and he had put aside the pile of books, the notebooks and the three large sketches to give Shuki his undivided attention.

But two times was not enough. Shuki wanted to talk, to tell everything, to pour his heart out and ask for advice — but the words wouldn't come. He knew that his father could take the heavy millstone that weighed on his heart and like a craftsman, crush it into fine dust, easing the burden. He needed his father. He couldn't do it alone.

At the same time, Shuki knew that he and he alone was to blame. His father had knocked on his heart twice, but he hadn't opened the locked gate.

Abba had tried, even though he was busy knocking on other doors. Yossi Nir couldn't free himself and get out from behind his locked cell on his own. He had a friend, Shuki's father, who, with Hashem's help, was trying to open his door to life.

Shuki stood outside the closed living-room door for a long time. He wasn't trying to eavesdrop. He couldn't understand what they were saying anyway. Besides, the explanations his father was making were complicated. He was pouring over thick volumes filled with strange concepts, drowning in obscure blueprints. To Shuki it might as well have been Chinese.

If he wasn't mistaken, his father was also having a hard time understanding what was going on. Maybe that was why his forehead was so wrinkled and his eyes blinked uncontrollably, a sure sign of exertion. It was because of this kind of strain that Shuki's mother would bring his father a vitamin tablet with a hot glass of tea every so often throughout the day.

Suddenly Shuki felt a wave of pity, a wave that brought in its wake a giant surge of appreciation. How dedicated and devoted his father was! Look what he was willing to do for a friend he hadn't seen for fifteen years. *And look at me*, Shuki thought. *I complain if I have to give up spending even a little time with my father, even though I know it's for a good cause.*

Duvi, his ten-month-old baby brother, crawled toward the door.

"Abba! Abba!" He banged on the closed door with his tiny fist. "Abba!" He sounded impatient. He was probably wondering why no one paid any attention to his calls or did anything to remove the barrier separating him from his beloved father.

Shuki hurried over to him. "Abba will come out soon," he said to distract the baby. "Come on, Duvi, let's play ball."

When Shuki picked up his brother, the baby burst out crying, as if to say, How unfair! I managed to crawl all the way from the kitchen to the living room all by myself, overcoming all obstacles in my path. Then, when I almost caught up with Abba, he disappeared without giving me a single hug. Instead, there's a big wall of wood blocking my way. And now Shuki's trying to take me away!

"Ima, what can we give him?" Shuki carried the frantic Duvi into the kitchen.

His mother remained calm. She smiled at Duvi. "You can put him down and let him crawl to his heart's content. Is he bothering anybody?"

"There's someone in there with Abba." Shuki put the baby on the floor.

"I know, but I don't think the baby's tiny knocks are bothering either Abba or his guest."

"Look, he's already heading for the door." Shuki was annoyed. "It's not nice to disturb them."

But his mother wasn't upset. She ignored Shuki's remarks, and Duvi, taking advantage of the situation, crawled toward the living room again.

Shuki stayed where he was in the kitchen. His father would probably open the living-room door to see what was going on, and he sure didn't want to be caught standing there. He would die of embarrassment. Under no circumstances did he want to be seen by the visitor.

"Aaabba," Duvi called with all his might.

But his father didn't hear a sound. Yitzchak Katz had begged Miki Sagiv to meet with him to discuss a pressing matter. It had taken a lot of effort to set up the meeting yesterday in his office and today at his home, and he wasn't about to waste a single precious moment.

Miki was a classmate of his from their university days. They had both studied agriculture together. In those days long ago, Miki had been nothing compared to him. He was the one to seek Yitzchak's friendship, ask his opinion and borrow his perfect notes and tests. But much water had flowed under the bridge since then, and many things had changed.

Today the tables were turned, and Yitzchak needed Miki. He wanted to hear his expert opinion of the idea he had thought of. It was an idea that would, if implemented, mean a breakthrough in water irrigation.

Miki had listened to him attentively yesterday. He was impressed with Tzachi's (as he still called him) simple, but brilliant innovation, although he didn't want to let on. Today, after a night spent reviewing the plan thoroughly, Miki presented Yitzchak with his suggestions for technical changes that would improve on the basic idea.

"You have to do something with this idea of yours," he said to Yitzchak as they sat in the living room in Arazim. "And you have to do something with yourself, too. It's unbelievable what's happened to you, Tzachi. You're wasting your life on rose gardens in this tiny, out-of-the-way settlement. Professor Linitz wouldn't believe me if I told him. Boy, did he think highly of you. He had great hopes for you."

Yitzchak didn't respond. He hadn't invited Miki to his home to discuss his supposedly wasted talents. If Miki were interested in knowing the truth, he'd be more than willing to spend all the time in the world talking to him about *Yiddishkeit*. But that wasn't the purpose of the meeting. What he wanted and needed was Miki's opinion of the plan — and his help with the presentation. Alone, Yitzchak knew he stood no chance of organizing his thoughts on such a complex subject, let alone of presenting it professionally. He had a hard enough time explaining it to Miki.

Didn't Miki realize how hard it was for him? Didn't he see his friend's clenched fists whitening under the strain of answering so many questions?

If he had noticed, how could he have been so callous as to ignore it?

What Yitzchak didn't know was that not all those who delve into the depths of technology are equally adept at delving into the depths of human emotion.

31

Not My Type

The circle of boys stood very close to Shuki's desk. He sat on the edge of his chair, elbows on the desk and head propped up on his hands, eagerly leaning forward to catch every word.

He was tempted several times to join in, to offer an opinion or tell a story, but someone always spoke up first. It took Shuki ages to decide what to say as he agonized over choosing the right word. The other boys were so much freer in their conversation.

If Avner wasn't the center of attention, Shuki thought bitterly, *maybe things would be different.*

It was seeing Avner, with the sharp look in his eyes, that made Shuki withdraw deeper into his shell.

Why do they spend every recess standing around talking? Shuki wondered. *Why don't they go out to the yard to play?* The weather was beautiful. The hot, dry winds were a thing of the past and the winter rains had not yet set in, so why not take advantage of it?

Pinchas Aharoni had just finished regaling the group with a story. Shuki waited for him to finish so that he could make his brilliant suggestion, one it seemed no one else had thought of.

"What do you think about —." Shuki stopped short. He still had one detail to work out. How would he explain his pause?

But no one even noticed. With all the talking going on, who had even heard the "what do you think about" uttered almost inaudibly by the shy new boy in class?

Shuki walked over to the window and looked out at the big school yard. *What a spacious play area,* he thought to himself, *yet they don't take advantage of it.* If he hadn't seen all the other kids playing outside he would have been positive you weren't allowed outside during recess in Haifa. But the cheder in Haifa was not much different, in that respect, from the cheder in Arazim or, for that matter, those in the rest of the country.

Shuki walked back to his desk. He began again, this time with more confidence. "What do you think about going down to the yard for recess? Do you know what great games we played during recess in Arazim? If you want, I can teach you some," he offered. "After sitting for so many hours learning, it's great to loosen up your muscles and run around."

Caught up with delivering his little speech, Shuki missed the looks the boys exchanged. It was only after he stopped talking that he noticed the strange expression on Avner's face and realized he had once again, as usual, said the wrong thing.

Gedalia Dalinsky patted Shuki on the shoulder in mock encouragement. "If you miss the baby games," he said, winking at Avner, "you can go back to the cheder in Arazim." The boys all laughed as if it was the best joke they had ever heard.

"We all like recess," Pinchas added, "but who needs to play games in the yard?"

Shuki bit his lower lip. *Why did I have to say anything?* he thought, mad at himself. From the way he said it, they must think running around with a ball was the most important thing in his life and that he wouldn't be able sleep at night if he hadn't played a good game.

He had made a fool of himself for no good reason. He had to learn that when Avner was around he should blend in with the woodwork. True, this time Avner hadn't said a thing, but something in the way he led the conversation signaled to Shuki that if Avner hadn't been there in the center of the circle, everything would have been different. Maybe the boys would have even gladly followed him down to the school yard.

Shuki had no idea how right he was.

The bell rang, signaling the end of recess. The boys returned to their seats, disappointed — as usual — that their free time had all too quickly come to an end.

But Shuki was pleased. If there was anything he really enjoyed at the new cheder it was Reb Moishe's lessons. And if there was anything he couldn't stand, it was the long breaks between classes. No, Shuki had no regrets that recess was over, not at all.

"Look over the last piece of Gemara we learned yesterday," Reb Moishe announced, "and we'll soon have a short review. Meanwhile, I will pass around a piece of paper for you to fill in with your personal information — name, address, phone number, date of birth and your father's occupation. Fill in the page fast, because it's a shame to waste time with this.

"Moshe, you start and pass it on." He handed the paper to Moshe Binder who sat in the first seat in the first row. Reb Moishe looked up at the rest of the class. "Until the paper reaches you, go over the *sugya* we learned yesterday."

Shuki opened his thin Gemara and nervously began to fold down the corners of the page. He folded the corner into a small triangle and then into a larger one, unable to concentrate. If his father saw the page of his Gemara today, he would conclude that Shuki had learned well. Unlike other fathers, his was never upset by a worn *Chumash* or a dog-eared *Mishnayos* looking like three generations had studied from it.

"A new book makes me scared," his father would always say

whenever an embarrassed Shuki took out one of his creased books. "True, you can learn from a *sefer* and still take care of it, but," he would at this point give Shuki a fatherly pinch on his cheek, "I'm pleased to see that you're learning so hard. So, even if there are notes written on the pages, don't feel bad."

When Abba sees my Gemara today, Shuki thought, *he'll assume the pages are creased from intense learning, from trying to understand a difficult passage.* Could Shuki tell his father that his fingers had crumpled the page before he even got a chance to look at it? His father wouldn't believe him.

His father wouldn't believe him because he would never understand how Shuki felt about the problem looming over him. How much longer would it be before the piece of paper reached his desk? He threw a troubled glance at the first row. Five boys had already entered their information. In a few minutes it would be passed to his row. Another six, seven boys and it would be on his desk. Would he be able to nonchalantly pick up his pen like everyone else and fill it out — Birthday: 23 Tammuz; Address: 309/75 Arazim; Telephone: (09) 430–0086; Father's Name: Yitzchak Katz; Occupation: gardener. Gardener? Could he really write that down, black on white, smack in the middle of the page for everyone to see?

No, he couldn't do it.

Shuki loved the beautiful garden that surrounded his house in Arazim. He loved to lie on the deep green blades of the meticulously kept lawn and enjoy the colorful petunias always in bloom and the other flowers that blossomed according to season.

But that was at home, where the green bushes hid the garden and all that went on there from the prying eyes of the outside world. Here, in the classroom, how could he write down for all to see that his father was a gardener?

It was impossible. Here in the new cheder in Haifa he wanted to begin from a totally different starting point, one much higher, not one connected to clumps of earth. It's not as if he wanted to lie. But what would be so terrible if his classmates thought his father was the Rav of Arazim or at least a *maggid shiur* in a yeshiva or an eighth-grade rebbe? There was no way he was going to let them know the truth.

Behind him he heard some kind of a commotion. Shuki turned around, his tension visible.

"Patience, Katz," Eliyahu Davidowitz said. "In another minute you'll have the page to fill in with your information." He flashed a smile.

Shuki quickly turned back to face the front of the classroom. *Boy,* he thought, *some kids just don't know how to read facial expressions.* Did he look like he was desperate to fill in the information? Of course not. Maybe, though, it was better for Eliyahu to think that. It would be pretty bad if he and the others knew what Shuki was really thinking.

The page was passed on. Cohen wrote in his details with a flourish and after two seconds passed the piece of paper to Shuki sitting to his left. To Shuki, the pen felt like a firebrand burning his hand. He tried to stop the trembling long enough fill in his address, phone number and date of birth. He left the space for "father's occupation" blank and quickly passed the paper to Avner's desk. After all the boys finished, he would ask for the paper again on the pretense of checking it for something. Then he would add the word gardener. But he would only do that at the end, when only Reb Moishe and the principal could see the information, not thirty-five new classmates.

Avner took the piece of paper and noticed the blank space in the otherwise complete lines. He turned to Shuki with the intention of helping him. *Maybe,* he thought, *this is a good opportunity to make amends. I'll show him that I don't hold a grudge, that I'm not mad at him for the way he acted when I tried to talk to him at the sink.*

"You didn't fill in the blank for father's occupation," Avner whispered to Shuki pointing to the empty line. "You have to write what your father does for a living. Here, look – *sofer stam*, owner of a gift store, a *mashgiach* in Yeshivas Bais Yitzchak."

Shuki felt the blood drain from his face.

"If your father doesn't have a job," Avner added, trying to be helpful, "write that he learns in a *kollel* just like all these boys." Avner's finger jumped around the page pointing to the places where *kollel* had been written. "You can't leave it blank."

Avner's soft tone of voice for some reason got Shuki's gall. "Don't you think I know how to read," he answered aggressively, practically shouting. "Take the page back and fill it in with your details. What's it your business what I wrote or didn't write?"

Avner's jaw dropped in open surprise. After filling in his information, he passed the page on.

Minutes passed before Shloime Levy handed the page to the rebbe.

"Just a minute," Shuki called out as if he suddenly remembered something important. "Let me check something." In great haste, as if trying to get rid of an unwelcome burden, Shuki filled in the word and gave the page to the rebbe.

"All finished?" the rebbe asked. A relieved Shuki nodded yes along with the rest of the class.

"Okay," the rebbe said. Turning to Shuki, he handed him the paper. "Take the list down to the principal. He's in the old office."

Shuki blushed. "I'm willing," he stammered, "but I don't know exactly where that is."

"I'll take it," Avner volunteered, reaching out for the page confidently.

"Are you sure?" the rebbe asked.

"No problem," Avner responded with a smile. "At most I'll miss a few minutes of class."

Shuki clearly noticed the warm look the rebbe gave Avner as he handed him the list. It was a look that spoke of the great admiration the revered rebbe had for his pupil. Shuki felt a wave of jealously sweep over him. He wouldn't have minded being on the receiving end of such a look himself. What did the rebbe find so admirable here? That Avner was ready to miss a few minutes from the lesson? Is that reason for admiration?

As such thoughts ran rampant in Shuki's mind, Avner got up and walked toward the door. Shuki stared at him, not believing his eyes. Avner's gait was heavy and lopsided. His right foot dragged along, trying to keep pace with the left. Avner limped? Confident Avner, with all that self-assurance, limped! Why hadn't he ever noticed it before?

Actually, it wasn't surprising. Avner's personality was so different from his. Avner was so filled with self-confidence that it overshadowed every possible physical defect.

Suddenly, Shuki realized the meaning of all those looks and comments at recess. All the boys stayed in the classroom because of Avner. It was probably hard for Avner to run around and play ball games. Shuki felt something close to admiration for the boy — but his heart grew stubborn. His own self-image seemed too fragile and hollow in comparison.

He remembered what Avner had said to him that first morning, as they stood there about to wash their hands to eat. Despite all that was admirable about Avner, as far as he, Shuki, was concerned, Avner just wasn't his type.

32

True Stories

Daniel sat in his easy chair, the daily newspaper lying on his lap, unread. The paper served as camouflage for his drooping eyelids and wandering thoughts. Someone was knocking impatiently at the front door. The knocks were followed by the doorbell ringing. The combination sounded urgent and ominous. As Daniel roused himself and rose to open the door, Yosefa gaily pranced inside.

"How many times have I told you not to ring the bell before you come in?" His voice was sharp.

Yosefa felt bad. Her teacher had taught the class that it was good manners to knock on a door before entering, whether it was your own home or anyone else's. Her teacher had said their parents would be so proud to have such polite children who knew to knock before entering. Why was her father so angry?

Daniel sank back down into his recliner. Yosefa didn't understand nor did his wife. She wouldn't understand why he gave their daughter such a hard time over such small irritations.

But what could he do if sudden knocks and the sharp ring of the doorbell reminded him of that terrible night when the bitter news was delivered? What he had been told then weighed heavily on his heart for years to come.

With effort, he was usually able to push the past to the back of his mind to make room for the present. But one ring of the doorbell, one sharp knock on the door and the dreadful memories were once again mercilessly evoked.

Back then, he had also been sitting in the easy chair reading the front-page headlines. He hadn't focused on the words, just the black border of the death notices.

Back then, he was sitting in Tel Aviv, a cup of coffee and a plate of homemade cake on the end table, while somewhere in northern Israel kids were trapped inside burning tanks. Yes, kids. What else could you call his Yossi if not a kid of nineteen?

At that moment, he had tried to picture Yossi but found he couldn't. Where was he? What was he doing? He hadn't heard a word from him in five days. If only he had a way of contacting him. Didn't Yossi know his parents were torn apart by worry, tormented by uncertainty?

If he wasn't calling, it must mean that he couldn't. But why? Why couldn't he pick up the phone and call? Was he up north on a complicated mission making his way through Lebanese villages or...

Everyone knew about the torturous battles. There were reports of heavy casualties, of numerous dead and wounded. His wife, Efrat, spent hours calling anyone and everyone who could give her any information, no matter how seemingly insignificant.

Daniel didn't interfere. It made more sense to leave the phone free for Yossi to get through, but he kept his opinion to himself. Everyone finds his own release from tension. The busy line allowed him to remain optimistic, picturing Yossi trying to get through.

He sat immobile, paralyzed with tension. He couldn't think,

he couldn't talk. If only he could close his eyes and keep them shut until the nightmare was over, until Yossi's cheerful voice was heard at the door.

He tried. He closed his eyes — not to sleep, for sleep was beyond reach — but to escape the crawl of time.

And then it came. The sharp knocks on the door, the ring of the doorbell that tore asunder their happily-ever-after life and turned it into a nightmare of tears and uncertainty.

Later on, Efrat would say that prior to the knock she had heard sounds of footsteps in the hallway and the doors of neighboring apartments opening and closing accompanied by loud voices. "Even then," she would tell all the visitors who came to encourage them and share their anguish, "my heart started beating faster. I had a premonition that bad news was coming our way. One more minute and our door would open, shattering all our hopes."

Efrat was the one to open the door. Daniel sat daydreaming. He envisioned himself putting his hand on Yossi's shoulder, touching his khaki uniform, gray from all the dust, and chiding him with a smile, "Next time you're away, give us a call, ask a friend to send regards. Do you know how worried we were?"

In his imagination, Yossi would answer with a smile, knowing his father was only giving vent to some of the pent-up tension he felt. It was the overwhelming love that shone through.

"Is this the Nir residence?" the nurse had asked.

Daniel didn't have to hear another word. The scenario was well known. This was the scene, this was the script.

With an expert motion, the nurse took the syringe and gave him an injection of tranquilizer in his arm — that's how all the tragedies began. And that's how the personal tragedy of the Nir family started.

// // //

Yosefa entered the living room. Soft slippers had replaced her school shoes. Her steps this time were slow and hesitant.

228 ❖ *True Stories*

"Abba?" she asked softly.

Daniel lifted his head, folding the newspaper that lay on his lap. "Yes, dear?" he replied, forcing a wide smile, sensing that she deserved it in lieu of an apology.

"We have homework to do," Yosefa cheerfully announced. "It's for our class project."

"Is there something I can do to help you?"

"Yes, Abba, please," Yosefa begged. "I want my notebook to be perfect. The teacher told us there'll be an exhibition of all our work, and very important people will be visiting the school. Morah Kochava said that our fourth grade is mature enough to be part of the exhibition.

"The topic is war and peace, and we'll be learning all about it," Yosefa went on breathlessly. "There are going to be lectures for the higher grades, and our class will be allowed to attend. That means we're really grown-up, doesn't it?" Yosefa paused, waiting for her father's approval.

Daniel nodded.

"Today," she continued, "we learned a long, long poem. The teacher called it a sonnet. It was about two wounded soldiers who keep on fighting. One soldier feels like he's dying and so he asks his buddy to leave him and run away so that he won't get captured. But his friend doesn't want to leave him. He helps him keep up with all the other soldiers.

"The end is so sad, Abba. Finally, the two soldiers have to separate and the wounded one waves goodbye. The whole class was really sad."

Daniel stared at his young daughter. She was growing up so fast, and he hadn't even noticed.

"What was this sonnet about?" he asked thickly. Could it be that the poem was based on their Yossi and his friend in his tank? "Which war did the teacher say it was from?" he asked, his voice cracking.

"It wasn't our war," Yosefa answered.

"It was probably on the Six Day War, wasn't it?"

Yosefa thought a minute, trying to remember the exact name. "No, that's a different war," she replied. "I can read a few lines from the poem so you can see for yourself."

Opening her notebook, she began to recite: "On the battlefield of Stalingrad they marched arm in arm. Together they walked, together they fought, together they fell, far from the flowing waters of the Volga—"

"Stop," Daniel's sad voice interrupted his daughter's recital. "Hasn't our country had enough of its own wars?"

"The teacher said it isn't a war in Israel," Yosefa suddenly remembered. "She said there's a lot to learn about Israel, but we won't learn poems about battles." Her voice took on the same lilt as her teacher's. "We will learn new Israeli poems about peace."

Daniel clenched his jaw and said nothing.

Yosefa waited. When her father looked up, she continued. "The teacher told us a lot about how soldiers help each other. She also gave us an assignment. Everyone is supposed to ask at home," she continued, imitating her teacher. "'Ask your father or older brothers, neighbors or friends, and bring a true story to class about bravery on the battlefield.' That's what she said. She asked us to think about why people who don't get along during regular life help each other during battle. Is it facing the enemy, is it facing death or is it something about the uniform?

"Abba, can you tell me a story about Yossi? I want to write about him."

Daniel sat up. "The war was a long time ago." He sounded tired. "I can tell you about a different kind of camaraderie. It's easy to discover an act of heroism in time of war but much harder to find such friendship during fifteen years filled with disappointment."

Yosefa listened without interrupting.

"Call my friend, Tzachi Katz, the one who comes here all the time, the friend who never gives up. You'll hear more than one story from him. I don't think anyone has more inspiring stories of camaraderie than he does.

"As to your second question, I don't have a clear-cut answer," her father continued. "But in our specific case, as far as Yossi and Tzachi Katz are concerned, it wasn't their uniform or fear that triggered their acts of heroism. It was the *kippa* on their heads and their faith."

Yosefa didn't waste a minute. As her father sank back into the recliner, she quietly took the family's phone book. She had bothered her father enough. She was a big girl now, a fourth grader who could make her own phone calls. Sure, she was shy and didn't really know what she was going to say. But she hoped she'd manage okay.

"Hello," she said as soon as she heard a voice on the other end. "May I please speak to Mr. Katz?"

Shuki was surprised to hear a child's voice on the other end of the line asking for his father.

"He's busy right now," he answered.

"Oh." The disappointment was apparent. "When will he be free?"

"I have no idea," came the reply.

Yosefa waited a second, wondering what to say next before deciding to say goodbye and hang up.

She waited another three minutes, nervously pacing back and forth near the telephone table, before dialing again.

"Hello, may I please speak to Mr. Katz?" she asked excitedly.

"I'm sorry," Shuki's mother answered. "He can't come to the phone right now. Whom exactly do you want to speak to?" She wanted to make sure the child calling hadn't dialed a wrong number what with all the Katzes listed in the phone book.

"I'm looking for Mr. Katz, the friend of my brother, my missing older brother," Yosefa answered. "Mrs. Katz, do you think he'll be able to come to the phone soon?"

❧ ❧ ❧

True Stories ❖ 231

"My homework isn't finished," Yosefa complained. "It's not very good and not very bad. It's just nothing."

"Why not?" her father asked solicitously, trying to recall what the homework assignment was all about. On principle, he didn't get involved with homework. They were between his daughter and her teachers and not for parents.

"Oh, Abba," Yosefa sighed. "Remember I told you about the poem our teacher read, and you said I should call Yossi's friend, Mr. Katz. I tried so many times, but they said he couldn't come to the phone — even when I said I was Yossi's sister."

"You called Tzachi Katz?" her father jumped up, incredulous.

"Yes," Yosefa answered, surprised at her father's reaction. "You told me to, remember?"

"I told you to?" her father repeated. "I didn't mean that you should actually go ahead and call him. I merely meant it was something you might think of doing at some future time. You mean to say you actually bothered him today, this evening, now?"

"I didn't bother him." Yosefa sounded defensive. "I only called him a couple of times. Couldn't he have come to the phone for a second?"

Daniel looked at her, suddenly struck by the absurdity of the situation. "Right this very moment, Yosefa, Tzachi is busy being a true comrade in arms. He is in the midst of an important meeting with two American experts — a meeting he spent much time and effort planning. It's no wonder he couldn't come to the phone!"

33

The Price

Shuki lay sprawled on his bedroom floor picking up the Duplo pieces his baby brother Duvi had strewn all over the room. "You mischief maker!" Shuki wagged his finger in mock anger as Duvi tried to get some pieces that had fallen between the bed and the floor. "How can anyone get used to a roommate like you?"

A gurgling laugh was his brother's only reply. As far as Duvi was concerned, Shuki was an ideal roommate, loving and entertaining, with never a dull moment between them. *How come Ima hadn't thought of it sooner?* he was probably thinking in his baby mind. *Why didn't they put my crib in this wonderful room of my big brother Shuki months ago?*

Shuki, though, was having a hard time getting used to the idea. The goings-on in the house were closing in on him, and he suddenly longed for privacy. His baby brother watched his every move, and his pudgy hands pulling notebooks off the desk annoyed Shuki no end.

Shuki put the bucket of Duplo next to Duvi and went out of the room. His thoughts accompanied him into the hall as he wondered what it was that he needed right then. The living-room door was locked, and a tense silence permeated the house. The door to the kitchen was half-closed as his mother prepared refreshments for the important guests. From time to time, the telephone rang, and a young girl kept asking for his father.

If anything comes out of all this, Shuki said to himself, surprised at the bitterness of his inner voice, *it will all be worth it.* But too much was being done in their house for Yossi with nothing to show for it. Would there ever be an end?

Shuki turned around and headed back to his room. Looking at him above the overturned Duplo bucket and colorful pieces strewn all over the floor was a very merry pair of eyes. Shuki gave no thought to straightening up again, nor did he pay attention to the crumpled notebook lying on the chair.

He picked up Duvi and put him in his crib. *Let him play by himself to his heart's content,* he thought as he went out of the room.

Looking for a quiet spot away from Duvi's laughter but without the oppressive silence of the house, Shuki went out to the garden. There, he had the chirping birds, the rustling leaves and the sound of passing cars. There, he could be alone with his thoughts.

He lay down on the grass and let his thoughts drift. *Let's say my friend would have come to visit me today.* He plucked aimlessly at the blades of grass. *Let's say that he would have gotten on the gray minivan and together we would have come here to my house, to the quiet, to the tension, to a house that's so different from all other houses.*

Shuki closed his eyes. He imagined Shloime Levy walking alongside him down the path, swinging his briefcase as he planned to spend the evening at his new friend's house. Shuki could imagine Shloime begging his parents to let him sleep over in Arazim. Shloime's mother — if she was like most other mothers — would probably be reluctant to let him come. Why should she let her son travel in a gray minivan to some faraway place? What would happen if Shloime felt homesick in the middle of the night and wanted to go home? Besides, what kind of family were those people in Arazim?

Just that morning Shloime had come over to him. He was one of the few boys who came over to him occasionally to ask questions — and not just questions about schoolwork.

"You know what, Shuki?" Shloime sounded excited. "My father said yes."

"Yes to what?" Shuki didn't know what Shloime was talking about.

"Don't you remember what we talked about last week?" Shloime asked, somewhat annoyed. "I've been pestering him all week, and today he finally agreed. It'll be terrific to go with you right after cheder, sleep over and ride to school the next morning," Shloime continued. "We'll be able to go bike riding all around the village just like you always describe. Okay?"

Shuki didn't answer. Shloime's stream of words and the enthusiasm that accompanied them bubbled with self-confidence. He spoke as if a contract between them had been signed and sealed ages ago, and that now all that was needed was a reminder. What was Shloime talking about?

It finally dawned on Shuki. He remembered the not-so-subtle hint Shloime had thrown out last week. While talking about the boys in class, Shuki had tossed out a comment here and there. Suddenly, Shuki found himself — he couldn't remember how he had been so open — talking about his unfulfilled dreams and expectations. No, not about Avner of course but about the difficulties of a new boy from out of town coming to a new school.

"I thought that every once in a while I would stay after class at one of my friends' houses," Shuki had said, almost swallowing the words. "We could *chazer* over the material we learned, prepare homework together and study for tests."

That's how he saw himself making friends.

"My father said it would be okay," he had continued. "Boys who live out of town sometimes sleep over at friends' houses. He's right. In our gray minivan there are exactly enough places for us. But practically every day, at least two places are empty. 'Where's Nachum?' I asked the eighth graders. 'He stayed over at Schwartz's house.' 'Where's Chaim?' I asked the next day. 'He has a test at the end of the week,' Bentzi explained, 'so he stayed over at Linder's, the best boy in the class. Tomorrow I'll be staying over,' he winked. 'I hope my father agrees because last week I already stayed over one night.'

"Sometimes the Haifa boys take advantage of the empty places," Shuki added, "and come along with us. Nachum had friends over a couple of times."

Just then the bell rang, and Shuki's uncharacteristic openness was cut short. He didn't bring up the subject again with Shloime or with anyone else for that matter. He had hoped that Shloime would get the hint and invite him over to his house today, tomorrow or next week. He really wanted to get to know the boys and become their friend, to be part of the crowd. Once Shloime opened the doors, the others would probably follow.

So here was his chance. Shloime had come over to him. But what puzzled Shuki was how he could be so misunderstood. Hadn't he made it clear that he was interested in going to the other kids' houses, not having them come to his?

"I've been begging my father for days," Shloime announced, the joy in his voice evident, "and today he agreed. At first, he wasn't too keen on the idea. After all, he doesn't know who you are or anything about your family. But in the end he gave in. He said that if you live in Arazim, you must be all right because all the families there are *bnei Torah*."

"Do you want to call your mother and tell her I'm coming? Let's use the pay phone. I have a card."

Shuki stared at the telephone card Shloime was holding in his hand. "Uh...I don't think so...that is, we have to first make sure there's room in the van. Recess time, I'll go up to the eighth grade and ask Nachum and Bentzi, okay?"

Whew! That was a close one. Good thing all the kids were going home that day and there was no room for the disappointed Shloime.

"How about tomorrow?" Shloime asked hopefully.

"Maybe." Shuki's answer was noncommittal.

That's all I needed, Shuki thought, lying there on the grass in the garden, that Shloime should see my father's scarred face. Shloime, who says the first thing that pops into his mind, would probably start right in asking all sorts of questions about how it happened and when. "Was your father in the army? Was he a real soldier fighting a real war?"

Shuki never liked his friends to invade his privacy — even friends he had known for a long time. If he felt this way about his old friends, how much more so new ones. He wanted to hold his new friends at bay — keep them away from Arazim and let them get to know just him, without any other details.

The door opened, and his mother appeared pushing Duvi in the blue stroller, her shopping bag blowing in the breeze. "I'm going to the store," she said as she hurried along. "I need a few things for supper. We're having company."

Oh. Now Shuki remembered. Guests. Good thing Shloime hadn't come! That was all he needed right then. Imagine Shloime coming and instead of finding a normal family with small kids running around the house, he'd see two bareheaded Americans. Later he'd probably tell his father that not all the families in Arazim were so terrific. There, in his friend Shuki's house, he'd seen two American *goyim* sitting in the living room for hours.

※ ※ ※

Neil Stevens and Jay Danker laid out the sketches and studied them in silence for a long time. Yitzchak watched them, his tension increasing. He silently murmured *Tehillim*. The scenario he had constructed was as fragile as a tower of cards.

He'd read one article in *The World of Nature,* and then his imagination had run wild. Two American experts who had been given a contract to design and plant luxurious gardens in Saudi Arabia were in Israel to learn water-saving irrigation techniques. Based on this scrap of information, Yitzchak had ingeniously built a whole plan on ifs and maybes.

But experience had taught him that even towers built on the most solid foundations can collapse in an instant; the thick files of Daniel Nir were filled with ample proof of such. And when Hashem willed it, even ifs and maybes could turn into a solid foundation — in this case, one that would hopefully lead to finding Yossi.

"Okay," Jay said to Yitzchak, after having studied the papers for hours. "I think we can say the idea is a good one. We've heard plenty of ideas in the past ten days, but yours may be the best one."

"As far as we're concerned," Neil said as he pulled up a chair, "we can draw up a preliminary agreement and set a date for your flight. We'll need you there with us, of course, to advise us on the irrigation system."

Yitzchak took a deep breath and said a silent prayer of thanks. "Before we finalize this," he said, drumming his fingers on the wooden desk, "I'd like to hear a few words about the Saudi sheik you'll be working for."

Neil and Jay exchanged knowing looks.

"You have nothing to worry about," Jay reassured Yitzchak. "You'll fly to the States, and from there we'll arrange for an American passport. You'll travel under our auspices. As far as Sheik Abdul Rachim al Shekari is concerned, he's a progressive man, one of the richest oil barons in the Middle East."

"You Israelis have preconceived notions regarding the Arab world," Neil added. "You think every Arab is interested in blowing up buses. Shekari is an intelligent person and very influential."

"He has financial dealings with Assad, the president of Syria," Jay added with a measure of pride.

"But that's not what's important." This time it was Neil speaking. "He's —"

"All right," Yitzchak interrupted. To him it was very important. "Let's continue."

"Your price?" Neil asked.

Yitzchak took out a picture of Yossi from his pocket and placed it on the table together with an English newspaper article. "Read this," he said. "That's my price."

34
Life's Purpose

"Can I get you a cup of coffee, Guy?" Manny offered. He stood up and stretched while looking around the hall as he waited for an answer.

"What did you say?" Guy sounded as if he was slowly awakening from a dream.

Manny suppressed a smile. He was used to reactions like Guy's. After a lecture like the one they had just heard, it was hard to come back to earth.

"That lecture was absolutely exceptional!" Guy could hardly contain his enthusiasm. He was still in a different world, transported there by the two-and-a-half-hour talk.

Manny got up and walked over to the electric coffee urn at the other end of the lobby. He poured two cups of coffee. Yes, the last lecture had been especially powerful. Exceptional, in fact, just as Guy had said. After being presented with pure truth, even a secular intellectual like him had to admit there was a lot he didn't know.

But Manny wasn't as impressed with the talk as Guy was. True, it caused a bit of soul-searching and aroused pangs of conscience. But the waves of enthusiasm that swept over the rest of the audience, drawing them all to the speaker like a magnet, passed him and his wife by. You can make a terrific impression the first time but not the tenth — and Manny and his wife had heard lectures like this one more than ten times.

Manny sipped the hot coffee. How many seminars had he already attended? The first one was ten years earlier, in the summer that followed the Peace for Galilee War. The next seminar was in the winter. He remembered the contrast between the storm raging outside and the inner warmth he felt for the first time in his life. He left the sessions a convinced man. He went out and bought a siddur and a pair of tefillin, tefillin that he still put on every morning in the privacy of his home. After that, there was an intense Shabbaton, then the seminar down south, then — had there really been so many?

He sighed. Deep inside, Manny was a believer. He wasn't antireligious, nor was he a skeptic. At the seminars he was fine. The problems started when he got home.

It was easy to believe at the luxurious hotel, where stately pines and green expanses buffered him from the outside world. Surrounded by spiritually oriented people who devoted themselves to helping others move forward, it was easy for him to feel strongly committed. It was when he returned to his regular environment and met the stares and disapproval that doubts crept in.

He recalled the second seminar he and Tali had gone to. They felt like they had found all the answers, and their motivation to go further was strong. They stayed up all night talking with the rabbanim and made plans to *kasher* their kitchen, send their four-year-old daughter Drorit to a religious kindergarten and look for a more suitable workplace for Tali.

"Just tell us when," the seminar organizers told them, "and we'll come to your house to *kasher* your kitchen. Just give us a date."

But the date was never given. They returned home, Manny

Life's Purpose ◆ 241

to his job at the hospital lab and Tali to her job editing at the newspaper. They returned to their friends and acquaintances, relatives and neighbors — and all the promises and newly made resolutions dissolved one after another, gone with the wind. Manny's determination, so pronounced when he sat with the Arachim team, evaporated into thin air when confronted with the cynicism of the outside world.

"Maybe next year," Tali said when they got home. "Maybe next fall we'll send Drorit to a religious kindergarten. Then we'll make our kitchen kosher, I'll cover my hair, we'll move forward..." But as time went by, their determination faded. Drorit graduated the local kindergarten and went on to first grade in public school, followed by her sister Iris and brother Neiri. Manny never had the courage to stand up and say, "Yes, I have transferred my daughter to a religious school. Actually, the whole family is moving in that direction." It was too hard for him to make a statement that would be so ridiculed by other people. Better, he felt, to keep his feelings to himself — until the next seminar.

The auditorium began to fill up. "Ron Gilad — His Story," Tali read from the program flyer as she looked for a seat. Personal histories were her favorite. She came away inspired and eager to start putting into practice all she had learned. Would the time ever come when her story would be added to the long list?

"I've heard his name before," Guy commented. "If I'm not mistaken, he became a *ba'al teshuva* after the Yom Kippur War."

Manny looked toward the entrance, curious to see this Ron Gilad. The Yom Kippur War, they said? Well, should the day ever come when he took the fateful step, he too would be able to pinpoint his turning point.

It happened when he was twenty-five. He couldn't say his life had changed, because he never had the courage to make real changes. It was more like a shift in direction, a time when he began to dream of change. He was called up for army reserve duty and stationed in the northern part of the country. There was tension along the border and talk of an unprecedented campaign to clean the area of enemy soldiers.

When the army chaplain was invited to give a short lecture, the organizers were sure the soldiers wouldn't pay too much attention. They assumed the lecture would be filed away in back of their minds to be forgotten, which is what happened more often than not. They never dreamed that the short talk with its simple words of truth would penetrate the hearts of three young soldiers — Yossi Nir, Tzachi Katz and Manny, the reserve medic — and take root.

Yossi and Tzachi were serious. They had a clear plan of how they wanted to proceed spiritually, and they pursued it. They knew what they were looking for and, even more so, how to find it. He, on the other hand, was hesitant. When he was with the other two, he talked like them. But when he was with other people, he became one of the boys, the joker, the clown who could rattle off five jokes in less than two minutes.

When they went out to battle something changed. He was sent to join the last tank in the convoy, knowing he faced a difficult task. Many long, tiring hours passed as they crept among the Lebanese villages, exposed to wild gunfire as RPG rockets went off on all sides. At the end of the second day, the situation worsened. The entire battalion went off to battle fully aware of the real possibility that an entire unit would not return.

To this day, whenever Manny thought of those first days of the war he shuddered, deeply mourning the tragedy. He remembered thinking, *What will the next few days hold in this bitter cruel battle? How much blood will yet be spilled?* Amid all the sorrow was the all-pervasive fear for the welfare of his two buddies, Yossi Nir and Tzachi Katz. Why hadn't they returned to the unit after the battle? They weren't among the wounded or the dead, either. What had happened to them?

The battle raged fiercely. There was no time for anyone to care that Manny was torn apart with worry over the fate of his best friends who had disappeared without a trace. War makes little room for personal considerations, nor do its cruel demands leave room for mercy. Manny joined a different battalion moving along a bypass road to surprise the Palestinian fighters from the north while the main force attacked from the south.

His only thoughts were of Yossi and Tzachi. Pictures of them flashed before his eyes like scenes in a movie. He felt he could hear their thoughts and sense their hopes and their dreams.

"G-d," Manny repeated during those long hours, "You know they wanted to come close to You. If You bring them home alive, if...I promise I'll join them and we'll seek You together."

This prayer of his, this silent cry brought him closer to Hashem. It was a prayer for his own life.

The tanks surrounded the Palestinian refugee camp, surprising it with heavy fire. The attack was stopped by a barrage of return shelling that found its target. A rapid exchange of gunfire ensued. The Israelis may have succeeded in surprising the terrorists, but the terrorists' response caught them by surprise too. No one dreamed that the refugee camp contained such artillery reserves.

In those fateful hours, Manny prayed for himself and, whenever he got a chance, in moments when the fighting let up, he prayed for Yossi and Tzachi. It was the first time in his life he had prayed.

His prayers were heard — and answered. Reinforcements arrived. The attack on the terrorists turned more forceful and sustained. The soldiers overran the main building and were able to divide the enemy territory in two. The end was in sight.

At that moment, desperate, the Palestinians played their trump card. A PLO ambulance appeared from an alley and headed toward the Israeli forces.

"Don't shoot," the Hebrew words echoed over the loudspeaker. "This is an injured Israeli soldier. Don't shoot!"

Manny sat bolt upright, intently alert to every word. "This is an injured Israeli soldier. Don't shoot!" The voice was familiar

and sounded so close. It was the same voice, only broken, clinging to a thin thread of hope.

The cease-fire order was given. A representative of the Red Cross went to bring the wounded captive in exchange for calling off the attack.

Many witnessed the heartrending moment from afar, but Manny saw it from close up. He was the medic brought to take care of the wounded soldier who, swaying on his feet, got out of the PLO ambulance. With one hand, the soldier held a bag of fluids attached by intravenous tubing to a needle in the other hand. Accompanied by a group of Palestinians, he marched toward the Israeli tank constantly calling out, "Don't shoot! This is an injured Israeli soldier. Don't shoot!"

Manny walked up to him, trying hard not to twist his face in an expression of repulsion. He'd seen plenty of things in that war, some grueling and some appalling, but he had never met up with the likes of what he was seeing now — a charred mass of a face from which stared a pair of eyes desperate to live.

After it was over, he returned home. Yaakov, their commander, and Shimshon, their communications officer, never returned. Nor did Rafi, Eli and Gil. They remained buried in the ground never again to see the light of day. Tzachi and so many others remained in the crowded hospital wards throughout northern Israel. Yossi Nir remained in enemy territory, dead or alive, while he, Manny returned home.

What is life and what is man? he asked himself many times. What's the point if man is here today and gone tomorrow? Today he dreams and plans, and tomorrow he suffers the agonies of purgatory? Today he desires, and tomorrow he is left with a big fat zero.

What is life and what is man? He searched for the answer to this question and found it. So why has life and the person living it still remained unchanged? Manny let out a sigh.

"The speaker still hasn't come," Tali broke into his reverie. "Maybe we should go up to the room now and call the kids."

Life's Purpose ✤ 245

Manny looked at his watch. "Five-forty. I hope they'll be home now. I heard the talk is supposed to take about two hours. If we wait till it's over, we're likely to miss the scheduled time again."

"We made a mistake with this phoning arrangement," Tali sighed. "It wasn't very smart of us to make up to call between five and six. I can imagine Iris's disappointment after sitting by the phone for an hour waiting for it to ring without be able to call us."

"There was no choice," Manny said. "You yourself said you didn't want everyone knowing exactly where we went, didn't you? This way, the children and the housekeeper know we went to a hotel for the weekend for a total vacation. As it is, without even mentioning that I went to an Arachim seminar, I'm considered by many people far too religious and not enough part of the crowd. Until we take the final step, we have to keep it as quiet as possible."

Tali nodded her agreement.

"In any case," Manny said, heading for the plush blue-carpeted stairs, "I'll go up to the room and try to call. Maybe one of them is home."

35

A Big Mistake

Sarah Mizrachi stood at the kitchen counter deftly peeling carrots and onions. The fish was already baking in the oven, and soon the soup would be bubbling on the stove. Later, she would do a last-minute straightening up of the house and then put the festive blue tablecloth on the table.

Oh, to be finally able to sit down and rest. She stretched her aching bones. Yes, it was pleasant working in the big house. Tali treated her well, always with respect and consideration. Her requests were certainly reasonable, and the salary was good. Still, age seemed to have taken its toll, and Sarah no longer had the strength of her younger years.

She recalled how she used to stay and take care of the three mischievous youngsters, five-year-old Drorit, three-year-old Iris and one-year-old Neiri. She would chase after them from room to room, play with them in the garden and try to see to it that they finished every drop of food on their plates.

Today the children were older, fairly self-sufficient and practically never at home. Still, she felt tired and looked forward to Sunday morning when Manny and Tali were to return from their minivacation. The responsibility would no longer be hers.

Music blared from the girls' room. Sarah put her hands over her ears and walked toward the room. Why bother? she thought as she stopped short at the kitchen entrance. It would only be a waste of her time and energy. After an argument, Drorit would do her a favor and lower the volume by one decibel. But as soon as her back was turned, the volume would be on maximum again. When Tali and Manny were home, they didn't allow it. Tali was like her. She couldn't stand the modern music kids listened to nowadays with both speakers blasting. With their parents away, Drorit and Iris took advantage to do as they pleased.

"I brought home two discs from Osnat," Drorit had told Iris over lunch.

"Great," Iris replied. "Now we'll have something to do over the weekend."

So now they were having a ball with the two discs. Sarah gave up on them. That's how it is when parents go away.

Neiri was also taking advantage of his parents' absence. After taking two bites out of his hamburger and eating a total of three French fries, he ran out to play ball. Happily for him the playing field was just two doors away, at the end of the block. This saved Sarah the worry of his crossing streets.

Why can't a boy of seven play at home at least some of the time? The house is certainly big enough for it, she wondered. She knew exactly how many games he had on the shelf in his room. But it was none of her business. She had brought up her own seven children within the walls of her home, *baruch Hashem.* If Tali wanted to let her son, Neiri, spend most of his free hours playing ball, that was her business.

The blaring music was suddenly silent. *I guess they're changing discs,* Sarah thought.

Little did she know her relief would be only temporary.

The doorbell rang, followed by loud knocks. *They've probably been ringing for quite some time.* Sarah wiped her wet hands on the striped apron around her waist as she went to answer. If it wasn't for that wild music...

"Who's there?" she asked cautiously, standing on tiptoes as she looked out the peephole. "Who is it?"

A babble of loud voices was the only reply. If she wasn't mistaken, it looked like a group of Neiri's friends.

"Neiri isn't home," she said through the locked door. "He's out playing ball."

"Neiri isn't playing ball," came a loud voice above the din. "He's right here with us. Open the door. He fell and got hurt. He's gotta go to the hospital."

Sarah's heart pounded. She retied the ends of her green kerchief, just as she always did when she was nervous, and wrung her hands. Her fingers shaking, she could barely turn the lock let alone slide the chain before opening the door.

Eight boys Neiri's age stood in the doorway, three of them carrying a crying Neiri in their arms.

"What happened this time?" Sarah asked. "That's what happens when you're wild! Come into the bathroom," she instructed, "and we'll wash off the scratch with some cold water. Then you'll go lie down to rest."

"He can't walk," one of the boys volunteered. "Maybe he broke his leg."

"Stand on the floor," Sarah commanded. "Stand up straight and let me see what happened. Who says it's broken? Let me take a look at it."

Neiri made no move to stand up. Exuding an aura of calm she didn't feel, Sarah told the boys to sit Neiri on the couch. When she bent down to inspect his leg and touched his torn, dirty pants, he screamed.

"Don't touch it!" Neiri waved his hands hysterically. His face

A Big Mistake ♦ 249

was flushed with pain. "Don't touch my leg. Don't move it. Ooowww!"

"Take him to the hospital," the tall boy advised. "He didn't just fall down, if that's what you're thinking. He fell from the roof of the storage shed when he climbed up to get the ball."

"You fell off a roof?" Sarah gently hugged Neiri who was sobbing uncontrollably. "My poor, poor boy. Why weren't you more careful? Do I let you climb onto roofs? Does your mother allow it?"

Neiri didn't answer. His friends filed out silently, one after the other.

Sarah looked at the leg again, now convinced it was broken. Even the slightest movement caused the boy excruciating pain. She knew she had to get him to a hospital. She also had to get in touch with his parents to let them know. The roads were empty at that time of day, and they could be home in an hour.

Neiri's screams of pain had brought his two sisters downstairs. "Drorit," Sarah said to the eleven year old, "where's the phone number of the hotel where your parents are?"

"Ima didn't write it down," Drorit answered. "Abba and Ima said they would call between five and six o'clock."

"I know." Sarah struggled to maintain her composure which was rapidly disintegrating with every passing minute. "But are you sure they didn't write down a number someplace on a piece of paper? Maybe they put it near the phone."

No, they hadn't. Sarah bit her lips. "When we go away, we want it to be a total vacation," Manny and Tali had said. "We'll make sure to be in touch with you."

But she needed to get in touch with them now.

Without wasting any more time, Sarah opened the thick Yellow Pages for the northern region of the country. Tali had mentioned they would be going there. Maybe she'd be able to find a hotel listed that sounded familiar.

"I heard Ima say something about the Kinneret," Drorit volunteered. "Maybe try calling hotels in Tiberias."

Sarah took her advice and dialed one number after another, listening to boring tunes while waiting for the reception desk to answer. All the polite clerks answered that no, there were no guests by that name and thank you for calling.

"We have no choice," Sarah said as she hung up the phone after the last attempt. "We'll just have to call a taxi and go to the hospital. We can't wait any longer."

"What about us?" nine-year-old Iris began to cry.

"You?" Sarah tried to remain calm. "I have no idea when we'll get back. We'll have to call one of your friends and ask her if you can sleep over. I really don't want you staying in the house alone."

Without waiting for the girls to reply, Sarah called a taxi. In the two-minute wait, she managed to stuff a carryall bag with whatever was at hand — pajamas and slippers (hopefully the time would come when Neiri would be able to walk around), several illustrated books and two electronic games. She dumped half of the pantry into the carryall and zipped it up.

Then she remembered the girls. "Where will you girls be going?" Sarah asked Drorit as she heard the taxi honking outside.

"It's okay, Sarah. I'll call Revital right away. I slept at her house lots of times even when Ima was home. Iris can come too. I'll just pack us a bag. Don't worry."

Sarah carried Neiri to the taxi and laid him down on the back seat, squeezing in next to him. Don't worry, Drorit had said to her. She couldn't be more worried.

Maybe she shouldn't have let Neiri go out and play for such a long time? Maybe she should have left immediately for the hospital without losing even a minute? Maybe she should have tried longer to find his parents and not undertake the responsibility herself?

The headache she felt was as real and strong as if steel hammers were pounding away on all sides.

A Big Mistake ✦ 251

"Where to, lady?" the driver asked.

Where to? He hadn't started the motor yet? Which hospital should they go to? How should she know. Thank G-d she didn't have much experience with hospitals.

"Go to..." She hesitated. "Uh, go to the nearest hospital — the best. Just go."

The driver glanced in the rearview mirror and saw a nervous woman, tying and untying the ends of her green kerchief, wringing her hands and muttering to herself.

The driver turned right. "We'll go to Ramat Mazor Hospital." He stepped on the gas. "We'll be there in ten minutes to a quarter of an hour."

Sarah wasn't even listening.

❀ ❀ ❀

At the small hotel it was rest hour, that peaceful, relaxing time to rest up for Shabbos. For many of those in attendance, this would be their first real Shabbos experience, and they looked forward to it with interest.

Manny and Tali looked forward to Shabbos no less, but instead of curiosity they felt excitement and anticipation. They looked forward to Shabbos the way one awaits a dear friend. They still felt the sweet taste of the last seminar about Shabbos, the spiritual uplift that accompanied them afterward. This time too it promised to be a special experience.

Maybe this Shabbos will accomplish what the previous ones failed to do, Manny mused. *Maybe Shabbos will now become a permanent once-a-week guest in our home, not the once-in-a-blue-moon type you meet only at a seminar at some distant hotels in northern Israel.*

"What lectures are scheduled for Shabbos?" Manny asked his wife, who kept the program in her pocket. Tali didn't take the paper out right away. Her fingers were busy redialing their home phone number.

"They're still not answering?" Manny frowned.

"No." Tali practically slammed down the receiver in aggravation and worry. "Why isn't anyone picking up the phone? They should all be home now." Puzzled, she again dialed. "I can understand that Drorit might be busy with schoolwork or friends. Maybe she's listening to a new disc. But what about Iris? Doesn't she miss us? She's the one who always makes such a fuss when we go away."

"I guess they don't miss us that much." Manny gave a weak smile. "Maybe they were angry at having to wait yesterday for a phone call that never came, so today they didn't bother to stop what they were doing to hang around waiting for our call. They must be too busy to stay home just to hear our voices and tell us that everything is okay. Besides," he concluded, "they're not babies. And don't forget that Sarah is with them."

"You're probably right," Tali conceded. "I'm not really angry. Maybe they're at friends and maybe Sarah is resting. But — we haven't spoken to them since we arrived Wednesday night. In a few hours it will be Shabbos, and the hotel's telephones will be disconnected. I'm afraid I won't be able to enjoy the wonderful Shabbos we've been looking forward to.

"What if Drorit suddenly needs money or Iris wants to ask us an important question or Neiri — I don't know what. How could we not have left them the hotel phone number? What a mistake that was. I'm in no mood to enjoy Shabbos here. I'll only be able to relax if we go home."

That was her only mistake. The Arachim Shabbos at the hotel was far more relaxing than the one at Ramat Mazor Hospital.

36
A Heavy Responsibility

The automatic doors at the hospital opened wide as Sarah strode through them with seven-year-old Neiri, moaning in pain, in her arms. She looked around the lobby, wondering where to go. Above her was a bright red sign whose bold white letters read, "Pediatric Emergency." The arrow pointed left. She quickly headed in that direction.

The large emergency room was filled to capacity. The long row of beds was occupied by children whose parents nervously paced back and forth. Even the colorful pictures on the wall did little to allay fears.

Sarah shifted positions. Neiri suddenly felt heavy in her arms.

"My leg!" Neiri cried out in pain, biting his lips.

Sarah looked up, expecting doctors and nurses to come rushing over. After all, there she was standing in the doorway, not knowing what to do or where to go with the obviously suffering boy. Anyone in his right mind could see that the situation required immediate attention.

Sarah murmured soothing sounds, trying to comfort Neiri. Where were the doctors and nurses?

She spotted a white gown in one of the cubicles and rushed over, the injured child languishing in her arms.

"Nurse," she said politely.

No answer.

Sarah swallowed hard and tried again. "Nurse!" she repeated, this time louder.

"Yes?" the nurse asked without turning around as she continued taking a patient's blood pressure.

"I'm here holding a child in my arms," Sarah explained. "Can someone take a look at him?"

The nurse barely glanced at the small woman holding a boy in her arms. She did not seem too impressed.

"We're very busy today," the nurse said. "Look around. All the beds are full. Go over to the desk" — she pointed to the admissions window — "and take care of the admission procedure."

The young nurse's aide sitting at the white Formica desk began entering information into the computer. A line formed behind Sarah, who struggled with her impatience at the bureaucracy.

"Okay," the aide said, after finally typing in all the pertinent information, including a description of what had happened to Neiri. The printer spewed out a ream of labels to be affixed to various forms. "There's an empty bed over there." She pointed to a bed alongside the wall. "Lay him down, and a nurse will come to you shortly." Before Sarah had made a move, the girl was working on the next admittance form.

Neiri looked around in bewilderment. The high bed with its iron railings and all sorts of medical equipment visible was intimidating. He clung to Sarah and demanded to see his mother.

"Look at this cute teddy bear," Sarah said, trying to distract him. "See the cute balloon the teddy is holding? Look at the small baby here in the bed next to you. Have you ever seen such a small baby? It looks less than a month old."

Neiri quieted down momentarily to look at the baby. He made a move to lift himself up to get a better look. "Ooww!" he screamed and fell back down on the bed. "Ooww," he continued to cry, "something happened to my leg. It hurts too much. Ima, Abba! Please...I can't take anymore."

Neiri's face was twisted in pain, his eyes full of tears. Sarah watched his eyes turn glassy, as his vision blurred. *The child is losing consciousness*, the terrifying thought struck her. *He's about to faint!*

Sarah left his bedside and ran hysterically to the first nurse in sight. "He's fainting!" She wanted to scream, but the words that barely left her lips were uttered softly, somewhat hesitatingly.

"It's all right," the nurse said reassuringly as she handed Sarah a thermometer. "The boy is in good hands here. We'll be right with him. Meanwhile, take his temperature."

Sarah ran back to Neiri. His eyes were closed and his hands hung limply by the side of the bed. She was petrified. His face was pale as could be, and his white lips were turning blue. Tears welled in her eyes. What was going to happen? What would Manny and Tali say?

A nurse appeared out of nowhere, bustling efficiently. "Sophie Aloni" read the ID tag. She pushed aside the curtain of the divider and went over to Neiri. "His temperature?" she asked in a stern tone as she took the thermometer out of Sarah's hands.

"You haven't taken it yet?" she asked with impatience. "Take his temperature first, and then I'll come back."

Sarah reached out and caught the nurse's sleeve. "Won't you please take it," she pleaded. "Look at him. He's passing out from pain. He doesn't seem to have a fever anyway," she said as she touched his forehead.

But it was like talking to the wall. Ten minutes passed before the nurse came back. Again Sarah was questioned about what had happened, when, how the boy had reacted following the fall, how he had reacted later on, was he generally in good health and on and on.

Sarah tried to concentrate so she could answer the questions accurately. After she answered them all, she allowed herself to ask the nurse one question. "What's going to happen to him?"

The nurse, unlike Sarah, felt no need to give comprehensive answers. "In a few minutes," she replied over her shoulder, "they'll take him to be X-rayed. Then they'll take a blood sample and a doctor will examine him. Be patient."

By the time Sarah and Neiri were sent up to the children's orthopedic ward on the second floor it was dark outside. On some of the windowsills in the hall stood small candles, long ago burned down, a reminder that it was Shabbos night. A kind nurse helped Neiri off the stretcher into an empty bed in room 4 while Sarah collapsed on the nearest chair, totally exhausted.

Neiri's moaning overshadowed the sound of heavy breathing coming from the three other children in the room. He no longer cried out loud; he had no more strength. The long hours of being moved from place to place, all the needle pricking for various tests and the doctor's exam had taken a heavy toll on the child.

Sarah tried to organize her thoughts. Here she was with Neiri in the hospital. He had three deep breaks in his thighbone and needed a very complicated operation. She had no way of contacting Manny and Tali, despite all her efforts. No one, neither friends nor relatives had their number. The arrangement was for them to do the calling. One can say over and over that the arrangement was a bad one, but what would that help?

The hospital asked Sarah to sign the form authorizing an operation. She clutched the pen in panic, but sign she did. *The doctors know better than I what to do*, she consoled herself. If they wanted to operate, all that was left for her was to sign.

From then on, Neiri wasn't allowed to eat or drink. Attached to an IV, he had to fast in preparation for the operation in the morning.

Sarah sat in the armchair resting her aching back. The small room was pitch-black. You could hear a pin drop. The darkness fit her mood, which was grim and filled with worry. She could imagine Neiri looking at her as the green door to the operating room opened, leaving her alone outside, helpless and racked with anxiety. She could almost hear his moans and the confrontation between her and his parents, with Manny and Tali accusing, "Why didn't you take better care of him?" Just the thought almost caused her to collapse.

Meanwhile, the doctors were examining Neiri's X-rays carefully. Dr. Rafi Shilon studied the slides longer than the others.

"I think," he said, a strange light in his pale gray eyes, "that the new operation would be just the thing in this case. Look over here," he pointed with his pen to a dark spot on the X-ray. "If the operation is successful, we will speed up the recuperation process and shorten the time needed for physiotherapy."

"What if the operation is not successful?" Dr. Weiss asked quietly.

"A person can always climb stairs," Dr. Shilon replied cynically, giving his colleague a sharp look. "The idea is to shorten the way by finding an elevator."

Dr. Weiss blushed, knowing the doctor was making a dig at his fear of elevators. As much as he tried to hide his phobia, it was no longer a secret.

"So we all agree?" Dr. Shilon pressed his point as he looked at the three doctors sitting around the table. "This is the only operation scheduled for this morning, and I will be able to operate using the new method. Do you all agree?"

"Perhaps we should explain the different options to the boy's parents," Dr. Weiss suggested, "and get their approval."

"I don't think there's a need for that," said Dr. Shilon

adamantly. "We are under no obligation to inform parents of all the minute details involved in the operation. They signed the hospital release form agreeing to an operation. The type of operation we do is our decision. Besides," he added as he looked over the forms, "the signature here isn't that of the parents. Sarah Mizrachi, their housekeeper, is the guardian in charge at this moment."

Dr. Weiss wanted to say something but swallowed his words. Something told him that that was exactly the point, but he decided not to intervene any longer. Why should he be the one to fight the battle for this anonymous patient and come out against the senior doctor? It was best to keep the relationship on an even keel. He kept his opinion to himself, forced a friendly smile on his lips and agreed.

At nine-thirty Neiri was wheeled into the operating room. Dr. Rafi Shilon was the chief surgeon in charge. Dr. Weiss and Dr. Tzur stood by his side to assist. The three of them leaned over the injured leg, working skillfully.

At nine forty-five they ran into trouble. Dr. Weiss saw the surgeon's eyes blink nervously and realized that something was wrong. The operation wasn't going as planned. He saw the exposed leg and realized what the problem was. The two fractures were far apart, further than it had appeared in the X-ray. This situation made the new procedure impossible.

It's still not too late, Dr. Weiss thought to himself. *We can start all over again with the standard procedure.* He was about to make the suggestion, but one glance at the haughty look on Dr. Shilon's face stopped him. *Don't interfere when no one is asking your opinion,* he told himself. Dr. Shilon wouldn't appreciate being faced with his mistake, and it was important to Dr. Weiss that he stay in his good graces.

Dr. Shilon bit his lip, trying to do the impossible, as Dr. Weiss watched silently.

When Neiri was taken to the recovery room, it was clear that the operation was not a success. What they didn't yet know was to what extent.

37

Zigzag

Manny parked the car and got out, slamming the door behind him. Gently, he helped Neiri get out of the back seat. Neiri gripped his father's arm and leaned on it heavily as he walked. Manny winced at the sight. Waves of pity washed over him.

That's how it was every Tuesday and Thursday. At first, it had been every Sunday as well. Before that, every waking minute. Now, two months after the accident, the physiotherapy sessions had been reduced to twice a week. After each one, Neiri would go home totally exhausted, intensely feeling the heavy weight of his right leg.

Manny pushed the front door to their home and helped Neiri into bed to rest. He glanced once more at the suffering boy, bit his lips and went out.

He slammed the front door shut behind him, just like he had the car door. Time was running out. The ground burned under his feet as he tried to verify every point needing clarification.

He was determined to do everything in his power — even if that meant an assertive and if necessary aggressive Manny for a change — even if doors were slammed shut in his face.

Until now, he had acted with restraint and self-control. Why blow things up out of proportion? Boys do fall, and sometimes they hurt themselves badly. Sometimes an operation is needed, and it sometimes happens that the operation isn't successful the first time and additional surgery is needed.

But his gnawing suspicion — confirmed today in its entirety — definitely pointed to a different story. What had happened to Neiri didn't just happen. It was the result of medical incompetence and negligence that couldn't be overlooked, even if it meant Manny's placing the blame squarely on the hospital staff he was part of. His son's limp and the irreversible damage to his right leg were more important.

The large parking lot at the hospital entrance was crowded at that early afternoon hour. Manny searched in vain for a space. When he didn't find one, he left and parked two blocks away.

I can walk the two blocks without any problem, he thought, *but my Neiri will have a hard time.* It will be difficult for him now and no less difficult in the future. He will always have a limp, with his right leg dragging behind.

A bitter pain accompanied Manny's thoughts as he quickened his pace. He entered the building and headed down the corridor. During the past few months he had gotten to know the building like the back of his hand. Before that, he had never been in this wing. His work as the head of the biochemical laboratory was in a totally different area of the hospital

He soon found himself outside the office where he had an appointment. He knocked on the door twice and then, as was customary between colleagues, entered the room without waiting. Dr. Weiss was sitting in his black leather swivel chair, nervously rocking. Buying time, he fidgeted with his silver-plated pen and glanced at several papers among those strewn across the desk.

Manny ignored it all as he sat down facing him and placed his two hands defiantly on the desk. His eyes demanded an explanation. *The* explanation.

"I can talk to you now as a friend," Dr. Weiss said as he composed himself. "I am prepared to tell you everything, and believe me, I have a lot to say. Look." He handed Manny two sheets of paper. "This is the official medical report. Read it, and as you go along, I'll fill you in on details to give you a clear picture."

Manny read the report, and Dr. Weiss filled in the rest of the information. Manny's expression remained stoic. Not a muscle moved as he heard Dr. Weiss describe the hasty decision to try the innovative operation instead of sticking with the usual accepted procedure. His frozen expression didn't change when the doctor told him in detail what happened in the operating room — how it suddenly became apparent that the operation wouldn't succeed under the circumstances, how there was still time to reverse the procedure and join the fracture of the femur in the conventional way, and how the decision was based on ulterior motives. How sheer dereliction caused the irreversible limp.

Dr. Weiss sat there in silence. Manny stared at him, not making any move to break the thick stillness filled with unspoken accusation.

"You surely understand," Dr. Weiss finally broke the long silence, "that my name cannot be mentioned. I told you the truth as a friend. I opposed the decision and said so at the time. But remember, if you decide to file a complaint or sue, don't mention my name. I can't afford to ruin my relationship with the chief, Dr. Shilon."

Manny smiled an ironic smile. "I'm not suing Dr. Shilon at this point. Right now I'm accusing you. Where were you, my faithful friend? How did you stand by and see what was happening yet remain silent?"

"How can you say such a thing?" Dr. Weiss asked in a conciliatory tone. "If I had known this was your son, would I have let this happen? But none of us knew. Some elderly woman stood there in a panic with some injured young kid. Had I dreamed it was your son, I would have stood up and made a terrible fuss in the department. I would have spoken out against Dr. Shilon without even considering the personal consequences. For you? How can you insult me this way?"

Manny remained unmoved. "If that's how you feel, let me add another accusation." He pointed a finger of indictment at his colleague. "Your action does not befit a doctor or a human being."

Dr. Weiss wanted to grab Manny's sleeve as he got up from the chair and answer him, but he changed his mind. His blue eyes turned icy.

"You're talking high and mighty," he spewed out the words, "but let's see what you would have done if you had to make a decision with a fidgety green-kerchiefed babysitter on one side and your career on the other. I wonder..."

Dr. Weiss stood up abruptly and walked out of the room with Manny.

Later, Manny met with Dr. Shilon himself. He couldn't lay all his cards on the table, obligated as he was to protect the confidential information he had received from Dr. Weiss, but he had enough cards in his hands to point an accusing finger. Dr. Shilon also apologized, saying he wasn't aware the patient was Manny's son, as if the limbs of anonymous youngsters were fair game for doctors.

"I acted according to all the rules of medical ethics," Dr. Shilon repeated over and over like a broken record. "A surgeon has every right to decide on the type of operation he will perform, even if it's innovative and unconventional. Every method has to be tried on somebody. I am sorry that it was your son who served as guinea pig. Why weren't you yourself here at the time?" the doctor inquired reproachfully. "How can you leave your children in the care of an aging babysitter who can't even locate the parents in time of emergency?"

Manny continued his crusade for quite some time. He complained both verbally and in writing, even reaching the board of directors of the hospital. Then, all of a sudden, he gave up. He stopped talking and started to think of all that had happened, analyzing every aspect in its minutest detail. How had Dr. Weiss put it? "Let's see what you would have done." He decided to see.

Manny put himself under the microscope and was taken aback by what he saw. In all honesty, he couldn't be sure he would have acted differently. Past incidents came to mind. Different in nature, some of them fairly insignificant, all were tied together by a consistent thread – or rather the absence of a consistent thread: the uneven line that zigged and zagged depending on the circumstances, and the ceaseless drive to win approval.

If it had been him, would he have stood up against the head of the department? Wasn't it better to turn a blind eye and a deaf ear, maintain your silence and let it pass? Why not keep on smiling at Dr. Shilon, let him run the show and play the role of assistant surgeon who understands little and knows less. After all, they didn't poison kids here. They meant well by trying a new surgical procedure that had a chance of success, and what was wrong with not taking a chance with a second operation? So the boy ended up with a limp? Who had thought of the possibility? Besides, even the standard operation is not without its risks. Three fractures of the femur is nothing to sneeze at.

Manny found these thoughts unsettling, but he was honest enough not to dismiss them. In a different scenario, on a different stage, with the roles switched, he could have easily played the part. No, not the role of Dr. Shilon, but the part played by his friend Dr. Weiss.

Something broke inside him under the pressure of this introspection. The discovery came as a shock. The thought that he — a person so honest and with such a high ethical standard — could easily step into the role of the cowardly physician, accomplice to an unscrupulous, coldhearted act crushed his soul and demolished his own self-image.

Manny never returned to his job at the hospital. The month he took off to care for Neiri was extended to a three-month leave of absence, followed by a year's leave without pay. He spent hours sitting at home, deep in thought, and consulted with other people until he finally came to a pragmatic conclusion. For ten years, this practical solution had been knocking on his door until Neiri, with his broken leg, opened it.

It is the Torah that provides us with the straight path, Manny now realized; all others are twisted by comparison. A line that changes direction with every whim, is neither straight nor honest — and he and Neiri had experienced the tragic results.

Manny no longer worried what others would think or say; no longer did he look over his shoulder to see how others were reacting. The time had come for him to turn his look inward, to the sincere and honest truth.

That summer, the entire Shaked family — Drorit, Iris and Neiri — went to one more seminar, this time a seminar for families. They were the talk of the neighborhood, but Manny paid no attention. Something in him did a complete 180-degree turn. The change brought him inner strength, the ability to chart his course and stick to it.

Manny found a new job, in a different hospital, this time in the northern region of the country, where he relocated his family. Their old neighborhood hadn't been willing to accept the changes made by the "crazy" family that, in its opinion, suddenly went off the deep end. So they sold their home and bought a pleasant apartment on one of Haifa's quiet streets. The move meant a new school, a new cheder, a new world with new concepts, a new set of values and new neighbors.

"Yes, we are, *baruch Hashem, ba'alei teshuva,*" the children said openly, proud and happy with their change. So what if the upstairs neighbor was called Sarah Leah, a friend at school was called Shaindy, and she was called Drorit? Did it matter if her name was different and unusual? That was her name, and there was no reason to be ashamed of it.

That's how the children saw themselves and that's how others accepted them — with respect and affection.

Together the family built a new home based on new, eternally strong foundations. Within its walls, Manny, or Menachem as he was now called, confidently led his family to a Torah-true life, sure of his faith and unswerving in his principles.

It was in this new home that Neiri became Avner Shaked.

38
A Tangle of Lies

The private plane landed in the small airport on the outskirts of Damascus. Three well-dressed gentlemen slowly walked down the tarmac looking at the usual contingent standing there ready to welcome visiting VIPs.

Sheik Abdul Rachim al Shekari was a most welcome visitor to Syria. The Syrians did everything to make his visits as long as possible, as often as possible — and as profitable as possible.

The three gentlemen didn't have long to wait. They were greeted with broad smiles under long black mustaches and warm handshakes all around.

"An elaborate welcome, as usual," Hamid whispered to Nabil, the second aide, as the royal committee hovered over them.

"They're probably hoping for some big business," Nabil replied. This wasn't the first time Nabil had accompanied the sheik on one of his visits to an Arab capital. The sheik, one of the richest oil magnates in the world, shuttled back and forth between various Arab countries, attending to his wide range of business dealings. This time, no doubt, he carried in his attaché case new plans that rang up dollar signs in the Syrians' eyes.

Three shiny black Mercedes limousines waited near the runway. A chauffeur opened the door of one, gesturing for the honored guests to enter, and drove off to the destination. It was the late afternoon rush hour, and the luxury vehicle crawled along the road amid the traffic jams. Masses of people walked through the gray dingy streets as heavy clouds of dust floated above the bustling city.

The chauffeur was an expert driver and wended his way through the gridlock effortlessly, driving as quickly as possible toward his destination, the exclusive section of Damascus, the capital city.

The well-tended gardens of beautiful villas were seen through the car window, and the sheik looked at them with interest. He envisioned the vast expanses surrounding his summer mansion soon to be filled with fragrant blossoms and lush foliage. The thought of it filled him with pleasure.

Like everything that belonged to Sheik Abdul Rachim al Shekari, the gardens, too, had to be absolutely perfect. He dreamed of this garden of his, one that would be among the most beautiful in the world, the envy of the world's rich and famous. Yes, the garden was of utmost importance to him, and he was willing to invest all the time and money needed to turn it into reality. He had already given hefty remuneration to the two Americans, Neil Stevens and Jay Danker, both international experts on landscape gardening. That was only the beginning, for he planned to spend much, much more.

This trip to Damascus was only tangentially related to his garden, yet necessary nonetheless. His plans for a major investment in Damascus, scheduled for several years hence, would be moved forward, that was all. A minor change to accommodate the Israeli.

The Americans said the whole plan hinged on the watering system. Fortunately for him, some unknown Israeli presented a reasonable solution, one no one else had thought of. His price was reasonable too, neither thousands of shekels nor rolls of greenbacks.

The Israeli was asking for a totally different kind of compensation for his efforts. And this is what brought the sheik to Syria, forcing him to reschedule his business plans by some two years. It was a small price to pay for seeing the garden of his dreams flourishing in the harsh desert climate of Saudi Arabia.

Al Shekari leaned back comfortably on the plush upholstered seat of the limousine. *It is but a small matter*, he thought to himself with complete assurance. He could take care of the Israeli's request with a minimum of effort.

There are those who scorn the power of money, he thought with a smile. These people would have brought the case of the Israeli as an example. But he, the sheik, thought otherwise. What one can't buy with money, one can buy with a lot of money. Even the strongest metal was not as strong as money. Money can break down walls, force open gates and slice through chains of steel.

The limousine stopped at the corner in front of a three-story building. The plain whitewash of the building belied the plush carpeting and opulence within. The sheik and his attendants stepped inside as the entourage waved goodbye. In a few hours, following time for rest and respite, a top-level group would be meeting with the sheik.

The meeting was held in the Round Room, the most magnificent room in the two-story office complex where important business dealings took place. Despite its name, the room was rectangular, not round. It was the large glass-topped table standing in the center that gave the room its name. Someone had once joked that it was called the Round Room because the endless meetings went in circles.

Everyone arrived at the meeting smiling and optimistic. Al Shekari, unlike many other Middle Eastern businessmen, was quick thinking and decisive. With him, there was no beating around the bush. Everyone knew he would come to the meeting with plans in his pocket and a precise, detailed schedule for carrying them out. All meetings with him usually came to a close with the signing of a contract and everything spelled out clearly.

Refreshments on the round, elegant black table were served on Limoges china; soft drinks sparkled in crystal goblets. The meeting opened with polite handshakes after which all waited for the sheik to speak. Al Shekari cleared his throat and removed a sheaf of papers from his attaché case.

"My financial investment this time is in the tourist industry. I have a new idea that will transform Damascus into the hub of tourism in the Middle East. It is as follows:

"One of the quaint quarters of the old city will be transformed into a modern tourist center. The government will begin by demolishing selected irreparable buildings, primarily those that have already been declared a safety hazard. In their place, a new, fully climate-controlled shopping mall will be constructed.

"The mall, to be designed by world-class architects, will be the biggest in the region and comparable in every way to the best in the Western world. It will draw the wealthiest of our Arab brothers, who will come to shop for all their purchases. All those sheiks we now find in London's finest stores will come here. The mall I envision will be the largest in the Middle East — and the most luxurious."

The sheik spoke quickly, glancing out of the corner of his eye at those sitting around the table.

"This is only the first stage of the project," Al Shekari lowered his voice. "The second stage will include an eighty-story hotel built over the mall. Each floor will encompass one private suite. The building itself will be hexagonal in shape, with the outer walls glass."

He unfolded an artist's rendering before the group. The design was striking. The two-story mall filled the page, with the six-sided hotel soaring skyward in the center.

"The glass windows of the hotel's facade will reflect the

ancient streets of Damascus and allow them to be seen at a distance. This unusual combination of new and old, modern and ancient, is quite popular nowadays."

The sheik gathered the papers and sat down, giving the others a chance to comment, an opportunity they took advantage of. They asked questions, got answers, clarified details, deliberated and analyzed for an hour and a half of lively discussion. The Syrian economic experts were enthusiastic. They saw in the investment potential to breathe new life into Syria's flagging tourist industry.

At that point, the sheik stood up to speak. He looked at the members of the Economic Development Council sitting around the table and stared at the two men from the Syrian Ministry of Defense who had been invited to join the meeting.

"My project can begin within the next two years," Abdul Rachim said, "but before we sign a contract I have one small condition. It may not be directly related, but due to certain business pressures it is an integral part of our project."

He paused, anticipating the impact of his next words.

"I want an Israeli captive soldier by the name of Nir, who has been in your hands since 1982, returned to his homeland. Dead or alive — it doesn't matter. I am willing to act as intermediary between you and the Israeli government and ready to demand that Palestinian fighters be released in exchange."

He stopped speaking and, when no one broke the silence, continued. "I imagine this won't create any problems. Between you and me," he lowered his voice and looked pointedly at the two officials from the Defense Ministry, "what good is this captive to you anyway? I will make sure you receive the maximum in return and, if you insist, I can see to it that Syria will not be officially implicated. I will arrange it so it appears that others are involved."

The smiling faces at the meeting turned ashen. Every Syrian, and certainly those holding influential positions, knows that some topics are taboo. One doesn't mention them out loud, not even in a whisper or through veiled reference.

The sheik took advantage of their silence to add a few words. "I want to meet with you again," he said to the defense officials, "in another two days. After we settle this minor issue, we will meet for a third time to finalize the project."

The sheik stood up, letting everyone know that as far as he was concerned the meeting was over.

The second meeting two days later was short and cold.

"We checked out all the data," the two officials from the Syrian Ministry of Defense said. "Syria is not holding captive any Israeli soldier by that name. There is information that the Lebanese were holding a soldier by the name of Nir two years after the war, in '84, but after that time he was handed over to others and contact with him was severed.

"That is the extent of our information," they continued. "We have documents to substantiate this. The Defense Department has gone above and beyond normal policy in disclosing this secret information, and we hope that you will reciprocate. When can we hold the next meeting to finalize project details?"

The sheik nervously scratched his forehead and took two steps back. "Not now," he said. "I will be flying back to Saudi Arabia today. If you have anything to add, contact me."

"We will have no reason to do that," one of the officials answered sharply. "We have told you everything we know. If you have anything to add, you contact us. We will be happy to cooperate in bringing this project to fruition."

All left disappointed. Abdul Rachim al Shekari left that same night on his private plane for Saudi Arabia. In midair, as the fluffy clouds caressed the metal wings of the plane, the tension began to subside.

The calming blue of the sky worked wonders to relax him. *They gave me all the information they have,* he consoled himself. *At least that is what they are saying. So that's what I'll tell Neil and Jay to say to that Israeli. How can I argue with the Syrians? Let the Israeli bring me proof, and I will confront the*

Syrians with it. With the few paltry facts they gave me, my information is far too inadequate.

Just thinking this made the sheik felt better. He could continue with his plans. *I made a special trip to Syria. I had two meetings with top officials. That's enough of a payment for the Israeli. Now we can begin working on the gardens. As for the tourist complex, I can put it off until after my gardens are complete.*

Sheik Abdul Rachim al Shekari could nap peacefully in his comfortable plane seat. He didn't know that at that very moment the two men he left behind were at another meeting, reporting to a top-level army officer.

"Not another word," the officer hissed, his teeth clenched as he pounded on the table. "Syria doesn't have any more information, not even in exchange for a grandiose project. No one can force you to give information you don't have. Is that clear?"

It was very clear.

Had the sheik been a partner to this conversation, he would have had the proof he wanted to demand return of the captive. But Syria carries on such conversations behind closed doors, in complete secrecy.

The sheik was left without even a shred of evidence that could be tied to Yossi Nir. Instead, he was left holding the frayed end of a lead that led nowhere.

But above was the One Who pulls all the strings. It is He and He alone Who chooses which strings to pull and when.

39
Chalk on the Blackboard

Shuki stood facing the big blackboard, clutching a piece of white chalk in his hand. His eyes followed the two other boys who were standing nearby writing on the green surface. One of the boys was Pinchas. For the first time, Shuki noticed the sad look on his face.

As he did every morning, Pinchas now stood in front of the blackboard, his hand trembling as he wrote the name of his beloved grandfather, Eliezer Mordechai *ben* Chana Rivka, who was very ill and in need of a *refua sheleima*.

How long has Pinchas been writing this name at the top of the board? Shuki wondered. He had seen it since the beginning of the year. Was it there last year, in the sixth grade?

Shuki thought of asking Pinchas and also asking about his grandfather. He would ask how he was feeling and listen carefully. In the quiet early morning hours, standing by an almost empty blackboard, things look different.

Usually Shuki rushed straight from the gray minivan into the bustling classroom, bursting with energy. He had half a minute — often less — to get organized and size up the goings on in the room before switching his mind into study mode. Before he knew it, Reb Moishe would be standing in the doorway and all distracting thoughts had to be pushed aside.

This morning it was different. Shuki couldn't enter the classroom at the sound of the bell and just write the name on the board. The bell obligated him to sit down in his seat and wait with *derech eretz* for the rebbe to enter the room. Only then could he raise his hand and ask permission to go up to the board to add another name. Then the curious eyes of every single boy in the room would follow him. They would also no doubt have questions and would want to ask him details. Nope, that sure wasn't for him.

"Abba, could you give me a ride to school tomorrow?" Shuki had asked his father yesterday afternoon.

It was his father who had asked Shuki to write the name on the blackboard. Surely he'd be willing to help him do it without attracting his classmates' attention and inviting awkward questions. Getting to school early was the solution. His father had considered the request. Take Shuki to Haifa? Actually the idea had been his.

In the summer, he had suggested to Shuki that from time to time, the forty-five minute drive with just the two of them in the car would be pleasant. But Shuki had never taken him up on the offer. Now, all of a sudden, when he was so pressed for time, Shuki asked to be driven.

Shuki's father hesitated for a second or two, picturing himself getting up early in the morning to daven with the early minyan after a few hours of sleep to make the round-trip to Haifa. He agreed.

"Okay, Shuki'le," he replied tenderly, putting his hand on his son's shoulder. If his Yehoshua, who was usually so closed and withdrawn, had made the request, maybe it signaled an opening in their relationship. Maybe they'd be able to have a real father-and-son talk as they drove. Yitzchak Katz wasn't about to close a door that only on rare occasions opened.

The trip passed without a word spoken. Yet the silence was better than long questions coming from behind the wheel and terse replies from the back seat. Shuki's father let him off at the cheder, watching the receding figure with a twinge of disappointment. Why had Shuki wanted a ride? Even the answer to this trivial question Shuki hadn't bothered to disclose.

Shuki's thoughts didn't reach that far. Pleased with himself, he walked toward the quiet building, enjoying the brisk morning air as he took a deep breath. It had been a good idea to ask his father to take him. If the long trip wasn't such an imposition, he would ask his father to drive him at least once a week. How could you compare a day that began with a tension-filled rush through the school gate trying to beat the bell to a relaxed peaceful saunter in the fresh air, your mind as clear as the blue sky above?

Only a few boys were in the classroom when Shuki arrived. He calmly walked between the rows to his desk and leisurely placed his briefcase on the floor. He then headed for the blackboard and picked up a piece of white chalk, getting ready to write the name. Pinchas had already slowly written his *zaidy's* name in the corner of the board, davening as he formed each letter, before sitting down in his seat.

Tzvi was still writing. He had a long list in his hand that he copied onto the board: Reuven Eliyahu *ben* Esther Toby, Shlomo Menachem *ben* Leah, Adina *bas* Sarah Hinda. Tzvi copied the letters from the paper onto the board. He didn't know who these people were. He didn't know a thing about them, the story of their lives, the tears, the prayers and hopes behind each and every name. He could only imagine.

Shuki never knew that it was Tzvi who was responsible for most of the names on the board. He never gave it much thought. He would glance at the list as his lips murmured "Refa'einu" in Shemoneh Esrei and that was it. Now, for the first time, he realized that Tzvi was behind it all.

"I copy the names from the newspaper," Tzvi told him in all simplicity. "All these people are mentioned in small notices. I can't say the entire *sefer Tehillim* by myself, but at least I can be instrumental in having thousands of kids mention them in their davening.

"I call up the people, if there's a phone number in the notice. Sometimes the person sounds cheered up when I tell them, and sometimes they sound broken and sad. It depends. Anyway, the davening works wonders," Tzvi added, believing it with all his heart.

"We can't always understand these things," he concluded as he added two more names to the list. "After I finish here, I go from room to room to all the other classes. That's why I come earlier than the rest of the class."

Shuki tossed the chalk to his other hand. His right hand was powdered white. *I hardly know any of my new friends*, he suddenly thought. *Why, Tzvi sits only a few desks away. I considered him an average student, sort of insignificant.* Shuki glanced at the long list that Tzvi had copied onto the board. Insignificant?

The class began to fill up as the boys arrived. Eliyahu Davidowitz walked over to the blackboard swinging his briefcase in his hand and in big letters printed the name Simcha Nota *ben* Shaindel Leah.

"He's a relative of one of my neighbors," Eliyahu whispered as he walked to his seat. "They asked me to write it on the list."

Shuki walked toward the center of the blackboard and in large round letters wrote Yosef *ben* Efrat. After a moment's hesitation, he added the words "missing in action" and in small letters underneath, "needs *rachamei Shamayim*." That was it. He put the chalk down and felt like someone who had just finished climbing a mountain. He stepped back to survey his handiwork. Yes, everything was fine. You could see every letter.

Now the whole class would daven for the missing Yosef *ben* Efrat, joining the many people all over the world who were dav-

Chalk on the Blackboard ◆ 277

ening for him on his birthday. Abba always said that a person's birthday was a good time for special requests, and this marked the sixteenth anniversary of Yosef's being held captive in some unknown place.

Hey, what was going on? Shuki rubbed his eyes, unbelieving. Avner Shaked stood by the blackboard and with bright colored chalk wrote in giant letters the very words he had just written! He drew a thick frame around the words and added two long lines. What was that all about?

Shuki walked up to the blackboard, a confused expression on his face. What did Avner have to do with their Yossi? It was his father who had persuaded Yossi's father, Daniel Nir, to organize a national day of prayer on behalf of his son. It was his father who had convinced Mr. Nir of the importance of *tefilla*. His father was the one who received a phone call one day from one of the other members of their army unit asking, in the name of Yossi's father, that prayers be said for his son who had been missing in action for so long. So what was Avner doing here now? How did he have the nerve to intrude on Shuki's private territory?

Avner still didn't understand the question in Shuki's eyes. After once again reading the name he had just written, Avner suddenly noticed in the upper corner of the board, the same name. The letters were smaller, but it was definitely the same name.

He turned around in surprise and found himself facing another surprised expression. "Was it...was it you who wrote that?" Avner asked Shuki.

"Yes," Shuki replied. "What...umm...how do you know?"

"He's a soldier missing in action since the Peace for Galilee War," Avner explained, obviously familiar with the details. "Yesterday, an old army buddy of my father's called him up and asked him, in the name of Yossi's father, to daven for his missing son. Today is his birthday."

"Your father...fought in the war?" Shuki's eyes opened wide

in astonishment. "My father was together with Yossi in the same tank. He was his best friend!"

"Yes, my father always says," Avner continued as he put his arm around Shuki's shoulder, "that it was during the war that he took his first step toward becoming a *ba'al teshuva*. He—"

"What!" Shuki's eyes opened even wider in absolute astonishment. "Your father is a *ba'al teshuva*?"

"Not only my father," Avner burst into a warm friendly smile, "but all of us. My mother, my two older sisters and me. I was seven when we changed our lives. Didn't you hear this from the other kids? Didn't you figure it out by yourself?"

Shuki was in a state of shock. He slowly put two and two together. Phrases began falling into place as pieces of the puzzle began to fit forming a clear picture, suddenly coherent, free from animosity and accusations.

"My father is also a *ba'al teshuva*," Shuki slowly let the words out of his mouth, surprised at his own candor. "He himself was wounded in the battle in which he lost his best friend. I was born into a regular *frum* family, but this war is something we live with day in and day out. My father doesn't look like every other person," Shuki explained. "He can't learn like every one else. I don't know exactly why. He—"

The hand on Shuki's shoulder practically hugged him and Shuki, feeling its warmth and understanding, stood silent, the tension in his body relaxing.

"Shuki, how about coming over to my house today," Avner asked, "or maybe tomorrow after school? I can introduce you to my father. He for sure knows your father. What was he called back then?"

"No." Shuki suddenly felt nervous. "I'm willing to come to your house but only on the condition that you don't say a thing to your father. Just tell him that I'm one of your friends. No more than that. I want him to...," Shuki tripped over his thoughts, "I want him to see me as...." Shuki wanted to add "the same as everyone else" but how could he say that, especially to Avner?

Chalk on the Blackboard ♦ 279

"No problem," Avner smiled understandingly. "I won't say a single word if you don't want me to. Ask your parents' permission to stay over tomorrow night. As far as I'm concerned," he said with a wink, "you can tell your father everything about me and my father."

Shuki smiled weakly. Avner sure didn't know him. He didn't need permission to discuss this with his father. These topics aren't the kind of subjects he would talk to his father about, no, not in a million years.

The bell rang. It sounded far away. Only then did Shuki realize that the classroom was as noisy as it was every morning before class started. Boys were talking, arguing and exchanging the latest news.

But Shuki was on a different planet. Avner clapped him on the shoulder as they exchanged a long look of understanding before walking to their desks.

What a great day, Shuki thought to himself as he basked in the sweetness he felt as he opened his siddur. Together with Avner, together with the entire class he would now daven and ask Hashem to help Yossi Nir.

Do any of the other boys feel this is a special day? he wondered.

40
All in One Night

"Come on in," Avner said, opening the door to Shuki. "My room is this way, straight ahead at the end of the hall." Shuki clutched his brown briefcase tightly in his hand, a sign of his nervousness at entering his classmate's home for the first time.

"Have a seat, Shuki," said Avner, motioning to a chair near the desk. "I'll bring us something to drink."

Shuki took advantage of his brief absence to look around. If there are similarities between homes and the people who live in them, then Avner's home was a perfect example. The house was spacious and airy. The large windows set deep in the thick walls were open wide, allowing the cool autumn evening air inside. The doors to all the rooms with their adjoining porches were wide open, too. The broad entryway welcomed all those who entered.

"Are you the friend Avner's always talking about?" asked a small boy who had seemingly appeared out of nowhere. His eyes sparkled mischievously.

"I guess so," Shuki answered. "I'm his friend. What has he told you about me?" he asked suspiciously. *You can't trust anyone*, the bitter thought flashed through his mind.

"A lot," the boy answered, his impish grin widening. "He said you're new at school and you're a good student. He also said you were nice and that he'd like to be your friend because you seem to have a lot in common. Is it true?"

Shuki felt his cheeks burning. "Is that exactly what he said?" he asked the small boy, unconsciously leaning forward anxiously to hear the yes.

"Yup," the youngster confirmed. "Exactly. You can ask him yourself."

Just then, Avner walked into the room carrying two glasses and a plate of cookies. "I hope tap water's okay," he said. "Here, in our house, we drink only water. We're so used to it, we don't like all the other sweet syrupy stuff."

He handed Shuki a glass, loudly said a *shehakol*, and started drinking. Shuki glanced at him out of the corner of his eye for a split second, then made a *bracha* and drank the water (which, in his not-so-humble opinion, wasn't that great).

"Have some cookies," Avner offered. "My sister Iris baked them. She's second in the family," he explained. "My older sister is Drorit, then comes Iris—"

"That's how you call them?" Shuki broke in, unable to keep from asking.

"Why not?" Avner answered nonchalantly. "I used to be called Neiri. We had all sorts of nicknames we no longer use. But our Rav said that there is no reason for us to change our names." Avner stood quietly for a moment. "At supper you'll get to meet Shlomo Dov and Chaim Yosef, my two younger brothers. They were born into our 'new' family here in Haifa and never knew any other life. Sometimes I stand and wonder what they will be like when they grow up. Will they be different from me? They won't wake up one fine day when they are seven years old and discover a whole new world full of surprises. They were born with *brachos* and davening and *peyos* and yarmulkes. It's so different, don't you think so?"

Shuki nodded. What Avner said really made sense. It was so interesting to hear his opinion on all kinds of subjects.

"Should we do our work sheets together now?" Avner asked, going back to his desk when Shuki didn't reply to his last comment. "This way we'll get it over with and have time to play."

Shuki agreed. It certainly would be good to leave Avner's house with all the questions of the homework assignment fully answered. He had such a hard time completing the assignment alone.

Shuki opened his briefcase and took out two work sheets. The pages were neatly printed with graphic designs. The heading boldly announced "General Jewish Knowledge." The Haifa cheder was having a special competition. The boys weren't obligated to participate, but any student who was halfway serious wanted to. The page contained a variety of questions related to the topic of general knowledge. Sometimes there would be hints where to look up the answers, and sometimes you were on your own.

"You can, you even should, ask your fathers for help," Reb Moishe had repeated more than once.

Shuki well understood why the rebbe emphasized this point. The questions were hard. Too hard, if you asked him. True, there was fascinating information to be discovered and very important facts that were worthwhile knowing, but it was all too difficult for a seventh-grade boy to figure out by himself. And Shuki so wanted to participate fully in the project to perfection! He wanted to hand in the weekly pages filled in their entirety, all meticulously written. He wanted to earn the maximum number of points and be among those who reached the finals. At times like this, he again strongly felt the agony of being different from everyone else. Of all the boys in the class, it was only his father who couldn't help, only his father who couldn't open the right *sefer* and read off the words confidently.

All in One Night ♦ 283

"It would be great if we could answer the questions now," Shuki said out loud. "Two heads are better than one."

He didn't know why, but something about the big house, the open rooms, the laughter that emanated within its walls, made him continue talking. "At my house, it's very hard for me to fill out the pages. I don't have anyone to help me, and I can't do it alone."

"Where's my green folder?" Avner wanted to get down to business. "I'm sure I put the pages into the special folder. I remember looking at the two pages when they were handed out. Where did I put them?"

Shuki followed Avner's look as he glanced around the room, but not a hint of the folder with the bold heading "General Jewish Knowledge" was seen. Avner got up and started to look carefully into every nook and cranny. Shuki hoped, for Avner's sake, that his friend would find it fast. No, it wasn't so that they could begin working on the project. It was because he imagined himself in a similar situation and felt the embarrassment and discomfort. Here a new friend comes to your house for the first time and you suggest they begin to do homework with you. What sort of impression does it make if you can't find your papers? It makes you look like an absentminded professor who doesn't remember where he puts things.

But Avner didn't seem at all embarrassed, and, interestingly enough, Shuki didn't see him as the absentminded professor type — which is how Shuki was sure he would look if the situation was reversed.

"Oh, I think I remember," Avner suddenly said. "Yesterday I showed the pages to my father. I must have left them on the living-room table. He was happy to see the assignment and interested in every single question."

"How lucky you are," Shuki said with some jealousy. "There's no point in my showing the work sheets to my father. He can't help me anyway."

"So what?" Avner smiled. "My father doesn't know enough

284 ♦ All in One Night

to help me either. He always says that I have to pay attention to every word the rebbe says and listen for the two of us. Then he asks me to explain it to him. But what difference does it make?" Avner continued. "My father enjoys seeing what we are learning. He loves to hear about all the projects and contests. I always tell him everything about the tests and lessons. Isn't your father interested in what's going on in cheder?"

Shuki nervously bit his lip. Interested? There wasn't another father in the world who was as interested in what his son learned in cheder as his father. But he, Shuki, was so distant that he didn't share any of it. Besides, his father didn't understand, so what was the point of telling him? But Avner seemed to think there was a point.

"My father is especially interested in the questions on general Jewish knowledge," Avner continued. "He's always trying to fill in the missing gaps in his life and admits that I know more than he. I've been learning in the cheder since I was seven, and I know practically as much as every other boy my age. But my father was already thirty-five when he began to learn, and it's harder when you're older. So there is still lots he doesn't know. He suggested that after I fill out all the pages, we sit together and I explain them to him. He's always ready to learn more new things."

There was a moment of silence and then Avner continued, a dreamy look in his brown eyes. "You know what? It's easy for me to talk to you because you probably feel the same way. When I think of my father and the great changes he made in his life, my heart fills with admiration. Do you know what it takes for a person to suddenly leave everything — all his friends and relatives, his whole way of life — and start a new life as if he was just born? I'm grateful to Hashem that I was only seven years old, because I'm not sure I would have had the courage to take such a step at age thirty-five like my father."

Avner stood up and walked to the door. "Not everybody can understand this," he said slowly. "It's said that even total tzaddikim can't stand in the place where *ba'alei teshuva* stand. I guess we can really understand why."

Shuki said not a word — not because he didn't have anything to say but because Avner's words threw him off balance.

"Did you see my papers?" Avner asked his mother and sister, who were standing in the kitchen. "Abba," he called to his father, who was standing by the phone, "do you remember the pages I showed you yesterday?" Yes, his father remembered. "I left them in the living room and now they're not there," Avner explained. "Did you take the green folder to look at?"

Menachem Shaked shook his head. "The pages really made a fine impression on me, and I did indeed want to look at them at the first opportunity, but I didn't get around to doing it yet. I had a very busy day at the hospital," he apologized. "Carefully look again among your things. All lost items are usually at the bottom, aren't they?"

Shuki heard the conversation and decided to save Avner from his predicament. "Let's leave the assignment for now and play a game," he suggested. "By the time we finish supper, the papers will show up."

Avner accepted the suggestion and took a board game off the shelf. "This game is called Submarines. Do you know how to play?"

"Yes," said Shuki. "I have the same game at home."

"Then let's look for something else. If you have it at home, it'll probably be boring for you."

"You probably won't find a game I don't have," Shuki said with a smile. "My grandmother always brings us games. You know how it is with grandmothers. They can't bring clothes or candy or books or cassettes, so board games are the ideal solution."

"My grandmother doesn't even bring games," Avner's face paled. "She hasn't been to our house in Haifa even once, and we haven't been to hers. Abba has tried to make peace but she refuses to see any of us. 'Not with your black clothes and *kippot*,' she says. Even when my two little brothers were born she didn't come to visit. They don't even know we have a grandmother living in Tel Aviv. Sometimes I miss her," Avner whispered into Shuki's ear. "I still remember her. She loved us so much. How can it be that she changed so much? How can she not be interested in how her Neiri is growing up?"

Shuki didn't know what to say. He suddenly felt fortunate and happy to have grandparents like his. True, Saba was bitter and sometimes even angry. He found it hard to come to terms with their way of life. Savta tried to smooth things over, making peace between everybody. Nevertheless, each family kept to its own ways. Shuki knew he meant a lot to them. They came for visits and showed how much they missed him. He felt a warmth creep into his heart. Until then, he hadn't thought the situation could be worse.

The board game was left untouched. Shuki had plenty of games at home but deep heart-to-heart talks like this one were something he had never before experienced. It would be a shame to miss out on it just to play a game.

So the two of them sat and talked till dinnertime and throughout the meal. Later, Avner found his green folder, and they studied. But most of the time was spent talking, and the more they talked, the harder it was to stop.

When Shuki said Shema before going to sleep late that night, he realized he would have plenty to think about for many nights to come.

41

Operation Tears

Street lamps went on, one after another. The skies of Beirut were still blue at this hour, as night began to fall. It was exactly 6:45 P.M. when the two European businessmen left their room at the posh Avia Hotel in the heart of the city.

"The time has come," the shorter of the two said.

"The moment has arrived," confirmed his well-dressed partner as he dug his hands into his pockets.

They nonchalantly walked down the long hallway, the thick shag carpet absorbing the sounds of their tense footsteps. The short one pressed the elevator button, and they waited in silence. There was only one topic that interested them at that moment — and on that topic, they weren't allowed to say even one word.

The elevator door opened. Some businessmen wearing traditional Arab dress were carrying on a lively conversation. They paid no attention to the two men who quickly entered the elevator. After all, there is nothing unusual about European businessman staying at luxurious Beirut hotels. Designer suits and handmade silk ties were common in the long quiet hallways of these hotels.

The elevator stopped at the underground parking lot. The two men got out and continued to exchange brief sentences in fluent English. The short one took a heavy key chain from his pocket and walked over to a purple Chevy. He opened the door for the man in the well-tailored suit, who took the wheel and turned on the ignition. A careful observer would have noted with surprise the swiftness with which he deftly maneuvered the car out of the crowded parking area and into the street. Fortunately for both of them, no one was watching.

The security guard of the hotel was sitting at the gate, a bored expression on his face. The short one smiled his broadest smile. "Hello, my friend," he said disarmingly, raising his right hand to his hat brim in a casual salute.

Nice fellows in that purple Chevy, the guard thought to himself as he pushed the button that raised the guard rail blocking the exit.

The men in the purple car smiled to themselves in satisfaction. "It's good he noticed us," the well-tailored one said.

"It's of no consequence," the short fellow remarked, looking out the window. "In another three days, when they start looking, we'll be gone. But it never hurts to take precautions."

His partner nervously put his fingers into his left pocket. Yes, he certainly hoped so. The time was 6:53.

The purple car glided along the wide roadway, moving from lane to lane along the winding road. Ten excruciatingly long minutes later the car stopped at the door of a large office building.

At 7:03, the man in the tailored suit stepped out of the car and turned right. He crossed the street, passing by the lit windows of the office buildings, all the while fingering the con-

Operation Tears ♦ 289

tents of his pocket. The small bottle, weighing only several grams, sat on his heart like a ton of bricks.

At 7:10, a white Renault pulled up to the curb next to him. He opened the back door and got in. Tension kept him sitting stiffly on the soft leather upholstery.

Meanwhile, the short man continued driving the purple Chevy to the outskirts of the city. There, in a bustling residential area, he parked the car according to plan. At 7:15 the white Renault picked him up.

"Are your tears ready?" the driver asked the man in the tailored suit. His attempt at humor fell flat.

"Ready," came the brusque answer from the back seat. He had no patience right then for any friendly conversations.

"Blue-Brown doesn't know how much he'll cry tonight," the driver grinned, using the code name.

There was no reaction. A thick silence fell on all three. Shrugging his shoulders, the driver made no response. Keeping his eyes glued to the familiar roadway ahead of him, he drove on.

Beirut is a beautiful city, the man in the tailored suit thought, *beautiful but devastated*. Bitter fighting had torn it apart. At the sight of the tall skyscrapers alongside bullet-riddled walls and rubble, he couldn't help but feel a tug at his heart. "The world's biggest disasters are man-made," he remembered hearing someone once say. How true.

He thought of Rafik Jamil, the one called Blue-Brown, and the comparison was unavoidable. Jamil brought about the biggest tragedies, not only to his Lebanese compatriots whose lives were shattered, but also to his very own brethren living in Israel.

He remembered the series of recent terrorist acts that turned the heart of Jerusalem into a scene of mass carnage, and he felt a desire for revenge. His job was clear-cut and absolutely necessary. He again fingered the small bottle in his pocket, but this time he touched it carefully, letting the feeling of destiny filter through to his fingertips.

At 7:27, a middle-aged man left Hizbullah headquarters, which was located in a building on the corner. At 7:30, he was scheduled to enter the Islamic Culture Center, a small building two blocks away.

The small bottle was destined to meet him before he got there.

The driver stopped the white Renault at the corner, letting the two men out. With astonishing agility, they jumped from the car, crossed the street and started to stroll along the sidewalk while engaged in lively conversation. They passed house number thirty-seven, thirty-five, thirty-three...

They saw the sign on the building written in flowing Arabic script: "The Islamic Culture Center."

They had taken this route many times in the past few weeks, changing cars to avoid suspicion. They hadn't overlooked even the smallest detail. They knew Blue-Brown's daily routine like the back of their hands. They had waited four days for the signal, and this evening they had gotten the go-ahead. Operation Tears was on its way.

They passed house number thirty-one, twenty-nine, twenty-seven. They slowed down, their hearts pounding. The digital wristwatch on the short man's wrist showed 7:28 and thirty seconds.

The man in the well-tailored suit took a newspaper out of his left pocket and opened it, pointing with his right hand to one of the articles. They continued to walk with the pages of English text covering their faces. No passerby would have dreamed that the pages were transparent, allowing them a clear view of all activity in the street.

With two fingers of his right hand, the man in the tailored suit continued to point to a small news article in a square box. In the middle of the square, there was a minuscule hole for the neck of the bottle he was clutching. The small bottle took up only half his fist.

Suddenly, he was on the alert. Heavy footsteps, fast and familiar, approached them. His fingers shook. His arm tightened around the bottle as he got ready to press the tripper.

"You don't understand," the short one said, raising his voice as he gave his partner a slight shove. "It is just like I..."

They looked like two European businessmen engrossed in a lively discussion over the financial pages of the international newspaper, seemingly oblivious that they were about to bump into the man walking toward them.

Rafik Jamil, veering slightly to the left in order to avoid the collision, suddenly felt a stinging sensation in his right eye.

The time was 7:29.

※ ※ ※

The large wall clock in the Mossad, Israel's secret service, showed 7:45. By this time, according to all plans, the two secret service agents should have given the agreed-upon signal that the operation was successfully accomplished.

The head of the Mossad cast a nervous eye at the green phone, waiting for the red light to blink. A third agent, the communications expert, was to call and say, "dry tears." At that signal, the boss would order the waiting naval commando forces to send a special unit to the shores of Lebanon.

At midnight, the agents would abandon their rented car and board the boat that was to bring them back to Israel.

The hands of the clock moved ahead at a threatening pace: 7:50, 7:58. The head of the secret service clenched his jaw. Every minute was precious. The strategy was based on the following plan: By the time the "tears" appeared — that is, when the poison began taking effect on Rafik Jamil, the head of Hizbullah — the Israeli agents would be far away.

The poison was specially formulated to begin taking effect two to three days after it made contact. One drop of the poison squirted in the victim's eye would cause a slight stinging sensation, an irritation barely felt. After a while, this would turn into a strong burning sensation. By the time the victim sought medical treatment, it would be too late. The poison would by then enter the bloodstream, sealing his fate.

It would be impossible, or so the brains in the Mossad thought, to connect the sudden strange death with a chance encounter on a bustling sidewalk. No one could point an accusing finger. Nevertheless, it would be best for the agents to be far away and to hear about the sudden death of Jamil together with all other Israeli citizens.

What's gone wrong? wondered the head of the Mossad.

He quickly punched in the numbers of the secret code, but replaced the receiver when he noticed the red light on the green telephone flashing. He picked up the receiver and listened.

Upon hearing the message, his face turned ashen.

/// /// ///

The two European businessmen continued to walk in long strides to blend in with the passersby. According to the plan that had been meticulously worked out in the days before the operation, they were to continue to the corner, where they would be picked up by the white Renault. The car would then be switched with the purple Chevy, which would take them back to the Avia Hotel.

A short time later, upon receipt of the prearranged signal, they would leave Beirut and head south. A walk would take them to the designated departure point marked on the seashore where a camouflaged boat would take them back to Israel.

But things didn't go according to plan.

The man in the well-tailored suit was supposed to spray two short spurts of the fatal poison from the bottle, one in each eye. Under the tension of the moment, he pressed too hard and too long.

There were seven steps separating Rafik Jamil from the newspaper hiding the bottle of poison when he felt a sharp stinging sensation in his eye. His head spun, and he saw everything in a blur. His life, he knew, was in danger.

Every terrorist lives with the knowledge that one day he may meet his end with a bullet aimed at him by the very people he is trying to annihilate. As he fought to retain consciousness, Rafik Jamil knew the inevitable had happened. He forced himself to stay alert long enough to reach for the instrument in his pocket. He pressed the round button four times and managed to shreik, "I've been attacked!"

Still conscious, he pointed in the direction of his assailants. A second later, his mind went blank, but the Beirut police were already chasing the white Renault.

42

Bitter Smile

"Haifa's sunset over the sea is impressive, isn't it?" Avner asked, noticing the dreamy look in Shuki's eyes. Shuki gazed at the blue horizon and the bright orange and purple rays of the sinking sun above it.

"I never thought much about different sunsets," Shuki said, "but speaking of sunsets, I must say that the sunsets in Arazim are tops. In Arazim, there's no pollution clouding the scenery or high-rise buildings obscuring the view. There, the streetlights don't go on so early." With a sweeping motion of his hand, he indicated the many lights dotting the sidewalk. "When the sun sets in Arazim, it's as if it's wishing the whole village good night — the small white cottages, the gardens, the bushes, the trees. If you're interested in seeing a really beautiful sunset," Shuki concluded, "come to Arazim."

"Really?" Avner asked with a mischievous twinkle in his eye. "Can I come tomorrow?"

"Tomorrow?" Shuki was taken by surprise. "Um...well...why not? I just have to tell my father and...actually, I'm sure you can come. It's a great idea!"

"Don't worry," Avner said, patting Shuki on the shoulder, "I'm not coming so fast. For the time being, it's better for both of us that you come to me. Right now, we have to get ahead with our project on general Jewish knowledge. And here in Haifa, we'll be able to go over the work sheets with the *bachur* my father spoke about. So it makes more sense for you to be at my house."

Shuki nodded in agreement. "Let's sit here on this fence," he suggested to his friend. "Does your father come from this direction?" Shuki pointed.

Avner didn't answer right away. "He does when he comes home from the hospital," Avner answered slowly. "He usually comes home at five, and it's almost seven now. Occasionally he is late, but never this late." Avner sounded concerned.

"He knows that you wanted to begin learning today, doesn't he?" Shuki asked.

"Of course," Avner answered, peering anxiously into the distance. "This morning, before my father went to daven, he told me he found someone to learn with me. Actually, he asked two boys, so in case one can't make it, we can always ask the other. They're both excellent students, and they learn in the yeshiva nearby.

"My father said he told them he'd pay them well for an hour of tutoring in the evening. He wants it to be done on a regular basis, so I'll be able to ask the *bachur* all the questions I would have wanted to ask my father. He wants me to be able to review all the hard Gemaras, and even get ahead of the class by learning new material.

"Do you understand, Shuki? My father may not be able to actually help me himself, but whatever he can do, he will do — no matter what it costs. It makes me feel that I really have to try hard and always pay attention in class. Do you feel that way too?"

Shuki, preoccupied with his thoughts, didn't answer. "So when do you think your father will arrive?" he asked.

"I have no idea," Avner replied, leaning against the wall, looking more worried all the time. "My father knows that we come home from cheder at five-thirty. He said he would be waiting at home for me with an answer, and let me know what the arrangements are with the *bachur* — where to meet him and when."

"Maybe he just forgot about it," Shuki suggested.

"Could be," Avner said. "My father is really a very busy person. He has a million things on his mind — but this one thing is more important to him than anything else in the world. It's not something he would forget about. No," Avner was certain now, "it's not possible."

Shuki didn't say anything. He just stared at Avner and marveled at the difference between them. Sure, Avner was anxious, waiting for his father to arrive, but he didn't give any thought to what his friend Shuki might be thinking. After all, Shuki had stayed over in Haifa especially to learn with him, and now Avner was just wasting time sitting on the fence. Avner wasn't even embarrassed or uncomfortable about the fact that his father had promised him something and then forgotten all about it.

Dusk became night. The stars were beginning to shine in the sky, and there was a chill to the early winter evening air.

"Let's go upstairs," Avner said, beginning to feel cold. "I'll ask my mother where my father is. Maybe she can call him and find out what the story is."

Avner's mother was busy putting the little ones to bed.

"Abba is very late today," Avner called out. "I can't understand it. He said that after school he would tell me all about the arrangement. Where is he now, Ima?"

Tali Shaked wasn't in a hurry to answer. "What's that you asked, Shlomo Dov?" she said, turning to her young son and patiently continuing the conversation Avner had interrupted.

"No, dear, the stars aren't cold," she said.

"But they don't have a blanket to cover themselves with," the young boy said, looking out the window.

"The dark sky is their blanket." Tali had said the first thing that came to her mind, hoping to satisfy his curiosity. "Now cover yourself with your blanket, and we'll say Shema together."

A few more minutes passed as they said Shema slowly, in a soft chant. Tali turned out the light, softly tiptoeing out of the room. She bumped into Avner, who had been standing by the door.

"Ima," he asked his mother, "where could Abba be at seven-thirty at night?"

"Where could he be?" Tali repeated. "What do you mean? He can be in a million and one places."

"I know," Avner said, following his mother into the kitchen. "But where is he now? Will he be home soon?"

Tali took a frying pan from the cupboard, greased it and put it on the fire. "What's that you asked?" she said, as though frying an egg required all her concentration. "Did you want something?"

"Yes, something very important," Avner continued. "Where is Abba's cell phone number?"

"There is a sticker with the number on the green telephone book," his mother replied. "But it won't help to call. Abba's cell phone is right here in the drawer."

"But Abba takes it with him to the hospital every day." Avner was surprised. "You mean he came home and went out again?"

"Something like that," his mother answered noncommittally as she flipped the egg. "Tomorrow afternoon, *im yirtzeh Hashem*, he'll be home. Try to manage alone meanwhile." His mother smiled, making it clear that she was counting on him to find a solution to his problem. "If you'll just think about it and try your best, I know you'll come up with something."

"We'll try," Avner acquiesced.

"I'm sure you'll do fine," Tali said encouragingly. "Are you coming in for supper?" she asked. "The omelets will be ready in a minute. The salad and bread are already on the table. How about some fresh orange juice?"

"No thanks, Ima," Avner answered. "You don't have to bother. I'll make some hot cocoa for the two of us when we finish eating."

Avner sensed that his mother was evading his questions. His fine-tuned antennae detected that there was something secret about his father's absence.

"Shuki," he said, turning to his friend, "let's wash."

"What about the work sheets?" Shuki whispered, the tension in his voice unmistakable. "Tomorrow is the last day for handing in this week's work sheets, and we haven't finished them yet. Where's the boy who is supposed to be helping us? What's with your father?"

"My father won't be coming home tonight," Avner replied, "and I haven't the faintest idea why. I can only guess that it's something especially urgent and important. Otherwise he would never have forgotten his promise."

"Is that how it is in your house?" Shuki asked hesitatingly. "Does this happen often? Does your father always go away on mysterious trips like this?"

"No, not at all," Avner answered. "Occasionally he comes home late from his hospital laboratory, but mysterious trips? I don't remember this ever happening before."

"Secret trips are really annoying," Shuki said. "I don't like it at all when there are secrets in our house. Sometimes my father gets busy with private telephone calls and doesn't even pay attention to me when I talk to him."

"Do you think your father always has to be available, exclusively for you?" Avner asked, flashing Shuki a sly grin.

"Well...yes," Shuki stammered. Shuki would have said

more, but he thought better of it, and dropped the subject. Yes, he wanted his father to give of himself completely for his sake. But was he willing to give of himself as well?

"So what's going to happen with those sheets?" Shuki asked again, the subject weighing heavily on his mind.

"We'll see after dinner," Avner replied, not at all fazed. "Anyway, we don't know what to do about the boy who's supposed to help us, because my father isn't here to tell us, so we'll have to come up with some other solution."

Shuki did not allow himself to answer. There was a lot that he would have liked to say to Avner, had their friendship not been so new. Besides, Shuki was too polite to insult Avner. But deep inside, he was amazed at Avner. How could he be so easygoing? Knowing what was at stake, how could he be so sure of himself?

Usually I look forward to these visits with Avner, and to staying over in Haifa, Shuki thought. *But today, of all days, I wanted to go home after cheder. Duvi is celebrating his first birthday, and even though Ima didn't plan a formal birthday party, I still wanted to be at home. I could have put Duvi on my shoulders and sung to him. Ima probably baked a delicious cake and prepared a special supper.*

Avner knew that I wanted to go home after school, but I stayed so we could go over the work sheets and learn together. It means so much to me to be among the finalists of the contest in the new cheder. I'm willing to put a lot of effort into it. So here I am, and the work sheets are incomplete. And Avner is not the least bit perturbed. Shuki gave him a glance. *If I were in his place, I would have been so embarrassed about the whole incident that I would have just wished the floor would open up so I could disappear.*

As if to verify Shuki's thoughts, Avner came over to him and put an encouraging arm around his shoulder. "Shuki, don't be so worried," he said. "Let's first eat something, and then we'll be able to concentrate better and to figure out what to do. Maybe my sister Drorit will be able to help us. I'm not sure, but it's a possibility. She always says that in Bais Yaakov the girls learn things even the boys don't know. The main thing is not to let it get us down."

Shuki smiled halfheartedly, even though Avner had described exactly how he felt at that moment — down in the dumps.

How is it that Avner — who is exactly the same age as I am — is so different? This new thought made Shuki feel even more miserable. *How is it that Avner is everything that I'm not?*

43

Blue-Brown

Beirut's skyline lit up the night as they neared. Menachem Shaked pressed his nose to the windowpane, trying to control his dizziness as the helicopter descended for a landing. Over the past years, he had visualized his first flight down to the minutest detail. Like many other things in life, the anticipation and the planning were more successful than the event itself.

Manny, unlike many of his contemporaries, had never ventured beyond the borders of Israel. *So now,* he smiled to himself, *I'm like all the others who go abroad, except I'm doing it under strange and mysterious circumstances!*

A half hour earlier they had boarded the helicopter at the Haifa airport, and in a few minutes they would be at the secret side entrance to the Beirut hospital. Menachem looked carefully at the two men who were with him: Dr. Ringel, one of the senior doctors at the hospital where he worked and an expert in his field, and next to him, Dr. Karp, his assistant and colleague. They sat in their seats totally relaxed, reading the daily news. One would think clandestine flights to Beirut were a daily occurrence and that the Mossad, Israel's secret service, called them out of important meetings at least once a week, telling them to put some other surgeon in charge and get on a helicopter.

"I think we should prepare the solution now," Dr. Ringel suggested to Menachem Shaked, head of the biochemical laboratories. "When we see our friend, we will be able to dilute the solution as necessary. But let's be prepared with the maximum strength."

Menachem took a small bottle from his bag and gently shook it. "The solution is ready. Five drops from this bottle in each eye. The yellow solution is to neutralize the negative effects of too much of the poisoned chemical being sprayed into his eye. Immediately following that, he'll need an injection to clean out his bloodstream quickly. If his condition warrants it, we may have to put some of the yellow solution into the IV to stop the poison from spreading through his body."

The helicopter descended deep into the thick black velvet night. Menachem looked at the lights below and the twinkling stars that seemed to encourage them from above. *How small and powerless is a human being*, he thought for a split second. *With a wave of His Hand, Hashem can create millions of sparkling lights.*

In his mind's eye he saw the two anonymous men who were assigned to confront the Arab terrorist. "What bad luck," Dr. Ringel said, when he heard a detailed description of all that had gone wrong. "It's like being chosen to be the first ever to perform a heart-transplant operation." He was trying to describe the intensity of his feelings to Dr. Karp, and his eyes were burning brightly. "You have this once-in-a-lifetime opportunity to become famous, and the whole world is looking at you and waiting with bated breath. But your hand is shaking and you fail. Your patient dies — and your chance of a lifetime dies with him. What a lost opportunity!"

Dr. Ringel vividly imagined the shaking hand. Dr. Karp's

Blue-Brown ✦ 303

thoughts were absorbed in the longer-than-necessary spray of the aerosol bottle, the drop that was one too many. But Menachem also saw the Hand of the One Above. It was He Who had guided the two drops as they were sprayed, followed by that third fateful drop. And it was Hashem Who was accompanying them now into the lion's den and Who would help them return safely home together with the others being held captive deep in Syria.

"Another thing before we go." Dr. Ringel opened his brown bag. "An opportunity like this doesn't come along every day. Today this undercover operation must be kept top secret. But a few years from now — and in a country like ours it may be only a matter of a few months or days — a person can make a lot of money from an incident like this." With a flip of his wrist, Dr. Ringel removed a silver pen from a long case. "This looks like an ordinary pen, doesn't it?" he asked, turning to the two as he clipped the pen inside his jacket pocket. "Not any different from your green pen, Dr. Karp, just a bit more elegant, as befits the occasion.

"This pen," Dr. Ringel went on as he carefully pressed the pen against his jacket, "will record the historic event in which we are to have the starring roles. This is a small movie camera," he caressed the pen lovingly, "a personal gift from one of my wealthy patients. It is worth thousands of dollars, and finally I have the opportunity to put it to good use. Not bad, eh?"

Dr. Karp smiled one of his pasted-on smiles, the kind he often flashed at his boss as a way of flattering him. Menachem Shaked was skeptical. The haughtiness of the senior doctors was repulsive. Unbidden, the image of the arrogant Dr. Shilon came to mind along with his son Avner's limp. He was grateful to Hashem that he no longer had to work under them. He was happy his job was in the laboratory, where the sharp smell of medications were what he contended with daily. In some other locations in the hospital, it was the smell of money that dominated.

Several minutes later, the three were standing inside a closed room, where they sensed the unfriendly stares of two security guards. The armed guards, dressed in the uniform of Beirut's police force, stood frozen in place. Near the hospital stretcher, on which lay the unconscious Rafik Jamil, stood two men dressed in white, coldly greeting the Israeli medical team. The two doctors from Damascus scrutinized Menachem suspiciously as he brought his equipment out of his medical bag. They clung to both sides of the stretcher as if they owned the patient lying there. Since they had no medical knowledge whatsoever about the poisonous substance that had been sprayed into Jamil's eyes, they couldn't really know anything about the treatment now being administered to counteract its lethal effect.

"Move over," Dr. Ringel commanded in a stern voice that bespoke three decades of experience. "If you want me to treat this patient, you have to make room."

The two stepped back three paces, continuing to follow intently every move of the senior doctor. The doctor examined the man lying on the stretcher quickly but thoroughly and carefully read the medical reports handed to him.

"I am now going to inject five drops of the medication from this bottle into each eye," Dr. Ringel said by way of explanation to all those standing around him. "Within ten minutes the medication will take effect" — he shot a look at the wall clock — "and you will begin to see the first signs of life."

With a dramatic movement of his hand, Dr. Ringel raised the small bottle and brought it close to Jamil's eyes. "Open his eyes," the doctor ordered Menachem. Menachem stepped forward, throwing a quick glance at the pen in the doctor's breast pocket. He stood at the head of the bed and, as Jamil lay in a state of total unconsciousness, pried open the closed eyelids.

"Is this a result of the poisonous spray?" Menachem asked aloud, a surprised look on his face.

"This is Blue-Brown," said Dr. Ringel tersely. "Each eye is a different color. One is blue and the other is brown. Keep the eyelids open. I am ready to insert the drops." Then, "What's the matter with you?" he hissed at Menachem. "Why are your hands shaking?"

He turned to his colleague. "Dr. Karp, come here," he commanded, giving the chalk-faced Menachem a stern look. "Since when does a professional medical man get so upset when he sees eyes of two different colors?"

Dr. Karp held Jamil's eyelids open as Dr. Ringel slowly dropped in the liquid, drop by drop. Menachem saw what they were doing, but the figures of the doctors became hazy as he focused on the two eyes, one blue and one brown. He saw there another pair of eyes, eyes without the harsh, bloodthirsty look of the two pupils he was staring into right now. The other eyes were big, wide, full of the desire to live — to live a true life, the kind of life that Menachem himself had discovered and had been living in recent years.

He saw those eyes in his mind, pleading with him, almost accusing him. *Where are you?* they cried out. *Where are you, all of you? Why aren't you doing more for me, so that I can see my loved ones? Why aren't you trying harder, so that I can escape this darkness and see the light?*

They were Yossi's eyes. Not many people knew, for Yossi Nir wore dark glasses. The hot summer sun was enough of a reason to wear them, but that wasn't the real purpose. The dark glasses served as a shield behind which his eyes — one brown and the other a deep blue — were free to probe.

Menachem now remembered the first time Yossi had come into his office. "I've been having excruciating headaches lately," he complained.

Menachem, an army medic in those days, studied the pale face before him. *No wonder,* he wanted to say, *with all the rigorous army drills by day and the evening exercises by night. What do you expect?*

Yossi was a serious fellow who thought a great deal about the meaning of life. He was torn apart with doubt. Unlike other young men his age, for him life wasn't just a picnic. He took life seriously and wanted to live each day with meaning. Was it any wonder that his cheeks were so pale and his head ached?

Menachem asked Yossi to take off his glasses so he could do a routine eye exam. It was then that he saw, for the first time in his life, someone whose eyes were each a different color. Not green and brown, which are closely related pigmentations, but brown and blue — two totally different, unrelated colors.

Oh, Yossi, his heart now cried out, *we're all torn apart. Here I am now in this cursed country that swallowed you up, never to return. Like me, you set out on a mission for the sake of others, but you were fated not to come back.*

Menachem felt Yossi's two eyes staring at him. The warm brown of mother earth and the blue of the sky, ever soaring upward. What have those eyes seen in the past fifteen years? Could they still see? Did they still have the will to see?

Menachem felt a pair of angry eyes staring at him. They weren't Yossi's eyes, exuding warmth and wisdom. It was the cold, steel stare of Dr. Ringel, wondering why Menachem was standing there stiffly, his mind in a different world.

Menachem coughed lightly. He was still staring at the patient's pupils as they slowly returned to normal size following the application of the eyedrops. "It is a very unusual phenomenon," he said to all those present. "Medical literature has practically no information about it," he explained, remembering how astonished he was when he first saw Yossi's eyes. He had searched through his medical journals, surprised to find how little was known about this most unusual occurrence. Yet here, out of nowhere, was another set of the same eyes.

The tension in the room suddenly eased a bit. As the patient showed signs of life, the suspicious Syrian doctors relaxed and began to trust the Israeli delegation treating Jamil.

"Are you referring to his different-colored pupils?" one of the Syrian doctors asked. "It isn't that unusual. Why, only two years ago I saw the exact same thing. It was in the eyes of one of your soldiers..."

44
Words That Hurt, Words That Heal

The dry, salty omelet stuck in Shuki's throat, and he searched the table for something to drink. He was surprised to find himself longing for his mother's hot cocoa. As far back as he could remember, his mother would say, "Cocoa, Shuki?" Always the same words, always the same sweet, hot cocoa prepared with love, just the way he liked it, cocoa that only a mother knows how to prepare.

Avner's voice broke into his thoughts. "Come on, let's make some cocoa. Do you like it hot?"

Shuki burst out laughing. "You know what? Just this second I was thinking of the hot cocoa my mother makes me every day before I leave the house in the morning and before I go to bed at night! "

"You've been here before," Avner exclaimed in surprise. "Why didn't you ever ask me for cocoa? Whenever I asked you what you usually drink you just shrugged your shoulders and said it didn't matter, that you drink anything — or nothing. What did you think — that we don't have milk or cocoa in our house?"

Shuki said nothing. He couldn't decide whether it was good manners that made him extra polite in a strange house or a chronic bashfulness. While Shuki stood quietly deciding whether or not to berate himself for his shyness, Avner filled the electric kettle with water and took out the ingredients to prepare two cups of hot cocoa.

"You are cordially invited to prepare cocoa according to your own personal tastes," Avner declared. "I'm all for homemade cocoa the way you like to drink it." Noticing Shuki's hesitation, he added, "Go ahead — take all the sugar you want and make it just the way you're used to drinking it."

But Shuki made no move. "I have no idea what I like or how it's made," he said finally, smiling sheepishly.

"But you just said you drink cocoa twice a day — and you still don't know how to make it?"

"I drink it. I don't make it," Shuki explained. "My mother always prepares it for me."

"Boy, are you spoiled." Avner's smile was friendly. He quickly prepared two cups of cocoa and put them on the table. "You're so spoiled you don't even realize how spoiled you are!"

With that, Avner gulped down his cocoa, *bentched* and went to the phone. Suddenly he was all business. "We have to do something about the work sheets for the general Jewish knowledge contest," he said to Shuki. "I'll call Yonasan or Shimmy. Neither of them lives too far from here, and they're both great students. If they haven't finished the work sheets yet, we can go over to one of their houses and do it together."

Shuki liked the idea and nodded his approval. Then he began to *bentch*, saying each word slowly and with careful concentration. Afterward, while Avner sat by the phone trying to get through to one of the boys, Shuki cleared the table and deposited their dishes in the sink.

Avner's great idea was proving difficult to arrange since the lines were busy in both Yonasan's and Shimmy's homes. Finally, he got through to Yonasan.

"You've already finished both pages?" Shuki heard Avner say in a disappointed voice. "Too bad. No, we don't want to copy your answers. Thanks. Maybe if we don't think of anything else, we'll call you up later for help. Thanks anyway. Goodbye."

Avner hung up and immediately tried Shimmy's line again. He was relieved when Shimmy answered right away this time.

"Great," Shuki listened to Avner say, "you haven't finished either? What do you say we do it together? Can we come over to you? Wonderful. Your father's going to help you? Terrific! This week's work sheets are really hard. I was able to fill in a lot of the answers, but there are still a bunch I couldn't figure out. So when should we come? A quarter of an hour? Okay. Be seeing you."

"You see?" Avner was ecstatic, and he pumped Shuki's hand. "Things really do fall in place."

"Sorry, this arrangement is not for me," Shuki said quietly.

"Why not? What's the matter?" Avner was taken by surprise. "I specifically mentioned the two of us. Shimmy invited you just like he invited me."

"He can invite whoever he wants." Shuki's voice sounded as if it was coming from far away. "That doesn't mean I have to accept his invitation."

"We're not talking about any obligations here," Avner responded in confusion as they headed for his room. "I told you before that I was going to call him so we could all do the homework together, and you agreed!"

"I agreed to do the homework with him," Shuki explained. "I never agreed to do it with his father. That's a different matter altogether."

"Oh," was all Avner could say as he thought about Shuki's last comment. He certainly didn't agree with his friend, but here it was again — that gap between the way they looked at things. He sure couldn't hope to bridge it in sixty seconds.

"But even Shimmy said the work sheets this week were especially tough," Avner finally continued. "You know he's one of the top students in the class, and even he couldn't fill in the answers without help. Listen, let's just go over to his house, and the three of us will do it together with his father's help and finish it fast. What could be the problem with that?"

"There wouldn't be any problem at all, if we would have arranged it in advance," Shuki declared. "But I'm not going to a friend's house on the spur of the moment to have his father help me. I didn't have to come here for that. I have a father too, don't I?"

"Sure," Avner replied placatingly, "but what does that have to do with it? You're here now, and your father's not. We thought we'd be able to manage on our own, but it didn't work out the way we planned. It's no secret that my father wouldn't have been able to help us with the work even if he were here — but now we found another solution. So what's wrong with going over to Shimmy's to prepare the sheets?"

Is there really something wrong with it? Shuki asked himself. The way Avner put it, everything seemed so simple and practical that Shuki couldn't understand why he had been against it in the first place. He couldn't come up with a quick answer because he just didn't have Avner's persuasive abilities. But something told him that going to Shimmy's house was not what he ought to be doing. He didn't feel like sitting in Shimmy's living room together with his father.

"You go," Shuki suggested. "I'll stay here, and when you get back you'll tell me what Shimmy's father explained to you. That way I'll be able to get through the questions without going."

"I suppose we could do that," Avner said, "but what a waste. Shimmy's father will explain the work better than I can. You'll understand it much better if you hear it from him, and you'll remember the answers better. You have nothing to be ashamed of, I promise you." Avner put everything he had into trying to convince Shuki. "Shimmy is a real nice kid. He's not the type who would go and tell the whole class that his father helped you, if that's what you're afraid of."

Shuki only shrugged.

"Okay," Avner gave in with a shrug. "If you don't want to come, I won't pressure you. If you'd rather stay, then stay. I'll close the bedroom door so nobody will bother you. You can have all the privacy you want. You can read any of the books on the shelf, and I'll put out some of my photo albums so you won't be bored." Avner took down four big albums and put them on the bed.

"I'd better get going now," Avner continued awkwardly. "It's getting late. Shimmy lives only a block away, but you know I can't walk so fast. A short distance like that can take me over ten minutes." He stood, hesitating for another minute.

"Hey" — Avner gave it one more try — "how about coming along with me anyway? I really don't like walking alone. When I'm by myself people seem to notice my limp more, and they stare. It's not that I mind so much when they stare, it's just nicer if I can avoid it. Of course, that's no reason for you to feel you have to join me. It's worth coming for your own sake — so you'll be better prepared for the contest."

Avner's simple, matter-of-fact words made Shuki start to unbend. Just as Avner had said, Shuki wasn't going in order to help him — he knew Avner didn't need his help. But there was something in the mature and candid way that Avner looked at reality that broke through the thick layer of protective armor that surrounded Shuki and that he tried to hide behind. He couldn't argue with Avner that the questions were complicated, and there was no one at Avner's house who could help them, so why not accept help from Shimmy's father?

For once, Shuki decided, he would be mature like Avner and

act with confidence. He would go. "All right," Shuki announced, knocking two albums onto the floor as he stood up, "you win. I'm coming."

The darkness of the sky and the soft rustling of the wind accompanied them as they walked side by side. There was something very tranquil about the enveloping night and their slow progress. The two boys walked together in silence, engrossed in thought.

Who says that people have to talk just because they're together? The trees sway in silence, the stars move in harmony. Words are only one way of communicating. There are many other ways, and many of them are no less meaningful than words.

Avner began to hum a melody they had learned the week before in cheder, and Shuki hummed along. Soft notes, the movement of feet — slow, even a bit cumbersome, but their hearts beat in unison.

Passersby may have heard the soft humming of the soulful melody. Maybe they noticed the boy whose walk was somewhat different, the boy whose right leg dragged, thought Shuki, or maybe they were too absorbed in their own thoughts to notice. Did some people shake their heads in pity? "Such a nice boy but look how he limps," they might be thinking. Or did they already know Avner from the neighborhood?

It mattered not at all what others thought, Shuki concluded. The two boys walked along the sidewalk, their hearts overflowing. And when the heart is full, when it is filled with contentment, it doesn't flutter like a leaf in the wind. Let people stare, let them shake their heads and say whatever they want. When you are at peace with yourself and you have faith in Hashem, what others say can't change anything for you. You are strong, steady and sure of yourself.

"Hi!"

They almost bumped into their classmates, Gedalia and Pinchas, heading in the other direction.

"What are you so engrossed in, that you didn't even notice us right here in front of you?" Gedalia asked with a smile.

Shuki and Avner exchanged glances. You didn't have to be a genius to sense that it wasn't some small, passing secret that bound the two. There was a strong connection between them. *When did all this happen?* Gedalia wondered. *When did their animosity turn into such deep friendship?* Those were his thoughts, but he spoke not a word about them.

"I see you're carrying your green folder too," Pinchas said, spying the thin binder peeking out of the plastic bag they were holding. "I'm just on my way home from shul. I've been sitting there with my father almost every night for weeks, going over the work sheets again and again. He tells me which *sefarim* to look into, and I find the answers there myself."

"I finished the work sheets on *motzaei Shabbos*," Gedalia added. "My older brother Yisrael was home from yeshiva for Shabbos and he helped me. He was really impressed with the level of the questions. He said they were on par with yeshiva-type learning!

"So where are you headed?" Gedalia asked.

"To Shimmy Cohen," Avner replied. "We finished some of the work sheets, but we ran into trouble with questions in the third part. There were no hints given where to look up the answers."

"Those really were tough questions," Pinchas agreed. "Good luck."

"Thanks. *Be'ezras Hashem*, we'll manage," Avner answered. "Shimmy's father will be helping us—"

Avner stopped in midstream and bit his lip, but he was too late. The words were out.

"Well, it's getting late," he said at last. The two friends waved goodbye to Avner and Shuki. "See you tomorrow."

Avner turned to Shuki and saw that the happy expression on his face was gone.

"I'm really sorry." How Avner regretted his slip of the tongue! "I don't know how that got out."

He looked at Shuki's pale face, which seemed even whiter against the black of the night. The darkness was no longer friendly as before. Now it was cold and embarrassing, as if it were trying to cover the unpleasant secret that Avner's slip had disclosed.

"I'm so sorry," Avner repeated, grasping Shuki's arm.

Shuki stared at him, a stubborn, angry look in his eyes.

Avner was scared Shuki would get mad at him — and with good reason. Avner realized that this time he was in the wrong. He could be as open as he pleased when it came to matters that concerned only himself, but he should never have spoken so openly when Shuki was involved, especially knowing what a sensitive subject it was for Shuki.

But his friend surprised him with words far gentler than what he had expected.

"It was nothing, Avner," Shuki said slowly. "Really."

"Then why are you so pale?"

"Oh, that? Don't pay any attention to that. I can't help it. When something embarrasses me, I just turn pale. But what you said was the right thing to say. What's so wrong about being helped by Shimmy's father? If I would have had the nerve," Shuki admitted, "I'd have said it myself. But you know me. I guess I'm made of putty."

"Not at all," Avner was quick to respond, and he meant every word he said. "You're made of top-notch stuff — but that stuff is just a little bit fragile. If you'll reinforce it with a bit of confidence and a different way of looking at things, you'll amaze everyone! You just proved you're on the right track."

As they walked up the steps to the Cohen apartment, the

gift of silence blessed them once again, as Avner's words echoed in Shuki's heart.

If Avner says so, Shuki thought, *maybe it's true.*

Avner looked at the boy climbing the three flights of stairs beside him, his chin set in determination, and he knew what a special friend he had found in Shuki.

45
Solution in Sight

Menachem Shaked locked the door to the room securely. The room was pitch dark and somewhat gloomy when small dots began to appear on the white screen that hung on the wall. Menachem scraped his chair across the floor and watched tensely as the undecipherable dots turned into clear figures. There was Dr. Karp wearing his smoothly pressed white coat, and there he was scrutinizing the test tube in his hands.

As the figures played across the screen, Menachem leaned forward, trying to decipher the fragmented conversation. *Dr. Ringel's wealthy patient gave him a gift that's not as impressive as he imagined*, Menachem thought ironically. It's not likely that Dr. Ringel will be able to make much money from this blurry video. However, for Yossi, this film — fuzzy as it is — may be the opportunity of a lifetime. Literally.

Menachem saw the terrorist Jamil's face fill the screen. Dr. Ringel had stood right by his side, Menachem remembered, so the pen was able to video the patient's face directly. His features seemed even more menacing when they covered the entire screen, and Menachem again felt the same disgust that had overcome him when he had stood next to the terrorist.

"Open his eyes," Menachem heard Dr. Ringel commanding, although his voice as recorded by the pen came out sounding hoarse. He now saw his own two hands taking hold of Jamil's eyelids, and there in the film were the two eyes that had brought back the burning memories: one blue and one brown.

The next frames were of Menachem's face as Dr. Ringel turned toward him. Even though the colors were blurred and out of focus, his paleness was obvious. His darting eyes, uncontrollable blinking and trembling lips reflected the waves of memories and longing.

Although the screen was not a mirror, it showed a realistic picture of how Menachem, sitting tensely on the living-room chair in his home watching the film, looked that very moment. In another minute the screen would show him the real evidence; he would hear the words that were spoken in the hospital room so that he could analyze them down to the last detail. He would be face-to-face with the truth, with the unadulterated reality, without the embellishments of imagination or emotional overtones.

Here it is — now! Menachem stood up as if trying to enter the picture on the screen, wanting to ask more questions and to demand answers. Would the tension never end?

"It is a very unusual phenomenon," Menachem clearly heard his own voice. "Medical literature has practically no information on it."

After an interlude of silence, the Syrian doctor moved his lips. "Are you referring to his different-colored pupils?" Menachem saw the magnificent mustache move on the screen. "It isn't that unusual."

Menachem's hands balled into fists. Was he imagining the loud echoes of the words in the closed room? "Why, only two years ago I saw the exact same thing. It was in the eyes of one of your soldiers."

That was it! The words of the Arab doctor spoke for themselves. It had not been his imagination blowing the proof out of proportion. The sad reality stood behind those words.

He watched the next few minutes of the video as if seeing it for the first time. Is that how Jamil rolled his eyes when the medication began to take effect? At what exact moment did Jamil lift his head? How could it be that Menachem had not noticed Dr. Ringel and Dr. Karp trying to steady the wild pattern of the patient's heartbeat? He must have been in a different world at that moment, somewhere in the world of brown and blue. The words of the Syrian doctor had echoed in his ears again and again until he realized that the words could have only one implication, an implication that had almost put an end to his hopes. Almost.

There in the hospital, after he had finally digested the words of the Arab doctor, Menachem suddenly realized what an important opportunity he had at that moment. There, not three paces away from him, stood a man who held the key to Yossi's whereabouts. It was not only the end of the thread that he held, but the entire thread, the thread that would lead to the longed-for solution. Fifteen and a half years of unfathomable mystery were about to come to an end in that room. At that very moment.

Menachem's heart beat faster. He uttered a silent prayer, and his soul called out pleadingly, "Only You can put the right words in my mouth, only You can turn the storm raging within me into an island of tranquility...only You."

On the screen, he watched his lips move before he uttered the words, "Two years ago, you say?" The conversation continued in a relaxed manner, despite the fact that Menachem's mind was running in circles. "Where is he today?" Fortunately, his words had come out coherently.

"Who?" asked the Syrian doctor nonchalantly.

"The Israeli soldier you just mentioned," Menachem said, wringing his hands nervously. "The one whose eyes are two different colors."

"Soldier? Did I say a soldier?" The doctor spoke in a normal conversational tone. "I meant he was 'one of yours.' I think it was someone involved with the Syrian Jewish community. Something like that."

"Where is he?" Menachem repeated the question.

"Where is he today?" the doctor echoed. "How should I know? I wasn't that interested in him. His eyes didn't really make an impression on me. They're not so unusual at all. Look, lying before us is another person with each eye of a different color. What's the big deal?"

"Where was he two years ago?" Menachem persisted.

"I have no idea," the doctor replied. "I told you I had no interest in him. I certainly wouldn't have bothered to keep track of him."

"But you saw him two years ago?" Menachem pressed.

"Did I say two years ago?" the doctor asked. "I didn't mean exactly two years. I meant several years ago. I don't remember exactly. It may have been three, five, maybe even seven or ten. It was during the past twenty years for sure."

"Where did you see him?" Menachem asked, unrelenting.

"What else do you expect me to remember?" the doctor asked. "I told you I didn't consider the incident important. I remember that he had two different eyes. Maybe it wasn't exactly blue and brown, maybe it was green and brown, or two different shades of blue. Yes, come to think of it, that's what it was. One eye was deep blue and the other a lighter kind of gray." His voice had the excitement of someone who finally remembered details. "It was quite interesting, seeing one eye dark blue and the second sort of grayish. But, of course, it wasn't something I would have written up in a medical report."

Here a long laugh was heard, as if signaling the end of the conversation. "So how's our patient?" the doctor asked as he walked toward the other end of the room. "Any improvement?"

The pictures flickered on the screen for another ten minutes, but Menachem didn't see a thing. Eventually he walked over to the projector and, with a whirring sound, the machine went off. There was nothing else of interest to him. Jamil received his treatment, they spent another two days in Beirut to keep their eye on the patient and then returned home to Israel.

Menachem was sworn to secrecy. "It's as if nothing happened," Dr. Ringel had told him when they returned to Israel, repeating the words of the head of the Israeli intelligence service. "In fact, forget the 'as if,'" he emphasized after a moment. "Nothing happened."

The sharp look he gave Menachem was a strong enough warning. There are other ways, not all of them pleasant, of making sure that secrets don't get out. Menachem wasn't about to take any chances.

Menachem glanced at the headlines in the newspaper that lay on the couch. Everything was normal. There was not a single word about the incident. Rafik Jamil was walking around Lebanon on his own two feet, still heading the Hizbullah terrorist organization, as if the best brains had never thought up "Operation Tears," as if two secret agents had never entered the lions' den, as if they hadn't gotten caught in the enemy's jaws, as if...

Jamil was never attacked, and he was never brought back to life. Nothing happened.

Menachem watched the videocassette rewinding itself, and waited. It wasn't safe for it to remain in Dr. Ringel's hands. Dr. Ringel was anxious to cash in on this video, to publicize the adventure to a population hungry for such information. But the film had a vital purpose right now, this minute — this second, in fact. But where?

Menachem wondered what he could do. Who could he interest in the film? To whom would he be allowed to show it at this stage?

He turned on the video again, fast-forwarding to the middle, to hear once more the fateful words.

"It isn't that unusual." The voice was loud and clear. "Why, only two years ago I saw the exact same thing. It was the eyes of one of your soldiers...."

One didn't need a lie detector to disclose the lies and pinpoint the one true sentence.

Menachem looked at the Syrian doctor he had caught contradicting himself at every turn, and he wished that the doctor were there right now so he could confront him. How he wished that he could somehow pin the doctor to the wall, in every sense.

Menachem took out his cell phone. Maybe he would contact the Mossad directly. Perhaps if they saw the video they would see things differently and would involve the proper parties. He began to dial, then reconsidered and quickly disconnected before he completed the call.

Something in the look of the Syrian doctor on the screen made him have second thoughts. It was a look of fear mingled with hatred. *The doctor is probably suspicious now.* Every step the Israelis took at this point would meet with a thick wall of resistance. It was best to wait a while. *Let's pretend we accept his feeble explanations. Let them think that we consider it just a coincidence now buried. One day we will be able to confront them with full proof, and place it directly before their eyes.*

Yet Menachem was impatient. Many would say, You waited over fifteen years, you can wait another few weeks. But Menachem felt, *We waited over fifteen years, can we afford to wait another few weeks or months? How can we sit idly by, knowing that the yearnings and hopes during all those sleepless nights are so close to being fulfilled? Shouldn't we try to grab at this opportunity with a thousand hands? How can we push it off for even one more day?*

From all over the country, there are people who have been forgotten. Their lives are one big question mark, a desperate cry for help. Can this one video lead to an answer?

First Steps

In one corner of the Haifa cheder's playground, boys were running happily after a yellow ball. At the other end, a group stood arguing loudly, almost coming to blows. In the center of the boisterous group stood a boy talking excitedly, as dozens of schoolmates listened intently. Over by the stone wall one student stood alone, his whole day ruined by this one recess.

Leaning against the green rail fence, Avner and Shuki were oblivious to all the goings-on. They sauntered to and fro, as if they were walking along the beach, their steps absorbed by the soft warm sand, with only the whooshing sounds of the waves to accompany their conversation.

"His name is Tuvia Weiner," Avner said, his eyes shining brightly, "and he's an excellent *bachur*. My father is paying him a lot for every hour of learning and agrees to have you join me for the sessions. Even Tuvia thinks it's a great idea. He says you'll be an asset. If we work together with him, then later on we'll be able to go over the Gemara together on our own. So what do you say — are you willing to stay over tonight?"

Shuki didn't answer right away. The words hung limply on the tip of his tongue, begging to be uttered, but held back as if by force. Avner continued to look at him with that special understanding look that Shuki so loved. But Shuki lowered his eyes, finding himself in a predicament.

"You always hesitate," Avner admonished. "You didn't want to go to Shimmy Cohen either, remember? But in the end, you were the one who suggested we go back a second time. So what do you say? Will you stay tonight?" This time Avner's tone demanded an answer.

Shuki didn't hear the patter of running feet, nor did he hear the hands clapping, applauding the winning team. He was oblivious to the arguments of the schoolboys around him. The sounds of laughter were so distant, they may as well have come from another planet. All that was happening in the big school yard, and the multitude of boys there, were nothing more than a silent sheet, a backdrop of mute scenery. Four words echoed in his ears, the four words that hung in the balance: Will you stay tonight?

The recess bell, which put an end to thirty minutes of freedom, released Shuki from the pressure of indecision that weighed heavily, mercilessly, on his mind. This reprieve would give him more time to deliberate what he ought to do.

Oh, how easy life can be when you take things as they come, without agonizing over every step along the way. But then life wouldn't be its truest, his father had told him once, when speaking about something else entirely. When you're merely a bystander, you see things superficially. If you're going to live life genuinely, though, at its deepest, you have to pay a price.

Shuki so wanted to say yes, to spend the night at Avner's welcoming home and talk till the wee hours of the morning; to walk the streets of Haifa together in the cool evening and review the topics in preparation for the forthcoming contest.

Learning with Avner and Tuvia could be a wonderful experience that would be enriching in many ways.

How could he compare studying at home alone — at a desk in a boring room, with his baby brother gurgling in the background — to a lively learning session with the three of them, with the sweet music of *niggunim* playing on the cassette? They were two different worlds.

Two different worlds, and both of them were his, both of them in his hands. But what about that other world, that world that was so close, while so very distant? Wasn't he obligated to open a crack in the door to that closed world, the world of his father?

Shuki again felt the pain in his heart as he recalled the conversation with his father.

"Hello, Yehoshua," his father had greeted him that Friday afternoon when he arrived home from cheder. "How is my Haifa boy?"

Shuki blushed and wished he could crawl into a corner.

"We sent you to the cheder in Haifa," his father continued, a broad smile — too broad — on his face. "But you've found yourself a home there, too, haven't you?"

Shuki again blushed in embarrassment, his face turning a deep red.

"We have all kinds of projects at this cheder," Shuki answered his father apologetically. "There are contests and quizzes, and all of them are really hard. When I stay in Haifa overnight, I get help. It's like…umm…going away to learn Torah."

"Of course, Shuki'le," his father said, as he placed his hand on Shuki's shoulder, still smiling. "No doubt about it. All our hopes and prayers are to that very end. All our wishes, all our desires are for the day you will go away to yeshiva. As difficult as it may be for us, it's what we want.

"It's just that you're starting a bit early, Yehoshua," his father explained, "that's all. If you get help there, and it helps your progress, we're willing to let you go for even another week!"

His father threw him a wink, the special signal that just the two of them understood, trying to lighten the earnestness of his last words.

Shuki's color began slowly to return to normal. The easygoing conversation that followed, about Haifa and what was happening at school, pushed the embarrassing moment away to a corner of his mind. It was only later, when each of them went off to prepare for Shabbos, that Shuki passed by the living-room door, which was slightly ajar.

Abba stood in the center of the room holding a big Gemara. The binding was sparkling new, the pages smooth and white. There were some *sefarim* in the large bookcase that Abba was able to understand with a great deal of effort. The Gemara was not one of them.

Shuki's father hugged the Gemara tightly in his arms. He fingered the brown leather binding lovingly. Shuki took a step back, but his eyes continued to follow his father's every move. He saw his father pace back and forth distraughtly, his eyes like two burning torches. Then suddenly, his father's expression changed, and his big eyes looked suspiciously moist. To Shuki it seemed that two polished diamonds sparkled with thousands of hues. Standing by the door, overcome with emotion, Shuki could clearly see two tears drop onto the dark binding, leaving a water stain on the leather.

Shuki's father put the Gemara on the dining-room table and opened it. He stared at the page in front of his eyes and began to cry. A muted sound reached Shuki's ears, a voiceless, silent sobbing. Now Shuki's heart was also crying; hot tears pierced deep into Shuki's soul like a searing burn. Shuki didn't hear the words, he didn't hear the cry. His father didn't realize that his latent well of tears lay ready to burst forth with terrific force at the first opportunity.

Hashem, he beseeched, *I left my father's house to come to You, to live a Torah life, to live a life of truth. My home is a living sefer Torah, one filled with sefarim with embossed golden letters that are more precious than pure gold. My son is also searching, but I, his loving father, can't even give him a helping hand.*

Is there no chance for me in this world? Yitzchak's heart cried out bitterly. *Am I destined to touch superficially only the very tip of Your wisdom, and not feel it in the depths of my soul? Will I ever be able to taste the sweetness of Torah, and most of all, to pass it on, with my own two hands, to my son?*

Shuki didn't hear the words, but he saw the tears, tears that dropped onto the leather binding and created two winding paths; tears that were absorbed by the large pages, replacing the smell of fresh ink with the fragrance of pure tears. Tears can etch deep lines on leather bindings and leave their indelible signature on the holy words. Tears can accomplish a great deal. How much more can they accomplish when they are the tears of a son crying to his Father Above, tears of a father for his son — and tears of a father, as his son looks on.

With Avner waiting for an answer, Shuki shook his head, as if trying to dispel the scene before his eyes. What would he say to him? His father had consented to his staying in Haifa to get ahead with his learning, but couldn't he get the same kind of help in Arazim, near his own home? Hadn't his father once suggested that Shuki speak to the Rav or one of the *avreichim* and ask them to help from time to time when he had difficulties? But it was he, Shuki, who had rejected the offer, causing his father such great pain. His father had never made the offer again.

It's time to think about Abba's world, Shuki said to himself, aware that he was using Avner's exact words. But Shuki wasn't aware that by doing so he would be building not only his father's world, but his own world as well.

He would go home and ask his father to find him someone to learn with, he decided, and then, in the big living room in their own home, the voice of Torah would be heard reviewing the Gemara each night. Maybe he'd have a question that would direct him to the very Gemara that Abba had held in his hand. Perhaps he would have to look up the answer on the very pages

First Steps ✦ 327

that had been dampened with tears.

He knew he wouldn't have to stifle a yawn, nor would he get up to walk lazily into the kitchen to find something sweet to eat.

His father couldn't help Shuki's brain deal with difficult passages, but he could help Shuki's heart struggle with obstacles so that he would not despair. Overcoming the difficulties that present themselves when trying to open one's heart to Torah study is more challenging by far than the difficulties that the learning presents.

"So, what do you say? Will you stay over tonight?" Avner asked Shuki at the end of the lesson, his voice filled with confidence. Avner was sure that, as always, Shuki would ultimately do what he wanted.

"Nope." Shuki looked straight into Avner's eyes, not trying to beat around the bush. "Thank you, really, for your good intentions, but I'll be going home."

Avner wanted to try to persuade Shuki to change his mind, to give him another reason or two. After all, Shuki was a softie, and it was so easy to get him to come around. You just had to pluck on the right strings.

But then Avner's jaw dropped. There was something different this time, something that Avner had never seen before, a new look in Shuki's eyes. It was a look of confidence and strong-mindedness, of knowing the rightness of his path. Before him now stood not merely another ball for others to toss as they pleased, but a young boy stepping firmly ahead along a newly trodden path. There was a lot for Shuki to learn from the boy who was standing at his side. But the ultimate path, the path that he would follow for the rest of his life, he himself, with *siyatta diShamaya*, would have to pave.

Avner, respecting his friend's wishes, did not say a word. Shuki wasn't about to plod along after him any longer, following him blindly. He was now taking his first steps down his own path, walking toward his father.

47
A Lot to Talk About

"Do you understand what the Gemara is saying?" Avner asked Shuki. "Tuvia Weiner, the *bachur* that I learn with at night, explained it to me. He said that—"

"Yes, I know," Shuki answered, his face lighting up. "I also had a hard time understanding this Gemara at first but then Aryeh's father explained it to me."

Aryeh Segal was a former classmate of Shuki's in Arazim. Shuki's father had spoken to Rabbi Segal, who was happy to give an hour or so of his time to learn with Shuki.

"Rabbi Segal said he was willing to learn with me any time I need help," Shuki continued, "but, now *baruch Hashem*, I'm managing on my own. When I run into something that isn't clear, I make a note of it so that I won't forget. Next week, I'll ask Aryeh's father all the questions I've written down.

"Now it's your turn to test me," Shuki reminded Avner, looking at his watch, anxious not to waste even a minute.

"Are you studying for the contest?" Menachem Shaked asked as he entered the room and spotted the green folders strewn over the table.

Avner nodded. His father took one of the folders, sat down in his easy chair and studied the pages with interest.

"I see you have not only the questions written here but the answers too," Avner's father remarked. "So, what do you say to my testing you fellows?"

Shuki shrugged his shoulders bashfully. For once, Avner's father seemed to have plenty of time. Shuki couldn't remember ever having seen him so relaxed, sitting in his recliner as he was now, drinking a cup of coffee and carrying on a conversation with his children. Mr. Shaked was a very busy man.

Shuki threw him a quick glance. He knew a lot about Avner's father. Mr. Shaked was one of the central figures in his son's life. Whenever Avner mentioned his father, Shuki could see his eyes fill with open admiration and hear the love in his voice. It was obvious that ties of love bound the two. It was hard for Shuki not to be jealous.

But Shuki rarely had a chance to actually see Avner's father, so he knew about him only from what Avner told him. During his frequent overnight visits, Shuki had gotten to know Shlomo Dov and Chaim Yosef, Avner's cute younger brothers. Now and then he would wonder when his baby brother Duvi would grow to be like them, saying things that were so funny and clever. He had also gotten to know Avner's kindhearted mother when he watched her prepare scrambled eggs and toast for them in her sparkling kitchen.

Now would be a perfect time to really get to know Avner's father. Shuki closed his green folder slowly and put it down on the table. Avner also sat ready to be tested. His father held the folder and sat up straight, ready for the first question.

Avner's father asked one question after another, changing

the order to make it more challenging. He was delighted to hear the boys answering him at length, explaining the material clearly. Yet once again, he felt that painful tug at his heart. How much more did he himself have to learn before he would reach the level of his twelve-year-old son?

"I think you are both very well prepared for the contest," Avner's father said, after twenty minutes of testing them. He closed the folder and, despite his fatigue, smiled broadly, his satisfaction obvious.

"Does everyone know the material as well as you boys do?" he asked Avner and Shuki.

"Everyone in the class is taking this pretty seriously." It was Shuki who spoke up first. "There's going to be a class trip as a special prize."

"It'll be a fourteen-hour trip up north," Avner told his father excitedly. "We'll be going to the holy places and seeing lots of beautiful sites. Some kids said we'll go right up to the border and be able to see Lebanon!"

Avner's father smiled.

"Is it really so beautiful, Abba?" Avner asked. "Is it interesting there? You probably know it, don't you?"

"Know it?" Avner's father's smile now filled his face. "There are places where I could walk with my eyes closed, where I know every rock and stone. I walked the region for hours and hours at a stretch — many more than fourteen hours. The views are breathtaking, but for us, it was sheer boredom. Imagine long nights of guard duty with your eyelids drooping from exhaustion. We walked back and forth, back and forth in patrols that seemed never to end. If only I had had then what I have now." He sighed. "If only I had known about the wealth of Torah that could have nurtured my soul during those long dark nights. But then, my well of Torah was dry.

"Do you understand what it means to sit with your buddy in a small hut on guard duty, talking and laughing at nonsense, feeling every minute crawling by? Only occasionally would patrol duty take on an added dimension," Avner's father continued, as he recalled with nostalgia those pleasant moments. "I had a few good friends in my unit who were searching for the meaning of life. The answers they found led them to become *ba'alei teshuva*. When I was on guard duty with one of them and we patrolled together, everything was different. Our conversations weren't just to pass the time and relieve the boredom. The talks we had together were something else entirely."

Was he talking over the boys' heads? He glanced at his son and Shuki. Both were listening intently, so he continued.

"It was like meeting my inner self. Getting to know who I am and what I am, what I want and what is expected of me. We asked questions, there under the stars in a sky that was so close to us. Even though none of us had perfect answers, we knew without a doubt that answers existed. The twinkling stars in the velvet black sky whispered that fact in our ears."

Avner's father stopped talking and again he smiled. Shuki's perceptive nature grasped that the smile was different this time, maybe even a bit melancholy.

"Much of what my two friends said still echoes in my ears." He continued to talk candidly, in the typically open manner of the Shaked family. "Their words went with me all those difficult years as I struggled, until I finally took my first steps toward doing *teshuva* — and they are still with me today."

"What happened to your friends?" Shuki whispered.

The smile on Menachem Shaked's face disappeared. "One of my friends is no longer with us. Where he is, only Hashem knows, and with His help we'll find him. As for the second friend, unfortunately, we lost contact with each other. We weren't good friends in the regular sense. We weren't the same age, we didn't go to the same school and we didn't live in the same city. But there was something about the special way he approached life — his honesty in the search for truth — that drew me to him like a magnet.

"That's enough," Avner's father stood up. "Just because I have time to sit around and talk doesn't mean that I have to take up your time. What are your plans for the rest of the evening? Will you continue to study, or are you going to take some time out to play?"

Shuki and Avner hadn't made any plans yet.

"Your father's stories are very, very interesting," Shuki whispered to Avner, a broad hint that he wouldn't mind sitting and listening to more of his experiences. "I guess my father also has stories like these to tell, but he's not a storyteller. He never talks. The little I know about his life I managed to pick up from him in bits and pieces over the years."

Menachem was already standing by the door ready to leave the room when he stopped and raised an eyebrow. He wanted to ask the boy something, but he quickly changed his mind. He realized that Shuki was shy, from the way he sat nervously biting his lip.

The phone rang, and Menachem lifted the receiver.

"Hello," he heard an unfamiliar voice at the other end. "This is Yehoshua Katz's father speaking. May I please speak to my son?"

It took a split second for Menachem to connect the soft-spoken, quiet Shuki to a boy called Yehoshua Katz.

"It's your father," Menachem said, putting the receiver down on the end table.

Shuki picked up the phone quickly, somewhat apprehensive. Why was his father calling? Had anything happened? His father had never before called him at this time of the night. What could be so important that it couldn't wait?

"Hello, Yehoshua," his father said, his voice even-toned. "Did you buy the salve for me?"

"Yes, Abba," Shuki answered. After school he had gone to the nearest drugstore and bought the prescribed medication for his father. His father had begun to apply the salve on his scar tissue, and the small drugstore in Arazim didn't carry the brand he needed. When Shuki was in Haifa, he could save his father a trip to the city by buying the salve for him.

"Can you find any way to send it to Arazim tonight?" Shuki's father asked. "I thought I had enough medication left to last me a few more days, but Duvi managed to get hold of the tube and smear it all over his clothes. If I wait for you to bring it, I won't have it before tomorrow night."

Shuki racked his brain for a solution. "Maybe we can find a way to send it with someone," he thought out loud. "Maybe someone here will have an idea. I'll talk to Avner and his father, and try to come up with something. If there's no way to send it," he added, "I'll come home tonight. There's a bus leaving at 8:45, in just a quarter of an hour. Don't worry, Abba. I'll get it to you." Shuki pressed the off button.

"Send it?" Avner's father furrowed his brow. "Now? It's not likely we'll find anyone. Is it so important?"

Shuki nodded. He took the tube out of the bag, preparing to put it in his pocket. "It's for a treatment," he said quietly, lowering his eyes. "It's for my father's face. My baby brother emptied the tube when he was playing, so my father really needs this new supply right away.

"There's no choice," Shuki said, packing his bags. "I think I'll take the next bus...even though I really don't like traveling alone at night." Turning to Avner he asked, "Where did you put my briefcase?"

"Here it is." Avner's father brought him the brown leather schoolbag that stood in the hall. "Avner and I will walk with you to the bus stop."

As he gave Shuki his bag, Menachem noticed the writing on the tube of medication. When he stopped to read it, he began to put two and two together. As an army medic, and with his current work in the hospital's biochemistry laboratory, he knew what this medication would have been prescribed for.

He walked slowly toward the first chair in sight and sat down, floored.

Was it possible? Menachem thought, as he stared at the young boy who had become his son's best friend.

"You're Shuki Katz, aren't you?" he asked, seemingly out of the blue. "Your father is Tzachi, right? Today he's probably called Yitzchak."

Shuki nodded his head as he stared at Avner's father, uncomprehending.

"Then it won't be necessary for you to travel home," Menachem Shaked said. "Call your father up and tell him to come here. He'll be able to pick up the package himself."

Shuki didn't understand what was happening. Avner was of no help either. He seemed just as confused as Shuki.

"What are you waiting for?" Avner's father asked Shuki impatiently. "Here's the phone. Go ahead and call."

Shuki hesitated, looking at Avner for some sort of explanation, but the puzzled expression on Avner's face was of no help.

"Go ahead," Menachem repeated. "Tell your father he's cordially invited to pick up the salve at the home of the Shaked family. Tell him Manny has a lot to talk to him about!"

48

Changes

The broad doors of the small community center in Arazim were opened wide. Mothers, walking in groups of three and four, made their way out after a lecture, dispersing along the quiet, dark paths of the village.

Shuki's mother adjusted her brown purse so it would rest comfortably on her shoulder, and headed for home with two of her friends. The evening's lecture had been interesting. She was hoping there'd be interesting news waiting for her at home as well.

What time is it? She glanced at her watch. Almost ten-thirty. By now Yitzchak was sure to be back from his visit with what's-his-name in Haifa, Shuki's friend's father. Oh, yes — Manny, his old army buddy.

Just thinking about the reunion made her smile. It was hard to believe that Avner's father Menachem, and Manny, the army medic, were one and the same.

Her friends' animated discussion penetrated her thoughts.

"It's impossible for someone to change his basic character traits," Shulamis was insisting. "A person can only redirect his basic character traits, sort of rechannel them, but he can't change them. That's just what Mrs. Rosen pointed out in her lecture, and I think it's important for us as mothers to know that.

"It would be a mistake to expect a child to change his basic personality," she continued adamantly. "A disorganized type will never win a prize for order, and a child who is a chronic dreamer will never be totally down-to-earth and practical. A parent's job is to guide the child so his innate traits find positive outlets. That, plus setting reasonable limits are what's needed in parenting."

Adina agreed with her. "When I look around, I see it's true. Sure, we see growth and changes in our children at times, but never in their basic attributes, only in the way these traits are expressed."

"A group of my former classmates recently met at a bar mitzva," Shulamis broke in. "It was a very interesting reunion. After so many years, each person had remained exactly the same. The ones who had self-confidence as kids still had it. Likewise for those with an inferiority complex. Even though their personalities were more developed, the classmates I remembered as always smiling and happy were still that way, while the ones who had found life tough still did.

"It was fascinating to see that when it came to their inner selves, nothing had changed. You could peel away the outer layers and underneath find the same group of high school girls. A person is what he is. Don't you agree?"

Adina and Shulamis carried on their conversation, repeating the same line of thought with a thousand and one variations, nodding their heads in agreement. They were so absorbed in their discussion, they didn't even notice Shuki's mother shaking her head. No, she didn't agree with them at all, but years of experience had taught her that not always, not with everyone and not on every topic, should one argue. In this instance, had she chosen to argue, she would have

Changes ❖ 337

had to disclose too many personal details to support her point of view.

So, smiling politely, she said good night to her friends and continued on to her next-door neighbor's house to pick up Duvi, still thinking about her different opinion.

Duvi lay sleeping, an angelic smile on his chubby face, exactly as she had left him in his blue stroller, snuggling in his blanket, hugging his cuddly teddy bear.

"He slept the whole time, didn't he?" she asked Leah, her neighbor.

"He's been a perfect angel."

Shuki's mother wasn't surprised. She patted the toddler's blond curls and started for home. At this stage of his life, Duvi was quite predictable. Her oldest son Shuki, on the other hand, was full of surprises these days. That very morning she had stood there with him openmouthed, hardly believing what her son was saying.

It was early, and Shuki was drinking his cocoa before leaving for the day. The van would soon arrive to take him to Haifa. It was cloudy outside and the wind was blowing, a sure sign that rain was on the way.

"Where's my umbrella?" Shuki had asked as he looked in the hallway closet where it usually hung. "Have you seen it, Ima?"

No, his mother hadn't seen it. He made a quick search of the house, to no avail. Any minute the driver would start honking the horn impatiently, leaving Shuki little time to improvise a solution.

"I guess you left your black umbrella at school," she had said to him. "Don't forget to look for it. For now, you have no choice but to take my umbrella. It's okay, I have two."

When she made the suggestion, she knew with certainty that it would be met with a shrug of the shoulders and a stubborn refusal. She could almost hear Shuki's excuses. He would argue that it was just cloudy and wouldn't really rain. He might say that he wasn't made of sugar and he wouldn't melt. He might even suggest that raindrops on his head were healthy. He might try to convince her that the few steps he'd have to take from the house to the van and from the van to the cheder building didn't justify taking an umbrella.

And that would be only the beginning. She had been sure he would absolutely refuse to take her flower-print umbrella and turn his nose up at the pink-and-purple-checked one too. She was ready to come to terms with the fact that her son would go out without any protection from the rain. Even if she did manage to force an umbrella into his hand as he walked out the door, he would hide it deep inside his briefcase so that none of his friends would see it and laugh at him.

But Shuki surprised her. He made a face for a just a fraction of a second, then picked up the checked one.

"At least the colors are almost dark," he said with a wisp of a smile. "I hope it rains only during class. But otherwise, I ought to have an umbrella. If it rains today like it did last week, it won't be comfortable to be caught in the downpour without it. I'm better off taking an umbrella – even one with flowers – than having to run madly for cover."

Those were Shuki's exact words. His mother didn't have to explain, convince, persuade or win him over. She simply stood there staring at her son in amazement, marveling at the change that had come over him.

Yes, the change in her son was certain and a real blessing. The Shuki who was always so hesitant, suspicious, meek and unsure, the boy who always looked to see what his friends would say before he made a move, that boy had changed.

Let her friends Shulamis and Adina say what they wanted; she had proof. Shuki, who in the past was always so unsure of himself, had become a different boy. Now he was marching along, facing life with determination and resolve. No longer did a raised eyebrow or a crinkled nose make him withhold his opinion when he wanted to speak or stop him in his tracks when he wanted to move on. Changes had taken place, many changes.

She walked into the house. A dim light was on in the living room, and the house was quiet. She placed Duvi gently in his crib and glanced over to the shelf where Shuki kept his games. Lately, the shelf was emptier than usual.

It had been a week and a half ago when she first noticed the change. Meir and Moishe, two of her son's former classmates who lived in the moshav, had knocked on the door one afternoon.

"Is Shuki home?" they had asked.

"No, he stayed over in Haifa," she had answered, somewhat surprised at the sudden visit. When Shuki was a student at the cheder in Arazim, hardly any of the boys visited him at home, so why would they come now?

"He's not back?" the more talkative of the two had asked. "They have afternoon classes even on Rosh Chodesh?"

"No," Shuki's mother had explained patiently, "he stayed over at a friend's house."

"If he calls," the boy had continued, "can you please tell him that Meir and Moishe came over. We arranged with him to meet here. Too bad he didn't tell us he wouldn't be home today." He sighed with disappointment.

Later that day, Shuki had called his mother from Avner's house and she told him about the visitors. "Oh, yeah." Shuki knew exactly what it was all about. "They asked to borrow some of my games. But they didn't mention that they would be coming on Rosh Chodesh. I would have left a bag of games ready for them."

This time, unlike other times when similar incidents had taken place, she hadn't sensed any disappointment or apology in Shuki's voice. He was sorry they wouldn't be able to play with his games that day, but that was all.

"Actually, Ima, I did set some games aside for them," Shuki had said as an afterthought. "There are five boxes on the left edge of the shelf. If they come again, you can give them those games. Just don't give them my Game Boy. They wanted that too, but Abba said it was too expensive to lend out. So if they ask for it, tell them they can come over and play with it in the house, okay?"

He had had a few more instructions to give. "Also, please tell Abba where I left the games for them, in case they come when you're busy with Duvi or when you're not home, okay?"

She had looked at the receiver, wondering what to say. Was that her son on the other end of the line, giving such clear instructions, so confidently? She could hardly believe her ears.

At first, she thought it was because he practically never saw his Arazim friends, since he no longer went to school with them. Maybe that was what made it easier for him to speak with such self-confidence. But when the scene repeated itself on another occasion, she realized there must be more to it. Was it the change to a new cheder that had brought on this turnabout?

The change went much further than Arazim and Haifa, the old cheder and the new one. It was Shuki himself who had changed — totally.

Shuki's mother walked into the living room and found her husband sitting there, head in hands, still stunned by what had taken place.

"I just got back a few minutes ago," he said, "but I still can't calm down. I sat for two and a half hours with Manny — Reb Menachem. We talked for two and a half hours, and I couldn't take my eyes off him for a second. I kept asking myself over and over, Could this be Manny? Is this the same Manny I once knew?"

He got up from his chair and paced the room as he talked. "If someone had asked me to describe Manny in a nutshell, it wouldn't have taken me more than two seconds. He had a lot of good qualities, true, but, basically, he was spineless. I never would have said that out loud," he hastened to assure his wife, "but that's what would have come to mind. Yet tonight, there was Manny sitting right across from me, the same — but so very different. He was solid as a rock.

"If he hadn't mentioned names and dates, reminiscing about all the times we spent together, I might not have believed it was him. Underneath the black beard and glasses, and with his serious demeanor, it was absolutely impossible to recognize the Manny I once knew. Why, in the old days, Manny would burst out laughing at the slightest hint of a joke, no matter how serious the moment.

"You couldn't keep up a serious conversation with him for more than five minutes at a stretch. You couldn't ask his opinion on any subject, because he never had an opinion of his own. His opinions swayed with the slightest breeze. He used to change sides according to what he thought was expected of him.

"Oh, if only Yossi were here with us now! What would he have said to Manny taking the big leap along with us? It's hard to believe Manny was able to ignore all the people who must have mocked him for his choice. I never thought that he, of all people, would be capable of doing it. Look how a person can change!"

Yes, people do change, Shuki's mother thought as she brought her exhausted husband a cup of coffee. *What about you? Haven't you changed, too?*

Her husband's whole set of values had made an about-face. All the rules of his earlier game, the game he had played for the first twenty years of his life, were null and void. Slowly, through perseverance and a certain doggedness, he had stuck to his new path — and along the way, learned a whole new set of rules, the rules used by Jews throughout the ages to seek their Father.

It wasn't often that Bruria thought about her husband's past, but on those rare occasions when she did, she was filled with admiration. She thought of all he had given up in the secular world: a chance to learn more in his chosen field, advanced degrees, his dreams and aspirations, the loving parents and brother that were now so distanced. There was a price to pay for change, a heavy price indeed.

Voices were heard beneath their kitchen window, followed

by the sound of footsteps. She glanced at the wall clock and smiled. The stragglers coming home from the evening lecture, she thought. Maybe they were still discussing whether or not people can change. They were right, but so was she.

Many people go through life steadily following the same path from beginning to end, placing one foot after the other, as they've done since they learned to walk. Their pace never speeds up or slows down, but remains the same.

Then there are others, people who work on themselves, who rise above the quagmire of complacency. They seek a path that is better, surer. Instead of dragging their feet through life, they learn to walk with strength and determination. When you see the world as one long path leading you ever closer to your Father, you find new energy coursing through your veins. You find the strength to make changes, to shift gears. You're more willing to make major changes that will take you forward.

How interesting, Bruria thought, that these people, who by all rights should be standing in the limelight, are often the ones standing unobtrusively at the sidelines.

49
Newfound Pride

It was Shuki who opened the front door. He had never seen the man standing there before. Perched on tufts of white hair sat a tiny, colorful yarmulke. Shuki perceived a deep sadness emanating from the blue eyes and could almost guess who the gentleman was.

"I've called several times over the past few days," the stranger said as Shuki led him to the living room, "and most of the time a boy answered the phone. That was you, wasn't it?" He pulled out a chair and sat down. "It's a real pleasure to meet Tzachi's son." The man smiled at Shuki. "Let's see, do you look like him?" He scrutinized the boy's features closely.

"Hmm...let's see," the man repeated. Shuki prepared himself for the comments that were bound to follow. Would this man find similarities between him and his father? Shuki found himself hoping the stranger would detect at least one thing they had in common.

"I definitely think so," the man continued. "The high forehead — a sure sign of a deep thinker. Large, round eyes — that shows sensitivity. Like your father, you impress me as being a sensitive fellow. Am I wrong?"

Shuki blushed deeply, as usual, and refrained from answering.

"Your father's been hard to reach these past days." The guest changed the subject as he drummed his fingers nervously on the dining-room table.

Shuki realized that his job had not ended with opening the door and welcoming the guest into the living room. Even the cup of hot coffee he would soon serve wouldn't complete his service to the guest. Daniel Nir, if he had correctly guessed the identity of the man who now stood before him, apparently considered Shuki his partner in conversation for the next twenty minutes or so, until his father arrived home. So Shuki, his cheeks still somewhat flushed, pulled over a chair and sat down across from the stranger.

"Today, I decided to drop by for a visit," the man continued. "Your line has been constantly busy since early this morning. I know your father, and he isn't a big talker. There are times when he's very busy with matters concerning my missing son — no doubt you've heard about him. What's been happening lately?"

Shuki opened his mouth to answer but immediately changed his mind. *Don't you know,* he wanted to shout, *that my father is busy again with your son? Busy from morning till night, worried and tense...but radiant and smiling as never before. Don't you know that he's just returned from a secret flight to Syria, which had to do with Yossi? How could it be that you don't know?*

But Shuki kept it all to himself. If Mr. Nir didn't know anything about these latest developments, it meant his father had decided it was better that way. Shuki certainly didn't have to be the one to give an up-to-date report.

Shuki heard his mother preparing coffee in the kitchen. He

excused himself and hurried to bring in the coffee and a plate of cookies.

Mr. Nir took the cup graciously and lifted it to his lips, then paused. "How do you say the blessing? You know, the one your father says with such concentration before he drinks?" Shuki said the words slowly, one by one, as his guest repeated them.

"Here, in your father's house, I feel obligated to do that, at the very least," he told Shuki somewhat apologetically. "Your father brought G-d into our house — actually, into my life and that of my family. I don't know much, and I find it hard to keep everything, but saying a blessing is the least I can do when I'm in this house."

"Come to think of it," he continued, "I never did properly thank your father for this. I've thanked him for all his efforts to bring Yossi home, of course, but for this, the feeling that G-d is close to me, too, the feeling that there is Someone Who listens and hears me as a father would a son, despite everything.... You have no idea what this does for a person in his most difficult moments, and believe me, I haven't lacked for trying times in my life."

Daniel sipped the hot coffee and tasted the cookies. "So, when will your father be home?" He glanced at his watch impatiently. "I would have waited another day or two. I wouldn't have barged in on you like this if I didn't have to give the bank an answer already."

Seeing Shuki's puzzled look, Yossi's father elaborated. "I've been working at the bank for the past thirty years, and I've just received an offer to be branch manager of a new branch they're opening in South Africa. There are so many pros and cons to the move, I can't decide what to do. When will Tzachi be here?" he again looked at his watch.

"What does that have to do with Yossi?" It didn't make sense to Shuki.

"Nothing." Mr. Nir seemed surprised by the question.

"Then..." Shuki searched for the right way to continue.

"Then how is my father involved in all this?"

"The only thing I want right now is to hear your father's opinion," Mr. Nir smiled. "No one else's — just his. There's no one else I would rely on for objective advice. Who, other than your father, knows how to analyze all angles of a question and come up with a clear answer? Who can I discuss this with and be sure that he will consider the matter fully, will want to help wholeheartedly, will be able to put himself in my place?

"Where else can you meet people today whose thinking is objective, who aren't out only for their own interests? Where can you find anyone who is willing to put himself out for somebody else? Where can you find people," and here his arms stretched out wide, "who are willing to give of their time, their energy and even their money to accomplish something? It's unbelievable that in fifteen years his enthusiasm hasn't waned."

Shuki saw the bright look of admiration in Mr. Nir's eyes. He sensed the feeling of respect and esteem in every single word, and something inside Shuki's heart swelled. *My father,* he thought proudly.

"It's because my father became a *ba'al teshuva,*" Shuki added in a whisper. "The Torah tells every Jew to be that way, to help other people without ulterior motives."

Daniel touched the yarmulke he had put on specially for the occasion to make sure it hadn't slid off.

"You're so very right," he said to Shuki. "But that's not all there is to it. Take his kindness, for instance. You can take all your problems and load them onto him, and his heart won't feel the heavier for it. And his sensitivity — he knows when to talk and when to keep quiet, what to say and how to say it. You can even cry, and put the pressure on him sometimes — even forcefully, if the situation warrants it — then wipe away the tears and get on with life. But I'm talking too much." He gave Shuki a broad smile. "Of course, you know all this better than I — you're his son!" Not expecting an answer to his last comment, he took another cookie and looked out the living-room window.

I know it better than him? Again Shuki blushed, and this time his face turned a deeper red than ever. No, Mr. Nir was mistaken. Shuki didn't know. He had never thought of his father, the quiet person who stood on the sidelines, the man who tended gardens, humble and even somewhat lackluster, in such a radiant, shining light. There are obviously bright sides to fathers that even sons are unaware of. Or, could it be that their own children never bother trying to see that part of them because they are satisfied with just a superficial glance?

Daniel carefully gathered some of the crumbs scattered on the tablecloth. He was still absorbed in thought and continued speaking as if there hadn't been a long moment of uninterrupted silence.

"I'm no longer a youngster," he told Shuki, as the furrows in his brow deepened. "I've met many people over the course of my life. I've learned to see people for what they are. I'm not making a mistake about your father. He is an outstanding individual. You should be very happy, young man — happy and proud."

Shuki lowered his eyes, unaware that he was fidgeting with the corners of the tablecloth. He was beginning to see his father in a new light.

But right now, the most pressing question was, where was his father? The father who was so good to him and so good to others? His father, whom a nonreligious stranger looked up to with such respect and admiration.

Shuki began to feel a happiness mixed with admiration flooding his heart. He was proud that he had such a father. Abba. The word sounded melodically in his ears, giving him a strong, sweet sense of belonging.

50

In Pursuit

Yitzchak parked his car near the house and opened the door. He had just returned from an important meeting with the head of army personnel in Jerusalem. The time had come to involve government officials. He and Manny had pulled all the strings they could, but Sheik Abdul Rachim al Shekari wasn't about to hand them Yossi Nir on a silver platter. Aside from the payment for Yitzchak's contribution to the sheik's gardens in Saudi Arabia, there were the Syrians and their demands to be dealt with.

Yitzchak sighed. Everything was so close, so close you could practically touch it — yet so far. Over the past fifteen years of disappointment after disappointment, there were moments when they had come so close to resolving the situation, but all those moments had evaporated into thin air. Was disappointment awaiting them once again? Please, Hashem, no more!

Yitzchak walked down the gravel path slowly, mentally reviewing the recent events that had occurred at a dizzying pace. It had all begun on his second trip to Manny — now Menachem — Shaked's home.

Manny had come to Arazim two days after that first reunion, and a week later Yitzchak had paid him a second visit. Their common language, one that went back to their shared army days, renewed itself on a level that was now more intense than ever before. Now their sons were best friends, and they had many common experiences yet to be discussed. Each of them still had much to hear and to tell.

They had sat next to the coffee table in Manny's living room, reminiscing and remembering Yossi, their hearts heavy with longing. When Yitzchak mentioned some of what he had done for Yossi over the years, Manny decided to share with Yitzchak the information he had. Instead of verbalizing what he knew, he simply walked over to the closet, took out the small videocassette and played it. Moments later, Yitzchak saw and heard it all for himself.

After he viewed the video, the rest of their visit had only one focus. Abdul Rachim al Shekari, an influential sheik who lived in Saudi Arabia, was willing to pressure the Syrians and knew how it could be done. But he needed clear, indisputable proof that the Syrians were holding Yossi — and here was that proof. "Why, only two years ago I saw the exact same thing. It was in the eyes of one of your soldiers."

All Yitzchak needed now was to get hold of medical documents proving that Yossi had two different-colored eyes — one brown and one blue — and send it on to the sheik, who would arrive at his own conclusion. And there could be only one conclusion.

It was Yitzchak who had met with the sheik to give him the medical report.

"Within a few days, we'll know where we stand," the rich oil magnate had told him during a flight in his private plane. "When I return from my trip to Syria, I'll update you on details."

Now, if the sheik could convince the Syrians to give him

information on Yossi Nir, Yitzchak would pass it on to Israeli officials. Most likely, Israel would have to pay a high price — the freeing of dozens, if not hundreds, of Palestinian prisoners, perhaps. The Foreign Ministry was awaiting a response from the sheik.

Walking up the path to his home, Yitzchak thought about the past few tension-fraught days. Those long moments, when millions of thoughts flooded his heart — the long, unending battle between hope and disappointment, disconnecting him from the here and now. Who will win this time? He felt his heart pound and butterflies nervously flutter in his stomach. Al Shekari had given their efforts an even chance. This time there was no denial on the part of the Syrians. Could one hope and believe that they were indeed holding Yossi? That he was there alive? That the negotiations the sheik was about to hold would end in success?

Yitzchak again mentally patted himself on the back for keeping Daniel in the dark about the latest developments. As the father, he was closer than anyone else, all the more reason for keeping him out of the picture at this stage. So many times Yitzchak had thought about how much more pleasant it would have been for him if he, too, could stay out of the picture during times of tension and just be there to accept the good news which would, *be'ezras Hashem*, be soon in coming.

But, of course, that was only fantasy. Someone had to be the *shaliach*, the one who takes action, so that there would be good news. This he had always done. He'd always made the maximum effort to be a faithful emissary.

"Shalom," Yitzchak called out as he opened the front door to his home, anxious to tell his wife the latest news. Unexpectedly, it was a different face he saw when he walked in.

"Hello," Daniel Nir greeted him. "Finally home?"

Yitzchak sat down with Daniel, who immediately began complaining about how busy Yitzchak had been of late and then went on to tell him every detail of the pros and cons of accepting the bank's job offer — never taking his eyes off Yitzchak, studying his reactions the whole time. Daniel told him about the new location, the language, the different mentality — a new beginning that surely would not be easy for a man of his age. He brought up the adjustment Yosefa would have to make to the new surroundings and the separation from her environment here.

"But the salary is a good one," Daniel explained, "and the conditions are excellent. We are talking about a trial period, of course.

"Do you understand?" Daniel continued, lowering his voice as sadness crept in. "The change might be good for me. Leaving the house where Yossi had his room; going away from the home that Yossi left and never returned to; leaving behind the streets we walked; going to a new, distant place. After all," Daniel's voice changed as he held back his tears, "with all the efforts we've put into this, we have to be realistic and practical. Almost sixteen years have passed. How long can one hope? Perhaps the time has come to bury our hopes and learn to live with the emptiness that will never be replaced."

Yitzchak finally spoke, unable to hold back the words any longer. "Let the bank send someone else to South Africa," he said decisively. "You stay here. Don't bury your hopes after all these years. Perhaps Hashem has heard our prayers, and these hopes will finally be fulfilled. Stay home, Daniel. Stay in the house where Yossi lived. Continue to pray there. Maybe you — maybe all of us — will hear Yossi's voice echoing through the walls of your quiet house once again."

// // //

Yitzchak sat across from the top-level officials at the Ministry of Defense, receiving his final briefing. The three gentlemen spoke quickly and tersely, one voice occasionally overriding another. With trembling hands and thoughts wandering constantly, Yitzchak had a hard time following what was being said.

Sheik Abdul Rachim al Shekari was convinced beyond the shadow of a doubt that Yossi Nir was alive and his place of captivity known. The sheik was in the midst of long, exhausting negotiations with the Israeli government over the number of terrorists to be released — the price of Yossi's freedom.

As optimistic as the sheik was, officials in Israel still detected some flaws in the rosy picture the sheik was trying to paint. Was Yossi really still alive? Perhaps he had been killed in the two years that passed since he was last seen alive?

What interested the Saudi Arabian sheik was something else entirely. "The captive soldier will be released in a few weeks," he announced over and over to Yitzchak. "If the Israeli government isn't too stubborn, you will soon be able to meet your friend face-to-face in your homeland. But meanwhile, it's a shame to put off my project — the flower gardens that were the start of all this — until the negotiations have been completed. The American experts who are designing the garden need more than just the general outline you submitted. They need your personal, on-the-spot guidance.

"I have fulfilled my end of the deal," the sheik said persuasively. "The man you want is on the way. Why can't you come now to Saudi Arabia, see the place, look over the soil and plan the irrigation system according to your specifications so we can get the project underway?"

Yitzchak was adamant. "Only after I clasp Yossi's hand in mine," he told Neil Stevens, one of the sheik's representatives. "Only after I see him with my own eyes and welcome him home, after I see the face that has haunted my mind all these years, only when I see him alive and well will I be able to pack my bags and go to Saudi Arabia to take care of the project's irrigation system."

"But then you'll be too emotional, too excited," Neil argued. "You'll be so busy celebrating, going to all the welcoming parties. It'll be harder for you to leave all the excitement and fly abroad. Wouldn't it be preferable to finish up everything now?"

No, it wouldn't be preferable. Yitzchak took a firm stand. He wasn't interested in the irrigation plan; in fact, he wasn't interested in the sheik's fancy gardens at all. The whole plan had been devised for Yossi's sake. He wasn't about to play the fool and cave in to pressure. This was the last card he held. If he threw it away, this last wisp of a chance, then his only hold — weak as it was — would be lost.

51
Irrefutable Evidence

At two past midnight, the phone rang. "Did I wake you?" The American accent gave away the caller's identity. Yes, Neil Stevens had woken Yitzchak from the deep sleep that had eluded him for so long.

"You don't have much time," Stevens continued. "Twelve hours from now we want to meet you in Turkey. The sheik doesn't have the patience to wait the weeks it will take to run this through official channels and complete the procedures. He is satisfied that he now has absolute, undeniable proof that Yossi is alive. I will meet you in twelve hours at the Ankara airport. Goodbye." He hung up.

Yitzchak didn't lose a moment. He had work to do, strings to pull, arrangements to make. Quite a few people were wakened from their sleep that night so he could arrange all that had to be taken care of before boarding the 8:00 A.M. flight to London. From London, he would change planes and head for Turkey;

there are times when the longer, less direct route proves to be the most practical. There had never been a guarantee that it would be an easy or direct path to reach Yossi.

Yitzchak was just receiving his last-minute instructions from three government officials before leaving for the airport, when two long honks from the waiting taxi filtered into the building. He would arrive at the airport only minutes before takeoff, but he knew he would not miss the flight. He had every official government document he needed to open all the gates and get him on the plane.

"This talk of absolute proof sounds extremely suspicious," one of the government officials was saying, deep concern evident in his voice. "I'm very uncomfortable with the whole thing. If Yossi is alive, and if the sheik knows where he is, why is he so anxious to give us proof? What kind of proof can there be that can only be shown in Turkey? Why can't he send his proof here, for everyone to see? Most unusual."

"That's why we've all come to this meeting on such short notice," the second official explained. "Shai Giladi here will give us a few pointers on how various forms of evidence can be tampered with, and how we can determine if they're fraudulent. You must know what to look out for; you have to be aware of every possibility, so you won't fall for fake evidence."

Shai, a man of slight build with large glasses that seemed to practically cover his entire small face, took over. "From all our experience thus far," he began to lecture, "we can cite some prime examples of fraudulent evidence. They could play you a cassette of Yossi talking. You may be able to recognize his voice and even hear him speaking clearly. He might say something like, 'Today is Monday, April 2, 1998. I am alive and well. All my needs are being taken care of, and I look forward to seeing you.'

"Even though you can identify his voice, and the date mentioned is recent, the cassette can be a fake. It is possible to take a two-year-old recording — or even one that is ten or fifteen years old — and recreate Yossi's voice saying different words.

Insist on a laboratory analysis. That it is the only way to check if an audio recording is authentic."

"A contact man will be on the plane with you," the main spokesman broke into Shai's words, showing Yitzchak a small photograph. "This is what he looks like. His code name is Signature. He will contact you at an opportune moment, and you will give him all the substantive information to check out."

Outside the taxi honked again, but Shai chose to ignore it. "Another commonly used type of evidence is a photograph — a picture showing Yossi at the age he would have been today, together with some other form of evidence from the present. For example, you might be shown a photo of Yossi holding a recent edition of the newspaper in which you'll be able to see clearly last week's date and headlines.

"This kind of proof, while very convincing, can be nothing more than a well-done photomontage — a combination of images that have been altered by computer. You can scan an old picture of Yossi into the computer, change his features to make him look older — a technique they call morphing — and place it in an image of a recent newspaper. Professionally done, the results are virtually flawless. So be aware of this technique too. A sensitive test, which Signature will do, will determine whether the photo is authentic or not.

"They can also show you a video of Yossi, in which case they could use both a faked voice and the morphing technique. It's complicated to prepare, but it can be done. This too would have to be checked to make sure it's genuine.

"That's it, more or less." Shai wrapped up what he had to say and sat back in his seat.

"Any other types of evidence?" Yitzchak asked.

"Other types of evidence?" Shai repeated the question in surprise, slowly enunciating every word. "What other types of evidence could there be that would be convincing? There's nothing else they could show you that would be considered irrefutable proof. A letter in Yossi's handwriting? That's too easy

Irrefutable Evidence ♦ 357

to forge. Personal belongings? That's no proof of anything. An eyewitness account by someone else? There's no reason to believe it. A photograph or a recording are worth investigating; any other proof is worthless."

Yitzchak sensed the truth of the logic that flowed through Shai Gilad's every word, and all his hopes sank. Stark reality doesn't fit well with dreams and hopes.

Yitzchak took his blue flight bag and stood up. Shai remained in his seat while the other two rose to accompany him to the door.

"One more very important thing," said the taller of the two men. "You are making this trip for the purpose of seeing the proof, but don't focus on that alone. Consider this a general mission. Keep your eyes and ears open — take in every single detail and keep it all etched in your mind. Make a mental note of all the people you come across, where you meet them, what names they mention, what they talk about. Every single detail of this kind can turn out to be very important data."

Yitzchak did his best to organize his wandering thoughts and concentrate on the man's words. "What's that you said?" he found himself asking. "I'm very sorry," Yitzchak quickly added, shaking his head from side to side. "I won't be able to concentrate on anything other than the matter at hand. I won't see or hear a thing that isn't related. The words will just pass me by as if they had never been spoken. Right now, all I can see in front of my eyes is Yossi's pleading face, and all I can hear are his last words during that awful, bloody battle. I am totally absorbed in just one question: Is Yossi still alive?"

Yitzchak opened the door. "I feel bad about this," he repeated, "but it's clear to me that I won't be able to concentrate on anything else." The other two men looked at him in silence, then shook his hand and wished him luck. They both had the same thought in mind: May he succeed in his mission.

Yitzchak spent the next six hours in a whirlwind of activity. From Ben Gurion Airport in Israel to Heathrow in London. Boarding, landing, boarding, landing. Goodbyes, warm welcomes, tension and then the release of tension.

Outwardly, Yitzchak seemed indifferent to all that was happening, but inside he was a knot of tension. How could one compare what the other passengers were feeling to his experience and to what Daniel Nir was experiencing? How could one liken the ordinary comings and goings in the airport to the reunion he dreamed of and prayed for? Even the bright, polished walls that were accustomed to the noisy clamor of emotional meetings would shake. Would these walls bear witness to the reunion of a father and his son returning home after a fifteen-year absence?

At 1:45 P.M., flight 354 from London landed at Ankara — fifteen minutes before the twelve-hour deadline. Neil Stevens walked up to Yitzchak and accompanied him to a small blue car. Sheik Abdul Rachim al Shekari was already sitting there, a broad smile on his face — too broad a smile, Yitzchak thought. When the sheik stretched out his right hand, Yitzchak flinched. The trembling of his fingers was strong, and he was afraid that his thin hands would quiver in the heavy fist of the sheik, like a small fish caught in a net. Nevertheless, he offered his hand in return greeting, trying mightily to overcome the tension that engulfed him.

The Turkish driver led them through the city with the smooth confidence of a native. The long drive to the outskirts of Ankara was exhausting, and the sheik and Neil occasionally dozed off. Only Yitzchak sat stiffly upright, his eyes open wide. Had he been traveling this road on his way to create a beautiful botanical garden, he could have managed a nap, but not when he was on the road with life and death hanging in the balance.

"We are nearing the border," Neil announced, wide awake after a long rest, "that separates Turkey from Syria."

"We will stop at the border, and there I will present the evidence," the sheik said to Neil, who translated his words from Arabic into English for Yitzchak's benefit. Yitzchak considered whether now was the time to raise the subject of his apprehension regarding the various possible types of evidence, but decided against it. *Let's wait until we have the bird in hand,* he thought, *and then we'll see whether it can fly.*

When the car stopped, the sheik was the first one out.

"From here the road continues to the city of Haleb," Neil said, translating the sheik's words as he pointed to the long train of cars in the distance. The three walked over to a sleek, black car parked several yards away. Dark curtains covering the windows hid the interior from view. Two hard-faced men leaped out of the car and exchanged a few words with the sheik.

"Here is your evidence," Neil said as he took hold of Yitzchak's arm and slowly led him toward to the car. As they neared it, Yitzchak tried to imagine the scene that was about to unfold before his eyes. Then, someone in the car pushed aside the dark curtain on the window, and the sheik motioned Yitzchak to peer inside.

"Here is your evidence," Neil repeated. "Here he is." The car door opened, and Yitzchak allowed himself to climb inside. Oversized clothing hung on a skeletal figure, and the ashen face gave the eyes an exaggerated largeness. There were no dark sunglasses covering those eyes, one blue and one brown.

Yitzchak stared for several seconds, long enough to identify the eyes that held a mere flicker of the spark that was so familiar to him, even after all these years.

It was Yossi.

52
Footsteps in the Sand

Raindrops fell onto the sandy soil, turning the wet earth muddy and marshy. Shuki stood alone by the school gate, a small overhang sheltering him from the sudden downpour but doing nothing to protect him from the blustering wind. Was he shivering from the cold or nervousness?

He peered into the distance, along the length of roadway, searching between the raindrops for the familiar face. It was a face that others might find frightening or even repulsive, but in him, that particular face — his father's face — evoked only pure love.

The already gloomy March sky began to fill with thick, gray clouds. Shuki felt the grayness seep into his heart. A sudden cloudburst sent buckets of rain pouring down on him. Wet and shivering, Shuki made his way into the cheder building, giving up the idea of waiting outside for his father. He would stand inside with the other boys.

Several minutes later, the rain eased. Protected by the overhang close to the fence, Shuki walked back to the outer gate, eager to be in the yard when his father arrived. His steps were slow and steady. His shoes, which sunk into the mud, made a squelching sound as they struggled to free themselves with each step. Under such circumstances, it's almost impossible to run enthusiastically. The most you can do is make the maximum effort possible and take one small step after another.

The idea had come up three days ago, while the class was discussing their get-together in honor of Rosh Chodesh Adar. They had chosen as their theme *hashgacha pratis* — how Hashem arranges everything, even what appears to be a chance occurrence — and they were trying to come up with a speaker.

"How about Shuki's father?" A smiling Gedalia had thrown out the suggestion. "He can tell us about that captive soldier — what's his name? — Yossi Nir. He probably has lots of exciting stories about *hashgacha pratis!*"

An out-and-out refusal— or a polite dodging of the issue — was what his classmates expected from Shuki to this spur-of-the-moment idea. Even Gedalia hadn't thought through his suggestion thoroughly before voicing it.

All eyes turned toward Shuki, none of them seeing the turmoil of emotions raging under the surface. In Shuki's mind, "No way!" wrestled with "Why not?". "Maybe" battled a definite "no." Yes. No. Yes.

Finally, he said, "It could be a great idea." Nervousness made the words come out raspy. "For sixteen years, my father's been doing everything he possibly could to find Yossi. He put his whole heart and soul into it. I'm sure he has plenty of really amazing stories to tell about it."

"So, will you invite him?" Reb Moishe asked.

"Yes, I'll ask him to come." Shuki sounded relaxed and comfortable with his answer. His face didn't flush with embarrassment, and the words came out matter-of-factly, as if he were asking the grocer for milk, or the baker for a cake.

When Shuki brought up the subject at home, his father was more than pleased. Journalists who had pressed for an interview were turned down, but this invitation to tell the story was different. It didn't involve reaching thousands, or even hundreds, of readers — only thirty-five seventh-grade boys. Nevertheless, the invitation filled him with intense joy. It wasn't even so much the invitation, but all that lay behind it.

Shuki made his way to the cheder's entrance and leaned against the big door. From inside the building came the sound of chairs being dragged across the floor. His classmates were probably setting up the room for his father's talk.

Shuki imagined how it would go. They'd all sit in a semicircle — Gedalia, Shimmy, Avner, Pinchas — everyone in the class fascinated, listening intently, their eyes glued to his father.

But maybe it was a mistake, he thought, as the biting wind blasted cold air at his back. *One big mistake. Should I have agreed to invite my father to speak to the class?*

Shuki had wanted to run away from everything that had to do with his home, to disconnect himself from anything connected to Arazim. He had wanted to move ahead with all his classmates, to be one among equals. Wouldn't this lecture of his father's be a setback? Everything he had tried so hard to hide would now be revealed. He had never said a thing, not even the slightest hint, about his father being a *ba'al teshuva*, and now his father would talk about his past. *Abba will have to tell about how he became friends with Yossi, about when they were both in the army, about their search for the truth.*

Everyone knew Shuki's father had been the moving force behind the search for the missing soldier. All people could talk about was the emotion-packed moment when Yitzchak Katz opened the car door and, to his utter amazement, found himself gazing into Yossi's eyes — eyes that sixteen years of absence couldn't make him forget.

In the weeks since, the whole country had been in a turmoil. No one had really believed that Yossi Nir was still alive, but now, with Hashem's help, he was not only alive but coming home.

Yet with all the publicity, Shuki was sure the boys in his class hadn't more than skimmed the headlines. As to how his father had come to be involved with the captive soldier, that was not a concern that occupied their minds. But now they would hear all the details firsthand.

None of Shuki's friends had ever been to his house in Arazim. None of them had ever met his father. Not one of the boys in his class had ever seen his father's scarred face. Now, by agreeing to invite his father to give a talk, Shuki was exposing his father to the entire class. They would see him, they would hear him, and all Shuki's secrets would be out in the open. No longer would he be able to hide behind the facade he had created. He would now be known to all as the son of this father.

Just that morning as he had left for cheder, he had been at peace with his decision. He had clasped his father's hand as he said goodbye and, with a broad smile, had wished his father success in his talk. He had left the house happy, not only for himself but for his father as well. How quickly had the silver lining behind the clouds turned to gloomy gray.

The thought suddenly crossed his mind that his father might not show up at all. Maybe the downpour was keeping him away. Shuki looked down the road, toying with the possibility. *No, Abba will come,* he told himself. Since when was his father afraid of a few drops of rain? Someone whose path is certain is not deterred by drops of rain, whether large or small. He walks with courage and determination toward his goal. Soon Abba would come and sit in the center of the room to begin his talk, telling the boys all about his own special experiences of *hashgacha pratis*.

Does Hashem watch over only those whose tracks have disappeared? Does He take special care only of missing soldiers in captive lands? Hadn't He been the One Who chose Arazim for the Katz family? Wasn't it He Who had surrounded Shuki's home with a beautiful garden for his father to tend?

Hashem had provided Shuki, too, with just the kind of soil he needed to grow; He had presented him with a path to follow for the rest of his life, with a father to walk by his side. If the path was a bit different from others, or if the soil had a different composition, what did it matter? After all, his own *hashgacha pratis* had given him this situation, tailor-made for Yehoshua Katz.

The rain eased off, and the winter sun showed itself from behind the clouds, casting its rays on the small puddles.

When you know there is meaning to your life, Shuki thought, *and that your deeds are accepted by the One Above, you don't worry about what's going on around you. You move forward with confidence, knowing that the path you're on and no other is the path that leads to Hashem.* Shuki felt he could almost see the path stretching beyond the gate and down the road to the rest of his life.

Let him come already, this wonderful father of his, who was so devoted to long-lost friends, this father who saw Hashem's guiding Hand every step of the way, this father who had given an immediate "yes" to his son's request. Shuki would greet him with love and pride.

Three of Shuki's friends appeared at his side.

"Isn't he here yet?" Pinchas echoed Shuki's thoughts.

"Too bad he's taking so long," Gedalia added. "I guess we'll start with the second part of the program first. I can hardly wait to meet your father and hear him speak!"

"I'm waiting for him a million times more," Avner said with a smile. "Your father will be talking about his life, but I'll be able to hear my father's story between the lines."

Shuki smiled back, his eyes still fixed on the green gate, searching, waiting. Finally, a small car stopped, the front door opened and a familiar figure appeared.

"My father's here!" Shuki called out as he rushed to the car, leaving his friends behind. He ran to his father, his arms stretched open wide to embrace him in a big bear hug. The three friends stood at a distance, welcoming Shuki's father shyly when he approached.

"I brought some flowers from our garden," Shuki's father said, showing the boys a colorful bouquet, "but they need a bit of green. Come, Shuki," he said, as he walked toward the sandy path that led to a patch of green. "Let's pick some green branches."

"My father is a gardener," Shuki said to his astonished friends. "He's an expert when it comes to plants. Go upstairs and tell Reb Moishe that my father's here. We'll be up in a few minutes. In the meantime, find a vase to put the flowers in and start singing."

Shuki's friends ran up the stairs as Shuki and his father slowly walked over to the green patch. Together they picked a few branches.

"Maybe you'll be the school gardener here one day," Shuki said to his father, handing him some carefully chosen leaves, a broad smile on his face. His father took the branch and added it to the bouquet. He thought a moment before answering, trying to read the thoughts that lay behind Shuki's surprising words.

"Maybe," he said finally, putting his arm around his son's shoulder.

*/ */ */

The smell of rain was still in the air. Dan Ariel stood at the edge of the school grounds, leaning over the damp, sandy soil. His fingers carefully touched the newly formed footprints, the clear tracks deeply embedded in the sand. These marked determined steps, ones that aren't erased easily by the passing wind.

Dan focused his camera lens. As soon as the heavy rain stopped he had taken his photography equipment and gone outdoors to the street that was now dotted with picturesque puddles, to the trees heavy with raindrop-laden leaves and to the wet muddy sand. This was the perfect time to photograph a topic that especially interested him — footprints in the rain. He noticed a long trail of what he considered perfect footprints and stopped in his tracks.

Two sets of footprints lay side by side, those left by large, purposeful strides that made a deep impression in the ground, and those of smaller footsteps hurrying alongside the larger ones. Dan bent down, looking for the best angle to take the shot. The smaller tracks were more numerous, as if trying to keep up with the other footprints.

He held the shutter release down, allowing for a long exposure. The tracks were dim and he had to open the aperture to allow for ample light, so that people would be able to sense the full dimension of the photograph and get the right feeling from it.

Dan stood up. Now his imprints marked the sandy surface too. It wasn't difficult to distinguish between the different sets. His own footprints marked the sand at random, spreading tiny grains of sand all around. Every step eradicated the previous one, making his movements impossible to decipher.

But the imprints of the other steps were clearly defined. In his mind's eye, the photographer could see a line drawn in the sand, an imaginary line along which two people walked together. Were they a teacher and student? Or were they a father and son?

He studied the footsteps, trying to decide which would be the best section to catch in the camera's lens, which steps were most worthy of being preserved for posterity. Should he choose the two sets of footprints that looked so natural side by side? Or should he take a shot of those at the end of the trail, where the two sets seemed to merge into one?

After a moment's hesitation, he adjusted the lens and pointed the camera straight at a set of large footprints with smaller ones following them. Both were headed in the same direction, toward the same destination.

Cameras can capture the flow of reality in an instant, the one single moment that will be gone forever. Yet no matter how sharp the focus, the future's mysteries remain forever hidden.

Dan Ariel's camera, though, in capturing on film the two sets of footprints, managed to record for posterity far more than a single moment. The shot caught part of a series of footsteps that extended from the past and would, *be'ezras Hashem*, carry the walkers far into the future.

Dan Ariel had no way of knowing that he was recording evidence of two lives deeply intertwined, that of a father and son. Their paths, made up of one step after another, were there for him to see because steps taken with great effort, steps fraught with trials and tribulations, don't disappear — they leave a lasting impression, a trail of footsteps.

FEB 20 2002

HEWLETT-WOODMERE PUBLIC LIBRARY
3 1327 00393 6952

28 Day Loan

Hewlett-Woodmere Public Library
Hewlett, New York 11557-2336

Business Phone 516-374-1967
Recorded Announcements 516-374-1667